Tales from a Gas-Lit Graveyard

Edited by
Hugh Lamb

Dover Publications, Inc.
Mineola, New York

Bibliographical Note

This Dover edition, first published in 2004, is an unabridged republication of
the edition published by W. H. Allen, London, 1979.

Library of Congress Cataloging-in-Publication Data

Tales from a gas-lit graveyard / edited by Hugh Lamb.
   p. cm.
ISBN 0-486-43429-X (pbk.)
   1. Horror tales, English. I. Lamb, Hugh.

PR1309.H6T33 2004
823'.0873808—dc22

2004043840

Manufactured in the United States of America
Dover Publications, Inc., 31 East 2nd Street, Mineola, N.Y. 11501

Contents

Acknowledgements

Nobody works in a vacuum. I certainly don't and there are many people who deserve a friendly mention for their help in compiling this book. There are the staff of Sutton Public Library who, despite the grandeur of their new surroundings, have not lost that magic touch of digging up old books for me, and still smile. Bob Hadji, a correspondent in Ontario, deserves a special vote of thanks for telling me about Lady Dilke. For his help with those awkward details of biography, Mike Ashley, the editor of *Who's Who in Horror and Fantasy Fiction*, should be awarded a medal. My thanks too, to Pat Ellender, who knows why. And finally, the usual, but still sincere, appreciation of the support and encouragement I receive from my wife, Susan; what would I have done without her?

Editor's Introduction

*The modern short story had its precocious youth in the eighties and
nineties; it now seems to be on the threshold of a burgeoning
maturity ... It should not be overlooked that the habit of the contemporary mind is no longer to regard human life as fixed within
plainly defined and immutable boundaries. Life is now depicted as
an affair of jagged and blurred edges, of hazy and indefinable outlines,
where dim half-lights afford little opportunity for clear discernment.
The conscious and subconscious intermingle; death and life are uncertainly poised; the subconscious impinges on the conscious. May it
not be that death itself is but a further remove from subconsciousness;
and that even death may prove, in the ultimate cycle, to be con-
tiguous to life, in a sense at present unfathomable?'*
Alfred C. Ward – *Aspects of the Modern Short Story* (1924)

I rather think Mr Ward put it perfectly, at least where ghost stories
and tales of terror are concerned. And I would go as far as to say
that, even in the eighties and nineties, authors were busily exploring that 'habit of the contemporary mind' he describes above – the
depiction of life with blurred edges, where death and life are uncertainly poised. It had, in the hands of some skilled writers,
reached that 'threshold of burgeoning maturity' he ascribes to
stories in the 1920s.

There is a widespread and perhaps understandable belief that
Victorian tales of terror were in the main childish things, full of
sheeted spectres and clanking chains, frightened heroines and manly
heroes, happy endings and ever-afters. Well, there were many such
stories, I won't deny it, especially in the earlier part of Victoria's
reign. And even today, many of these stories are repeatedly
anthologised, thus continuing the childish myth. But this is just
not the whole picture: towards the end of the last century, there
were authors busily producing stories that would not have disgraced
the work of such modern masters of mature terror as Robert
Aickman or America's Russell Kirk. Admittedly, their literary
hands were often tied by the moral climate of the day and spectres
of the Freudian subconscious were, of necessity, crudely drawn or
disguised. But does that necessarily mean that the authors were
ignorant of the symbolism of their work?

In my past three Victorian collections, readers may have noted an increasing emphasis not only on forgotten stories but also on forgotten authors. At the risk of repeating myself, even now, nearly eighty years after the Victorian reign, there are still many unknown tales by famous writers and even more unknown tales by unknown writers. I have always thought that the unknown authors deserved their moment of triumph and have tried to include more and more in each book. Well, in *Tales from a Gas-lit Graveyard*, I think I've managed to satisfy both the arguments above: there are forgotten authors in here with mature stories, all worthy of standing on Mr Ward's 'threshold of burgeoning maturity'.

Perhaps the most startling 'discovery' (I hate the word, it seems presumptuous, but as archaeologists feel competent to use it, then so do I – their work and mine is not too far removed) is Bernard Capes. He died in 1918 and has been completely overlooked ever since. I cannot trace a story of his in any collection of ghost stories since his death. Yet, as his work here will show you, he was a superlative writer, with a style and themes that would not look out of place in today's subtler markets. And, to make his neglect even more startling, Capes was no casual writer of ghost stories, contributing the odd story here and there to magazines – he wrote no less than *five* complete collections of ghostly tales.

And for works dealing with the blurred edges of life, try the forgotten talents of J. H. Pearce, Lady Dilke and the Countess of Munster – all three forgotten masters.

Readers of my previous Victorian collections will have made the acquaintance of such names as Robert Barr, R. Murray Gilchrist, Mrs J. H. Riddell, Ambrose Bierce, Richard Marsh and Guy Boothby. They are all neglected names from the Victorian era, represented here with stories that have not been reprinted since their original publication. In fact, of the seventeen stories here, only two have ever been included in an anthology before – and that anthology appeared in the Victorian era itself.

So, here are the *Tales from a Gas-lit Graveyard*. I can promise you pleasant surprises, for these are no tales for children, no stories for the undiscerning reader. These are forgotten mature works, from the era described by Alfred Ward as the 'precocious youth' of the short story. I hope you will agree with me that Mr Ward's idea of precocity was slightly wrong.

HUGH LAMB
Sutton, Surrey

THE HAUNTED STATION

by

Hume Nisbet

Our first tale from the gas-lit graveyard comes from Hume Nisbet, a long-forgotten Scottish author who spent several years in Australia and eventually returned there, dying some time in the 1920s.

Nisbet was born in 1849 and first went to Australia in 1865. He returned to England in 1872 and an unsuccessful attempt to make teaching art his career led him to take up writing for a living. Noted for his ghost stories and adventure romances, Nisbet wrote many books in the macabre vein, including Paths of the Dead *(1899) and* Stories Weird and Wonderful *(1900).*

Hume Nisbet neatly pointed out the paradox between Victorian practicality and the passion for spiritualism and the occult. 'We have become very hard-headed, so that it takes a great deal of heat to warm our languid and chilled blood,' he said. 'And yet, never, even during the most flourishing days of witches and warlocks, have we been so prone to believe in the presence of spirits, good and evil.'

The ghost stories in his remarkable volume The Haunted Station *(1894) were in his own words 'psychological studies gleaned in most instances from reliable sources or personal experience ... malignant influences, more awful in their consequences to poor humanity than the life-sucking vampires of olden times, I have attempted to define in such sketches as 'The Haunted Station'.*

Bearing in mind Nisbet's words about personal experience, and the many years he spent in Australia, this tale of an outback station with decidedly unwelcome tenants takes on a whole new significance. As the first stop on this tour of the Victorian graveyard, it is eminently suitable.

It looked as if a curse rested upon it, even under that glorious southern morn which transformed all that it touched into old oak and silver-bronze.

I use the term silver-bronze, because I can think of no other combination to express that peculiar bronzy tarnish, like silver that has lain covered for a time, which the moonlight in the tropics gives to the near objects upon which it falls – tarnished silver surfaces and deep sepia-tinted shadows.

I felt the weird influence of that curse even as I crawled into the gully that led to it; a shiver ran over me as one feels when they say some stranger is passing over your future grave; a chill gripped at my vitals as I glanced about me apprehensively, expectant of something ghoulish and unnatural to come upon me from the sepulchral gloom and mystery of the overhanging boulders under which I was dragging my wearied limbs. A deathly silence brooded within this rut-like and treeless gully that formed the only passage from the arid desert over which I had struggled, famishing and desperate; where it led to I neither knew nor cared, so that it did not end in a *cul-de-sac*.

At last I came to what I least expected to see in that part, a house of two storeys, with the double gables facing me, as it stood on a mound in front of a water-hole, the mellow full moon behind the shingly roof, and glittering whitely as it repeated itself in the still water against the inky blackness of the reflections cast by the denser masses of the house and vegetation about it.

It seemed to be a wooden erection, such as squatters first raise for their homesteads after they have decided to stay; the intermediate kind of station, which takes the place of the temporary shanty while the proprietor's bank account is rapidly swelling, and his children are being educated in the city boarding schools to know their own social importance. By and by, when he is out of the mortgagee's hands, he may discard this comfortable house, as he has done his shanty, and go in for stateliness and stone-work, but to the tramp or the bushranger, the present house is the most welcome sight, for it promises to the one shelter, and to the other a prospect of loot.

There was a verandah round the basement that stood clear above the earth on piles, with a broad ladder stair leading down to the garden walk which terminated at the edge of the pool or water-hole; under the iron roofing of the verandah I could make out the vague indications of French doors that led to the reception rooms, etc., while above them were bedroom windows, all dark with the exception of one of the upper windows, the second one from the end gable, through which a pale greenish light streamed faintly.

Behind the house, or rather from the centre of it, as I afterwards found out, projected a gigantic and lifeless gum tree, which spread its fantastic limbs and branches wildly over the roof, and behind that again a mass of chaotic and planted greenery, all softened and generalised in the thin silvery mist which emanated from the pool and hovered over the ground.

At the first glance it appeared to be the abode of a romantic owner, who had fixed upon a picturesque site, and afterwards devoted himself to making it comfortable as well as beautiful. He had planted creepers and trained them over the walls, passion-fruit and vines clung closely to the posts and trellis work and broke the square outlines of windows and angles, a wild tangle of shrubs and flowers covered the mound in front and trailed into the water without much order, so that it looked like the abode of an imaginative poet rather than the station of a practical, money-grabbing squatter.

As I quitted the desolate and rock-bound gully and entered upon this romantic domain, I could not help admiring the artful manner in which the owner had left Nature alone where he could do so; the gum trees which he had found there were still left as they must have been for ages, great trees shooting up hundreds of feet into the air, some of them gaunt and bald with time, others with their leafage still in a flourishing condition, while the more youthful trees were springing out of the fertile soil in all directions, giving the approach the appearance of an English park, particularly with the heavy night-dew that glistened over them.

But the chill was still upon me that had gripped me at the entrance of the gully, and the same lifeless silence brooded over the house, garden, pool and forest which had awed me amongst the boulders, so that as I paused at the edge of the water and regarded the house, I again shuddered as if spectres were round me, and murmured to myself, 'Yes, it looks like a place upon which has fallen a curse.'

Two years before this night, I had been tried and condemned to death for murder, the murder of the one I loved best on earth, but, through the energy of the press and the intercession of a number of influential friends, my sentence had been *mercifully* commuted to transportation for life in Western Australia.

The victim, whom I was proved by circumstantial evidence to have murdered, was my young wife, to whom I had been married only six months before; ours was a love match, and until I saw her lying stark before me, those six months had been an uninterrupted honeymoon, without a cloud to cross it, a brief term of heaven, which accentuated the after misery.

I was a medical practitioner in a small country village which I need not name, as my supposed crime rang through England. My practice was new but growing, so that, although not too well off, we were fairly comfortable as to position, and, as my wife was modest in her desires, we were more than contented with our lot.

I suppose the evidence was strong enough to place my guilt beyond a doubt to those who could not read my heart and the heart of the woman I loved more than life. She had not been very well of late, yet, as it was nothing serious, I attended her myself; then the end came with appalling suddenness, a post-mortem examination proved that she had been poisoned, and that the drug had been taken from my surgery, by whom or for what reason is still a mystery to me, for I do not think that I had an enemy in the world, nor do I think my poor darling had one either.

At the time of my sentence, I had only one wish, and that was to join the victim of this mysterious crime, so that I saw the judge put on the fatal black cap with a feeling of pleasure, but when afterwards I heard it was to be transportation instead, then I flung myself down in my cell and hurled imprecations on those officious friends who had given me slavery and misery instead of release. Where was the mercy in letting me have life, since all had been taken from it which made it worth holding? – the woman who had lain in my arms while together we built up glowing pictures of an impossible future, my good name lost, my place amongst men destroyed; henceforward I would be only recognised by a number, my companions the vilest, my days dragged out in chains, until the degradation of my lot encrusted over that previous memory of tenderness and fidelity, and I grew to be like the other numbered felons, a mindless and emotionless animal.

Fortunately, at this point of my sufferings, oblivion came in the form of delirium, so that the weeks passed in a dream, during which my lost wife lived once more with me as we had been in the past, and by the time the ship's doctor pronounced me recovered, we were within a few days of our dreary destination. Then my wife went from me to her own place, and I woke up to find that I had made some friends amongst my fellow-convicts, who had taken care of me during my insanity.

We landed at Fremantle, and began our life, road-making; that is, each morning we were driven out of the prison like cattle, chained together in groups, and kept in the open until sundown, when we were once more driven back to sleep.

For fourteen months this dull monotony of eating, working and sleeping went on without variation, and then the chance came that I had been hungering for all along; not that liberty was likely to do me much good, only that the hope of accomplishing it kept me alive.

Three of us made a run for it one afternoon, just before the gun sounded for our recall, while the rest of the gang, being in our confidence, covered our escape until we had got beyond gun-shot distance. We had managed to file through the chain which linked us together, and we ran towards the bush with the broken pieces in our hands as weapons of defence.

My two comrades were desperate criminals, who, like myself, had been sentenced for life, and, as they confessed themselves, were ready to commit any atrocity rather than be caught and taken back.

That night and the next day we walked in a straight line about forty miles through the bush, and then, being hungry and tired, and considering ourselves fairly safe, we lay down to sleep without any thought of keeping watch.

But we had reckoned too confidently upon our escape, for about daybreak the next morning we were roused up by the sound of galloping horses, and, springing to our feet and climbing a gum tree, we saw a dozen of mounted police, led by two black trackers, coming straight in our direction. Under the circumstances there were but two things left for us to do, either to wait until they came and caught us, or run for it until we were beaten or shot down.

One of my companions decided to wait and be taken back, in spite of his bravado the night before; an empty stomach demoralises most men; the other one made up his mind, as I did, to run as long as we could. We started in different directions, leaving our mate sitting under the gum tree, he promising to keep them off our track as long as possible.

The fact of him being there when the police arrived gave us a good start. I put all my speed out, and dashed along until I had covered, I daresay, about a couple of miles, when all at once the scrub came to an end, and before me I saw an open space, with another stretch of bush about half a mile distant, and no shelter between me and it.

As I stood for a few minutes to recover my breath, I heard two or three shots fired to the right, the direction my companion had taken, and on looking that way I saw that he also had gained the open, and was followed by one of the trackers and a couple of the police. He was still running, but I could see that he was wounded from the way he went.

Another shot was sent after him, that went straight to its mark, for all at once he threw up his arms and fell prone upon his face, then, hearing the sounds of pursuit in my direction, I waited no longer, but bounded full into the morning sunlight, hoping, as I ran, that I might be as lucky as he had been, and get a bullet between my shoulders and so end my troubles.

I knew that they had seen me, and were after me almost as soon as I had left the cover, for I could hear them shouting for me to stop, as well as the clatter of their horses' hoofs on the hard soil, but still I kept to my course, waiting upon the shots to sound which would terminate my wretched existence, my back-nerves quivering in anticipation and my teeth meeting in my under-lip.

One!

Two!!

Two reports sounded in my ears; a second after the bullets had whistled past my head; and then, before the third and fourth reports came, something like hot iron touched me above my left elbow, while the other bullet whirred past me with a singing wail, cooling my cheek with the wind it raised, and then I saw it ricochet in front of me on the hill side, for I was going up a slight rise at the time.

I had no pain in my arm, although I knew that my humerus was splintered by that third last shot, but I put on a final spurt in order to tempt them to fire again.

What were they doing? I glanced over my shoulder as I rushed, and saw that they were spreading out, fan-like, and riding like fury, while they hurriedly reloaded. Once more they were taking aim at me, and then I looked again in front.

Before me yawned a gulf, the depth of which I could not estimate, yet in width it was over a hundred feet. My pursuers had seen this impediment also, for they were reining up their horses, while they shouted to me, more frantically than ever, to stop.

Why should I stop? flashed the thought across my mind as I neared the edge. Since their bullets had denied me the death I courted, why should I pause at the death spread out for me so opportunely?

As the question flashed through me, I answered it by making the leap, and as I went down I could hear the reports of the rifles above me.

Down into shadow from the sun-glare I dropped, the outer branches of a tree breaking with me as I fell through them. Another obstacle caught me a little lower, and gave way under my weight, and then with an awful wrench, that nearly stunned me, I felt myself hanging by the remnant of the chain which was still rivetted to my waist-band, about ten feet from the surface, and with a hundred and fifty feet of a drop below me before I could reach the bottom. The chain had somehow got entangled in a fork of the last tree through which I had broken.

Although that sudden wrench was excruciating, the exigency of my position compelled me to collect my faculties without loss of time. Perhaps my months of serfdom and intercourse with felons had blunted my sensibility, and rendered me more callous to danger and bodily pain than I had been in my former and happier days, or the excitement of that terrible chase was still surging within me, for without more than a second's pause, and an almost indifferent glance downwards to those distant boulders, I made a wild clutch with my unwounded arm at the branch which had caught me, and with an effort drew myself up to it, so that the next instant I was astride it, or rather crouching, where my loose chain had caught. Then, once more secure, I looked upwards to where I expected my hunters to appear.

When I think upon it now, it was a marvel how I ever got to be placed where I was, for I was under the shelving ledge from which I had leapt, that is, it spread over me like a roof, therefore I must conclude that the first tier of branches must have bent inwards, and so landed me on to the second tree at a slant.

At least, this is the only way in which I can account for my position.

The tree on which I sat grew from a crevice on the side of the precipice, and from the top could not be seen by those above, neither could I see them, although they looked down after me, but I could hear them plainly enough and what they said.

'That fellow has gone right enough, Jack, although I don't see his remains below; shall we try to get down and make sure?' I heard one say, while another replied:

'What's the good of wasting time, he's as dead as the other chap, after that drop, and they will both be picked clean enough, so let us get back to Fremantle with the living one, and report the other two as wiped out; we have a long enough journey before us, sergeant.'

'Yes, I suppose so,' answered the sergeant. 'Well, boys, we may say that there are two promising bushrangers the less for this colony to support, so right about, home's the word.'

I heard their horses wheel round and go off at a canter after this final speech, and then I was left alone on my airy perch, to plan out how best I was to get down with my broken arm, for it was impossible to get up, and also what I was likely to do with my liberty in that desolate region.

Desperate men are not very particular about the risks they run, and I ran not a few before I finally reached the bottom of that gulch, risky drops from one ledge to another, frantic clutchings at branches and tree roots; sufficient that I did reach the level ground at last more nearly dead than alive, so that I was fain to lie under the shadow of a boulder for hours without making an effort to rise and continue my journey.

Then, as night was approaching, I dragged myself along until I came to some water, where, after drinking and bracing up my broken arm with a few gum-trunk shards, and binding them round with some native grasses, while I made my supper of the young leaves of the eucalyptus bushes, I went on.

On, on, on for weeks, until I had lost all count of time, I wandered, carrying my broken fetters with me, and my broken arm gradually mending of its own accord. Sometimes I killed a snake or an iguana during the day with the branch I used for a stick, or a 'possum or wild cat at night, which I devoured raw. Often I existed for days on grass roots or the leaves of the gum-tree, for anything was good enough to fill up the gap.

My convict garb was in tatters and my feet bootless by this time, and my hair and beard hung over my shoulders and chest, while often I went for days in a semi-conscious state, for the fierce sun seemed to wither up my blood and set fire to my brain.

Where I was going I could not tell, and still, with all the privation and misery, the love of life was once again stronger in me than it had been since I had lost my place amongst civilised men, for I was at liberty and alone to indulge in fancy.

And yet it did not seem altogether fancy that my lost wife was with me on that journey. At first she came only when I lay down to sleep, but after a time she walked with me hand in hand during the day as well as in my dreams.

Dora was her name, and soon I forgot that she had been dead, for she was as living and beautiful as ever as we went along together, day after day, speaking to each other like lovers as we used to speak, and she did not seem to mind my ragged, degraded costume, or my dirty, tangled beard, but caressed me with the same tenderness as of yore.

Through the bush, down lonely gullies, over bitter deserts and salt marshes, we passed as happy and affectionate as fond lovers could be who are newly married, and whom the world cannot part, my broken chain rattling as I staggered onwards while she smiled as if pleased with the music, because it was the chain which I was wearing for her dear sake.

Let me think for a moment – was she with me through that last desert before I came to that gloomy gully? I cannot be quite sure of that, but this I do know, that she was not with me after the chill shadows of the boulders drew me into them, and I was quite alone when I stood by the water-hole looking upon that strange and silent house.

It was singular that the house should be here at all in this far-off and as yet unnamed portion of Western Australia, for I naturally supposed that I had walked hundreds of miles since leaving the convict settlement, and as I had encountered no one, not even a single tribe of wandering blacks, it seemed impossible to believe that I was not the first white man who had penetrated so far, and yet there it loomed before me, substantial-looking in its masses, with painted weather-boards, shingles, iron sheeting, carved posts and trellis-work, French windows, and the signs of cultivation about it, although bearing the traces of late neglect.

Was it inhabited? I next asked myself as I looked steadily at that dimly-illumined window; seemingly it was, for as I mentally asked the question, a darkness blotted out the light for a few moments and then moved slowly aside, while the faint pallor once more shone out; it appeared to be from the distance a window with a pale green blind drawn down, behind which a lamp turned low was burning, possibly for some invalid who was restlessly walking about, while the rest of the household slept.

Would it be well to rouse them up at this hour of the night? I next queried as I paused, watching the chimney tops from which no wreath of smoke came, for although it did not seem late, judging from the height of the moon, yet it was only natural to suppose that in this isolated place the people would retire early. Perhaps it would be better to wait where I was till morning and see what they were like before I ventured to ask hospitality from them, in my ragged yet unmistakably convict dress. I would rather go on as I was than run the risk of being dragged back to prison.

How chilly the night vapours were which rose from this large pool, for it was more like the moat from some ancient ruin than an ordinary Australian water-hole. How ominous the shadows that gathered over this dwelling, and which even the great and lustrous moon, now clear of the gable end, seemed unable to dissipate, and what a dismal effect that dimly-burning lamp behind the pale green blind gave to it.

I turned my eyes from the window to the pond from which the ghostly vapours were steaming upwards in such strange shapes; they crossed the reflections like grey shadows and floated over the white glitter which the moon cast down, like spectres following each other in a stately procession, curling upwards interlaced, while the gaunt trees behind them altered their shapes and looked demoniac in their fantastic outlines, shadows passing along and sending back doleful sighs, which I tried with all my might to think was the night breeze but without succeeding.

Hush! was that a laugh that wafted from the house, a low, but blood-curdling cachinnation such as an exultant devil might utter who had witnessed his fell mischief accomplished, followed by the wail of a woman, intermixed with the cry of a child!

Ah! what a fool I was to forget the cry of the Australian king-fisher; of course that was it, of course, of course, but –

The shapes are thickening over that mirror-like pool, and as I look I see a woman with a chalk-white face and eyes distended in horror, with a child in her hands – a little girl – and beside them the form of a man whose face changes into two different men, one the face of death, and the other like that of a demon with glaring eyeballs, while he points from the woman and child to the sleeping pool.

What is the devil-spectre pointing at, as he laughs once more while the woman and child shrink with affright?

The face that he himself wore a moment ago, the face of the dead man whom I can see floating amongst that silver lustre.

I must have fainted at the weird visions of the night before, or else I may have fallen asleep and dreamt them, for when I opened my eyes again, the morning sun was pouring over the landscape and all appeared changed.

The pool was still there but it looked like a natural Australian water-hole which had been deepened and lengthened, and artificially arranged by a tasteful proprietor to beautify his estate; water-lilies grew round the edges and spread themselves in graceful patches about; it was only in the centre portion, where the moonlight had glinted and the other reflections cast themselves, that the water was clear of weeds, and there it still lay inky and dangerous-like in its depth.

Over the building itself clustered a perfect tangle of vegetable parasites, Star-of-Bethlehem, Maiden-blush roses, and Gloire-de-Dijon, passion-flowers and convolvulus, intermingling with a large grape-laden vine going to waste, and hanging about in half-wild, neglected festoons; a woman's hand had planted these tendrils, as well as the garden in front, for I could see that flowers predominated.

As for the house itself, it still stood silent and deserted-looking, the weather-boards had shrunk a good deal with the heat of many suns beating upon them, while the paint, once tasteful in its varied tints, was bleached into dry powder; the trellis-work also on the verandah had in many places been torn away by the weight of the clinging vines, and between the window-frames and the windows yawned wide fissures where they had shrunk from each other.

I looked round at the landscape, but could see no trace of sheep, cattle, nor humanity; it spread out a sun-lit solitude where Nature, for a little while trained to order, had once more asserted her independent lavishness.

A little of my former awe came upon me as I stood for a few moments hesitating to advance, but at the sight of those luscious-looking bunches of grapes, which seemed to promise some fare more substantial inside, the dormant cravings for food which I had so long subdued came upon me with tenfold force, and, without more than a slight tremor of superstitious dread, I hurriedly crushed my way through the tangle of vegetation, and made for the verandah and open door of the hall.

Delicious grapes they were, as I found when, after tearing off a huge bunch, and eating them greedily, I entered the silent hall and began my exploration.

The dust and fine sand of many 'brick-fielders', i.e., sand storms, lay thickly on every object inside, so that as I walked I left my footprints behind me as plainly as if I had been walking over snow. In the hall I found a handsome stand and carved table with chairs, a hat and riding-whip lay on the table, while on the rack I saw two or three coats and hats hanging, with sticks and umbrellas beneath, all white with dust.

The dining-room door stood ajar, and as I entered I could see that it also had been undisturbed for months, if not for years. It had been handsomely furnished, with artistic hangings and stuffed leather chairs and couches, while on the elaborately carved chiffonier was a plentiful supply of spirit and wine decanters, with cut glasses standing ready for use. On the table stood a bottle of Three-star brandy, half-emptied, and by its side a water-filter and glass as they had been left by the last user.

I smelt the bottle, and found that the contents were mellow and good, and when, after dusting the top, I put it to my mouth, I discovered that the bouquet was delicious; then, invigorated by that sip, I continued my voyage of discovery.

The chiffonier was not locked, and inside I discovered rows of sealed bottles, which satisfied me that I was not likely to run short of refreshments in the liquid form at any rate, so, content with this pleasant prospect, I ventured into the other apartments.

The drawing-room was like the room I had left, a picture of comfort and elegance, when once the accumulation of dust and sand had been removed.

The library or study came next, which I found in perfect order, although I left the details for a more leisurely examination.

I next penetrated the kitchen, which I saw was comfortable, roomy and well-provided, although in more disorder than the other rooms; pans stood rusting in the fireplace, dishes lay dirty and in an accumulated pile on the table, as if the servants had left in a hurry and the owners had been forced to make what shifts they could during their absence.

Yet there was no lack of such provisions as an up-country station would be sure to lay in; the pantry I found stored like a provision shop, with flitches of bacon, hams sewn in canvas, tinned meats and soups of all kinds, with barrels and bags and boxes of flour, sugar, tea and other sundries, enough to keep me going for years if I was lucky enough to be in possession.

I next went upstairs to the bedrooms, up a thickly-carpeted staircase, with the white linen overcloth still upon it. In the first room I found the bed with the bedclothes tumbled about as if the sleeper had lately left it; the master of the house I supposed, as I examined the wardrobe and found it well stocked with male apparel. At last I could cast aside my degrading rags, and fit myself out like a free man, after I had visited the workshop and filed my fetters from me.

Another door attracted me on the opposite side of the lobby, and this I opened with some considerable trepidation because it led into the room which I had seen lighted up the night before.

It seemed untenanted, as I looked in cautiously, and like the other bedroom was in a tumble of confusion, a woman's room, for the dresses and underclothing were lying about, a bedroom which had been occupied by a woman and a child, for a crib stood in one corner, and on a chair lay the frock and other articles belonging to a little girl of about five or six years of age.

I looked at the window, it had venetian blinds upon it, and they were drawn up, so that my surmise had been wrong about the pale green blind, but on the end side of the room was another window with the blinds also drawn up, and thus satisfied I walked in boldly; what I had thought to be a light, had only been the moonlight streaming from the one window to the other, while the momentary blackening of the light had been caused, doubtless, by the branches of the trees outside, moved forward by the night breeze. Yes, that must have been the cause, so that I had nothing to fear, the house was deserted, and my own property, for the time at least.

There was a strange and musty odour in this bedroom, which blended with the perfume that the owner had used, and made me for a moment almost giddy, so the first thing I did was to open both windows and let in the morning air, after which I looked over to the unmade bed, and then I staggered back with a cry of horror.

There amongst the tumble of bedclothes lay the skeletons of what had been two human beings, clad in embroidered night-dresses. One glance was enough to convince me, with my medical knowledge, that the gleaming bones were those of a woman and a child, the original wearers of those dresses which lay scattered about.

What awful tragedy had taken place in this richly furnished but accursed house? Recovering myself, I examined the remains more particularly, but could find no clue, they were lying reposefully enough, with arms interlacing as if they had died or been done to death in their sleep, while those tiny anatomists, the ants, had found their way in, and cleaned the bones completely, as they very soon do in this country.

With a sick sensation at my heart, I continued my investigations throughout the other portions of the station. In the servants' quarters I learnt the cause of the unwashed dishes; three skeletons lay on the floor in different positions as they had fallen, while their shattered skulls proved the cause of their end, even if the empty revolver that I picked up from the floor had not been evidence enough. Some one must have entered their rooms and woke them rudely from their sleep in the night time, for they lay also in their blood-stained nightdresses, and beside them, on the boards, were dried-up markings which were unmistakable.

The rest of the house was as it had been left by the murderer or murderers. Three domestics, with their mistress and child, had been slaughtered, and then the guilty wretches had fled without disturbing anything else.

It was once again night, and I was still in the house which my first impulse had been to leave with all haste after the gruesome discoveries that I had made.

But several potent reasons restrained me from yielding to that impulse. I had been wandering for months, and living like a wild beast, while here I had everything to my hand which I needed to recruit my exhausted system. My curiosity was roused, so that I wanted to penetrate the strange mystery if I could, by hunting after and reading all the letters and papers that I might be able to find, and to do this required leisure; thirdly, as a medical practitioner who had passed through the anatomical schools, the presence of five skeletons did not have much effect upon me, and lastly, before sun-down the weather had broken, and one of those fierce storms of rain, wind, thunder and lightning had come on, which utterly prevented any one who had the chance of a roof to shelter him from turning out to the dangers of the night.

These were some of my reasons for staying where I was, at least the reasons that I explained to myself, but there was another and a more subtle motive which I could not logically explain, and which yet influenced me more than any of the others. *I could not leave the house, now that I had taken possession of it,* or rather, if I may say it, now that *the house had taken possession of me.*

I had lifted the bucket from the kitchen, and found my way to the draw-well in the back-garden, with the uncomfortable feeling that some unseen force was compelling me to stay here. I discovered a large file and freed myself from my fetters, and then, throwing my rags from me with disgust, I clad myself in one of the suits that I found in the wardrobe upstairs. Then I set to work dusting and sweeping out the dining-room, after which I lit a fire, retrimmed the lamps, and cooked a substantial meal for myself. The storm coming on decided me, so that I spent the remainder of the afternoon making the place comfortable, and when darkness did come, I had drawn the blinds down and secured the shutters, and with a lighted lamp, a bottle of good wine, and a box of first-class cigars which I also found in the chiffonier, with a few volumes that I had taken from the book shelves at random, and an album of photographs that I picked up from the drawing-room table, I felt a different man from what I had been the night previous, particularly with that glowing log fire in the grate.

I left the half-emptied bottle of brandy where I had found it, on the table, with the used glass and water filter untouched, as I did also the chair that had been beside them. I had repugnance to those articles which I could not overcome; the murderer had used them last, possibly as a reviver after his crimes, for by this time I had reasoned out that one hand only had been at the work, and that man's the owner of the suit which I was then wearing and which fitted me so exactly, otherwise why should the house have been left in the condition that it was?

As I sat at the end of the table and smoked the cigar, I rebuilt the whole tragedy, although as yet the motive was not so clear, and as I thought the matter out, I turned over the leaves of the album and looked at the photographs.

Before me, on the walls, hung three oil portraits, enlargements they were, and as works of art vile things, yet doubtless they were faithful enough likenesses. In the album, I found three cabinet portraits from which the paintings had been enlarged.

They were the portraits of a woman of about twenty-six, a girl of five years, and a man of about thirty-two.

The woman was good-looking, with fresh colour, blue eyes and golden-brown hair. The girl – evidently her daughter – for the likeness was marked between the two, had one of those seraphic expressions which some delicate children have who are marked out for early death, that places them above the plane of grosser humanity. She looked, as she hung between the two portraits, with her glory of golden hair, like the guardian angel of the woman who was smiling so contentedly and consciously from her gilded frame.

The man was pallid-faced and dark, clean-shaven, all except the small black moustache, with lips which, except the artist had grossly exaggerated the colour, were excessively and disagreeably vivid. His eyes were deep set, and glowing as if with the glitter of a fever.

'These would be the likenesses of the woman and child whose skeletons lay unburied upstairs, and that pallid-faced, feverish-eyed ghoul, the fiend who had murdered them, his wife and child,' I murmured to myself as I watched the last portrait with morbid interest.

'Right and wrong, Doctor, as you medical men mostly are,' answered a deep voice from the other end of the table.

I started with amazement, and looked from the painting to the vacant chair beside the brandy bottle, which was now occupied by what appeared to be the original of the picture I had been looking at, face, hair, vivid scarlet lips were identical, and the same deep-set fiery eyes, which were fixed upon me intently and mockingly.

How had he entered without my observing him? By the window? No, for that I had firmly closed and secured myself, and as I glanced at it I saw that it still remained the same. By the door? Perhaps so, although he must have closed it again after he had entered without my hearing him, as he might easily have done during one of the claps of thunder which were now almost incessant, as were the vivid flashes of wild fire or lightning that darted about, while the rain lashed against the shutters outside.

He was dripping wet, as I could see, so that he must have come from that deluge, bare-headed and dripping, with his hair and moustache draggling over his glistening, ashy cheeks and bluish chin, as if he had been submerged in water, while weeds and slime hung about his saturated garments; a gruesome sight for a man who fancied himself alone to see start up all of a sudden, and no wonder that it paralysed me and prevented me from finding the words I wanted at the moment. Had he lain hidden somewhere watching me take possession of his premises, and being, as solitary men sometimes are, fond of dramatic effect, slipped in while my back was turned from the door to give me a surprise? If so he had succeeded, for I never before felt so craven-spirited or horror-stricken, my flesh was creeping and my hair bristling, while my blood grew to ice within me. The very lamp seemed to turn dim, and the fire smouldered down on the hearth, while the air was chill as a charnel vault, as I sat with shivering limbs and chattering teeth before this evil visitor.

Outside, the warring elements raged and fought, shaking the wooden walls, while the forked flames darted between us, lighting up his face with a ghastly effect. He must have seen my horror, for he once more laughed that low, malicious chuckle that I had heard the night before, as he again spoke.

'Make yourself at home, Doctor, and try some of this cognac instead of that washy stuff you are drinking. I am only sorry that I cannot join you in it, but I cannot *just yet*.'

I found words at last and asked him questions, which seemed impertinent in the extreme, considering where I was.

'Who are you? Where do you come from? What do you want?'

Again that hateful chuckle, as he fixed his burning eyes upon me with a regard which fascinated me in spite of myself.

'Who am I, do you ask? Well, before you took possession of this place I was its owner. Where do I come from? From out of *there* last.'

He pointed backwards towards the window, which burst open as he uttered the words, while through the driving rain a flash of lightning seemed to dart from his outstretched finger and disappear into the centre of the lake, then after that hurried glimpse, the shutters clashed together again and we were as before.

'What do I want? You, for lack of a better.'

'What do you want with me?' I gasped.

'To make you myself.'

'I do not understand you, what are you?'

'At present nothing, yet with your help, I shall be a man once more, while you shall be free and rich, for you shall have more gold than you ever could dream of.'

'What can I do for you?'

'Listen to my story and you will see. Ten years ago I was a successful gold finder, the trusting husband of that woman, and the fond father of that girl. I had likewise a friend whom I trusted, and took to live with me as a partner. We lived here together, my friend, myself, my wife and my daughter, for I was romantic and had raised this house to be close to the mine which I had discovered, and which I will show you if you consent to my terms.

'One night my friend murdered me and pitched my body into that water-hole, where the bones still lie. He did this because he coveted my wife and my share of the money.'

I was calm now, but watchful, for it appeared that I had to deal with a madman.

'In my lifetime I had been a trusting and guileless simpleton, but no sooner was my spirit set free than vengeance transformed its nature. I hovered about the place where all my affections had been centred, watching him beguile the woman who had been mine until he won her. She waited three years for me to return, and then she believed his story that I had been killed by the natives, and married him. They travelled to where you came from, to be married, and I followed them closely, for that was the chance I waited upon. The union of those two once accomplished he was in my power for ever, for this had established the link that was needed for me to take forcible possession of him.'

'And where was his spirit meantime?' I asked, to humour the maniac.

'In my grasp also, a spirit rendered impotent by murder and ingratitude; a spirit which I could do with as I pleased, so long as the wish I had was evil. I took possession of his body, the mirage of which you see now, and from that moment until the hour that our daughter rescued her from his clutches, he made the life of my former wife a hell on earth. I prompted his murder-embrued spirit to madness, leaving him only long enough to himself after I had braced him up to do the deed of vengeance.'

'How did the daughter save the mother?'

'By dying with her, and by her own purity tearing the freed spirit from my clutches. I did not intend the animal to do all that he did, for I wanted the mother only, but once the murder lust was on him, I found that he was beyond my influence. He slew the two by poison, as he had done me, then, frenzied, he murdered the servants, and finally exterminated himself by flinging himself into the pool. That was why I said that I came last from out of there, where both my own remains and his lie together.'

'Yes, and what is my share in this business?'

'To look on me passively for a few moments, as you are at present doing, that is all I require.'

I did not believe his story about his being only a mirage or spectre, for he appeared at this moment corporal enough to do me a considerable amount of bodily harm, and therefore to humour him, until I could plan a way to overpower him, I fixed my eyes upon his steadfastly, as he desired.

Was I falling asleep, or being mesmerised by this homicidal lunatic? As he glared at me with those fiery orbs and an evil contortion curling the blood-red lips, while the forked lightning played around him, I became helpless. He was creeping slowly towards me as a cat might steal upon a mouse, and I was unable to move, or take my eyes from his eyes which seemed to be charming my life-blood from me, when suddenly I heard the distant sound of music, through a lull of the tempest, the rippling of a piano from the drawing-room with the mingling of a child's silvery voice as it sang its evening hymn, and at the sound his eyes shifted while he fell back a step or two, with an agonised spasm crossing his ghastly and dripping wet face.

Then the hurricane broke loose once more, with a resistless fury, while the door and window burst open, and the shutters were dashed into the room.

I leapt to my feet in a paroxysm of horror, and sprang towards the open door with that demon, or maniac, behind me.

Merciful heavens! the drawing-room was brilliantly lighted up, and there, seated at the open piano, was the woman whose bones I had seen bleaching upstairs, with the seraphic-faced child singing her hymn.

Out to the tempest I rushed madly, and heedless of where I went, so that I escaped from that accursed and haunted house, on, past the water-hole and into the glade, where I turned my head back instinctively, as I heard a wilder roar of thunder and the crash as if a tree had been struck.

What a flash that was which lighted up the scene and showed me the house collapsing as an erection of cards. It went down like an avalanche before that zig-zag flame, which seemed to lick round it for a moment, and then disappear into the earth.

Next instant I was thrown off my feet by the earthquake that shook the ground under me, while, as I still looked on where the house had been, I saw that the ruin had caught fire, and was blazing up in spite of the torrents that still poured down, and as it burned, I saw the mound sink slowly out of sight, while the reddened smoke eddied about in the same strange shapes which the vapours had assumed the night before, scarlet ghosts of the demon and his victims.

Two months after this, I woke up to find myself in a Queensland back-country station. They had found me wandering in a delirious condition over one of their distant runs six weeks before my return to consciousness, and as they could not believe that a pedestrian, without provisions, could get over that unknown stretch of country from Fremantle, they paid no attention to my ravings about being an escaped convict, particularly as the rags I had on could never have been prison made. Learning, however, that I had medical knowledge, by the simple method of putting it to the test, my good rescuers set me up in my old profession, where I still remain – a Queensland back-country doctor.

THE HOUR AND THE MAN

by

Robert Barr

*Like his contemporary, Hume Nisbet, Robert Barr (1850–1912)
spent a lot of time abroad, in Canada and North America, before
returning to England to find literary fame.*

*Barr emigrated to Canada with his family at the age of four.
He was educated in Toronto, and after a spell as headmaster of a
school, he moved to Detroit where he became a reporter on the* Free
Press. *He returned to England in 1881 when his paper sent him to
set up a British edition. After a time, Barr started his own publish-
ing house and, together with the humorist Jerome K. Jerome,
founded and edited the magazine* The Idler *in 1892. Much of his
journalism appeared under the pseudonym of Luke Sharp and it was
this name that he used for his first book* Strange Happenings
(1883).*

*It was not until nine years later that he published a book under
his own name; this was his skilled collection of short stories* In a
Steamer Chair *(1892) and he followed this up with other volumes
of tales, among them* The Face and the Mask *(1894) and a post-
humous work* The Helping Hand *(1920).*

*Robert Barr is still remembered for his detective stories, wherein
he created the renowned Eugene Valmont. His ghost stories failed to
achieve such lasting fame, though they included an original short
novel* From Whose Bourne *(1893) and a fine collection of short
grim tales* Revenge! *(1896).*

'The Hour and the Man' comes from Revenge! *and, while it is
clearly modelled on the style of the* conte cruel *authors, such as
Villiers de L'Isle Adam, it is nevertheless a splendidly macabre
story that deserves to see the light of day once more.*

Prince Lotarno rose slowly to his feet, casting one malignant glance at the prisoner before him.

'You have heard,' he said, 'what is alleged against you. Have you anything to say in your defence?'

The captured brigand laughed.

'The time for talk is past,' he cried. 'This has been a fine farce of a fair trial. You need not have wasted so much time over what you call evidence. I knew my doom when I fell into your hands. I killed your brother; you will kill me. You have proven that I am a murderer and a robber; I could prove the same of you if you were bound hand and foot in my camp as I am bound in your castle. It is useless for me to tell you that I did not know he was your brother, else it would not have happened, for the small robber always respects the larger and more powerful thief. When a wolf is down, the other wolves devour him. I am down, and you will have my head cut off, or my body drawn asunder in your court-yard, whichever pleases your Excellency best. It is the fortune of war, and I do not complain. When I say that I am sorry I killed your brother, I merely mean I am sorry you were not the man who stood in his shoes when the shot was fired. You, having more men than I had, have scattered my followers and captured me. You may do with me what you please. My consolation is that killing me will not bring to life the man who is shot, therefore conclude the farce that has dragged through so many weary hours. Pronounce my sentence. I am ready.'

There was a moment's silence after the brigand had ceased speaking. Then the Prince said, in low tones, but in a voice that made itself heard in every part of the judgement-hall –

'Your sentence is that on the fifteenth of January you shall be taken from your cell at four o'clock, conducted to the room of execution, and there beheaded.'

The Prince hesitated for a moment as he concluded the sentence, and seemed about to add something more, but apparently he remembered that a report of the trial was to go before the King, whose representative was present, and he was particularly desirous that nothing should go on the records which savoured of old-time malignity; for it was well known that his Majesty had a par-ticular aversion to the ancient forms of torture that had obtained heretofore in his kingdom. Recollecting this, the Prince sat down.

The brigand laughed again. His sentence was evidently not so gruesome as he had expected. He was a man who had lived all his life in the mountains, and he had had no means of knowing that more merciful measures had been introduced into the policy of the Government.

'I will keep the appointment,' he said jauntily, 'unless I have a more pressing engagement.'

The brigand was led away to his cell. 'I hope,' said the Prince, 'that you noted the defiant attitude of the prisoner.'

'I have not failed to do so, your Excellency,' replied the ambassador.

'I think,' said the Prince, 'that under the circumstances, his treatment has been most merciful.'

'I am certain, your Excellency,' said the ambassador, 'that his Majesty will be of the same opinion. For such a miscreant beheading is too easy a death.'

The Prince was pleased to know that the opinion of the ambassador coincided so entirely with his own.

The brigand Toza was taken to a cell in the northern tower, where, by climbing on a bench, he could get a view of the profound valley at the mouth of which the castle was situated. He well knew its impregnable position, commanding, as it did, the entrance to the valley. He knew also that if he succeeded in escaping from the castle he was hemmed in by mountains practically unscalable, while the mouth of the gorge was so well guarded by the castle that it was impossible to get to the outer world through that gateway. Although he knew the mountains well, he realised that, with his band scattered, many killed, and the others fugitives, he would have a better chance of starving to death in the valley than of escaping out of it. He sat on the bench and thought over the situation. Why had the Prince been so merciful? He had expected torture, whereas he was to meet the easiest death that a man could die. He felt satisfied there was something in this that he could not understand. Perhaps they intended to starve him to death, now that the appearance of a fair trial was over. Things could be done in the dungeon of a castle that the outside world knew nothing of. His fears of starvation were speedily put to an end by the appearance of his gaoler with a better meal than he had had for some time; for during the last week he had wandered a fugitive in the mountains until captured by the Prince's men, who evidently had orders to bring him in alive. Why then were they so anxious not to kill him in a fair fight if he were now to be merely beheaded?

'What is your name?' asked Toza of his gaoler.

'I am called Paulo,' was the answer.

'Do you know that I am to be beheaded on the fifteenth of the month?'

'I have heard so,' answered the man.

'And do you attend me until that time?'

'I attend you while I am ordered to do so. If you talk much I may be replaced.'

'That, then, is a tip for silence, good Paulo,' said the brigand. 'I always treat well those who serve me well; I regret, therefore, that I have no money with me, and so cannot recompense you for good service.'

'That is not necessary,' answered Paulo. 'I receive my recompense from the steward.'

'Ah, but the recompense of the steward and the recompense of a brigand chief are two very different things. Are there so many pickings in your position that you are rich, Paulo?'

'No; I am a poor man.'

'Well, under certain circumstances, I could make you rich.'

Paulo's eyes glistened, but he made no direct reply. Finally he said, in a frightened whisper, 'I have tarried too long, I am watched. By-and-by the vigilance will be relaxed, and then we may perhaps talk of riches.'

With that the gaoler took his departure. The brigand laughed softly to himself. 'Evidently,' he said, 'Paulo is not above the reach of a bribe. We will have further talk on the subject when the watchfulness is relaxed.'

And so it grew to be a question of which should trust the other. The brigand asserted that hidden in the mountains he had gold and jewels, and these he would give to Paulo if he could contrive his escape from the castle.

'Once free of the castle, I can soon make my way out of the valley,' said the brigand.

'I am not so sure of that,' answered Paulo. 'The castle is well guarded, and when it is discovered that you have escaped, the alarm-bell will be rung, and after that not a mouse can leave the valley without the soldiers knowing it.'

The brigand pondered on the situation for some time, and at last said, 'I know the mountains well.'

'Yes,' said Paulo; 'but you are one man, and the soldiers of the Prince are many. Perhaps,' he added, 'if it were made worth my while, I could show you that I know the mountains even better than you do.'

'What do you mean?' asked the brigand, in an excited whisper.

'Do you know the tunnel?' inquired Paulo, with an anxious glance towards the door.

'What tunnel? I never heard of any.'

'But it exists, nevertheless; a tunnel through the mountains to the world outside.'

'A tunnel through the mountains? Nonsense!' cried the brigand. 'I should have known of it if one existed. The work would be too great to accomplish.'

'It was made long before your day, or mine either. If the castle had fallen, then those who were inside could escape through the tunnel. Few know of the entrance; it is near the waterfall up the valley, and is covered with brushwood. What will you give me to place you at the entrance of that tunnel?'

The brigand looked at Paulo sternly for a few moments, then he answered slowly, 'Everything I possess.'

'And how much is that?' asked Paulo.

'It is more than you will ever earn by serving the Prince.'

'Will you tell me where it is before I help you to escape from the castle and lead you to the tunnel?'

'Yes,' said Toza.

'Will you tell me now?'

'No; bring me a paper tomorrow, and I will draw a plan showing you how to get it.'

When his gaoler appeared, the day after Toza had given the plan, the brigand asked eagerly, 'Did you find the treasure?'

'I did,' said Paulo quietly.

'And will you keep your word? – will you get me out of the castle?'

'I will get you out of the castle and lead you to the entrance of the tunnel, but after that you must look to yourself.'

'Certainly,' said Toza, 'that was the bargain. Once out of this accursed valley, I can defy all the princes in Christendom. Have you a rope?'

'We shall need none,' said the gaoler. 'I will come for you at midnight, and take you out of the castle by the secret passage; then your escape will not be noticed until morning.'

At midnight his gaoler came and led Toza through many a tortuous passage, the two men pausing now and then, holding their breaths anxiously as they came to an open court through which a guard paced. At last they were outside of the castle at one hour past midnight.

The brigand drew a long breath of relief when he was once again out in the free air.

'Where is your tunnel?' he asked, in a somewhat distrustful whisper of his guide.

'Hush!' was the low answer. 'It is only a short distance from the castle, but every inch is guarded, and we cannot go direct; we must make for the other side of the valley and come to it from the north.'

'What!' cried Toza in amazement, 'traverse the whole valley for a tunnel a few yards away?'

'It is the only safe plan,' said Paulo. 'If you wish to go by the direct way, I must leave you to your own devices.'

'I am in your hands,' said the brigand with a sigh. 'Take me where you will, so long as you lead me to the entrance of the tunnel.'

They passed down and down around the heights on which the castle stood, and crossed the purling little river by means of stepping-stones. Once Toza fell into the water, but was rescued by his guide. There was still no alarm from the castle as daylight began to break. As it grew more light they both crawled into a cave which had a low opening difficult to find, and there Paulo gave the brigand his breakfast, which he took from a little bag slung by a strap across his shoulder.

'What are we going to do for food if we are to be days between here and the tunnel?' asked Toza.

'Oh, I have arranged for that, and a quantity of food has been placed where we are most likely to want it. I will get it while you sleep.'

'But if you are captured, what am I to do?' asked Toza. 'Can you not tell me now how to find the tunnel, as I told you how to find the treasure?'

Paulo pondered over this for a moment, and then said, 'Yes; I think it would be the safer way. You must follow the stream until you reach the place where the torrent from the east joins it. Among the hills there is a waterfall, and halfway up the precipice on a shelf of rock there are sticks and bushes. Clear them away, and you will find the entrance to the tunnel. Go through the tunnel until you come to a door, which is bolted on this side. When you have passed through, you will see the end of your journey.'

Shortly after daybreak the big bell of the castle began to toll, and before noon the soldiers were beating the bushes all around them. They were so close that the two men could hear their voices from their hiding-place, where they lay in their wet clothes, breathlessly expecting every moment to be discovered.

The conversation of two soldiers, who were nearest them, nearly caused the hearts of the hiding listeners to stop beating.

'Is there not a cave near here?' asked one. 'Let us search for it!'

'Nonsense,' said the other. 'I tell you that they could not have come this far already.'

'Why could they not have escaped when the guard changed at midnight?' insisted the first speaker.

'Because Paulo was seen crossing the courtyard at midnight, and they could have had no other chance of getting away until just before daybreak.'

This answer seemed to satisfy his comrade, and the search was given up just as they were about to come upon the fugitives. It was a narrow escape, and, brave as the robber was, he looked pale, while Paulo was in a state of collapse.

Many times during the nights and days that followed, the brigand and his guide almost fell into the hands of the minions of the Prince. Exposure, privation, semi-starvation, and, worse than all, the alternate wrenchings of hope and fear, began to tell upon the stalwart frame of the brigand. Some days and nights of cold winter rain added to their misery. They dare not seek shelter, for every habitable place was watched.

When daylight overtook them on their last night's crawl through the valley, they were within a short distance of the waterfall, whose low roar now came soothingly down to them.

'Never mind the daylight,' said Toza; 'let us push on and reach the tunnel.'

'I can go no farther,' moaned Paulo; 'I am exhausted.'

'Nonsense,' cried Toza; 'it is but a short distance.'

'The distance is greater than you think; besides, we are in full view of the castle. Would you risk everything now that the game is nearly won? You must not forget that the stake is your head; and remember what day this is.'

'What day is it?' asked the brigand, turning on his guide.

'It is the fifteenth of January, the day on which you were to be executed.'

Toza caught his breath sharply. Danger and want had made a coward of him, and he shuddered now, which he had not done when he was on his trial and condemned to death.

'How do you know it is the fifteenth?' he asked at last.

Paulo held up his stick, notched after the method of Robinson Crusoe.

'I am not so strong as you are, and if you will let me rest here until the afternoon, I am willing to make a last effort, and try to reach the entrance of the tunnel.'

'Very well,' said Toza shortly.

As they lay there that morning neither could sleep. The noise of the waterfall was music to the ears of both; their long toilsome journey was almost over.

'What did you do with the gold that you found in the mountains?' asked Toza suddenly.

Paulo was taken unawares, and answered, without thinking, 'I left it where it was. I will get it after.'

The brigand said nothing, but that remark condemned Paulo to death. Toza resolved to murder him as soon as they were well out of the tunnel, and get the gold himself.

They left their hiding-place shortly before twelve o'clock, but their progress was so slow, crawling, as they had to do, up the steep side of the mountain, under cover of bushes and trees, that it was well after three when they came to the waterfall, which they crossed, as best they could, on stones and logs.

'There,' said Toza, shaking himself, 'that is our last wetting. Now for the tunnel!'

The rocky sides of the waterfall hid them from view of the castle, but Paulo called the brigand's attention to the fact that they could be easily seen from the other side of the valley.

'It doesn't matter now,' said Toza; 'lead the way as quickly as you can to the mouth of the cavern.'

Paulo scrambled on until he reached a shelf about halfway up the cataract; he threw aside bushes, brambles, and logs, speedily disclosing a hole large enough to admit a man.

'You go first,' said Paulo, standing aside.

'No,' answered Toza; 'you know the way, and must go first. You cannot think that I wish to harm you – I am completely unarmed.'

'Nevertheless,' said Paulo, 'I shall not go first. I did not like the way you looked at me when I told you the gold was still in the hills. I admit that I distrust you.'

'Oh, very well,' laughed Toza, 'it doesn't really matter.' And he crawled into the hole in the rock, Paulo following him.

Before long the tunnel enlarged so that a man could stand upright.

'Stop!' said Paulo; 'there is the door near here.'

'Yes,' said the robber, 'I remember that you spoke of a door,' adding, however, 'What is it for, and why is it locked?'

'It is bolted on this side,' answered Paulo, 'and we shall have no difficulty in opening it.'

'What is it for?' repeated the brigand.

'It is to prevent the current of air running through the tunnel and blowing away the obstruction at this end,' said the guide.

'Here it is,' said Toza, as he felt down its edge for the bolt.

The bolt drew back easily, and the door opened. The next instant the brigand was pushed rudely into a room, and he heard the bolt thrust back into its place almost simultaneously with the noise of the closing door. For a moment his eyes were dazzled by the light. He was in an apartment blazing with torches held by a dozen men standing about.

In the centre of the room was a block covered with black cloth, and beside it stood a masked executioner, resting the corner of a gleaming axe on the black draped block, with his hands crossed over the end of the axe's handle.

The Prince stood there surrounded by his ministers. Above his head was a clock, with the minute hand pointed to the hour of four.

'You are just in time!' said the Prince grimly; 'we are waiting for you!'

NUT BUSH FARM

by

Mrs J. H. Riddell

The life of Mrs J. H. Riddell (1832–1906) was marred by tragedy, illness and poverty, reading like a scriptwriter's dream: rags to riches and back to rags again. Yet, as her biographer S. M. Ellis records, she was one of the most cheerful people he ever met.

Born Charlotte Cowan, daughter of the High Sheriff of the County of Antrim, she wrote from childhood and Ellis notes that she had written a novel by the time she was fifteen. In 1855 her father died and she moved with her mother, who was already dying of cancer, to London. Casting about for a means of support, she engaged in a fairly short, but grim, search for a publisher for her works. Her first book Zuriel's Grandchild *appeared anonymously that same year, and her second* The Moors and the Fens *(1858) appeared under the pen-name F. G. Trafford. It took some years for her to establish her reputation but by 1866 she was able to publish under her own name. Her most famous and successful novel* George Geith of Fen Court *was first published pseudonymously in 1864 and was later reprinted many times under her own name.*

By 1867 she had reached the peak of her career, that same year becoming editor and part-proprietor of The St James's Maga-zine. *As she is reputed to have lost all count of her works, it is more than likely that to this day, many of her stories lie undiscovered and unidentified in this and other magazines.*

For many years, Mrs Riddell enjoyed huge success and financial comfort. But it was not to last. In 1857, she had married Joseph Riddell, a civil engineer with bad business instinct. He died in 1880 in financial ruin and, with no legal obligation to do so, his wife undertook to repay all his debts. For years she struggled to cancel his liabilities, crippling herself financially in later years when her books no longer enjoyed great success. The final tragedy came when she found she had the same disease that killed her mother. She

spent her last years in poverty and ill-health, dying in Hounslow in
1906.

Mrs Riddell had a most extraordinary method of composition.
She remarked to her publisher one day that she had finished her
latest novel. He asked when he could see the manuscript and was
startled to find that she had not committed a single word to paper.
She would 'write' her books mentally, down to the last conversation,
before she actually wrote a word.

Today, Charlotte Riddell is remembered mainly for her ghost
stories, which were some of the best to be written by Victorian
women. She produced several volumes, among them The Haunted
River *(1877),* The Nun's Curse *(1888) and* The Banshee's
Warning *(1894). Her most famous collection,* Weird Stories
(1884), was a short but masterly set of fine tales, from which comes
'Nut Bush Farm'. In it, Mrs Riddell goes against the most
hallowed traditions of Victorian ghost stories – she produces her
ghost in broad daylight.

Chapter one

When I entered upon the tenancy of Nut Bush Farm almost the
first piece of news which met me, in the shape of a whispered
rumour, was that 'something' had been seen in the 'long field'.

Pressed closely as to what he meant, my informant reluctantly
stated that the 'something' took the 'form of a man', and that the
wood and the path leading thereto from Whittleby were supposed
to be haunted.

Now, all this annoyed me exceedingly. I do not know when
I was more put out than by this intelligence. It is unnecessary to
say I did not believe in ghosts or anything of that kind, but my
wife being a very nervous, impressionable woman, and our only
child a delicate weakling, in the habit of crying himself into fits if
left alone at night without a candle, I really felt at my wits' end to
imagine what I should do if a story of this sort reached their ears.

And reach them I knew it must if they came to Nut Bush
Farm, so the first thing I did when I heard people did not care to
venture down the Beech Walk or through the copse, or across the
long field after dark, or indeed by day, was to write to say I thought
they had both better remain on at my father-in-law's till I could
get the house thoroughly to rights.

After that I lit my pipe and went out for a stroll; when I knocked the ashes out of my pipe and re-entered the sitting-room I had made up my mind. I could not afford to be frightened away from my tenancy. For weal or for woe I must stick to Nut Bush Farm. It was quite by chance I happened to know anything of the place at first. When I met with that accident in my employers' service, which they rated far too highly and recompensed with a liberality I never can feel sufficiently grateful for, the doctors told me plainly if I could not give up office work and leave London altogether, they would not give a year's purchase for my life.

Life seemed very sweet to me then – it always has done – but just at that period I felt the pleasant hopes of convalescence, and with that thousand pounds safely banked, I *could* not let it slip away from me.

'Take a farm,' advised my father-in-law. 'Though people say a farmer's is a bad trade, I know many a man who is making money out of it. Take a farm, and if you want a helping hand to enable you to stand the racket for a year or two, why, you know I am always ready.'

I had been bred and born on a farm. My father held something like fifteen hundred acres under the principal landowner in his county, and though it so happened I could not content myself at home, but must needs come up to London to see the lions and seek my fortune, still I had never forgotten the meadows and the corn-fields, and the cattle, and the orchards, and the woods and the streams, amongst which my happy boyhood had been spent. Yes, I thought I should like a farm – one not too far from London; and 'not too big', advised my wife's father.

'The error people make nowadays,' he went on, 'is spreading their butter over too large a surface. It is the same in business as in land – they stretch their arms out too far – they will try to wade in deep waters – and the consequence is they never know a day's peace, and end mostly in the bankruptcy court.'

He spoke as one having authority, and I knew what he said was quite right. He had made his money by a very different course of procedure, and I felt I could not follow a better example.

I knew something about farming, though not very much. Still, agriculture is like arithmetic: when once one knows the multiplication table the rest is not so difficult. I had learned unconsciously the alphabet of soils and crops and stock when I was an idle young dog, and liked nothing better than talking to the labourers, and accompanying the woodman when he went out felling trees; and so I did not feel much afraid of what the result would be, more especially as I had a good business head on my shoulders, and enough money to 'stand the racket', as my father-in-law put it, till the land began to bring in her increase.

When I got strong and well again after my long illness – I mean strong and well enough to go about – I went down to look at a farm which was advertised as to let in Kent.

According to the statement in the newspaper, there was no charm that farm lacked; when I saw it I discovered the place did not possess one virtue, unless, indeed, an old Tudor house fast falling to ruins, which would have proved invaluable to an artist, could be so considered. Far from a railway, having no advantages of water carriage, remote from a market, apparently destitute of society. Nor could these drawbacks be accounted the worst against it. The land, poor originally, seemed to have been totally exhausted. There were fields on which I do not think a goose could have found subsistence – nothing grew luxuriantly save weeds; it would have taken all my capital to get the ground clean. Then I saw the fences were dilapidated, the hedges in a deplorable condition, and the farm buildings in such a state of decay I would not have stabled a donkey in one of them.

Clearly, the King's Manor, which was the modest name of the place, would not do at any price, and yet I felt sorry, for the country around was beautiful, and already the sweet, pure air seemed to have braced up my nerves and given me fresh energy. Talking to mine host at the 'Bunch of Hops', in Whittleby, he advised me to look over the local paper before returning to London.

'There be many farms vacant,' he said, 'mayhap you'll light on one to suit.'

To cut a long story short, I did look in the local paper and found many farms to let, but not one to suit. There was a drawback to each – a drawback at least so far as I was concerned. I felt determined I would not take a large farm. My conviction was then what my conviction still remains, that it is better to cultivate fifty acres thoroughly than to crop, stock, clean, and manure a hundred insufficiently. Besides, I did not want to spend my strength on wages, or take a place so large I could not oversee the workmen on foot. For all these reasons and many more I came reluctantly to the conclusion that there was nothing in that part of the country to suit a poor unspeculative plodder like myself.

It was a lovely afternoon in May when I turned my face towards Whittleby, as I thought, for the last time. In the morning I had taken train for a farm some ten miles distant and worked my way back on foot to a 'small cottage with land' a local agent thought might suit me. But neither the big place nor the little answered my requirements much to the disgust of the auctioneer, who had himself accompanied us to the cottage under the impression I would immediately purchase it and so secure his commission.

Somewhat sulkily he told me a short cut back to Whittleby, and added, as a sort of rider to all previous statements, the remark:

'You had best look out for what you want in Middlesex. You'll find nothing of that sort hereabouts.'

As to the last part of the foregoing sentence I was quite of his opinion, but I felt so oppressed with the result of all my wanderings that I thought upon the whole I had better abandon my search altogether, or else pursue it in some county very far away indeed – perhaps in the land of dreams for that matter!

As has been said, it was a lovely afternoon in May – the hedges were snowy with hawthorn blossom, the chestnuts were bursting into flower, the birds were singing fit to split their little throats, the lambs were dotting the hillsides, and I – ah, well, I was a boy again, able to relish all the rich banquet God spreads out day by day for the delight and nourishment of His too often thankless children.

When I came to a point half way up some rising ground where four lanes met and then wound off each on some picturesque diverse way, I paused to look around regretfully.

As I did so – some distance below me – along what appeared to be a never-before-traversed lane, I saw the gleam of white letters on a black board.

'Come,' I thought, 'I'll see what this is at all events,' and bent my steps towards the place, which might, for all I knew about it, have been a ducal mansion or a cockney's country villa.

The board appeared modestly conspicuous in the foreground of a young fir plantation, and simply bore this legend:

To be let, House and Land,
Apply at the 'White Dragon.'

'It is a mansion,' I thought, and I walked on slowly, disappointed.

All of a sudden the road turned a sharp corner and I came in an instant upon the prettiest place I had ever seen or ever desire to see.

I looked at it over a low laurel hedge growing inside an open paling about four feet high. Beyond the hedge there was a strip of turf, green as emeralds, smooth as a bowling green – then came a sunk fence, the most picturesque sort of protection the ingenuity of man ever devised; beyond that, a close-cut lawn which sloped down to the sunk fence from a house with projecting gables in the front, the recessed portion of the building having three windows on the first floor. Both gables were covered with creepers, the lawn was girt in by a semi-circular sweep of forest trees, the afternoon sun streamed over the grass and tinted the swaying foliage with a thousand tender lights. Hawthorn bushes, pink and white, mingled with their taller and grander brothers. The chestnuts here were in flower, the copper beech made a delightful contrast of colour, and a birch rose delicate and graceful close beside.

It was like a fairy scene. I passed my hand across my eyes to assure myself it was all real. Then I thought 'if this place be even nearly within my means I will settle here. My wife will grow stronger in this paradise – my boy get more like other lads. Such things as nerves must be unknown where there is not a sight or sound to excite them. Nothing but health, purity, and peace.'

Thus thinking, I tore myself away in search of the 'White Dragon', the landlord of which small public-house sent a lad to show me over the farm.

'As for the rent,' he said, 'you will have to speak to Miss Gostock herself – she lives at Chalmont, on the road between here and Whittleby.'

In every respect the place suited me; it was large enough, but not too large; had been well farmed, and was amply supplied with water – a stream indeed flowing through it; a station was shortly to be opened, at about half-a-mile's distance; and most of the produce could be disposed of to dealers and tradesmen at Crayshill, a town to which the communication by rail was direct.

I felt so anxious about the matter, it was quite a disappointment to find Miss Gostock from home. Judging from the look of her house, I did not suppose she could afford to stick out for a long rent, or to let a farm lie idle for any considerable period. The servant who appeared in answer to my summons was a singularly red armed and rough handed Phyllis. There was only a strip of carpeting laid down in the hall, the windows were bare of draperies, and the avenue gate, set a little back from the main road, was such as I should have felt ashamed to put in a farmyard.

Next morning I betook myself to Chalmont, anxiously wondering as I walked along what the result of my interview would prove.

When I neared the gate, to which uncomplimentary reference has already been made, I saw standing on the other side a figure wearing a man's broad-brimmed straw hat, a man's coat, and a woman's skirt.

I raised my hat in deference to the supposed sex of this stranger. She put up one finger to the brim of hers, and said, 'Servant, sir.'

Not knowing exactly what to do, I laid my hand upon the latch of the gate and raised it, but she did not alter her position in the least.

She only asked, 'What do you want?'

'I want to see Miss Gostock,' was my answer.

'I am Miss Gostock,' she said; 'what is your business with me?'

I replied meekly that I had come to ask the rent of Nut Bush Farm.

'Have you viewed it?' she inquired.

'Yes.' I told her I had been over the place on the previous afternoon.

'And have you a mind to take it?' she persisted. 'For I am not going to trouble myself answering a lot of idle inquiries.'

So far from my being an idle inquirer, I assured the lady that if we could come to terms about the rent, I should be very glad indeed to take the farm. I said I had been searching the neighbourhood within a circuit of ten miles for some time unsuccessfully, and added, somewhat unguardedly, I suppose, Nut Bush Farm was the only place I had met with which at all met my views.

Standing in an easy attitude, with one arm resting on the top bar of the gate and one foot crossed over the other, Miss Gostock surveyed me, who had unconsciously taken up a similar position, with an amused smile.

'You must think me a very honest person, young man,' she remarked.

I answered that I hoped she was, but I had not thought at all about the matter.

'Or else,' proceeded this extraordinary lady, 'you fancy I am a much greater fool than I am.'

'On the contrary,' was my reply. 'If there be one impression stronger than another which our short interview has made upon me it is that you are a wonderfully direct and capable woman of business.'

She looked at me steadily, and then closed one eye, which performance, done under the canopy of that broad-brimmed straw hat, had the most ludicrous effect imaginable.

'You won't catch me napping,' she observed, 'but, however, as you seem to mean dealing, come in; I can tell you my terms in two minutes,' and opening the gate – a trouble she would not allow me to take off her hands – she gave me admission.

Then Miss Gostock took off her hat, and swinging it to and fro began slowly walking up the ascent leading to Chalmont, I beside her.

'I have quite made up my mind,' she said, 'not to let the farm again without a premium; my last tenant treated me abominably –'

I intimated I was sorry to hear that, and waited for further information.

'He had the place at a low rent – a very low rent. He should not have got it so cheap but for his covenanting to put so much money in the soil; and well – I'm bound to say he acted fair so far as that – he fulfilled that part of his contract. Nearly two years ago we had a bit of a quarrel about – well, it's no matter what we fell out over – only the upshot of the affair was he gave me due notice to leave at last winter quarter. At that time he owed about a year-and-a-half's rent – for he was a man who never could bear parting with money – and like a fool I did not push him for it. What trick do you suppose he served me for my pains?'

It was simply impossible for me to guess, so I did not try.

'On the twentieth of December,' went on Miss Gostock, turning her broad face and curly grey hair – she wore her hair short like a man – towards me, 'he went over to Whittleby, drew five thousand pounds out of the bank, was afterwards met going towards home by a gentleman named Waite, a friend of his. Since then he has never been seen nor heard of.'

'Bless my soul!' I exclaimed involuntarily.

'You may be very sure I did not bless his soul,' she snarled out angrily. 'The man bolted with the five thousand pounds, having

previously sold off all his stock and the bulk of his produce, and
when I distrained for my rent, which I did pretty smart, I can tell
you, there was scarce enough on the premises to pay the levy.'

'But what in the world made him bolt?' I asked, quite unconsciously adopting Miss Gostock's expressive phrase; 'as he had so
much money, why did he not pay you your rent?'

'Ah! Why, indeed?' mocked Miss Gostock. 'Young sir, I am
afraid you are a bit of a humbug, or you would have suggested
at once there was a pretty girl at the bottom of the affair. He left
his wife and children, and me – all in the lurch – and went off with
a slip of a girl, whom I once took, thinking to train up as a better
sort of servant, but was forced to discharge. Oh, the little hussy!'

Somehow I did not fancy I wanted to hear anything more about
her late tenant and the pretty girl, and consequently ventured to
inquire how that gentleman's defalcations bore upon the question
of the rent I should have to pay.

'I tell you directly,' she said, and as we had by this time arrived
at the house, she invited me to enter, and led the way into an old-
fashioned parlour that must have been furnished about the time
chairs and tables were first invented and which did not contain a
single feminine belonging – not even a thimble.

'Sit down,' she commanded, and I sat. 'I have quite made up my
mind,' she began, 'not to let the farm again, unless I get a premium
sufficient to insure me against the chances of possible loss. I mean
to ask a very low rent and – a premium.'

'And what amount of premium do you expect?' I inquired,
doubtfully.

'I want – ' and here Miss Gostock named a sum which fairly
took my breath away.

'In that case,' I said as soon as I got it again, 'it is useless to
prolong this interview; I can only express my regret for having
intruded, and wish you good morning.' And arising, I was bowing
myself out when she stopped me.

'Don't be so fast,' she cried, 'I only said what I wanted. Now
what are you prepared to give?'

'I can't be buyer and seller too,' I answered, repeating a phrase
the precise meaning of which, it may here be confessed, I have
never been able exactly to understand.

'Nonsense,' exclaimed Miss Gostock – I am really afraid the lady
used a stronger term – 'if you are anything of a man of business,

fit at all to commence farming, you must have an idea on the subject. You shall have the land at a pound an acre, and you will give me for premium – come, how much?'

By what mental process I instantly jumped to an amount it would be impossible to say, but I did mention one which elicited from Miss Gostock the remark:

'That won't do at any price.'

'Very well, then,' I said, 'we need not talk any more about the matter.'

'But what *will* you give?' asked the lady.

'I have told you,' was my answer, 'and I am not given either to haggling or beating down.'

'You won't make a good farmer,' she observed.

'If a farmer's time were of any value, which it generally seems as if it were not,' I answered, 'he would not waste it in splitting a sixpence.'

She laughed, and her laugh was not musical.

'Come now,' she said, 'make another bid.'

'No,' I replied, 'I have made one and that is enough. I won't offer another penny.'

'Done then,' cried Miss Gostock, 'I accept your offer – we'll just sign a little memorandum of agreement, and the formal deeds can be prepared afterwards. You'll pay a deposit, I suppose?'

I was so totally taken aback by her acceptance of my offer I could only stammer out I was willing to do anything that might be usual.

'It does not matter much whether it is usual or not,' she said; 'either pay it or I won't keep the place for you. I am not going to have my land lying idle and my time taken up for your pleasure.'

'I have no objection to paying you a deposit,' I answered.

'That's right,' she exclaimed; 'now if you will just hand me over the writing-desk we can settle the matter, so far as those thieves of lawyers will let us, in five minutes.'

Like one in a dream I sat and watched Miss Gostock while she wrote. Nothing about the transaction seemed to me real. The farm itself resembled nothing I had ever before seen with my waking eyes, and Miss Gostock appeared to me but as some monstrous figure in a story of giants and hobgoblins. The man's coat, the woman's skirt, the hob-nailed shoes, the grisly hair, the old straw hat, the bare, unfurnished room, the bright sunshine outside, all struck me as mere accessories in a play – as nothing which had any hold on the outside, everyday world.

It was drawn – we signed our names. I handed Miss Gostock over a cheque. She locked one document in an iron box let into the wall, and handed me the other, adding, as a rider, a word of caution about 'keeping it safe and taking care it was not lost.'

Then she went to a corner cupboard, and producing a square decanter half full of spirits, set that and two tumblers on the table.

'You don't like much water, I suppose,' she said, pouring out a measure which frightened me.

'I could not touch it, thank you, Miss Gostock,' I exclaimed; 'I dare not do so; I should never get back to Whittleby.'

For answer she only looked at me contemptuously and said, 'D—d nonsense.'

'No nonsense, indeed,' I persisted; 'I am not accustomed to anything of that sort.'

Miss Gostock laughed again, then crossing to the sideboard she returned with a jug of water, a very small portion of the contents of which she mixed with the stronger liquor, and raised the glass to her lips.

'To your good health and prosperity,' she said, and in one instant the fiery potion was swallowed.

'You'll mend of all that,' she remarked, as she laid down her glass, and wiped her lips in the simplest manner by passing the back of her hand over them.

'I hope not, Miss Gostock,' I ventured to observe.

'Why, you look quite shocked,' she said; 'did you never see a lady take a mouthful of brandy before?'

I ventured to hint that I had not, more particularly so early in the morning.

'Pooh!' she said. 'Early in the morning or late at night, where's the difference? However, there was a time when I – but that was before I had come through so much trouble. Goodbye for the present, and I hope we shall get on well together.'

I answered I trusted we should, and was half-way to the hall-door, when she called me back.

'I forgot to ask you if you were married,' she said.

'Yes, I have been married some years,' I answered.

'That's a pity,' she remarked, and dismissed me with a wave of her hand.

'What on earth would have happened had I not been married?'
I considered as I hurried down the drive. 'Surely she never con-
templated proposing to me herself? But nothing she could do
would surprise me.'

Chapter two

There were some repairs I had mentioned it would be necessary to
have executed before I came to live at Nut Bush Farm, but when
I found Miss Gostock intended to do them herself – nay, was doing
them all herself – I felt thunderstruck.

On one memorable occasion I came upon her with a red hand-
kerchief tied round her head, standing at a carpenter's bench in a
stable yard, planing away, under a sun which would have killed
anybody but a negro or my landlady.

She painted the gates, and put sash lines in some of the windows;
she took off the locks, oiled, and replaced them; she mowed the
lawn, and offered to teach me how to mow; and lastly, she showed
me a book where she charged herself and paid herself for every
hour's work done.

'I've made at least twenty pounds out of your place,' she said
triumphantly. 'Higgs at Whittleby would not have charged me a
halfpenny less for the repairs. The tradesmen here won't give me
a contract – they say it is just time thrown away, but I know that
would have been about his figure. Well, the place is ready for you
now, and if you take my advice, you'll get your grass up as soon as
possible. It's a splendid crop, and if you hire hands enough, not a
drop of rain need spoil it. If this weather stands you might cut one
day and carry the next.'

I took her advice, and stacked my hay in magnificent condition.
Miss Gostock was good enough to come over and superintend the
building of the stack, and threatened to split one man's head open
with the pitchfork, and proposed burying another – she called him
a 'lazy blackguard' – under a pile of hay.

'I will say this much for Hascot,' she remarked, as we stood
together beside the stream; 'he was a good farmer; where will you
see better or cleaner land? A pattern I call it – and to lose his whole
future for the sake of a girl like Sally Powner; leaving his wife
and children on the parish, too!'

'You don't mean that?' I said.

'Indeed I do. They are all at Crayshill. The authorities did talk of shifting them, but I know nothing about what they have done.'

I stood appalled. I thought of my own poor wife and the little lad, and wondered if any Sally on the face of the earth could make me desert them.

'It has given the place a bad sort of name,' remarked Miss Gostock, looking at me sideways: 'but, of course, that does not signify anything to you.'

'Oh, of course not,' I agreed.

'And don't you be minding any stories; there are always a lot of stories going about places.'

I said I did not mind stories. I had lived too long in London to pay much attention to them.

'That's right,' remarked Miss Gostock, and negativing my offer to see her home she started off to Chalmont.

It was not half an hour after her departure when I happened to be walking slowly round the meadows, from which the newly mown hay had been carted, that I heard the rumour which vexed me – 'Nut Bush Farm haunted.' I thought, 'I said the whole thing was too good to last.'

'What, Jack, lost in reverie?' cried my sister, who had come up from Devonshire to keep me company, and help to get the furniture a little to rights, entering at the moment, carrying lights; 'supper will be ready in a minute, and you can dream as much as you like after you have had something to eat.'

I did not say anything to her about my trouble, which was then indeed no bigger than a man's hand, but which grew and grew till it attained terrible proportions.

What was I to do with my wife and child? I never could bring them to a place reputed to be haunted. All in vain I sauntered up and down the Beech Walk night after night; walked through the wood – as a rule selected that route when I went to Whittleby. It did not produce the slightest effect. Not a farm servant but eschewed that path townward; not a girl but preferred spending her Sunday at home rather than venture under the interlacing branches of the beech trees, or through the dark recesses of the wood.

It was becoming serious – I did not know what to do.

One wet afternoon Lolly came in draggled but beaming.

'I've made a new acquaintance, Jack,' she said; 'a Mrs Waite –

such a nice creature, but in dreadfully bad health. It came on to rain when I was coming home, and so I took refuge under a great tree at the gate of a most picturesque old house. I had not stood there long before a servant with an umbrella appeared at the porch to ask if I would not please to walk in until the storm abated. I waited there ever so long, and we had such a pleasant talk. She is a most delightful woman, with a melancholy, pathetic sort of expression that has been haunting me ever since. She apologised for not having called – said she was not strong and could not walk so far. They keep no conveyance she can drive. Mr Waite, who is not at home at present, rides into Whittleby when anything is wanted.'

'I hoped she would not think of standing on ceremony with me. I was only a farmer's daughter, and accustomed to plain, homely ways, and I asked her if I might walk round and bid her goodbye before I went home.'

'You must not go home yet, Lolly,' I cried, alarmed; 'what in the world should I do without you?'

'Well, you would be a lonely boy,' she answered, complacently, 'with no one to sew on a button or darn your socks, or make you eat or go to bed, or do anything you ought to do.'

I had not spoken a word to her about the report which was troubling me, and I knew there must be times when she wondered why I did not go up to London and fetch my wife and child to enjoy the bright summer-time; but Lolly was as good as gold, and never asked me a question, or even indirectly inquired if Lucy and I had quarrelled, as many another sister might.

She was as pleasant and fresh to look upon as a spring morning, with her pretty brown hair smoothly braided, her cotton or muslin dresses never soiled or crumpled, but as nice as though the laundress had that moment sent them home – a rose in her belt and her hands never idle – for ever busy with curtain or blind, or something her housewifely eyes thought had need of making or mending.

About ten days after that showery afternoon when she found shelter under Mr Waite's hospitable roof, I felt surprised when, entering the parlour a few minutes before our early dinner, I found Lolly standing beside one of the windows apparently hopelessly lost in the depths of a brown study.

'Why, Lolly,' I exclaimed, finding she took no notice of me, 'where have you gone to now? A penny for your thoughts, young lady.'

'They are not worth a penny,' she said, and turning from the window took some work and sat down at a little distance from the spot where I was standing.

I was so accustomed to women, even the best and gayest of them, having occasional fits of temper or depression – times when silence on my part seemed the truest wisdom – that, taking no notice of my sister's manner, I occupied myself with the newspaper till dinner was announced.

During the progress of that meal she talked little and ate still less, but when I was leaving the room, in order to go out to a field of barley where the reapers were at work, she asked me to stop a moment.

'I want to speak to you, Jack,' she said.

'Speak, then,' I answered, with that lack of ceremony which obtained amongst brothers and sisters.

She hesitated for a moment, but did not speak.

'What on earth is the matter with you, Lolly?' I exclaimed. 'Are you sick, or cross, or sorry, or what?'

'If it must be one of the four,' she answered, with a dash of her usual manner, 'it is "or what," Jack,' and she came close up to where I stood and took me sorrowfully by the buttonhole.

'Well?' I said, amused, for this had always been a favourite habit of Lolly's when she wanted anything from one of the males of her family.

'Jack, you won't laugh at me?'

'I feel much more inclined to be cross with you,' I answered. 'What are you beating about the bush for, Lolly?'

She lifted her fair face a moment and I saw she was crying.

'Lolly, Lolly!' I cried, clasping her to my heart, 'what is it, dear? Have you bad news from home, or have you heard anything about Lucy or the boy? Don't keep me in suspense, there's a darling. No matter what has happened, let me know the worst.'

She smiled through her tears, and Lolly has the rarest smile! It quieted my anxious heart in a moment, even before she said:

'No, Jack – it is nothing about home, or Lucy, or Teddy, but – but – but –' and then she relinquished her hold on the buttonhole, and fingered each button on the front of my coat carefully and lingeringly. 'Did you ever hear – Jack – anybody say anything about this place?'

I knew in a moment what she meant; I knew the cursed tattle had reached her ears, but I only asked:

'What sort of thing, Lolly?'

She did not answer me; instead, she put another question.

'Is that the reason you have not brought Lucy down?'

I felt vexed – but I had so much confidence in her good sense, I could not avoid answering without a moment's delay.

'Well, yes; I do not want her to come till this foolish report has completely died away.'

'Are you quite sure it is a foolish report?' she inquired.

'Why, of course; it could not be anything else.'

She did not speak immediately, then all at once:

'Jack,' she said, 'I must tell you something. Lock the door that we may not be interrupted.'

'No,' I answered; 'come into the barley field. Don't you remember Mr Fenimore Cooper advised, if you want to talk secrets, choose the middle of a plain?'

I tried to put a good face on the matter, but the sight of Lolly's tears, the sound of Lolly's doleful voice, darkened my very heart. What had she to tell me which required locked doors or the greater privacy of a half-reaped barley field. I could trust my sister – she was no fool – and I felt perfectly satisfied that no old woman's story had wrought the effect produced on her.

'Now, Lolly,' I said, as we paced side by side along the top of the barley field in a solitude all the more complete because life and plenty of it was close at hand.

'You know what they say about the place, Jack?'

This was interrogative, and so I answered. 'Well, no, Lolly, I can't say that I do, for the very good reason that I have always refused to listen to the gossip. What do they say?'

'That a man haunts the Beech Walk, the long meadow, and the wood.'

'Yes, I have heard that,' I replied.

'And they say further, the man is Mr Hascot, the late tenant.'

'But he is not dead,' I exclaimed; 'how, then, can they see his ghost?'

'I cannot tell. I know nothing but what I saw this morning. After breakfast I went to Whittleby, and as I came back I observed a man before me on the road. Following him, I noticed a curious thing, that none of the people he met made way for him or he for them. He walked straight on, without any regard to the persons on the side path, and yet no one seemed to come into collision with him. When I reached the field path I saw him going on still at the same pace. He did not look to right or left, and did not seem to walk – the motion was gliding –'

'Yes, dear.'

'He went on, and so did I, till we reached the hollow where the nutbushes grow, then he disappeared from sight. I looked down among the trees, thinking I should be able to catch a glimpse of his figure through the underwood, but no, I could see no signs of him, neither could I hear any. Everything was as still as death; it seemed to me that my ear had a spell of silence laid upon it.'

'And then?' I asked hoarsely, as she paused.

'Why, Jack, I walked on and crossed the little footbridge and was just turning into the Beech Walk when the same man bustled suddenly across my path, so close to me if I had put out my hands I could have touched him. I drew back, frightened for a minute, then, as he had not seemed to see me, I turned and looked at him as he sped along down the little winding path to the wood. I thought he must be some silly creature, some harmless sort of idiot, to be running here and there without any apparent object. All at once, as he neared the wood, he stopped, and, half wheeling round, beckoned to me to follow him.'

'You did not, Lolly?'

'No, I was afraid. I walked a few steps quietly till I got among the beech trees and so screened from sight, and then I began to run. I could not run fast, for my knees trembled under me; but still I did run as far nearly as that seat round the "Priest's Tree". I had not got quite up to the seat when I saw a man rise from it and stand upright as if waiting for me. *It was the same person, Jack!* I recognised him instantly, though I had not seen his face clearly before. He stood quiet for a moment, and then, with the same gliding motion, silently disappeared.'

'Someone must be playing a very nice game about Nut Bush Farm,' I exclaimed.

'Perhaps so, dear,' she said doubtfully.

'Why, Lolly, you don't believe it was a ghost you met in the broad daylight?' I cried incredulously.

'I don't think it was a living man, Jack,' she answered.

'Living or dead, he dare not bring himself into close quarters with me,' was my somewhat braggart remark. 'Why, Lolly, I have walked the ground day after day and night after night in the hope of seeing your friend, and not a sign of an intruder, in the flesh or out of it, could I find. Put the matter away, child, and don't ramble in that direction again. If I can ascertain the name of the person who is trying to frighten the household and disgust me with Nut Bush Farm he shall go to jail if the magistrates are of my way of thinking. Now, as you have told me this terrible story, and we have reduced your great mountain to a molehill, I will walk back with you to the house.'

She did not make any reply: we talked over indifferent matters as we paced along. I went with her into the pleasant sunshiny drawing-room and looked her out a book and made her promise to read something amusing; then I was going, when she put up her lips for me to kiss her, and said –

'Jack, you won't run any risks?'

'Risks – pooh, you silly little woman!' I answered; and so left my sister and repaired to the barley field once more.

When it was time for the men to leave off work I noticed that one after another began to take a path leading immediately to the main road, which was a very circuitous route to the hamlet, where most of them had either cottages or lodgings.

I noticed this for some time, and then asked a brawny young fellow.

'Why don't you go home through the Beech Walk? It is not above half the distance.'

He smiled and made some almost unintelligible answer.

'Why are you all afraid of taking the shortest way,' I remarked, 'seeing there are enough of you to put half a dozen ghosts to the rout?'

'Likely, sir,' was the answer; 'but the old master was a hard man living, and there is not many would care to meet him dead.'

'What old master?' I inquired.

'Mr Hascot: it's him as walks. I saw him as plain as I see you now, sir, one moonlight night, just this side of the wood, and so did Nat Tyler and James Monsey, and James Monsey's father – wise Ben.'

'But Mr Hascot is not dead; how can he "walk", as you call it?' was my natural exclamation.

'If he is living, then, sir, where is he?' asked the man. 'There is nobody can tell that, and there is a many, especially just lately, think he must have been made away with. He had a cruel lot of money about him – where is all that money gone to?'

The fellow had waxed quite earnest in his interrogations, and really for the first time the singularity of Mr Hascot's disappearance seemed to strike me.

I said, after an instant's pause, 'The money is wherever he is. He went off with some girl, did he not?'

'It suited the old people to say so,' he answered; 'but there is many a one thinks they know more about the matter than is good for them. I can't help hearing, and one of the neighbours did say Mrs Ockfield was seen in church last Sunday with a new dress on and a shawl any lady might have worn.'

'And who is Mrs Ockfield?' I inquired.

'Why, Sally Powner's grandmother. The old people treated the girl shameful while she was with them, and now they want to make her out no better than she should be.'

And with a wrathful look the young man, who I subsequently discovered had long been fond of Sally, took up his coat and his tin bottle and his sickle, and with a brief 'I think I'll be going, sir; good night,' departed.

It was easy to return to the house, but I found it impossible to shake the effect produced by this dialogue off my mind.

For the first time I began seriously to consider the manner of Mr Hascot's disappearance, and more seriously still commenced trying to piece together the various hints I had received as to his character.

A hard man – a hard master, all I ever heard speak considered him, but just, and in the main not unkind. He had sent coals to one widow, and kept a poor old labourer off the parish, and then in a minute, for the sake of a girl's face, left his own wife and children to the mercy of the nearest Union.

As I paced along it seemed to me monstrous, and yet how did it happen that till a few minutes previously I had never heard even a suspicion of foul play?

Was it not more natural to conclude the man must have been made away with, than that, in one brief day, he should have changed his nature and the whole current of his former life?

Upon the other hand, people must have had some strong reason for imagining he was gone off with Miss Powner. The notion of a man disappearing in this way – vanishing as if the earth had opened to receive him and closed again – for the sake of any girl, however attractive, was too unnatural an idea for anyone to have evolved out of his internal consciousness. There must have been some substratum of fact, and then, upon the other hand, there seemed to me more than a substratum of possibility in the theory started of his having been murdered.

Supposing he had been murdered, I went on to argue, what then? Did I imagine he 'walked'? Did I believe he could not rest wherever he was laid?

Pooh – nonsense! It might be that the murderer haunted the place of his crime – that he hovered about to see if his guilt were still undetected, but as to anything in the shape of a ghost tenanting the Beech Walk, long meadow, and wood, I did not believe it – I could not, and I added, 'if I saw it with my own eyes, I would not.'

Having arrived at which decided and sensible conclusion, I went in to supper.

Usually a sound sleeper, I found it impossible that night when I lay down to close my eyes. I tossed and turned, threw off the bedclothes under the impression I was too hot and drew them tight up round me the next instant, feeling cold. I tried to think of my crops, of my land, of my wife, of my boy, of my future – all in vain. A dark shadow, a wall-like night stood between me and all the ordinary interests of my life – I could not get the notion of Mr Hascot's strange disappearance out of my mind. I wondered if there was anything about the place which made it in the slightest degree probable I should ever learn to forget the wife who loved, the boy who was dependent on me. Should I ever begin to think I might have done better as regards my choice of a wife, that it would be nicer to have healthy merry children than my affectionate delicate lad?

When I got to this point, I could stand it no longer. I felt as though some mocking spirit were taking possession of me, which eventually would destroy all my peace of mind, if I did not cast it out promptly and effectually.

I would not lie there supine to let any demon torment me; and, accordingly, springing to the floor, I dressed in hot haste, and flinging wide the window, looked out over a landscape bathed in the clear light of a most lovely moon.

'How beautiful!' I thought. 'I have never yet seen the farm by

night, I'll just go and take a stroll round it and then turn in again
– after a short walk I shall likely be able to sleep.'

So saying, I slipped downstairs, closed the hall door softly after
me, and went out into the moonlight.

Chapter three

As I stood upon the lawn, looking around with a keen and subtle
pleasure, I felt, almost for the first time in my life, the full charm
and beauty of night. Every object was as clearly revealed as though
the time had been noon instead of an hour past midnight, but
there lay a mystic spell on tree and field and stream the garish day
could never equal. It was a fairy light and a fairy scene, and it would
scarcely have astonished me to see fantastic elves issue from the
foxglove's flowers or dart from the shelter of concealing leaves and
dance a measure on the emerald sward.

For a minute I felt – as I fancy many and many a commonplace
man must have done when first wedded to some miracle of grace
and beauty – a sense of amazement and unreality.

All this loveliness was mine – the moonlit lawn – the stream
murmuring through the fir plantation, singing soft melodies as it
pursued its glittering way – the trees with a silvery gleam tinting
their foliage – the roses giving out their sweetest, tenderest perfumes
– the wonderful silence around – the fresh, pure air – the soft
night wind – the prosperity with which God had blessed me. My
heart grew full, as I turned and gazed first on this side and then on
that, and I felt vexed and angry to remember I had ever suffered
myself to listen to idle stories and to be made uncomfortable by
reason of village gossip.

On such a night it really seemed a shame to go to bed, and,
accordingly, though the restlessness which first induced me to rise
had vanished, and in doing so left the most soothing calm behind,
I wandered on away from the house, now beside the stream, and
again across a meadow, where faint odours from the lately carried
hay still lingered.

Still the same unreal light over field and copse – still the same
witching glamour – still the same secret feeling. I was seeing something and experiencing some sensation I might never again recall
on this side of the grave!

A most lovely night – one most certainly not for drawn curtains
and closed eyelids – one rather for lovers' tête-à-tête or a dreamy

reverie – for two young hearts to reveal their secrets to each other or one soul to commune along with God.

Still rambling, I found myself at last beside a stile, opening upon a patch, which, winding upwards, led past the hollow where the nut trees grew, and then joined the footway leading through the long field to Whittleby. The long field was the last in that direction belonging to Nut Bush Farm. It joined upon a portion of the land surrounding Chalmont, and the field path continued consequently to pass through Miss Gostock's property till the main road was reached. It cut off a long distance, and had been used generally by the inhabitants of the villages and hamlets dotted about my place until the rumour being circulated that something might be 'seen' or 'met' deterred people from venturing by a route concerning which such evil things were whispered. I had walked it constantly, both on account of the time it saved and also in order to set a good example to my labourers and my neighbours, but I might as well have saved my pains.

I was regarded merely as foolhardy, and I knew people generally supposed I should one day have cause to repent my temerity.

As I cleared the stile and began winding my upward way to the higher ground beyond, the thought did strike me what a likely place for a murder Nut Bush Hollow looked. It was a deep excavation, out of which, as no one supposed it to be natural, hundreds and thousands of loads of earth must at some time or other have been carted. From top to bottom it was clothed with nut trees – they grew on every side, and in thick, almost impenetrable masses. For years and years they seemed to have had no care bestowed on them, the Hollow forming in this respect a remarkable contrast to the rest of Mr Hascot's careful farming, and, as a fir plantation ran along the base of the Hollow, while the moon's light fell clear and full on some of the bushes, the others lay in densest shadow.

The road that once led down into the pit was now completely overgrown with nut bushes which grew luxuriantly to the very edge of the Beech Walk, and threatened ere long to push their way between the trunks of the great trees, which were the beauty and the pride of my lovely farm.

At one time, so far as I could understand, the nut bushes had the whole place almost to themselves, and old inhabitants told me that formerly, in the days when their parents were boys and girls, the nuts used to pay the whole of the rent. As years passed, however, whether from want of care or some natural cause, they gradually ceased to bear, and had to be cut down and cleared off the ground – those in the dell, however, being suffered to remain, the hollow being useless for husbandry, and the bushes which flourished there producing a crop of nuts sufficient for the farmer's family.

All this recurred to my mind as I stood for a moment and looked down into the depths of rustling green below me. I thought of the boys who must have gone nutting there, of all the nests birds had built in the branches so closely interlaced, of the summers' suns which had shone full and strong upon that mass of foliage, of the winters' snows which had lain heavy on twig and stem and happed the strong roots in a warm covering of purest white.

And then the former idea again asserted itself – what a splendid place for a tragedy; a sudden blow – a swift stab – even a treacherous push – and the deed could be done – a man might be alive and well one minute, and dead the next!

False friend, or secret enemy; rival or thief, it was competent for either in such a place at any lonely hour to send a man upon his last long journey. Had Mr Hascot been so served? Down, far down, was he lying in a quiet, dreamless sleep? At that very moment was there anyone starting from fitful slumber to grapple with his remorse for crime committed, or shrink with horror from the dread of detection?

'Where was my fancy leading me?' I suddenly asked myself. This was worse than in my own chamber preventing the night watches. Since I had been standing there my heart felt heavier than when tossing from side to side in bed, and wooing unsuccessfully the slumber which refused to come for my asking.

What folly! what nonsense! and into what an insane course of speculation had I not embarked. I would leave the eerie place and get once again into the full light of the moon's bright beams.

Hush! hark! what was that? deep down amongst the underwood – a rustle, a rush, and a scurry – then silence – then a stealthy movement amongst the bushes – then whilst I was peering down into the abyss lined with waving green below, SOMETHING passed by me swiftly, something which brought with it a cold chill as though the hand of one dead had been laid suddenly on my heart.

Instantly I turned and looked around. There was not a living thing in sight – neither on the path, nor on the sward, nor on the hillside, nor skirting the horizon as I turned my eyes upward.

For a moment I stood still in order to steady my nerves, then reassuring myself with the thought it must have been an animal of some kind, I completed the remainder of the ascent without further delay.

'The ghost, I suspect,' I said to myself as I reached the long field and the path leading back to the farm, 'will resolve itself into a hare or pheasant – is not the whirr of a cock pheasant rising, for instance, enough, when coming unexpectedly, to frighten any nervous person out of his wits? And might not a hare, or a cat, or, better still, a stoat – yes, a stoat, with its gliding, almost noiseless, movements – mimic the footfall of a suppositious ghost?'

By this time I had gained the summit of the incline, and slightly out of breath with breasting the ascent, stood for a moment contemplating the exquisite panorama stretched out beneath me. I linger on that moment because it was the last time I ever saw beauty in the moonlight. Now I cannot endure the silvery gleam of the queen of night – weird, mournful, fantastic if you like, but to be desired – no.

Whenever possible I draw the blinds and close the shutters, yet withal on moonlight nights I cannot sleep, the horror of darkness is to my mind nothing in comparison to the terror of a full moon. But I drivel; let me hasten on.

From the crest of the hill I could see lying below a valley of dreamlike beauty – woods in the foreground – a champagne country spreading away into the indefinite distance – a stream winding in and out, dancing and glittering under the moon's beams – a line of hills dimly seen against the horizon, and already a stream of light appearing above them – the first faint harbinger of dawn.

'It is morning, then, already,' I said, and with the words turned my face homewards. As I did so I saw before me on the path – *clearly* – the figure of a man.

He was walking rapidly and I hurried my pace in order to overtake him. Now to this part of the story I desire to draw particular attention. *Let me hurry as I might I never seemed able to get a foot nearer to him.*

At intervals he paused, as if on purpose to assist my desire, but the moment I seemed gaining upon him the distance between us suddenly increased. I could not tell how he did it, the fact only remained – it was like pursuing some phantom in a dream. All at once when he reached the bridge he stood quite still. He did not move hand or limb as I drew near – the way was so narrow I knew I should have to touch him in passing; nevertheless, I pressed forward. My foot was on the bridge – I was close to him – I felt my breath coming thick and fast – I clasped a stick I had picked up in the plantation firmly in my hand – I stopped, intending to speak – I opened my mouth, intending to do so – and then – without any movement on his part – I was alone!

Yes, as totally alone as though he had never stood on the bridge – never preceded me along the field-path – never loitered upon my footsteps – never paused for my coming.

I was appalled.

'Lord, what is this?' I thought. 'Am I going mad?' I felt as if I were. On my honour, I know I was as nearly insane at that moment as a man ever can be who is still in the possession of his senses.

Beyond lay the farm of which in my folly I had felt so proud to be the owner, where I once meant to be so happy and win health for my wife and strength for my boy. I saw the Beech Walk I had gloried in – the ricks of hay it seemed so good to get thatched geometrically as only one man in the neighbourhood was said to be able to lay the straw.

What was farm, or riches, or beech trees, or anything, to me now? Over the place there seemed a curse – better the meanest cottage than a palace with such accessories.

If I had been incredulous before, I was not so now – I could not distrust the evidence of my own eyes – and yet as I walked along, I tried after a minute or two to persuade myself imagination had been playing some juggler's trick with me. The moon, I argued, always lent herself readily to a game of hide-and-seek. She is always open to join in fantastic gambols with shadows – with thorn bushes – with a waving branch – aye, even with a clump of gorse. I must have been mistaken – I had been thinking weird thoughts as I stood by that dismal dell – I had seen no man walking – beheld no figure disappear!

Just as I arrived at this conclusion I beheld someone coming towards me down the Beech Walk. It was a man walking leisurely with a firm, free step. The sight did me good. Here was something tangible – something to question. I stood still, in the middle of the path – the Beech Walk being rather a grassy glade with a narrow footway dividing it, than anything usually understood by the term walk – so that I might speak to the intruder when he drew near, and ask him what he meant by trespassing on my property, more especially at such an hour. There were no public rights on my land except as regarded the path across the long field and through the wood. No one had any right or business to be in the Beech Walk, by day or night, save those employed about the farm, and this person was a gentleman; even in the distance I could distinguish that. As he came closer I saw he was dressed in a loose Palmerston suit, that he wore a low-crowned hat, and that he carried a light cane. The moonbeams dancing down amongst the branches and between the leaves fell full upon his face, and catching sight of a ring he had on his right hand, made it glitter with as many different colours as a prism.

A middle-aged man, so far as I could judge, with a set, determined expression of countenance, dark hair, no beard or whiskers, only a small moustache. A total stranger to me. I had never seen him nor any one like him in the neighbourhood. Who could he be, and what in the wide world was he doing on my premises at that unearthly hour of the morning?

He came straight on, never moving to right or left – taking no more notice of me than if he had been blind. His easy indifference, his contemptuous coolness, angered me, and planting myself a little more in his way, I began:

'Are you aware, sir –'

I got no further. Without swerving in the slightest degree from the path, he passed me! I felt something like a cold mist touch me for an instant, and the next, I saw him pursuing his steady walk down the centre of the glade. I was sick with fear, but for all that I ran after him faster than I had ever done since boyhood.

All to no purpose! I might as well have tried to catch the wind. Just where three ways joined I stood still and looked around. I was quite alone! Neither sign nor token of the intruder could I discover. On my left lay the dell where the nut trees grew, and above it the field path to Whittleby showing white and clear in the moonlight; close at hand was the bridge; straight in front the wood looked dark and solemn. Between me and it lay a little hollow, down which a narrow path wound tortuously. As I gazed I saw that, where a moment before no one had been, a man was walking now. But

I could not follow. My limbs refused their office. He turned his head, and lifting his hand on which the ring glittered, beckoned me to come. He might as well have asked one seized with paralysis. On the confines of the wood he stood motionless as if awaiting my approach; then, when I made no sign of movement, he wrung his hands with a despairing gesture, and disappeared.

At the same moment, moon, dell, bridge, and stream faded from my sight – and I fainted.

Chapter four

It was not much past eight o'clock when I knocked at Miss Gostock's hall door, and asked if I could see that lady.

After that terrible night vision I had made up my mind. Behind Mr Hascot's disappearance I felt sure there lurked some terrible tragedy – living, no man should have implored my help with such passionate earnestness without avail, and if indeed one had appeared to me from the dead I would right him if I could.

But never for a moment did I think of giving up the farm. The resolve I had come to seemed to have braced up my courage – let what might come or go, let crops remain unreaped and men neglect their labour, let monetary loss and weary, anxious days be in store if they would, I meant to go on to the end.

The first step on my road clearly led in the direction of Miss Gostock's house. She alone could give me all the information I required – to her alone could I speak freely and fully about what I had seen.

I was instantly admitted, and found the lady, as I had expected, at breakfast. It was her habit, I knew, to partake of that meal while the labourers she employed were similarly engaged. She was attired in an easy *négligé* of a white skirt and a linen coat which had formerly belonged to her brother. She was not taking tea or coffee like any other woman – but was engaged upon about a pound of smoking steak which she ate covered with mustard and washed down with copious draughts of home-brewed beer.

She received me cordially and invited me to join in the banquet – a request I ungallantly declined, eliciting in return the remark I should never be good for much till I ceased living on 'slops' and took to 'good old English' fare.

After these preliminaries I drew my chair near the table and said:

'I want you to give me some information, Miss Gostock, about my predecessor.'

'What sort of information?' she asked, with a species of frost at once coming over her manner.

'Can you tell me anything of his personal appearance?'

'Why do you ask?'

I did not immediately answer, and seeing my hesitation she went on:

'Because if you mean to tell me you or anyone else have seen him about your place I would not believe it if you swore it – there!'

'I do not ask you to believe it, Miss Gostock,' I said.

'And I give you fair warning, it is of no use coming here and asking me to relieve you of your bargain, because I won't do it. I like you well enough – better than I ever liked a tenant; but I don't intend to be a shilling out of pocket by you.'

'I hope you never may be,' I answered meekly.

'I'll take very good care I never am,' she retorted; 'and so don't come here talking about Mr Hascot. He served me a dirty turn, and I would not put it one bit past him to try and get the place a bad name.'

'Will you tell me what sort of looking man he was?' I asked determinedly.

'No, I won't,' she snapped, and while she spoke she rose, drained the last drop out of a pewter measure, and after tossing on the straw hat with a defiant gesture, thumped its crown well down on her head. I took the hint, and rising, said I must endeavour to ascertain the particulars I wanted elsewhere.

'You won't ascertain them from me,' retorted Miss Gostock, and so we parted as we had never done before – on bad terms.

Considerably perplexed, I walked out of the house. A rebuff of this sort was certainly the last thing I could have expected, and as I paced along I puzzled myself by trying to account for Miss Gostock's extraordinary conduct, and anxiously considering what I was to do under present circumstances. All at once the recollection of mine host of the 'Bunch of Hops' flashed across my mind. He must have seen Mr Hascot often, and I could address a few casual questions to him without exciting his curiosity.

No sooner thought than done. Turning my face towards Whittleby, I stepped briskly on.

'Did I ever see Mr Hascot?' repeated the landlord – when after some general conversation about politics, the weather, the crops, and many other subjects, I adroitly turned it upon the late tenant of Nut Bush Farm. 'Often, sir. I never had much communication with him, for he was one of your stand-aloof, keep-your-distance, sort of gentlemen – fair dealing and honourable – but neither free nor generous. He has often sat where you are sitting now, sir, and not so much as said – 'it is a fine day,' or, 'I am afraid we shall have rain.'

'You had but to see him walking down the street to know what he was. As erect as a grenadier, with a firm easy sort of marching step, he looked every inch a gentleman – just in his everyday clothes, a *Palmerston suit* and a *round hat*, he was, as many a one said, fit to go to court. His hands were not a bit like a farmer's, but white and delicate as any lady's, and the *diamond ring* he wore flashed like a star when he stroked the *slight bit of a moustache* that was *all the hair he had upon his face*. No – not a handsome gentleman, but fine looking, with a presence – bless and save us all to think of his giving up everything for the sake of that slip of a girl.'

'She was very pretty, wasn't she?' I inquired.

'Beautiful – we all said she was too pretty to come to any good. The old grandmother, you see, had serious cause for keeping so tight a hold over her, but it was in her, and 'what's bred in bone,' you know, sir.'

'And you really think they did go off together?'

'Oh, yes, sir; nobody had ever any doubt about that.'

On this subject his tone was so decided I felt it was useless to continue the conversation, and having paid him for the modest refreshment of which I had partaken I sauntered down the High Street and turned into the Bank, where I thought of opening an account.

When I had settled all preliminaries with the manager he saved me the trouble of beating about the bush by breaking cover himself and asking if anything had been heard of Mr Hascot.

'Not that I know of,' I answered.

'Curious affair, wasn't it?' he said.

'It appears so, but I have not heard the whole story.'

'Well, the whole story is brief,' returned the manager. 'He comes over here one day and without assigning any reason withdraws the whole of his balance, which was very heavy – is met on the road homeward but never returns home – the same day the girl Powner is also missing – what do you think of that?'

'It is singular,' I said, 'very.'

'Yes, and to leave his wife and family totally unprovided for.'

'I cannot understand that at all.'

'Nor I – it was always known he had an extreme partiality for the young person – he and Miss Gostock quarrelled desperately on the subject – but no one could have imagined an attachment of that sort would have led a man so far astray – Hascot more especially. If I had been asked to name the last person in the world likely to make a fool of himself for the sake of a pretty face I should have named the late tenant of Nut Bush Farm.'

'There never was a suspicion of foul play,' I suggested.

'Oh, dear, no! It was broad daylight when he was last seen on the Whittleby road. The same morning it is known he and the girl were talking earnestly together beside the little wood on your pro-perty, and two persons answering to their description were traced to London, that is to say, a gentleman came forward to say he believed he had travelled up with them as far as New Cross on the afternoon in question.'

'He was an affectionate father I have heard,' I said.

'A *most* affectionate parent – a most devoted husband. Dear, dear! It is dreadfully sad to think how a bad woman may drag the best of men down to destruction. It is terrible to think of his wife and family being inmates of the Union.'

'Yes, and it is terrible to consider not a soul has tried to get them out of it,' I answered, a little tartly.

'H—m, perhaps so; but we all know we are contributing to their support,' he returned with an effort at jocularity, which, in my then frame of mind, seemed singularly *mal-apropos*.

'There is something in that,' I replied with an effort, and leaving the Bank next turned my attention to the Poorhouse at Crayshill.

At that time many persons thought what I did quixotic. It is so much the way of the world to let the innocent suffer for the guilty, that I believe Mr Hascot's wife might have ended her days in Crayshill Union but for the action I took in the matter.

Another night I felt I could not rest till I had arranged for a humble lodging she and her family could occupy till I was able to form some plan for their permanent relief. I found her a quiet, ladylike woman, totally unable to give me the slightest clue as to where her husband might be found. 'He was just at the stile on the Chalmont fields,' she said, 'when Mr Waite met him; no one saw him afterwards, unless it might be the Ockfields, but, of course, there is no information to be got from them. The guardians have tried every possible means to discover his whereabouts without success. My own impression is he and Sally Powner have gone to America, and that some day we may hear from him. He cannot harden his heart for ever and forget –' Here Mrs Hascot's sentence trailed off into passionate weeping.

'It is too monstrous!' I considered; 'the man never did such a thing as desert his wife and children. Someone knows all about the matter,' and then in a moment I paused in the course of my meditations.

Was that person Miss Gostock?

It was an ugly idea, and yet it haunted me. When I remembered the woman's masculine strength, when I recalled her furious impetuosity when I asked her a not very exasperating question, as I recalled the way she tossed off that brandy, when I considered her love of money, her eagerness to speak ill of her late tenant, her semi-references to some great trouble prior to which she was more like other women, or, perhaps, to speak more correctly, less unlike them – doubts came crowding upon my mind.

It was when entering her ground Mr Hascot was last seen. He had a large sum of money in his possession. She was notoriously fond of rambling about Nut Bush Farm, and what my labouring men called 'spying around', which had been the cause of more than one pitched battle between herself and Mr Hascot.

'The old master could not a-bear her,' said one young fellow.

I hated myself for the suspicion; and yet, do what I would, I could not shake it off. Not for a moment did I imagine Miss Gostock had killed her former tenant in cold blood; but it certainly occurred to me that the dell was deep, and the verge treacherous, that it would be easy to push a man over, either by accident or design, that the nutbushes grew thick, that a body might lie amongst them till it rotted, ere even the boys who went nutting there, season after season, happened to find it.

Should I let the matter drop? No, I decided. With that mute appeal haunting my memory, I should know no rest or peace till I had solved the mystery of Mr Hascot's disappearance, and cleared his memory from the shameful stain circumstances had cast upon it.

What should I do next? I thought the matter over for a few days, and then decided to call on Mr Waite, who never yet had called on me. As usual, he was not at home; but I saw his wife, whom I found just the sort of woman Lolly described – a fair, delicate creature who seemed fading into the grave.

She had not much to tell me. It was her husband who saw Mr Hascot at the Chalmont stile; it was he also who had seen Mr Hascot and the girl Powner talking together on the morning of their disappearance. It so happened he had often chanced to notice them together before. 'She was a very, very pretty girl,' Mrs Waite added, 'and I always thought a modest. She had a very sweet way of speaking – quite above her station – inherited, no doubt, for her father was a gentleman. Poor little Sally!'

The words were not much, but the manner touched me sensibly. I felt drawn to Mrs Waite from that moment, and told her more of what I had beheld and what I suspected than I had mentioned to anyone else.

As to my doubts concerning Miss Gostock, I was, of course, silent but I said quite plainly I did not believe Mr Hascot had gone off with any girl or woman either, that I thought he had come to an unfair end, and that I was of opinion the stories circulated, concerning a portion of Nut Bush Farm being haunted, had some foundation in fact.

'Do you believe in ghosts then?' she asked, with a curious smile.

'I believe in the evidence of my senses,' I answered, 'and I declare to you, Mrs Waite, that one night, not long since, I saw as plainly as I see you what I can only conclude to have been the semblance of Mr Hascot.'

She did not make any reply, she only turned very pale, and blaming myself for having alarmed one in her feeble state of health, I hastened to apologise and take my leave.

As we shook hands, she retained mine for a moment, and said, 'When you hear anything more, if you should, that is, you will tell us, will you not? Naturally we feel interested in the matter, he was such a near neighbour, and – we knew him.'

I assured her I would not fail to do so, and left the room.

Before I reached the front door I found I had forgotten one of my gloves, and immediately retraced my steps.

The drawing-room door was ajar, and somewhat unceremoniously, perhaps, I pushed it open and entered.

To my horror and surprise, Mrs Waite, whom I had left apparently in her ordinary state of languid health, lay full length on the sofa, sobbing as if her heart would break. What I said so indiscreetly had brought on an attack of violent hysterics – a malady with the signs and tokens of which I was not altogether unacquainted.

Silently I stole out of the room without my glove, and left the house, closing the front door noiselessly behind me.

A couple of days elapsed, and then I decided to pay a visit to Mrs Ockfield. If she liked to throw any light on the matter, I felt satisfied she could. It was, to say the least of it, most improbable her grand-daughter, whether she had been murdered or gone away with Mr Hascot, should disappear and not leave a clue by which her relatives could trace her.

The Ockfields were not liked, I found, and I flattered myself if they had any hand in Mr Hascot's sudden disappearance I should soon hit on some weak spot in their story.

I found the old woman, who was sixty-seven, and who looked two hundred, standing over her washing tub.

'Can I tell you where my grand-daughter is,' she repeated, drawing her hands out of the suds and wiping them on her apron. 'Surely, sir, and very glad I am to be able to tell everybody, gentle and simple, where to find our Sally. She is in a good service down in Cheshire. Mr Hascot got her the place, but we knew nothing about it till yesterday; she left us in a bit of a pet, and said she wouldn't have written me only something seemed to tell her she must. Ah! she'll have a sore heart when she gets my letter and hears how it has been said that the master and she went off together. She thought a deal of the master, did Sally; he was always kind and stood between her and her grand-father.'

'Then do you mean to say,' I asked, 'that she knows nothing of Mr Hascot's disappearance?'

'Nothing, sir, thank God for all His mercies; the whole of the time since the day she left here she has been in service with a friend of his. You can read her letter if you like.'

Though I confess old Mrs Ockfield neither charmed nor inspired me with confidence, I answered that I should like to see the letter very much indeed.

When I took it in my hand I am bound to say I thought it had been written with a purpose, and intended less for a private than for the public eye, but as I read I fancied there was a ring of truth about the epistle, more especially as the writer made passing reference to a very bitter quarrel which had preceded her departure from the grand-paternal roof.

'It is very strange,' I said, as I returned the letter, 'it is a most singular coincidence that your grand-daughter and Mr Hascot should have left Whittleby on the same day, and yet she should know nothing of his whereabouts, as judging from her letter seems to be the case.'

'Are you quite sure Mr Hascot ever did leave Whittleby, sir?' asked the old woman with a vindictive look in her still bright old eyes. 'There are those as think he never went very far from home, and that the whole truth will come out some day.'

'What do you mean?' I exclaimed, surprised.

'Least said soonest mended,' she answered shortly; 'only I hopes if ever we do know the rights of it, people as do hold their heads high enough, and have had plenty to say about our girl, and us too for that matter, will find things not so pleasant as they find them at present. The master had a heap of money about him, and we know that often those as has are those as wants more!'

'I cannot imagine what you are driving at,' I said, for I feared every moment she would mention Miss Gostock, and bring her name into the discussion. 'If you think Mr Hascot met with any foul play you ought to go to the police about the matter.'

'Maybe I will some time,' she answered, 'but just now I have my washing to do.'

'This will buy you some tea to have afterwards,' I said, laying down half-a-crown, and feeling angry with myself for this momentary irritation. After all, the woman had as much right to her suspicions as I to mine.

Thinking over Miss Powner's letter, I came to the conclusion it might be well to see the young lady for myself. If I went to the address she wrote from I could ascertain at all events whether her statement regarding her employment was correct. Yes, I would take train and travel to Cheshire; I had commenced the investigation and I would follow it to the end.

I travelled so much faster than Mrs Ockfield's letter – which, indeed, that worthy woman had not then posted – that when I arrived at my journey's end I found the fair Sally in total ignorance of Mr Hascot's disappearance and the surmises to which her own absence had given rise.

Appearances might be against the girl's truth and honesty, yet I felt she was dealing fairly with me.

'A better gentleman, sir,' she said, 'than Mr Hascot never drew breath. And so they set it about he had gone off with me – they little know – they little know! Why, sir, he thought of me and was careful for me as he might for a daughter. The first time ever I saw him grandfather was beating me, and he interfered to save me. He knew they treated me badly, and it was after a dreadful quarrel I had at home he advised me to go away. He gave me a letter to the lady I am now with, and a ten-pound note to pay my travelling expenses and keep something in my pocket. "You'll be better away from the farm, little girl," he said the morning I left; "people are beginning to talk, and we can't shut their mouths if you come running to me every time your grandmother speaks sharply to you." '

'But why did you not write sooner to your relatives?' I asked.

'Because I was angry with my grandmother, sir, and I thought I would give her a fright. I did not bring any clothes or anything and I hoped – it was a wicked thing I know, sir – but I hoped she would believe I had made away with myself. Just lately, however, I began to consider that if she and grandfather had not treated me well, I was treating them worse, so I made up a parcel of some things my mistress gave me and sent it to them with a letter. I am glad it reached them safely.'

'What time was it when you saw Mr Hascot last?' I inquired.

'About two o'clock, sir, I know that, because he was in a hurry. He had got some news about the Bank at Whittleby not being quite safe, and he said he had too much money there to run any risk of loss. "Be a good girl," were the last words he said, and he walked off sharp and quick by the field path to Whittleby. I stood near the bridge crying for a while. Oh, sir! do you think anything ill can have happened to him?'

For answer, I only said the whole thing seemed most mysterious.

'He'd never have left his wife and children, sir,' she went on; 'never. He must have been made away with.'

'Had he any enemies, do you think?' I asked.

'No, sir; not to say enemies. He was called hard because he would have a day's work for a day's wage, but no one that ever I heard of had a grudge against him. Except Miss Gostock and Mr Waite, he agreed well with all the people about. He did not like Miss Gostock, and Mr Waite was always borrowing money from him. Now Mr Hascot did not mind giving, but he could not bear lending.'

I returned to Nut Bush Farm perfectly satisfied that Mr Hascot had been, as the girl expressed the matter, 'made away with'. On the threshold of my house I was met with a catalogue of disasters. The female servants had gone in a body; the male professed a dislike to be in the stable-yard in the twilight. Rumour had decided that Nut Bush Farm was an unlucky place even to pass. The cattle were out of condition because the men would not go down the Beech Walk, or turn a single sheep into the long field. Reapers wanted higher wages. The labourers were looking out for other service.

'Poor fellow! This is a nice state of things for you to come home to,' said Lolly compassionately. 'Even the poachers won't venture into the wood, and the boys don't go nutting.'

'I will clear away the nut trees and cut down the wood,' I declared savagely.

'I don't know who you are going to get to cut them,' answered Lolly, 'unless you bring men down from London.'

As for Miss Gostock, she only laughed at my dilemma, and said, 'You're a pretty fellow to be frightened by a ghost. If he was seen at Chalmont I'd ghost him.'

While I was in a state of the most cruel perplexity, I bethought me of my promise to Mrs Waite, and walked over one day to tell her the result of my inquiries.

I found her at home, and Mr Waite, for a wonder, in the drawing-room. He was not a bad-looking fellow, and welcomed my visit with a heartiness which ill accorded with the discourtesy he had shown in never calling upon me.

Very succinctly I told what I had done, and where I had been. I mentioned the terms in which Sally Powner spoke of her benefactor. We discussed the whole matter fully – the *pros* and *cons* of anyone knowing Mr Hascot had such a sum of money on his person, and the possibility of his having been murdered. I mentioned what I had done about Mrs Hascot, and begged Mr Waite to afford me his help and co-operation in raising such a sum of money as might start the poor lady in some business.

'I'll do all that lies in my power,' he said heartily, shaking hands at the same time, for I had risen to go.

'And for my part,' I remarked, 'it seems to me there are only two things more I can do to elucidate the mystery, and those are – root every nut-tree out of the dell and set the axe to work in the wood.

There was a second's silence. Then Mrs Waite dropped to the floor as if she had been shot.

As he stooped over her he and I exchanged glances, and then *I knew*. Mr Hascot *had* been murdered, and Mr Waite was the murderer!

That night I was smoking and Lolly at needlework. The parlour windows were wide open, for it was warm, and not a breath of air seemed stirring.

There was a stillness on everything which betokened a coming thunderstorm; and we both were silent, for my mind was busy and Lolly's heart anxious. She did not see, as she said, how I was to get on at all, and for my part I could not tell what I ought to do.

All at once something whizzed through the window furthest from where we sat, and fell noisily to the floor.

'What is that?' Lolly cried, springing to her feet. 'Oh, Jack! What is it?'

Surprised and shaken myself, I closed the windows and drew down the blinds before I examined the cause of our alarm. It proved to be an oblong package weighted with a stone. Unfastening it cautiously, for I did not know whether it might not contain some explosive, I came at length to a pocket book. Opening the pocket book, I found it stuffed full of bank notes.

'What are they? Where can they have come from?' exclaimed Lolly.

'They are the notes Mr Hascot drew from Whittleby bank the day he disappeared,' I answered with a sort of inspiration, but I took no notice of Lolly's last question.

For good or for evil that was a secret which lay between myself and the Waites, and which I have never revealed till now.

If the vessel in which they sailed for New Zealand had not gone to the bottom I should have kept the secret still.

When they were out of the country and the autumn well advanced, I had the wood thoroughly examined, and there in a gully, covered with a mass of leaves and twigs and dead branches, we found Mr Hascot's body. His watch was in his waistcoat pocket – his ring on his finger; save for these possessions no one could have identified him.

His wife married again about a year afterwards and my brother took Nut Bush Farm off my hands. He says the place never was haunted – that I never saw Mr Hascot except in my own imagination – that the whole thing originated in a poor state of health and a too credulous disposition!

I leave the reader to judge between us.

THE MAN WHO COINED HIS BLOOD INTO GOLD

by

J. H. Pearce

In reviewing Drolls from Shadowland (1893), The Illustrated
London News said of Joseph Henry Pearce that 'his little book
will give him an assured place.' Sadly, the journal was mistaken; I
am unable to find out much about Mr Pearce other than that he was
born in 1856. His works, however, show a writing talent quite
extraordinary and it is regrettable that he faded into obscurity.

J. H. Pearce's first book was Esther Pentreath (1891), one of
several Cornish novels he wrote, including Jaco Treloar (1893) and
Ezekiel's Sin (1898). His last book seems to have been The
Dreamer's Book (1905).

Drolls from Shadowland certainly appears to have been his best
received book, described variously as 'clever and powerful, highly
imaginative and weirdly fantastic' (The Guardian), 'curdling the
blood with a few strokes of the pen' (Academy), and 'as consummate
as Daudet – a masterpiece' (Boston Traveller).

Judge for yourself the quality of Pearce's work from 'The Man
Who Coined His Blood into Gold', a Cornish tale from Drolls
from Shadowland. It is a distinctive story for Victorian times, an
exceedingly gruesome fairy tale for adults.

The yoke of Poverty galled him exceedingly, and he hated his
taskmistress with a most rancorous hatred.

As he climbed up or down the dripping ladders, descending
from sollar to sollar towards the level where he worked, he would
set his teeth grimly that he might not curse aloud – an oath under-
ground being an invitation to the Evil One – but in his heart the
muffled curses were audible enough. And when he was at work in
the dreary level, with the darkness lying on his shoulder like a

hand, and the candles shining unsteadily through the gloom, like little evil winking eyes, he brooded so moodily over his bondage to Poverty, that he desired to break from it at any cost.

'I'd risk a lem for its weight in gowld: darned ef I wedn'!' he muttered savagely, as he dug at the stubborn rock with his pick.

He could hear the sounds of blasting in other levels – the explosions travelling to him in a muffled boom – and above him, for he was working beneath the bed of the ocean, he could faintly distinguish the grinding of the sea as the huge waves wallowed and roared across the beach.

'I'm sick to death o' this here life,' he grumbled; 'I'd give a haand or a' eye for a pot o' suvrins. Iss, I'd risk more than that,' he added darkly: letting the words ooze out as if under his breath.

At that moment his pick detached a piece of rock which came crashing down on the floor of the level, splintering into great jagged fragments as it fell.

He started back with an exclamation of uncontrollable surprise. The falling rock had disclosed the interior of a cavern whose outlines were lost in impenetrable gloom, but which here and there in a vague fashion, as it caught the light of the candle flickering in his hat, seemed to sparkle as if its walls were crusted with silver.

'Lor' Jimmeny, this es bra' an' queer!' he gasped.

As he leaned on his pick, peering into the cavern with covetous eyes, but with a wildly-leaping heart, he was aware of an odd movement among the shadows which were elusively outlined by the light of his dip.

It was almost as though some of them had an independent individuality, and could have detached themselves from their roots if they wished.

It was certain a squat, hump-backed blotch, that was sprawling blackly beside a misshapen block, was either wriggling on the floor as if trying to stand upright ... or else there was something wrong with his eyes.

He stared at the wavering gloom in the cavern, with its quaint, angular splashes of glister, where heads of quartz and patches of mundic caught the light from the unsteady flame of the candle, and presently he was *certain* that the shadows were alive.

Most of all he was sure that the little hump-backed oddity had risen to its feet and was a veritable creature: an actual uncouth, shambling grotesque, instead of a mere flat blotch of shadow.

Up waddled the little hump-back to the hole in the wall where Joel stood staring leaning on his pick.

'What can I do for'ee, friend?' he asked huskily: his voice sounding faint, hoarse, and muffled, as if it were coming from an immense distance, or as if the squat little frame had merely borrowed it for the nonce.

Joel stared at the speaker, with his lower jaw dropping.

'What can I do for'ee, friend?' asked the hump-back; peering at the grimy, half-naked miner, with his little ferrety eyes glowing luminously.

Joel moistened his lips with his tongue before he answered. 'Nawthin', plaise, sir,' he gasped out, quakingly.

'Nonsense, my man!' said the hump-back pleasantly, rubbing his hands cheerfully together as he spoke. And Joel noticed that the fingers, though long and skinny – almost wrinkled and lean enough, in fact, to pass for claws – were adorned with several sparkling rings. 'Nonsense, my man! I'm your friend – if you'll let me be. O never mind my hump, if it's that that's frightening you, I got that through a fall a long while ago,' and the lean brown face puckered into a smile. 'Come! In what way can I oblige'ee, friend? I can grant you any wish you like. Say the word – and it's done! Just think what you could do if you had heaps of money, now – piles of suvrins in that owld chest in your bedroom, instead o' they paltry two-an'-twenty suvrins which you now got heeded away in the skibbet.'

Joel stared at the speaker with distended eyes: the great beads of perspiration gathering on his forehead.

'How ded'ee come to knaw they was there?' he asked.

'I know more than that,' said the hump-back, laughing. 'I could tell'ee a thing or two, b'leeve, if I wanted to. I knaw tin,* cumraade, as well as the next.' And with that he began to chuckle to himself.

'Wedn'ee like they two-an'-twenty suvrins in the skibbet made a hundred-an'-twenty?' asked the hump-back insinuatingly.

'Iss, by Gosh, I should!' said Joel.

'Then gi'me your haand on it, cumraade; an' you shall have 'em!'

---

*To 'knaw tin' is among the miners of Cornwall a sign of, and a colloquial euphemism for, cleverness.

'Here goes, then!' said Joel, thrusting out his hand.

The hump-back seized the proffered hand in an instant, covering the grimy fingers with his own lean claws.

'Oh, le'go! *le'go!*' shouted Joel.

The hump-back grinned; his black eyes glittering.

'I waan't be niggardly to'ee, cumraade,' said he. 'Every drop o' blood you choose to shed for the purpose shall turn into a golden suvrin for'ee – there!'

'Darn'ee! thee ben an' run thy nails in me – see!'

And Joel shewed a drop of blood oozing from his wrist.

'Try the charm, man! Wish! Hold un out, an' say, *Wan!*'

Joel held out his punctured wrist mechanically.

'Wan!'

There was a sudden gleam – and down dropped a sovereign: a bright gold coin that rang sharply as it fell.

'Try agen!' said the hump-back, grinning delightedly.

Joel stooped first to pick up the coin, and bit it eagerly.

'Ay, good Gosh! 'tes gowld, sure 'nuff!'

'Try agen!' said the hump-back 'Make up a pile!'

Joel held out his wrist and repeated the formula.

'Wan!'

And another coin clinked at his feet.

'I needn' wait no longer, s'pose?' said the hump-back.

'Wan!' cried Joel. And a third coin dropped.

He leaned on his pick and kept coining his blood eagerly, till presently there was quite a little pile at his feet.

The hump-back watched him intently for a time: but Joel appeared to be oblivious of his presence; and the squat little figure stealthily disappeared.

The falling coins kept chiming melodiously, till presently the great stalwart miner had to lean against the wall of the level to support himself. So tired as he was, he had ever felt before. But give over his task he either could not, or would not. The chink of the gold-pieces he must hear if he died for it. He looked down at them greedily. 'Wan! ... Wan! ... Wan! ...'

Presently he tottered, and fell over on his heap.

At that same moment the halting little hump-back stole out from the shadows immediately behind him, and leaned over Joel, rubbing his hands gleefully.

'I must catch his soul,' said the little black man.

And with that he turned Joel's head round sharply, and held his hand to the dying man's mouth.

Just then there fluttered up to Joel's lips a tiny yellow flame, which, for some reason or other, seemed as agitated as if it had a human consciousness. One might almost have imagined it perceived the little hump-back, and knew full well who and what he was. But there on Joel's lips the flame hung quivering. And now a deeper shadow fell upon his face.

Surely the tiny thing shuddered with horror as the hump-back's black paws closed upon it!

But, in any case, it now was safely prisoned. And the little black man laughed long and loudly.

'Not so bad a bargain after all!' chuckled he.

THE SHRINE OF DEATH

and

THE BLACK VEIL

by

Lady Dilke

Like Mrs Riddell, our next forgotten Victorian authoress was the victim of tragedy, though of a much different kind. Lady Dilke (1840–1904) was one of the principal actors in a drama that ruined the career of a Cabinet minister and rocked Victorian society.

Born Emilia Strong, she married Mark Pattison, a clergyman twenty-one years her senior, in 1861. The Pattisons lived in Oxford, where they were host to several famous literary names, such as Browning and George Eliot. A great traveller (mainly for her health), Emilia Pattison was intensely interested in art and visited most of the European galleries.

Mark Pattison died in 1884 and the following year, in India, Emilia met, and fell in love with, Sir Charles Wentworth Dilke. Dilke was a member of Gladstone's Cabinet and Deputy Leader of the Liberal Party, and was widely thought to be a future Prime Minister. Shortly after the couple's return to England, the famous Dilke scandal broke out, and the divorce case that ruined Sir Charles followed. Emilia Pattison married Dilke in 1886, the same year that she published her first collection of strange stories.

The divorce case had finished Sir Charles in Victorian society, and, though Lady Dilke spent the rest of her life trying to restore his name, she was unsuccessful. The effort of this and her constant illness wore her out and she died in 1904, Sir Charles Dilke surviving her by only seven years.

While the scandal is remembered, Lady Dilke and her books have been almost forgotten. I am indebted to a Canadian correspondent, Bob Hadji, for drawing my attention to the following stories. They come from Lady Dilke's first book of short stories The Shrine of Death (*1886*), *a volume she emulated again in* The Shrine of Love (*1891*). *These are very strange tales indeed, quite remarkable discoveries, and reveal Lady Dilke as yet another forgotten Victorian master of the macabre.*

THE SHRINE OF DEATH

Ah! Life has many secrets! – These were the first words that fell on the ears of a little girl-baby, whose mother had just been brought to bed. As she grew up she pondered their meaning, and, before all things, she desired to know the secrets of life. Thus, longing and brooding, she grew apart from other children, and her dreams were ever of how the secrets of life should be revealed to her.

Now, when she was about fifteen years of age, a famous witch passed through the town in which she dwelt, and the child heard much talk of her, and people said that her knowledge of all things was great, and that even as the past lay open before her, so there was nothing in the future that could be hidden from her. Then the child thought to herself, 'This woman, if by any means I get speech of her, can, if she will, tell me all the secrets of life.'

Nor was it long after, that walking late in the evening with other and lesser children, along the ramparts on the east side of the town, she came to a corner of the wall which lay in deep shadow, and out of the shadow there sprang a large black dog, baying loudly, and the children were terrified, and fled, crying out, 'It is the witch's dog!' and one, the least of all, fell in its terror, so the elder one tarried, and lifted it from the ground, and, as she comforted it – for it was shaken by its fall, and the dog continued baying – the witch herself came out of the shadow, and said, 'Off with you, you little fools, and break my peace no more with your folly.' And the little one ran for fear, but the elder girl stood still, and laying hold of the witch's mantle, she said, 'Before I go, tell me, where are the secrets of life?' And the witch answered, 'Marry Death, fair child, and you will know.'

At the first, the saying of the witch fell like a stone in the girl's heart, but ere long her words, and the words which she had heard in the hour of her birth, filled all her thoughts, and when other girls jested or spoke of feasts and merriment, of happy love and all the joys of life, such talk seemed to her mere wind of idle tales, and the gossips who would have made a match for her schemed in vain, for she had but one desire, the desire to woo Death, and learn the secrets of life. Often now she would seek the ramparts in late evening, hoping that in the shadows she might once more find the witch, and learn from her the way to her desire; but she found her not.

Returning in the darkness, it so happened, after one of these fruitless journeys, that she passed under the walls of an ancient church, and looking up at the windows, she saw the flickering of a low, unsteady light upon the coloured panes, and she drew near to the door, and, seeing it ajar, she pushed it open and entered, and passing between the mighty columns of the nave, she stepped aside to the spot whence the light proceeded. Having done so, she found herself standing in front of a great tomb, in one side of which were brazen gates, and beyond the gates a long flight of marble steps leading down to a vast hall or chapel below; and above the gates, in a silver lamp, was a light burning, and as the chains by which the lamp was suspended moved slightly in the draught from the open door of the church, the light which burnt in it flickered, and all the shadows around shifted so that nothing seemed still, and this constant recurrence of change was like the dance of phantoms in the air. And the girl, seeing the blackness, thought of the corner on the ramparts where she had met the witch, and almost she expected to see her, and to hear her dog baying in the shadows.

When she drew nearer, she found that the walls were loaded with sculpture, and the niches along the sides were filled with statues of the wise men of all time; but at the corners were four women whose heads were bowed, and whose hands were bound in chains. Then, looking at them as they sat thus, discrowned but majestic, the soul of the girl was filled with sorrow, and she fell weeping, and, clasping her hands in her grief, she cast her eyes to heaven. As she did so, the lamp swayed a little forwards, and its rays touched with light a figure seated on the top of the monument. When the girl caught sight of this figure she ceased weeping, and when she had withdrawn a step or two backwards, so as to get a fuller view, she fell upon her knees, and a gleam of wondrous expectation shone out of her face; for, on the top of the tomb, robed and crowned, sat the image of Death, and a great gladness and awe filled her soul, for she thought, 'If I may but be found worthy to enter his portals, all the secrets of life will be mine.' And laying her hands on the gates, she sought to open them, but they were locked, so after a little while she went sadly away.

Each day, from this time forth, when twilight fell, the girl returned to the church, and would there remain kneeling for many hours before the shrine of Death, nor could she by any means be drawn away from her purpose. Her mind was fixed on her desire, so that she became insensible to all else; and the whole town mocked her, and her own people held her for mad. So then, at last, they took her before a priest, and the priest, when he had talked with her awhile, said, 'Let her have her way. Let her pass a night within the shrine; on the morrow it may be that her wits will have returned to her.'

So a day was set, and they robed her in white as a bride, and in great state, with youths bearing torches, and many maidens, whose hands were full of flowers, she was brought through the city at nightfall to the church; and the gates of the shrine were opened, and as she passed within, the youths put out their torches and the maidens threw their roses on the steps beneath her feet. When the gates closed upon her, she stood still awhile upon the upper steps, and so she waited until the last footfall had ceased to echo in the church, and she knew herself to be alone in the long desired presence. Then, full of reverent longing and awe, she drew her veil about her, and as she did so, she found a red rose that had caught in it, and, striving to dislodge it, she brought it close to her face, and its perfume was very strong, and she saw, as in a vision, the rose garden of her mother's house, and the face of one who had wooed her there in the sun; but, even as she stood irresolute, the baying of a hound in the distant street fell on her ears, and she remembered the words of the witch, 'Marry Death, fair child, if you would know the secrets of life,' and casting the rose from her, she began to descend the steps.

As she went down, she heard, as it were, the light pattering of feet behind her; but turning, when she came to the foot, to look, she found that this sound was only the echoing fall from step to step of the flowers which her long robes had drawn after her, and she heeded them not, for she was now within the shrine, and looking to the right hand and to the left, she saw long rows of tombs, each one hewn in marble and covered with sculpture of wondrous beauty.

All this, though, she saw dimly; the plainest thing to view was the long black shadow of her own form, cast before her by the light from the lamp above, and as she looked beyond the uttermost rim of shadow, she became aware of an awful shape seated at a marble table whereon lay an open book. Looking on this dread shape, she trembled, for she knew that she was in the presence of Death. Then, seeing the book, her heart was uplifted within her, and stepping boldly forwards, she seated herself before it, and as she did so, it seemed to her that she heard a shiver from within the tombs.

Now, when she came near, Death had raised his finger, and he pointed to the writing on the open page, but, as she put her hands upon the book, the blood rushed back to her heart, for it was ice-cold, and again it seemed to her that something moved within the tombs. It was but for a minute, then her courage returned, and she fixed her eyes eagerly upon the lines before her and began to read, but the very letters were at first strange to her, and even when she knew them she could by no means frame them into words, or make any sentence out of them, so that, at the last, she looked up in her wonderment to seek aid. But he, the terrible one, before whom she sat, again lifted his finger, and as he pointed to the page, a weight as of lead forced down her eyes upon the book; and now the letters shifted strangely, and when she thought to have seized a word or a phrase it would suddenly be gone, for, if the text shone out plain for an instant, the strange shadows, moving with the movements of the silver lamp, would blot it again as quickly from sight.

At this, distraction filled her mind, and she heard her own breathing like sobs in the darkness, and fear choked her; for ever, when she would have appealed for help, her eyes saw the same deadly menace, the same uplifted and threatening finger. Then, glancing to left and right, a new horror took possession of her, for the lids of the tombs were yawning wide, and whenever her thoughts turned to flight, their awful tenants peered at her from above the edges, and they made as though they would have stayed her.

Thus she sat till it was long past midnight, and her heart was sick within her, when again the distant baying of a hound reached her ears; but this sound, instead of giving her fresh courage, seemed to her but a bitter mockery, for she thought, 'What shall the secrets of life profit me, if I must make my bed with Death?' And she became mad with anger, and she cursed the counsels of the witch, and in her desperation, like a creature caught in the toils, she sprang from her seat and made towards the steps by which she had come. Ere she could reach them, all the dreadful dwellers in the tombs were before her, and she, seeing the way to life was barred for ever, fell to the ground at their feet and gave up her spirit in a great agony. Then each terrible one returned to his place, and the book which lay open before Death closed with a noise as of thunder, and the light which burnt before his shrine went out, so that all was darkness.

In the morning, when that company which had brought her came back to the church, they wondered much to see the lamp extinguished, and, fetching a taper, some went down fearfully into the vault. There all was as it had ever been, only the girl lay face downwards amongst the withered roses, and when they lifted her up they saw that she was dead; but her eyes were wide with horror. And so another tomb was hewn in marble, and she was laid with the rest, and when men tell the tale of her strange bridal they say, 'She had but the reward of her folly. God rest her soul!'

THE BLACK VEIL

There is a village in Norway which stands in a plain near a lake, not far from the mountains, but far from the sea, and equally far from any city. In this isolated spot there once lived a couple of ill-fame; they were evil to each other, and to all the world beside. He was the stronger of the two, so she suffered the most; and the more she suffered, the more her will to repay evil with evil grew within her, till at last one night she slew him. But she did not grow strong with her crime; she felt the shame of it; so even then, when she could say, 'I am free,' nothing seemed well with her, and a fear came on her lest the neighbours should know or should suspect her guilt.

So he was buried, and she bemoaned him, and she bought for herself a veil of mourning, longer and thicker than common. This veil, which was cumbersome at first, grew day by day more cumbersome, until, when some months had passed, it was so long that it trailed behind her, and so heavy that it weighed her to the ground, and so thick that she could see neither the sun, nor the moon, nor any stars. And day by day her fears grew heavier, and her thoughts were ever, 'How shall this my veil be shortened; how shall it be lightened; and how shall my eyes be cleared?'

Some of the people then said, 'It is her over-sorrow has angered the spirits of the mountain, that have sent this curse upon her.' She herself looked towards the mountains, where afar off there dwelt a wise woman, and when the others said, 'Go, ask counsel of the wise woman of the mountain,' she went.

It was a weary journey, but at last it was done, and she stood before the wise woman, and said, 'How shall this my veil be shortened? How shall this my veil, which is heavy, be made light? How shall this my veil, which obscures all things, so that I can see neither the sun, nor the moon, nor any star, be made clear to my sight?'

Then the wise woman, after a pause, made answer, 'Go; pray three times in the night on the grave of him who is no more. Go; pray three times in the night on the grave of him who is not here. Go; pray three times in the night on the grave of him who lies in the earth.'

With this answer she went heavily back to the village, and they met her eagerly and questioned her, but she made no reply, for she shrank from the task set to her, and she shut herself indoors and thought, 'Peradventure if I go not over the threshold it will be a less weighty burden.' But it was not so, and outside the neighbours watched, for they marvelled more and more.

At last, one night of thick blackness covered the sky, and the woman arose and said, 'If I go forth now none will see me; here I can sit no longer.' And she went forth and betook herself to the churchyard, but she was not alone, for the neighbours watched, and when they saw her go forth they followed her. And she heard them behind her, and turned in fear and anger, and saw that they pressed on her close. Then she made haste, and, coming to the high gate in the wall of the churchyard, she entered quickly and made it fast, so that none should disturb her and play the spy, but she trembled with a great fear, and the darkness was so thick that it stifled the words on her lips. But, at last, they outside heard her pray, and they listened, and there was silence for a space – silence till, with a great cry, she said, 'Help me, O friends and neighbours! He drags me down; he holds it, and draws me to him!'

And they outside shook the gate, but within she had made it too fast for all their strength; and she said, 'I cannot pray. He draws me! I am going down into the earth!' And her voice grew fainter, and they shook the gate like madmen, and some strove to climb the wall, and when they paused for an instant to listen, all was still.

When the day came, and the gates were broken, and they had come to the grave, they saw nothing; then with frenzied hands they laid bare the earth, and they found nothing, and next they opened the very coffin itself; the dead man was there alone, but in his hand they found a piece of her black veil clutched fast within his fingers.

THE WAYS OF GHOSTS

by

Ambrose Bierce

The life of Ambrose Bierce (1842–1913?) was one long paradox, being neatly summarised in the American critic E. F. Bleiler's view of Bierce's stories: 'a strange mixture of sincerity and contrivance, remarkable insights and astonishing stupidities, dazzling technique and leaden crudities, high mindedness often turning out to be simply vulgarity and coarseness in a bright uniform.'

Bierce was the most notorious member of a very strange family, which included the leader of an unsuccessful attempt to invade Canada, a circus strong man, and a missionary sister reputed to have been eaten by cannibals in Africa. Bierce's father had thirteen children, all of whom he christened with names beginning with the letter 'A'. Ambrose left home to fight in the Civil War, where he distinguished himself by his bravery, and after leaving the army took various jobs, before turning to journalism for a living.

His reputation as a writer can be gauged from his nickname of 'Bitter' Bierce. In a newspaper world where few libel laws restrained the journalist, and a gunfight would often settle a simple slander quarrel, Ambrose Bierce shone out as a leading exponent of the art of editorial character assassination.

Eventually, old and even more bitter than ever, Bierce left for Mexico in 1913, to cover the civil war then raging. He was never seen again. Many theories still abound about the disappearance of Ambrose Bierce, including his murder by Pancho Villa and his own contrived disappearance followed by suicide.

Despite having his collected works published by his friend and admirer Walter Neale, a twelve-volume set much prized by macabre enthusiasts, Bierce's reputation, small in his lifetime, now rests solely on his ghost stories. These gruesome tales, quite unlike anything written before or since in America, reveal a fascinating and complex creator.

Some of them are classics. 'The Death of Halpin Frayser', where a son is murdered by his mother's soulless corpse, is probably the most frightening story to emerge from America in the nineteenth century. 'A Tough Tussle', a Civil war story (Bierce was a master of these) deals with a soldier's encounter with a dead opponent. Probably his most famous story 'An Occurrence at Owl Creek Bridge' is also a Civil War tale, but is remarkable for being among the first to describe a dead man's feelings before he knows he is dead. This story was filmed in 1961; any film-maker in search of good plots could do worse than look in the direction of Ambrose Bierce.

Strangely, for all Bierce's revellings in tales of the supernatural, it is not certain that he believed in ghosts himself (more paradox) despite his having claimed to see a wind-wraith rush past him at the moment of his friend Tom Hood's death. He violently refuted the idea of survival after death, yet many of his stories deal with such survival. In later years he collected stories of supernatural events and (ironically) strange disappearances.

It is not widely known that Bierce published several of these true tales of the supernatural. Some can be found in his article 'Some Haunted Houses' (in my anthology A Tide of Terror*); here are some more, forgotten for many years. They are an interesting insight into the mind of macabre fiction's greatest paradox: Ambrose Bierce.*

Present at a Hanging

An old man named Daniel Baker, living near Lebanon, Iowa, was suspected by his neighbours of having murdered a peddler who had obtained permission to pass the night at his house. This was in 1853, when peddling was more common in the Western country than it is now, and was attended with considerable danger. The peddler with his pack traversed the country by all manner of lonely roads, and was compelled to rely upon the country people for hospitality. This brought him into relation with queer characters, some of whom were not altogether scrupulous in their methods of making a living, murder being an acceptable means to that end. It occasionally occurred that a peddler with diminished pack and swollen purse would be traced to the lonely dwelling of some rough character and never could be traced beyond. This was so in the case of 'old man Baker', as he was always called. (Such names are given in the western 'settlements' only to elderly persons who

.are not esteemed; to the general disrepute of social unworth is affixed the special reproach of age.) A peddler came to his house and none went away – that is all that anybody knew.

Seven years later the Rev. Mr Cummings, a Baptist minister well known in that part of the country, was driving by Baker's farm one night. It was not very dark: there was a bit of moon somewhere above the light veil of mist that lay along the earth. Mr Cummings, who was at all times a cheerful person, was whistling a tune, which he would occasionally interrupt to speak a word of friendly encouragement to his horse. As he came to a little bridge across a dry ravine he saw the figure of a man standing upon it, clearly outlined against the grey background of a misty forest. The man had something strapped on his back and carried a heavy stick – obviously an itinerant peddler. His attitude had in it a suggestion of abstraction, like that of a sleep-walker. Mr Cummings reined in his horse when he arrived in front of him, gave him a pleasant salutation and invited him to a seat in the vehicle – 'if you are going my way,' he added. The man raised his head, looked him full in the face, but neither answered nor made any further movement. The minister, with good-natured persistence, repeated his invitation. At this the man threw his right hand forward from his side and pointed downward as he stood on the extreme edge of the bridge. Mr Cummings looked past him, over into the ravine, saw nothing unusual and withdrew his eyes to address the man again. He had disappeared. The horse, which all this time had been uncommonly restless, gave at the same moment a snort of terror and started to run away. Before he had regained control of the animal the minister was at the crest of the hill a hundred yards along. He looked back and saw the figure again, at the same place and in the same attitude as when he had first observed it. Then for the first time he was conscious of a sense of the supernatural and drove home as rapidly as his willing horse would go.

On arriving at home he related his adventure to his family, and early the next morning, accompanied by two neighbours, John White Corwell and Abner Raiser, returned to the spot. They found the body of old man Baker hanging by the neck from one of the beams of the bridge, immediately beneath the spot where the apparition had stood. A thick coating of dust, slightly dampened by the mist, covered the floor of the bridge, but the only footprints were those of Mr Cummings' horse.

In taking down the body the men disturbed the loose, friable earth of the slope below it, disclosing human bones already nearly uncovered by the action of water and frost. They were identified as those of the lost peddler. At the double inquest the coroner's jury found that Daniel Baker died by his own hand while suffering from temporary insanity, and that Samuel Morritz was murdered by some person or persons to the jury unknown.

A cold greeting

This is a story told by the late Benson Foley of San Francisco:

'In the summer of 1881 I met a man named James H. Conway, a resident of Franklin, Tennessee. He was visiting San Francisco for his health, deluded man, and brought me a note of introduction from Mr Lawrence Barting. I had known Barting as a captain in the Federal army during the civil war. At its close he had settled in Franklin, and in time became, I had reason to think, somewhat prominent as a lawyer. Barting had always seemed to me an honorable and truthful man, and the warm friendship which he expressed in his note for Mr Conway was to me sufficient evidence that the latter was in every way worthy of my confidence and esteem. At dinner one day Conway told me that it had been solemnly agreed between him and Barting that the one who died first should, if possible, communicate with the other from beyond the grave, in some unmistakable way – just how, they had left (wisely, it seemed to me) to be decided by the deceased, according to the opportunities that his altered circumstances might present.

'A few weeks after the conversation in which Mr Conway spoke of this agreement, I met him one day, walking slowly down Montgomery Street, apparently, from his abstracted air, in deep thought. He greeted me coldly with merely a movement of the head and passed on, leaving me standing on the walk, with half-proffered hand, surprised and naturally somewhat piqued. The next day I met him again in the office of the Palace Hotel, and seeing him about to repeat the disagreeable performance of the day before, intercepted him in a doorway, with a friendly salutation, and bluntly requested an explanation of his altered manner. He hesitated a moment; then, looking me frankly in the eyes, said:

' "I do not think, Mr Foley, that I have any longer a claim to your friendship, since Mr Barting appears to have withdrawn his own from me – for what reason, I protest I do not know. If he has not already informed you he probably will do so."

' "But," I replied, "I have not heard from Mr Barting."

' "Heard from him!" he repeated, with apparent surprise. "Why, he is here. I met him yesterday ten minutes before meeting you. I gave you exactly the same greeting that he gave me. I met him again not a quarter of an hour ago, and his manner was precisely the same: he merely bowed and passed on. I shall not soon forget your civility to me. Good morning, or – as it may please you – farewell."

'All this seemed to be singularly considerate and delicate behaviour on the part of Mr Conway.

'As dramatic situations and literary effects are foreign to my purpose I will explain at once that Mr Barting was dead. He had died in Nashville four days before this conversation. Calling on Mr Conway, I apprised him of our friend's death, showing him the letters announcing it. He was visibly affected in a way that forbade me to entertain a doubt of his sincerity.

' "It seems incredible," he said, after a period of reflection. "I suppose I must have mistaken another man for Barting, and that man's cold greeting was merely a stranger's civil acknowledgement of my own. I remember, indeed, that he lacked Barting's moustache."

' "Doubtless it was another man," I assented; and the subject was never afterward mentioned between us. But I had in my pocket a photograph of Barting, which had been inclosed in the letter from his widow. It had been taken a week before his death, and was without a moustache.'

A wireless message

In the summer of 1896 Mr William Holt, a wealthy manufacturer of Chicago, was living temporarily in a little town of central New York, the name of which the writer's memory has not retained. Mr Holt had had 'trouble with his wife', from whom he had parted a year before. Whether the trouble was anything more serious than 'incompatibility of temper', he is probably the only living person that knows: he is not addicted to the vice of confidences. Yet he has related the incident herein set down to at least one person without exacting a pledge of secrecy. He is now living in Europe.

One evening he had left the house of a brother whom he was visiting, for a stroll in the country. It may be assumed – whatever the value of the assumption in connection with what is said to have occurred – that his mind was occupied with reflections on his domestic infelicities and the distressing changes that they had wrought in his life. Whatever may have been his thoughts, they so possessed him that he observed neither the lapse of time nor whither his feet were carrying him; he knew only that he had passed far beyond the town limits and was traversing a lonely region by a road that bore no resemblance to the one by which he had left the village. In brief, he was 'lost'.

Realising his mischance, he smiled; central New York is not a region of perils, nor does one long remain lost in it. He turned about and went back the way that he had come. Before he had gone far he observed that the landscape was growing more distinct – was brightening. Everything was suffused with a soft, red glow in which he saw his shadow projected in the road before him. 'The moon is rising,' he said to himself. Then he remembered that it was about the time of the new moon, and if that tricksy orb was in one of its stages of visibility it had set long before. He stopped and faced about, seeking the source of the rapidly broadening light. As he did so, his shadow turned and lay along the road in front of him as before. The light still came from behind him. That was surprising; he could not understand. Again he turned, and again, facing successively to every point of the horizon. Always the shadow was before – always the light behind, 'a still and awful red'.

Holt was astonished – 'dumfounded' is the word that he used in telling it – yet seems to have retained a certain intelligent curiosity. To test the intensity of the light whose nature and cause he could not determine, he took out his watch to see if he could make out the figures on the dial. They were plainly visible, and the hands indicated the hour of eleven o'clock and twenty-five minutes. At that moment the mysterious illumination suddenly flared to an intense, an almost blinding splendour, flushing the entire sky, extinguishing the stars and throwing the monstrous shadow of himself athwart the landscape. In that unearthly illumination he saw near him, but apparently in the air at a considerable elevation, the figure of his wife, clad in her night-clothing and holding to her breast the figure of his child. Her eyes were fixed upon his with an expression which he afterwards professed himself unable to name or describe, further than that it was 'not of this life'.

The flare was momentary, followed by black darkness, in which, however, the apparition still showed white and motionless; then by insensible degrees it faded and vanished, like a bright image on the retina after the closing of the eyes. A peculiarity of the apparition, hardly noted at the time, but afterwards recalled, was that it showed only the upper half of the woman's figure: nothing was seen below the waist.

The sudden darkness was comparative, not absolute, for gradually all objects of his environment became again visible.

In the dawn of the morning Holt found himself entering the village at a point opposite to that at which he had left it. He soon arrived at the house of his brother, who hardly knew him. He was wild-eyed, haggard, and grey as a rat. Almost incoherently, he related his night's experience.

'Go to bed, my poor fellow,' said his brother, 'and – wait. We shall hear more of this.'

An hour later came the predestined telegram. Holt's dwelling in one of the suburbs of Chicago had been destroyed by fire. Her escape cut off by the flames, his wife had appeared at an upper window, her child in her arms. There she had stood, motionless, apparently dazed. Just as the firemen had arrived with a ladder, the floor had given way, and she was seen no more.

The moment of this culminating horror was eleven o'clock and twenty-five minutes, standard time.

An arrest

Having murdered his brother-in-law, Orrin Brower of Kentucky was a fugitive from justice. From the county jail where he had been confined to await his trial he had escaped by knocking down his jailer with an iron bar, robbing him of his keys and, opening the outer door, walking out into the night. The jailer being unarmed, Brower got no weapon with which to defend his recovered liberty. As soon as he was out of the town he had the folly to enter a forest; this was many years ago, when that region was wilder than it is now.

The night was pretty dark, with neither moon nor stars visible, and as Brower had never dwelt thereabout, and knew nothing of the lay of the land, he was, naturally, not long in losing himself.

He could not have said if he were getting farther away from the town or going back to it – a most important matter to Orrin Brower. He knew that in either case a posse of citizens with a pack of bloodhounds would soon be on his track and his chance of escape was very slender; but he did not wish to assist in his own pursuit. Even an added hour of freedom was worth having.

Suddenly he emerged from the forest into an old road, and there before him saw, indistinctly, the figure of a man, motionless in the gloom. It was too late to retreat: the fugitive felt that at the first movement back towards the wood he would be, as he afterward explained, 'filled with buckshot'. So the two stood there like trees, Brower nearly suffocated by the activity of his own heart; the other – the emotions of the other are not recorded.

A moment later – it may have been an hour – the moon sailed into a patch of unclouded sky and the hunted man saw that visible embodiment of Law lift an arm and point significantly towards and beyond him. He understood. Turning his back to his captor, he walked submissively away in the direction indicated, looking to neither the right nor the left; hardly daring to breathe, his head and back actually aching with a prophecy of buckshot.

Brower was as courageous a criminal as ever lived to be hanged; that was shown by the conditions of awful personal peril in which he had coolly killed his brother-in-law. It is needless to relate them here; they came out at his trial, and the revelation of his calmness in confronting them came near to saving his neck. But what would you have? – when a brave man is beaten, he submits.

So they pursued their journey jailward along the old road through the woods. Only once did Brower venture a turn of the head: just once, when he was in deep shadow and he knew that the other was in moonlight, he looked backwards. His captor was Burton Duff, the jailer, as white as death and bearing upon his brow the livid mark of the iron bar. Orrin Brower had no further curiosity.

Eventually they entered the town, which was all alight, but deserted; only the women and children remained, and they were off the streets. Straight towards the jail the criminal held his way. Straight up to the main entrance he walked, laid his hand upon the knob of the heavy iron door, pushed it open without command, entered and found himself in the presence of a half-dozen armed men. Then he turned. Nobody else entered.

On a table in the corridor lay the dead body of Burton Duff.

THE FEVER QUEEN

by

K. and H. Prichard

Kate Ryall Prichard and Hesketh Vernon Prichard were mother and son who collaborated on several books, the most notable being a volume of tales about Flaxman Low, psychic detective.

Hesketh was born in India shortly after his father's death in 1876, and returned with his mother to England. He grew up to become a famous big-game hunter and explorer, and a county cricketer. Together, the Prichards travelled all over the world until Kate's death shortly before the First World War. Hesketh Prichard continued to write, served in the war as a major, and died in 1922 of a rare disease.

Flaxman Low was the Prichard's most enduring creation. A scientific investigator of ghosts, he made his first appearance in Pearson's Magazine in 1898, under the Prichard's pen-names E. and H. Heron. There were twelve Flaxman Low stories in all, which were collected into Ghosts (1899). For some reason, the Prichards published Ghosts under their real names, yet they returned to the Heron pseudonym for a 1916 volume called Ghost Stories which reprinted half the original Flaxman Low tales.

Now completely forgotten is their excellent collection of short stories Roving Hearts (1903), a title which sums up the life of the Prichards very neatly. At the zenith of the British Empire, Kate and Hesketh had seen life in its outposts, and in Roving Hearts they collected together the stories they had written over the years about their experiences, which had originally appeared in such journals as the Cornhill Magazine. 'The Fever Queen', despite being built around a flamboyant and romantic gesture that could only have been in Victorian times, is still a sharply painted picture of how grim life must have been for some of the servants of the Empire in their lonely outposts.

I

He was not of a melancholy disposition, but he was greatly given to brooding over his artistic shortcomings. He lived for Art and in Art, and Art treated him as a heartless woman treats a boy who brings his all to her feet. She absorbed and crushed him.

He was utterly unconventional, and had trouble in arriving at technical detail. Yet there burned in him something of the sacred fire. He was a man marked out for critical depreciation, and that because he travelled to his effects by paths that were not the old well-trodden ones, but new, hewn out at first hand and at a magnificent cost of experience and labour.

He painted a picture which lives today. It is called 'The Inspiration', and the subject is a single figure tense with the glory of a new idea. In the face, I have heard men say, they can read the story of their own personal efforts, which is synonymous with calling the picture genius.

Art critics found fault with it from many points of view, and the greatest art critic of all objected seriously to the lacing of the sandals, which he said was so egregiously faulty that it eclipsed any merit or meaning the production might have possessed. The picture was sold for two figures to a dealer, and he passed it on for three to a man who later refused 4,000*l.* for it. Meantime the artist, carrying with him the curse of the critical world, slipped out of ken.

Anon came the reaction. Public opinion slowly trampled down the new raw path into the smoothness which permits of the passing of the tender-footed critic. Then 'The Inspiration' was bespattered with loud praise. Brodrick the painter was enquired for, but Brodrick the painter was nowhere to be found.

A man answering to his description was reported to have died in beggary in Liverpool. The Press added sombre and well-worn regrets. 'Poor Brodrick! he has joined the band of which Keats is the head and front.'

A few bewailed him for his art's sake, and the critics raised their voices in eulogising the technical perfection of his work, which was perhaps not the greatest part of it. The man's tragedy had its little boom. It droned into nothingness, yet Brodrick the lost remained, on the fame of his one picture, a shining planet in the sky of Art.

Such is shortly the history of Sidney Brodrick as it is known to everyone. The sequel was given me to read in living characters, and follows in due course.

I had left the mail at a certain small and unimportant port, and dived with my scanty band of natives into the primeval forest. The district was practically unexplored; what I was doing there is of no consequence.

For days and days we had bored our way worm-like through the gloomy airless density of the forest, and at last on a quiet evening (it was Sunday at home, but all days are alike in those unfathomed depths of growth) we emerged upon a swamp, where in the rainy season long lagoons string themselves out along the river bed.

But as we drew away from the skirts of the forest land, it appeared to me as if the world had aged since last I looked upon its face three weeks before. The time was towards the close of the dry season, and all was stale and withered. Grey scummy pools broke the foreshores of the river, which itself had dwindled to a mean stream in a spread of black and caking mud. Silence and heat lay heavy-handed there.

In England it was the hour of church bells and the long blue cool summer evening. I tramped on at the head of my small party, dreaming listlessly of home and feeling lonely and remote. At length we picked up the edge of a shrunken lagoon, at the further end of which gleamed a deeper pool. Skirting along it, we came suddenly upon a man's dwelling-place.

I shouted.

At the noise something dived from a thicket of reeds, breaking the oily glare of the lagoon into long ripples that quaked themselves into peace on the verge.

I shouted again.

The small wattle hut was humped against a background of sunset, the whole scene iridescent with a thousand delicate colours.

We were now come very near, and the place continued deadly still. Once more I broke the silence with a shout.

This time there was an answer in a cracked high scream, and a figure appeared in the doorway – a man naked to the waist and sun-blackened, with wild eyes peering out at us from a wilderness of hair.

'Hullo!' I called.

'I'm mad – mad – mad!' ejaculated the figure hoarsely. 'Possessed of a legion of devils! Mad – mad, you know – mad since I buried Arroga!' he laughed, clinging to the doorpost and laughing again.

The horror of the thing held us dumb. When I found my voice I said:

'Mad? Nonsense! You have fever and nerves – that's all! You can't wonder at that, seeing where you've stranded yourself. In a month you'll be all right and on your way back to England.'

'England? I? I don't want to go! No, no, I'm happy here with the moon for company by night and the stars by day. Big purple stars staring out in a great dull-red sky, overhung by the nakedness of space! And Arroga's soul comes to me – he had a soul, you know – whining and talking in the lurid nights. Go away, I say!'

But I only asked permission to camp near by for a few hours, hoping he might show himself in a more reasonable mood by morning.

'Yes, stay with me – stay tonight,' his fever-struck brain vacillating with my words. Then he pulled me closer. 'I'm afraid of the nights when there is no moon. Sometimes the darkness is a mouth – waiting! Sometimes it has black velvet hands gripping and feeling round the hut.' He shivered and laughed woefully, with an apeish twisting of the features. Then his eyes changed, he looked hard at me, and the thoughts of a man lit up his face. 'Sorry' – he spoke in a changed tone, and with evident difficulty now – 'I hardly know what I've been saying. I'm shaky, you see – malaria, and that kind of thing. Forgive me; it's very lonesome since Arroga died – he came here with me – long, long ago. Come in.'

II

I made my men camp close at hand, and I myself proposed to share the sick man's hut. He was wrung with fever and needed tending. Through his delirium ran the broken story of his sufferings. How the days and the nights had passed over him with the roar of a train passing through a tunnel, and the turmoil beat in upon his brain until it was bruised and tender, and he prayed for rest. But there was no respite; thousands of thoughts with little trampling feet swarmed upon him, until his head quivered in the agony of over-use.

'And Arroga – what of him?' I asked.

'Don't you know?' muttered the sick man feebly; 'he's dead. He didn't go away with the rest; he was a poor, stupid creature, but he would not leave me here alone. And then he sickened, too – he struggled for his life – yes, he struggled – of course it was useless, because' – he raised himself upon his elbows and stared about him nervously with flaming eyes as he whispered, 'because *she* was there.'

He sank down again. I involuntarily glanced back over my shoulder.

'Arroga died – died in the swamp and left me alone with *her*. About that time something seemed to give way' – he held his head between his hands – 'here, I think. Hush, hush! They'll hear you. Round and round and round they fly! *She* sends them. Where are you? I can't see you.'

And this was how the night passed. He raved continually, but I could gather nothing definite as to why he had come to that God-forsaken place. Before morning he slept, and with the light awoke sane and collected enough.

The hut was tumble-down, and on the floor the black mud of the soil had broken into an ankle-deep dust. My host was full of apologies.

'I have not many visitors, you see,' he said, with a pathetic jocularity. 'As far as I remember, you're the first, and I've been here' – he pressed his forehead – 'a long time. I've lost count of days and weeks; sometimes I fancy I have lost count of years, too. Come, you shall tell me how the world is wagging, the world I once thought would miss me,' he laughed painfully – 'but I know better, much better now.'

This conversation took place at the rather hollow ceremony of breakfast. For food we levied toll upon the natural products of the district – rainbow-hued fish from the lagoon, and the fat, pulpy fruit of the tropics. To these I added whisky and a wild duck I had shot, besides biscuit. My companion spoke little, and the world of which he did speak was the world of five years ago. I let my tongue wander among the subsequent events and happenings. He sat and listened with clenched hands and something not far removed from anguish upon his face. The more I observed him the more I laid the blame of his desperate exile upon some woman. He was a man with a strange charm of his own, one who had been lovable once in those old days which had either sinned against him cruelly or given him some vital disillusionment. He avoided all reference to the past regarding himself.

I urged him to return with me to the coast, and to this he consented. As soon as he picked up a little strength we were to start upon our homeward march.

'Five years have passed since I came here,' he said, after a long silence, 'and yet I am always seeing something new. I cannot exhaust the forms and colours Nature wears in this single spot. How can one man master all her revelations? Sunset and sunrise, and the moon when the quivering air seems full of powdered glass. And the nights – the moonrise' – he stopped abruptly and a troubled dimness covered his eyes – 'then I dream,' he ended uncertainly.

To this I answered in a dull, practical way that I wondered he should have chosen a place so obviously unhealthy.

'When I came here I never noticed that,' he said simply. 'My mind was full of other things. There seemed to me much here which few before had seen and none knew by heart. I came to learn.'

'Then you had better go and give the world the benefit of your knowledge,' I said, half banteringly; the man's mental condition was such I hardly dared touch him with serious speech. 'You've been here quite long enough. You have fever, and from the look of you, you have had it a long time.'

He was gazing at me in a puzzled kind of way, and I noticed a subtle change in his expression. The border line between sanity and delirium was perilously thin; he overstepped it a hundred times a day, while the fever raged in his drying veins.

'Yes,' he cried eagerly, after a pause. 'I have fever. I have it badly, but I work better when I have fever.'

'Work?'

'Yes, you know I paint. I have tried to paint for many years – tried to paint the truth as I saw it. But I didn't succeed somehow, although when alone, as I looked at my finished pictures, I could have sworn they reflected truth, and truth only. But I was wrong – quite wrong!'

He lay in dejected silence for a long time, then rambled away into disconnected sentences.

I gave him nourishment and remedies to the best of my knowledge, and it almost seemed as the days went by that he was gaining ground. He moaned and muttered less and slept better. But with gaining strength a strange reticence grew upon him. He avoided all reference to himself or his past, and yet I felt that his was no inherent reserve, but the reserve born of a wounded spirit.

The rains broke early that season, earlier than I had counted upon. First a few days of hot puffing breezes with long sweltering lulls between, through which one continued to breathe only by an effort. Then in a terrific burst of storm the rain fell. No downpour of close-set, heavy lines, but a solid mass of water tumbling from the clouds.

All the night through, huddled in a corner, he babbled incessantly, yet never for a moment lost consciousness of my presence.

'When the light comes, the moonlight – moonlight and fever are great aids – I will paint again. You are blind, you know, as I was when I came. You see nothing. God! man! there are terrible scenes in the valley of fever! *She* is there. Fever materialised, a pale woman, young, cruel, and beautiful, with deep eyes shining and red lips. She stoops – stoops over the dying and laughs low – so low that it is like the wind stirring. And the poor human thing she has stricken gasps and battles for failing life, and she sucks away his breath with kisses. She was there when Arroga died. We were out in the moon, she on one side of the dying, I on the other, and I took sketches of her.

> By the cruelty deaf as a fire
> And blind as the night.

I'll show you those sketches some time. No eyes have seen that face but mine.'

I had contrived a light, but it burned feebly in the heavy damp of the atmosphere. Still, by its means I could keep some sort of watch upon my companion.

'Then Arroga died,' he went on presently, 'and I saw her no more for a time. But one night as I lay here she came again. She came in the dark. I saw her, for a pale light fell all around her, like the shining of sick men's eyes – thousands and thousands of burning sleepless eyes. Yes, she came again – for me this time, and she used to break my sleep, so that I took to sketching things, and when she glanced away I would draw her face, dark and bloodless and beautiful, and her pale white hands. But she knew, and she laughed low till my ears tingled at the sound and –

The man was silent on a sudden, yet his lips moved with voiceless words. Some harmony of inspiration wandered in his brain perhaps, and his lips moved to its music.

'I have the sketches for that picture, my great picture that will be,' he whispered, dragging his weak limbs nearer me. 'The background, a grey pool with crawling things upon the scum – you can't see them, only you know they are there – and drifted over with fever-mist. It is her home; this pale woman waits there, lovely as a she-devil, for those who pass by. No one has ever done anything like that picture because no one else knows. Once they said I had striven to paint that of which I knew nothing. But now I know, and not one other living soul beside!'

He brooded upon the thought a while, a strange rapture on his face. 'It is alone and mine! – that picture which must stand and blaze matchless in the world. I will paint it when I reach England again, and people will stop before it and thrill with the wonder and the nearness of it. And that picture will be mine! I have paid for it – for my right to paint it in sickness, in terror, and in the loneliness of the damned!'

His earnestness was awful.

I made some common-place remark as he seemed to wait for an answer. 'No,' he shook his head, 'I am not overwrought. Only loneliness and dreams have enlightened my eyes to see the phantoms that haunt the world.'

III

It was a palsied earth, palsied and dripping with continuous rain. By day the sick man lay on his back half asleep and half awake, by night he raved.

Altogether it seemed to me that he was very nearly broken, and his fancy had turned into a new channel.

'Take me away,' he would moan at intervals, 'take me away from this accursed place. I stifle here, take me away! See, the very colours are wrong,' pointing outside where, under the level evening light, the sodden spread of swamp was patched with vivid unwholesome green.

From appearances I imagined we were about to have a break in the rains, of which I had resolved to take due advantage by beginning our return march to the coast.

'Tomorrow,' I said; 'we will move on tomorrow!'

He seemed to grow easier at the promise, and as the darkness came on he dropped into dozing fitfully.

It was a dreadful night; the sky drooped above us close as a dish-cover, the ground beneath steamed with clamminess and chill. Marsh exhalations made the air foul. In the midst of it all I slept. When I woke night was still at its deepest, but a late moon streamed in across the floor. I turned and looked towards the place where my companion had been lying. It was empty, save for a huge uncouth spider.

I sprang up and ran out. Under the low moon nothing stirred. The cessation of the swamp noises had in it something weird and awful. I seemed to hear far-off echoes not of this world.

It was a ghastly moon; within its circle of pallid light wild and ravening terror moved abroad. The hour was one of influences.

I looked across the lagoon. It was ashift with moonlight, the dark trees written black upon its surface.

At one side the camp lay stirless in its tired slumber. I thought of rousing the men, but at the instant a suggestion struck me almost as if it had been spoken in my ear aloud.

There was another pool up the river, a pool coated with festering scum and bubbles, which in my mind had somehow come to represent the scene of Arroga's death and my poor friend's vision. With an unreasoning certainty that I should find him there, I started towards it, finding my way as quickly as I was able round beds of reed and treacherous morass. But since the rains the place had become unrecognisable. The lagoons had extended on all sides, swallowing up their daughter pools as the water rose.

Feeling foolishly thrown out by these changes, which at any other time I should have been prepared for, I stopped at a point where the water touched the foot of an open bank, and looked round.

To my relief I saw my man at a little distance. He was walking and stumbling up and down, a ragged spectre of despair. I called to him, and he stood still waiting for me to come up, yet he did not, I believe, so much as see me.

As I came abreast of him he shambled away towards a clump of low-growing shrubs; amongst the twisted branches of one of them he had propped up the end of a packing-case, much as a canvas is set upon an easel, and in the strengthening light of the moon I could make out a face painted upon it. I could use many words to describe that face, but unless a man had looked upon it with his own eyes he could by no means imagine it.

Marvellous in its beautiful malignancy, it seemed to overpower the senses. At one moment it was all glorious beauty, at the next evil submerged its loveliness.

He began to work upon it, talking wildly as he worked.

'You laugh' – his brush flickered over the surface – 'as you have often laughed. I had no canvas, no paper, nothing left to me. You laboured to defeat me. You drowned away the pool out of my sight, but it is cut in upon my memory. And now you are here – here, your very self, my Fever Queen!'

The moonless half of the night made a background, and against it the lagoon, with its white reflected light, aided the moonbeams.

'I have won you to my brush after all,' his tongue ran wildly on. 'Your image is mine. And I shall be famous! Everyone will look at you – at you! I have despaired for many days, but I should have known that you could not evade me at the last!'

He staggered as he ended, and caught at the branch to steady himself.

'You say I am dying? Then let me die. You may kill me, but I have won! I am immortal with your immortality here.' He raised his arm towards the picture, and I caught him as he sank slowly to the ground.

I carried him back to the hut somehow, but in that obstinate swoon he lay all the day through until evening. Then I could not hide from myself that he was dying. I gave him stimulant, and as he began to find power he spoke.

'I am ebbing out,' he said, 'and there is one thing I must ask of you.'

It was evident he was now in full possession of his senses. I told him I would do all he wished.

'Bury me here and forget you have ever seen me.'

To this I demurred, recalling his picture to his mind, the picture I had left overnight by the lagoon. But he shook his head wearily.

'Too late,' he said. 'My cunning has gone. She – I almost fancy she is real sometimes.' He smiled faintly. 'She has robbed me of all – health and mind, and the cunning of my right hand. No, bury it with me, the picture as nameless as the painter who created it.'

I urged him no more, this broken man, and he, reading the pity in my face perhaps, panted slowly on:

'Once I dreamed of God knows what fame! I would not be denied. I have toiled, and I have followed Art into the portals of Death, but they've been too quick for me, and have caught me in the gate. Leave me my picture, it is all I have. I made many sketches, but you will not find them now: this climate destroys all things, from life downwards. Fame, you say? Oh, God, I so wanted fame! I lived for fame! I never doubted *really* but that I should get it some day – and now!' the man sobbed.

I was moved out of the common, and I said more of the wonderful picture I had seen than I can remember.

'Fame! you tempt me,' he whispered, weak and eager. 'It would have been dear to me to know I had won it even when I was dead! But no, no! You don't know the past, you have not felt my shame. Once I painted a picture and the critics laughed at it. And I had painted with my heart's blood!' He waited, as if the remembrance suffocated him. 'I left England. I had believed in myself and been mistaken, and the cancer of it ate into me. Now you understand?'

I told him that I understood, but that he had banished himself most cruelly.

'I wanted to hide myself,' the thin voice resumed; 'hide myself until I had attained knowledge and master-craft. I wanted to gain local colour, and the local colour gained me,' he laughed hoarsely. 'Now do you not see why you cannot take my new picture home? I could not endure to have my name bandied about again with sneers when I am dead. Leave me to my lost art and my nameless grave.'

I could only say I wished he would let me do differently.

'What would you write above me? "Here lies Sidney Brodrick, who dreamed of a National Funeral. Fool!"'

I started.

'The name of your picture – what was it?' I asked.

'You will never have heard of it. It adorns some servant's bedroom, I expect. It was called "The Inspiration".'

' "The Inspiration"! Why, man,' I cried, 'you are famous! Last year five thousand pounds was paid for your picture by the nation. Your name is amongst the great names of the land.'

But Sidney Brodrick, new-found, was on the Borderland.

'Famous?' he whispered, and again, 'famous?'

Then he lay so long silent with closed eyes that I began to fear he had known too late. But after a time he smiled, and I saw that all was well.

'I will take your last picture,' I said; 'you cannot refuse to grant me that now. When I get home I will show it to all the world. It will make a fitting Omega to your Alpha of "The Inspiration." '

He smiled again.

'They throng the rooms,' he said suddenly; 'they say it is false, immoral, degrading to Art.' In mind he was back in that long-past bitter day of humiliation. 'Yet when Time has hallowed the work it takes its own place. See them passing with a stare! "What meaning has it?" "None!"

'So they talk under the skylights and move on. Better to follow the worn groove and spill common tints in the well-worn way upon some subject staled by use. The critic comes, you look for his judgement with a throb – he only laughs at that which you have given a life to create! Laughter and gibes – they have been long in my heart, but now above and beyond I hear the thunder and the tumult of a higher applause.'

THE PERMANENT STILETTO

by

W. C. Morrow

Few books are more eagerly pursued by macabre fiction enthusiasts than The Ape, The Idiot and Other People, *the only volume of short stories written by William Chambers Morrow (1853–1923). Originally published in America by Lippincott in 1897, it appeared the following year in a British edition, issued by an enterprising young publisher called Grant Richards, whose list included the names of Arthur Machen, M. P. Shiel, Barry Pain, R. Murray Gilchrist, Maurice Level and Grant Allen.*

W. C. Morrow, born in Selma, Alabama and a long-time resident of California, wrote only two more books, both novels: A Man, His Mark *(1900) and* Lentala of the South Seas *(1908). He also wrote many stories for magazines, which are now being hunted down by researchers like America's Sam Moskowitz, but he faded into obscurity.*

The Ape, The Idiot and Other People *has steadily gained in reputation over the years as a source of some of the finest tales of the macabre ever to appear in America. Perhaps the most widely-known story is 'The Monster Maker', where a scientist replaces a man's head with a silver ball – but keeps him alive. Other notable tales include 'Over an Absinthe Bottle' and 'His Unconquerable Enemy' (which can be found in my anthology* A Tide of Terror*).*

Happily, 'The Permanent Stiletto' seems to have escaped the wider circulation of his other tales. This really is a strange story, based on a medical premise that, in those days, could well have been possible.

I had sent in all haste for Dr Rowell, but as yet he had not arrived, and the strain was terrible. There lay my young friend upon his bed in the hotel, and I believed that he was dying. Only the jewelled handle of the knife was visible at his breast; the blade was wholly sheathed in his body.

'Pull it out, old fellow,' begged the sufferer, through white, drawn lips, his gasping voice being hardly less distressing than the unearthly look in his eyes.

'No, Arnold,' said I, as I held his hand and gently stroked his forehead. It may have been instinct, it may have been a certain knowledge of anatomy that made me refuse.

'Why not? It hurts,' he gasped. It was pitiful to see him suffer, this strong, healthy, daring, reckless young fellow.

Dr Rowell walked in – a tall, grave man, with grey hair. He went to the bed, and I pointed to the knife-handle, with its great, bold ruby in the end and its diamonds and emeralds alternating in quaint designs in the sides. The physician started. He felt Arnold's pulse and looked puzzled.

'When was this done?' he asked.

'About twenty minutes ago,' I answered.

The physician started out, beckoning me to follow.

'Stop!' said Arnold. We obeyed. 'Do you wish to speak of me?' he asked.

'Yes,' replied the physician, hesitating.

'Speak in my presence, then,' said my friend; 'I fear nothing.' It was said in his old, imperious way, although his suffering must have been great.

'If you insist –'

'I do.'

'Then,' said the physician, 'if you have any matters to adjust they should be attended to at once. I can do nothing for you.'

'How long can I live?' asked Arnold.

The physician thoughtfully stroked his grey beard. 'It depends,' he finally said; 'if the knife be withdrawn you may live three minutes; if it be allowed to remain you may possibly live an hour or two – not longer.'

Arnold never flinched.

'Thank you,' he said, smiling faintly through his pain; 'my friend here will pay you. I have some things to do. Let the knife remain.' He turned his eyes to mine, and, pressing my hand, said, affectionately, 'And I thank you too, old fellow, for not pulling it out.'

The physician, moved by a sense of delicacy, left the room, saying, 'Ring if there is a change. I will be in the hotel office.' He had not gone far when he turned and came back. 'Pardon me,' said he, 'but there is a young surgeon in the hotel who is said to be a very skilful man. My specialty is not surgery, but medicine. May I call him?'

'Yes,' said I, eagerly; but Arnold smiled and shook his head. 'I fear there will not be time,' he said. But I refused to heed him and directed that the surgeon be called immediately. I was writing at Arnold's dictation when the two men entered the room. There was something of nerve and assurance in the young surgeon that struck my attention. His manner, though quiet, was bold and straightforward, and his movements sure and quick. This young man had already distinguished himself in the performance of some difficult hospital laparotomies, and he was at that sanguine age when ambition looks through the spectacles of experiment. Dr Raoul Entrefort was the newcomer's name. He was a Creole, small and dark, and he had travelled and studied in Europe.

'Speak freely,' gasped Arnold, after Dr Entrefort had made an examination.

'What think you, doctor?' asked Entrefort of the older man.

'I think,' was the reply, 'that the knife-blade has penetrated the ascending aorta, about two inches above the heart. So long as the blade remains in the wound the escape of blood is comparatively small, though certain; were the blade withdrawn the heart would almost instantly empty itself through the aortal wound.'

Meanwhile, Entrefort was deftly cutting away the white shirt and the undershirt, and soon had the breast exposed. He examined the gem-studded hilt with the keenest interest.

'You are proceeding on the assumption, doctor,' he said, 'that this weapon is a knife.'

'Certainly,' answered Dr Rowell, smiling; 'what else can it be?'

'It *is* a knife,' faintly interposed Arnold.

'Did you see the blade?' Entrefort asked him, quickly.

'I did – for a moment.'

Entrefort shot a quick look at Dr Rowell and whispered, 'Then it is *not* suicide.' Dr Rowell looked puzzled and said nothing.

'I must disagree with you, gentlemen,' quietly remarked Entrefort; 'this is not a knife.' He examined the handle very narrowly. Not only was the blade entirely concealed from view within Arnold's body, but the blow has been so strongly delivered that the skin was depressed by the guard. 'The fact that it is not a knife presents a very curious series of facts and contingencies,' pursued Entrefort, with amazing coolness, 'some of which are, so far as I am informed, entirely novel in the history of surgery.'

A quizzical expression, faintly amused and manifestly interested, was upon Dr Rowell's face. 'What is the weapon, doctor?' he asked.

'A stiletto.'

Arnold started. Dr Rowell appeared confused. 'I must confess,' he said, 'my ignorance of the differences among these penetrating weapons, whether dirks, daggers, stilettos, poniards, or bowie-knives.'

'With the exception of the stiletto,' explained Entrefort, 'all the weapons you mention have one or two edges, so that in penetrating they cut their way. A stiletto is round, is ordinarily about half an inch or less in diameter at the guard, and tapers to a sharp point. It penetrates solely by pushing the tissues aside in all directions. You will understand the importance of that point.'

Dr Rowell nodded, more deeply interested than ever.

'How do you know it is a stiletto, Dr Entrefort?' I asked.

'The cutting of these stones is the work of Italian lapidaries,' he said, 'and they were set in Genoa. Notice, too, the guard. It is much broader and shorter than the guard of an edged weapon; in fact, it is nearly round. This weapon is about four hundred years old, and would be cheap at twenty thousand florins. Observe, also, the darkening colour of your friend's breast in the immediate vicinity of the guard; this indicates that the tissues have been bruised by the crowding of the "blade", if I may use the term.'

'What has all this to do with me?' asked the dying man.

'Perhaps a great deal, perhaps nothing. It brings a single ray of hope into your desperate condition.'

Arnold's eyes sparkled and he caught his breath. A tremor passed all through him, and I felt it in the hand I was holding. Life was sweet to him, then, after all – sweet to this wild dare-devil who had just faced death with such calmness! Dr Rowell, though showing no sign of jealousy, could not conceal a look of incredulity.

'With your permission,' said Entrefort, addressing Arnold, 'I will do what I can to save your life.'

'You may,' said the poor boy.

'But I shall have to hurt you.'

'Well.'

'Perhaps very much.'

'Well.'

'And even if I succeed (the chance is one in a thousand) you will never be a sound man, and a constant and terrible danger will always be present.'

'Well.'

Entrefort wrote a note and sent it away in haste by a bell-boy.

'Meanwhile,' he resumed, 'your life is in imminent danger from shock, and the end may come in a few minutes or hours from that cause. Attend without delay to whatever matters may require settling, and Dr Rowell,' glancing at that gentleman, 'will give you something to brace you up. I speak frankly, for I see that you are a man of extraordinary nerve. Am I right?'

'Be perfectly candid,' said Arnold.

Dr Rowell, evidently bewildered by his cyclonic young associate, wrote a prescription, which I sent by a boy to be filled. With unwise zeal I asked Entrefort –

'Is there not danger of lockjaw?'

'No,' he replied; 'there is not a sufficiently extensive injury to peripheral nerves to induce traumatic tetanus.'

I subsided. Dr Rowell's medicine came and I administered a dose. The physician and the surgeon then retired. The poor sufferer straightened up his business. When it was done he asked me –

'What is that crazy Frenchman going to do to me?'

'I have no idea; be patient.'

In less than an hour they returned, bringing with them a keen-eyed, tall young man, who had a number of tools wrapped in an apron. Evidently he was unused to such scenes, for he became deathly pale upon seeing the ghastly spectacle on my bed. With staring eyes and open mouth he began to retreat towards the door, stammering –

'I – I can't do it.'

'Nonsense, Hippolyte! Don't be a baby. Why, man, it is a case of life and death!'

'But – look at his eyes! he is dying!'

Arnold smiled. 'I am not dead, though,' he gasped.

'I – I beg your pardon,' said Hippolyte.

Dr Entrefort gave the nervous man a drink of brandy and then said –

'No more nonsense, my boy; it must be done. Gentlemen, allow me to introduce Mr Hippolyte, one of the most original, ingenious, and skilful machinists in the country.'

Hippolyte, being modest, blushed as he bowed. In order to conceal his confusion he unrolled his apron on the table with considerable noise of rattling tools.

'I have to make some preparations before you may begin, Hippolyte, and I want you to observe me that you may become used not only to the sight of fresh blood, but also, what is more trying, the odour of it.'

Hippolyte shivered. Entrefort opened a case of surgical instruments.

'Now, doctor, the chloroform,' he said, to Dr Rowell.

'I will not take it,' promptly interposed the sufferer; 'I want to know when I die.'

'Very well,' said Entrefort; 'but you have little nerve now to spare. We may try it without chloroform, however. It will be better if you can do without. Try your best to lie still while I cut.'

'What are you going to do?' asked Arnold.

'Save your life, if possible.'

'How? Tell me all about it.'

'Must you know?'

'Yes.'

'Very well, then. The point of the stiletto has passed entirely through the aorta, which is the great vessel rising out of the heart and carrying the aerated blood to the arteries. If I should withdraw the weapon the blood would rush from the two holes in the aorta and you would soon be dead. If the weapon had been a knife, the parted tissue would have yielded, and the blood would have been forced out on either side of the blade and would have caused death. As it is, not a drop of blood has escaped from the aorta into the thoracic cavity. All that is left for us to do, then, is to allow the stiletto to remain permanently in the aorta. Many difficulties at once present themselves, and I do not wonder at Dr Rowell's look of surprise and incredulity.'

That gentleman smiled and shook his head.

'It is a desperate chance,' continued Entrefort, 'and is a novel case in surgery; but it is the only chance. The fact that the weapon is a stiletto is the important point – a stupid weapon, but a blessing to us now. If the assassin had known more she would have used –'

Upon his employment of the noun 'assassin' and the feminine pronoun 'she', both Arnold and I started violently, and I cried out to the man to stop.

'Let him proceed,' said Arnold, who, by a remarkable effort, had calmed himself.

'Not if the subject is painful,' Entrefort said.

'It is not,' protested Arnold; 'why do you think the blow was struck by a woman?'

'Because, first, no man capable of being an assassin would use so gaudy and valuable a weapon; second, no man would be so stupid as to carry so antiquated and inadequate a thing as a stiletto, when that most murderous and satisfactory of all penetrating and cutting weapons, the bowie-knife, is available. She was a strong woman, too, for it requires a good hand to drive a stiletto to the guard, even though it miss the sternum by a hair's breadth and slip between the ribs, for the muscles here are hard and the intercostal spaces narrow. She was not only a strong woman, but a desperate one also.'

'That will do,' said Arnold. He beckoned me to bend closer. 'You must watch this man; he is too sharp; he is dangerous.'

'Then,' resumed Entrefort, 'I shall tell you what I intend to do. There will undoubtedly be inflammation of the aorta, which, if it persist, will cause a fatal aneurism by a breaking down of the aortal walls; but we hope, with the help of your youth and health, to check it.

'Another serious difficulty is this: With every inhalation, the entire thorax (or bony structure of the chest) considerably expands. The aorta remains stationary. You will see, therefore, that as your aorta and your breast are now held in rigid relation to each other by the stiletto, the chest, with every inhalation, pulls the aorta foward out of place about half an inch. I am certain that it is doing this, because there is no indication of an escape of arterial blood into the thoracic cavity; in other words, the mouths of the two aortal wounds have seized upon the blade with a firm hold and thus prevent it from slipping in and out. This is a very fortunate occurrence, but one which will cause pain for some time. The aorta, you may understand, being made by the stiletto to move with the breathing, pulls the heart backward and forward with every breath you take; but that organ, though now undoubtedly much surprised, will accustom itself in its new condition.

'What I fear most, however, is the formation of a clot around the blade. You see, the presence of the blade in the aorta has already reduced the blood-carrying capacity of that vessel; a clot, therefore, need not be very large to stop up the aorta, and, of course, if that should occur, death would ensue. But the clot, if one form, may be dislodged and driven forward, in which event it may lodge in any one of the numerous branches from the aorta, and produce results more or less serious, possibly fatal. If, for instance, it should choke either the right or the left carotid, there would ensue atrophy of one side of the brain, and consequently paralysis of half the entire body; but it is possible that in time there would come about a secondary circulation from the other side of the brain, and thus restore a healthy condition. Or the clot (which, in passing always from larger arteries to smaller, must unavoidably find one not sufficiently large to carry it, and must lodge somewhere) may either necessitate amputation of one of the four limbs, or lodge itself so deep within the body that it cannot be reached with the knife. You are beginning to realise some of the dangers which await you.'

Arnold smiled faintly.

'But we shall do our best to prevent the formation of a clot,' continued Entrefort; 'there are drugs which may be used with effect.'

'Are there more dangers?'

'Many more; some of the more serious have not been mentioned. One of these is the probability of the aortal tissues pressing upon the weapon relaxing their hold and allowing the blade to slip. That would let out the blood and cause death. I am uncertain whether the hold is now maintained by the pressure of the tissues or the adhesive quality of the serum which was set free by the puncture. I am convinced, though, that in either event the hold is easily broken, and that it may give way at any moment, for it is under several kinds of strains. Every time the heart contracts and crowds the blood into the aorta, the latter expands a little, and then contracts when the pressure is removed. Any unusual exercise or excitement produces stronger and quicker heart-beats, and increases the strain on the adhesion of the aorta to the weapon. A fright, fall, a jump, a blow on the chest – any of these might so jar the heart and aorta as to break the hold.'

Entrefort stopped.

'Is that all?' asked Arnold.

'No; but is not that enough?'

'More than enough,' said Arnold, with a sudden and dangerous sparkle in his eyes. Before any of us could think, the desperate fellow had seized the handle of the stiletto with both hands in a determined effort to withdraw it and die. I had had no time to order my faculties to the movement of a muscle, when Entrefort, with incredible alertness and swiftness, had Arnold's wrists. Slowly Arnold relaxed his hold.

'There, now!' said Entrefort, soothingly; 'that was a careless act and might have broken the adhesion! You'll have to be careful.'

Arnold looked at him with a curious combination of expressions.

'Dr Entrefort,' he quietly remarked, 'you are the devil.'

Bowing profoundly, Entrefort replied: 'You do me too great honour;' then he whispered to his patient: 'If you do *that*' – with a motion towards the hilt – 'I will have *her* hanged for murder.'

Arnold started and choked, and a look of horror overspread his face. He withdrew his hands, took one of mine in both of his, threw his arms upon the pillow about his head, and, holding my hand, firmly said to Entrefort, –

'Proceed with your work.'

'Come closer, Hippolyte,' said Entrefort, and observe narrowly. 'Will you kindly assist me, Dr Rowell?' That gentleman had sat in wondering silence.

Entrefort's hand was quick and sure, and he used the knife with marvellous dexterity. First he made four equidistant incisions outward from the guard and just through the skin. Arnold held his breath and ground his teeth at the first cut, but soon regained command of himself. Each incision was about two inches long. Hippolyte shuddered and turned his head aside. Entrefort, whom nothing escaped, exclaimed, –

'Steady, Hippolyte! Observe!'

Quickly was the skin peeled back to the limit of the incisions. This must have been excruciatingly painful. Arnold groaned, and his hands were moist and cold. Down sank the knife into the flesh from which the skin had been raised, and blood flowed freely; Dr Rowell handled the sponge. The keen knife worked rapidly. Arnold's marvellous nerve was breaking down. He clutched my hand fiercely; his eyes danced; his mind was weakening. Almost in a moment the flesh had been cut away to the bones, which were now exposed – two ribs and the sternum. A few quick cuts cleared the weapon between the guard and the ribs.

'To work, Hippolyte – be quick!'

The machinist had evidently been coached before he came. With slender, long-fingered hands, which trembled at first, he selected certain tools with nice precision, made some rapid measurements of the weapon and of the cleared space around it, and began to adjust the parts of a queer little machine. Arnold watched him curiously.

'What – ' he began to say; but he ceased; a deeper pallor set on his face, his hands relaxed, and his eyelids fell.

'Thank God!' exclaimed Entrefort; 'he has fainted – he can't stop us now. Quick, Hippolyte!'

The machinist attached the queer little machine to the handle of the weapon, seized the stiletto in his left hand, and with his right began a series of sharp, rapid movements backward and forward.

'Hurry, Hippolyte!' urged Entrefort.

'The metal is very hard.'

'Is it cutting?'

'I can't see for the blood.'

In another moment something snapped. Hippolyte started; he was very nervous. He removed the little machine.

'The metal is very hard,' he said; 'it breaks the saws.'

He adjusted another tiny saw and resumed work. After a little while he picked up the handle of the stiletto and laid it on the table. He had cut it off, leaving the blade inside Arnold's body.

'Good, Hippolyte!' exclaimed Entrefort. In a minute he had closed the bright end of the blade from view by drawing together the skin-flaps and sewing them firmly.

Arnold returned to consciousness and glanced down at his breast. He seemed puzzled. 'Where is the weapon?' he asked.

'Here is part of it,' answered Entrefort, holding up the handle.

'And the blade –

'That is an irremovable part of your internal machinery.' Arnold was silent. 'It had to be cut off,' pursued Entrefort, 'not only because it would be troublesome and an undesirable ornament, but also because it was advisable to remove every possibility of its withdrawal.' Arnold said nothing. 'Here is a prescription,' said Entrefort; 'take the medicine as directed for the next five years without fail.'

'What for? I see that it contains muriatic acid.'

'If necessary I will explain five years from now.'

'If I live.'

'If you live.'

Arnold drew me down to him and whispered, 'Tell her to fly at once; this man may make trouble for her.'

Was there ever a more generous fellow?

I thought that I recognised a thin, pale, bright face among the passengers who were leaving an Australian steamer which had just arrived at San Francisco.

'Dr Entrefort!' I cried.

'Ah!' he said, peering up into my face and grasping my hand; 'I know you now, but you have changed. You remember that I was called away immediately after I had performed that crazy operation on your friend. I have spent the intervening four years in India, China, Tibet, Siberia, the South Seas, and God knows where not. But wasn't that a most absurd, hare-brained experiment that I tried on your friend! Still, it was all that could have been done. I have dropped all that nonsense long ago. It is better, for more reasons than one, to let them die at once. Poor fellow! he bore it so bravely! Did he suffer much afterwards? How long did he live? A week – perhaps a month?'

'He is alive yet.'

'What!' exclaimed Entrefort, startled.

'He is, indeed, and is in this city.'

'Incredible!'

'It is true; you shall see him.'

'But tell me about him now!' cried the surgeon, his eager eyes glittering with the peculiar light which I had seen in them on the night of the operation. 'Has he regularly taken the medicine which I prescribed.'

'He has. Well, the change in him, from what he was before the operation, is shocking. Imagine a young daredevil of twenty-two, who had no greater fear of danger or death than of a cold, now a cringing, cowering fellow; apparently an old man, nursing his life with pitiful tenderness, fearful that at any moment something may happen to break the hold of his aorta-walls on the stiletto-blade; a confirmed hypochondriac, peevish, melancholic, unhappy in the extreme. He keeps himself confined as closely as possible, avoiding all excitement and exercise, and even reads nothing exciting. The constant danger has worn out the last shred of his manhood and left him a pitiful wreck. Can nothing be done for him?'

'Possibly. But has he consulted no physician?'

'None whatever; he has been afraid that he might learn the worst.'

'Let us find him at once. Ah, here comes my wife to meet me! She arrived by the other steamer.'

I recognised her immediately and was overcome with astonishment.

'Charming woman,' said Entrefort; 'you'll like her. We were married three years ago at Bombay. She belongs to a noble Italian family and has travelled a great deal.'

He introduced us. To my unspeakable relief she remembered neither my name nor my face. I must have appeared odd to her, but it was impossible for me to be perfectly unconcerned. We went to Arnold's rooms, I with much dread. I left her in the reception-room and took Entrefort within. Arnold was too greatly absorbed in his own troubles to be dangerously excited by meeting Entrefort, whom he greeted with indifferent hospitality.

'But I heard a woman's voice,' he said. 'It sounds – ' He checked himself, and before I could intercept him he had gone to the reception-room; and there he stood face to face with the beautiful adventuress – none other than Entrefort's wife now – who, wickedly desperate, had driven a stiletto into Arnold's vitals in a hotel four years before because he had refused to marry her. They recognised each other instantly and both grew pale; but she, quicker witted, recovered her composure at once, and advanced towards him with a smile and an extended hand. He stepped back, his face ghastly with fear.

'Oh!' he gasped, 'the excitement, the shock, – it has made the blade slip out! The blood is pouring from the opening, – it burns, – I am dying!' and he fell into my arms and instantly expired.

The autopsy revealed the surprising fact that there was no blade in his thorax at all; it had been gradually consumed by the muriatic acid which Entrefort had prescribed for that very purpose, and the perforations in the aorta had closed up gradually with the wasting of the blade, and had been perfectly healed for a long time. All his vital organs were sound. My poor friend, once so reckless and brave, had died simply of a childish and groundless fear, and the woman unwittingly had accomplished her revenge.

THE HOUSEBOAT

by

Richard Marsh

It seems likely that Richard Marsh will always be remembered for his macabre novel The Beetle (1897), *which is as good a work as any to be associated with, but it really is time that some more of his stories and books were returned to print. I regard Marsh as one of the best writers of tales of terror to be found in the Victorian era but very few of his stories have been resurrected.*

Marsh was born in 1857 and started writing at an early age, selling stories to boys magazines when he was twelve. He went on to write for a living, producing over seventy successful works, ranging from humorous stories through detective fiction to downright horror.

He was a prolific writer of short stories, and continued writing until his death in 1915. If any ghost story enthusiasts are in search of good rare material, then I urge them to sample some of Marsh's collections. The best tales are to be found in his four books Marvels and Mysteries (1900), The Seen and the Unseen (1900), Both Sides of the Veil (1901) *and* Between the Dark and the Daylight (1902).

In addition to his short stories, Marsh wrote several novels with supernatural or macabre overtones, among them The Death Whistle (1903), A Metamorphosis (1903) *and* Tom Ossington's Ghost (1898). *His notable contribution to detective fiction were the adventures of Miss Judith Lee, one of the first fictional women detectives.*

'The Houseboat' is a fine ghost story, which comes from The Seen and the Unseen. *Perhaps it will encourage others to take an interest in Richard Marsh, one of our most unjustly neglected masters of terror.*

Chapter I

'I am sure of it!'

Inglis laid down his knife and fork. He stared round and round the small apartment in a manner which was distinctly strange. My wife caught him up. She laid down her knife and fork.

'You're sure of what?'

Inglis seemed disturbed. He appeared unwilling to give a direct answer. 'Perhaps, after all, it's only a coincidence.'

But Violet insisted. 'What is a coincidence?'

Inglis addressed himself to me.

'The fact is, Millen, directly I came on board I thought I had seen this boat before.'

'But I thought you said that you had never heard of the *Water Lily*.'

'Nor have I. The truth is that when I knew it, it wasn't the *Water Lily*.'

'I don't understand.'

'They must have changed the name. Unless I am very much mistaken this – this used to be the *Sylph*.'

'The *Sylph*?'

'You don't mean to say that you have never heard of the *Sylph*?'

Inglis asked this question in a tone of voice which was peculiar.

'My dear fellow, I'm not a riparian authority. I am not acquainted with every houseboat between Richmond and Oxford. It was only at your special recommendation that I took the *Water Lily*.'

'Excuse me, Millen, I advised a houseboat. I didn't specify the *Water Lily*.'

'But,' asked my wife, 'what was the matter with the *Sylph* that she should so mysteriously have become the *Water Lily*?'

Inglis fenced with this question in a manner which seemed to suggest a state of mental confusion.

'Of course, Millen, I know that that sort of thing would not have the slightest influence on you. It is only people of a very different sort who would allow it to have any effect on them. Then, after all, I may be wrong. And, in any case, I don't see that it matters.'

'Mr Inglis, are you suggesting that the *Sylph* was haunted?'

'Haunted!' Inglis started. 'I never dropped a hint about its being haunted. So far as I remember I never heard a word of anything of the kind.' Violet placed her knife and fork together on her plate. She folded her hands upon her lap.

'Mr Inglis, there is a mystery. Will you this mystery unfold?'
'Didn't you really ever hear about the *Sylph* – two years ago?'
'Two years ago we were out of England.'
'So you were. Perhaps that explains it. You understand, this mayn't be the *Sylph*. I may be wrong – though I don't think I am.'
Inglis glanced uncomfortably at the chair on which he was sitting.
'Why, I believe this is the very chair on which I sat! I remember noticing what a queer shape it was.'
It was rather an odd-shaped chair. For that matter, all the things on board were odd.
'Then have you been on board this boat before?'
'Yes.' Inglis positively shuddered. 'I was, once; if it is the *Sylph*, that is.' He thrust his hands into his trouser pockets. He leaned back in his chair. A curious look came into his face. 'It is the *Sylph*, I'll swear to it. It all comes back to me. What an extraordinary coincidence! One might almost think there was something supernatural in the thing.'
His manner fairly roused me.
'I wish you would stop speaking in riddles, and tell us what you are driving at.'
He became preternaturally solemn.
'Millen, I'm afraid I have made rather an ass of myself; I ought to have held my tongue. But the coincidence is such a strange one that it took me unawares, and since I have said so much I suppose I may as well say more. After dinner I will tell you all there is to tell. I don't think it's a story which Mrs Millen would like to listen to.'
Violet's face was a study.
'I don't understand you, Mr Inglis, because you are quite well aware it is a principle of mine that what is good for a husband to hear is good for a wife. Come, don't be silly. Let us hear what the fuss is about. I daresay it's about nothing after all.'
'You think so? Well, Mrs Millen, you shall hear.' He carefully wiped his moustache. He began: 'Two years ago there was a houseboat on the river called the *Sylph*. It belonged to a man named Hambro. He lent it to a lady and a gentleman. She was rather a pretty woman, with a lot of fluffy, golden hair. He was a quiet unassuming-looking man, who looked as though he had something to do with horses. I made their acquaintance on the river. One evening he asked me on board to dine. I sat, as I believe, on

this very chair, at this very table. Three days afterwards they disappeared.'

'Well?' I asked. Inglis had paused.

'So far as I know, he has never been seen or heard of since.'

'And the lady?'

'Some of us were getting up a picnic. We wanted them to come with us. We couldn't quite make out their sudden disappearance. So, two days after we had missed them, I and another man tried to rout them out, I looked through the window. I saw something lying on the floor. "Jarvis," I whispered, "I believe that Mrs Bush is lying on the floor dead drunk." "She can't have been drunk two days," he said. He came to my side. "Why, she's in her nightdress. This is very queer. Inglis, I wonder if the door is locked." It wasn't. We opened it and went inside.'

Inglis emptied his glass of wine.

'The woman we had known as Mrs Bush lay in her nightdress, dead upon the floor. She had been stabbed to the heart. She was lying just about where Mrs Millen is sitting now.'

'Mr Inglis!' Violet rose suddenly.

'There is reason to believe that, from one point of view, the woman was no better than she ought to have been. That is the story.'

'But' – I confess it was not at all the story I had expected it was going to be; I did not altogether like it – 'who killed her?'

'That is the question. There was no direct evidence to show. No weapon was discovered. The man we had known as Bush had vanished, as it seemed, off the face of the earth. He had not left so much as a pocket-handkerchief behind him. Everything both of his and hers had gone. It turned out that nobody knew anything at all about him. They had no servant. What meals they had on board were sent in from the hotel. Hambro had advertised the *Sylph*. Bush had replied to the advertisement. He had paid the rent in advance, and Hambro had asked no questions.'

'And what became of the *Sylph*?'

'She also vanished. She had become a little too notorious. One doesn't fancy living on board a houseboat on which a murder has been committed; one is at too close quarters. I suppose Hambro sold her for what he could get, and the purchaser painted her, and rechristened her the *Water Lily*.'

'But are you sure this is the *Sylph*?'

'As sure as that I am sitting here. It is impossible that I could be mistaken. I still seem to see that woman lying dead just about where Mrs Millen is standing now.'

'Mr Inglis!'

Violet was standing up. She moved away – towards me. Inglis left soon afterwards. He did not seem to care to stop. He had scarcely eaten any dinner. In fact, that was the case with all of us. Mason had exerted herself to prepare a decent meal in her cramped little kitchen, and we had been so ungrateful as not even to reach the end of her bill of fare. When Inglis had gone she appeared in her bonnet and cloak. We supposed that, very naturally, she had taken umbrage.

'If you please, ma'am, I'm going.'

'Mason! What do you mean?'

'I couldn't think of stopping in no place in which murder was committed, least of all a houseboat. Not to mention that last night I heard ghosts, if ever anyone heard them yet.'

'Mason! Don't be absurd. I thought you had more sense.'

'All I can say is, ma'am, that last night as I lay awake, listening to the splashing of the water, all at once I heard in here the sound of quarrelling. I couldn't make it out. I thought that you and the master was having words. Yet it didn't sound like your voice. Besides, you went on awful. Still, I didn't like to say nothing, because it might have been, and it wasn't my place to say that I had heard. But now I know that it was ghosts.'

She went. She was not to be persuaded to stay any more than Inglis. She did not even stay to clear the table. I have seldom seen a woman in a greater hurry. As for wages, there was not a hint of them. Staid, elderly, self-possessed female though she was, she seemed to be a perfect panic of fear. Nothing would satisfy her but that she should, with the greatest possible expedition, shake from her feet the dust of the *Water Lily*. When we were quit of her I looked at Violet and Violet looked at me. I laughed. I will not go so far as to say that I laughed genially; still, I laughed.

'We seem to be in for a pleasant river holiday.'

'Eric, let us get outside.'

We went on deck. The sun had already set. There was no moon, but there was a cloudless sky. The air was languorous and heavy. Boats were stealing over the waters. Someone in the distance was playing a banjo accompaniment while a clear girlish voice was singing 'The Garden of Sleep'. The other houseboats were radiant with Chinese lanterns. The *Water Lily* alone was still in shadow. We drew our deck-chairs close together. Violet's hand stole into mine.

'Eric, do you know that last night I, too, heard voices?'

'You!' I laughed again. 'Violet!'

'I couldn't make it out at all. I was just going to wake you when they were still.'

'You were dreaming, child. Inglis's story – confound him and his story! – has recalled your dream to mind. I hope you don't wish to follow Mason's example, and make a bolt of it. I have paid pretty stiffly for the honour of being the *Water Lily* tenant for a month, not to mention the fact of disarranging all our plans.'

Violet paused before she answered.

'No; I don't think I want, as you say, to make a bolt of it. Indeed,' she nestled closer to my side, 'it is rather the other way. I should like to see it through. I have sometimes thought that I should like to be with someone I can trust in a situation such as this. Perhaps we may be able to fathom the mystery – who knows?'

This tickled me. 'I thought you had done with romance.'

'With one sort of romance I hope I shall never have done.' She pressed my hand. She looked up archly into my face. I knew it, although we were in shadow. 'With another sort of romance I may be only just beginning. I have never yet had dealings with a ghost.'

Chapter II

At first I could not make out what it was that had roused me. Then I felt Violet's hand steal into mine. Her voice whispered in my ear, 'Eric!' I turned over towards her on the pillow. 'Be still. They're here.' I did as she bade me. I was still. I heard no sound but the lazy rippling of the river.

'Who's here?' I asked, when, as I deemed, I had been silent long enough.

'S–sh!' I felt her finger pressed against my lips. I was still again. The silence was broken in rather a peculiar manner.

'I don't think you quite understand me.'

The words were spoken in a man's voice, as it seemed to me, close behind my back. I was so startled by the unexpected presence of a third person that I made as if to spring up in bed. My wife caught me by the arm. Before I could remonstrate or shake off

her grasp a woman's laughter rang through the little cabin. It was too metallic to be agreeable. And a woman's voice replied –
'I understand you well enough, don't you make any error!'
There was a momentary pause.
'You don't understand me, fool!'
The first four words were spoken with a deliberation which meant volumes, while the final epithet came with a sudden malignant ferocity which took me aback. The speaker, whoever he might be, meant mischief. I sprang up and out of bed.
'What are you doing here?' I cried.
I addressed the inquiry apparently to the vacant air. The moonlight flooded the little cabin. It showed clearly enough that it was empty. My wife sat up in bed.
'Now,' she observed, 'you've done it.'
'Done what? Who was that speaking?'
'The voices.'
'The voices! What voices? I'll voice them! Where the dickens have they gone?'
I moved towards the cabin door, with the intention of pursuing my inquiries further. Violet's voice arrested me.
'It is no use your going to look for them. They will not be found by searching. The speakers were Mr and Mrs Bush.'
'Mr and Mrs Bush?'
Violet's voice dropped to an awful whisper. 'The murderer and his victim.'
I stared at her in the moonlight. Inglis's pleasant little story had momentarily escaped my memory. Suddenly roused from a dreamless slumber, I had not yet had time to recall such trivialities. Now it all came back in a flash.
'Violet,' I exclaimed, 'have you gone mad?'
'They are the voices which I heard last night. They are the voices which Mason heard. Now you have heard them. If you had kept still the mystery might have been unravelled. The crime might have been re-enacted before our eyes, or at least within sound of our ears.'
I sat down upon the ingenious piece of furniture which did duty as a bed. I seemed to have struck upon a novel phase in my wife's character. It was not altogether a pleasing novelty. She spoke with a degree of judicial calmness which, under all the circumstances, I did not altogether relish.

'Violet, I wish you wouldn't talk like that. It makes my blood run cold.'

'Why should it? My dear Eric, I have heard you yourself say that in the presence of the seemingly mysterious our attitude should be one of passionless criticism. A mysterious crime has been committed in this very chamber.' I shivered. 'Surely it is our duty to avail ourselves of any opportunities which may offer, and which may enable us to probe it to the bottom.'

I made no answer. I examined the doors. They were locked and bolted. There was no sign that anyone had tampered with the fastenings. I returned to bed. As I was arranging myself between the sheets Violet whispered in my ear. 'Perhaps if we are perfectly quiet they may come back again.'

I am not a man given to adjectives; but I felt adjectival then. I was about to explain, in language which would not have been wanting in force, that I had no desire that they should come back again, when –

'You had better give it to me.'

The words were spoken in a woman's voice, as it seemed, within twelve inches of my back. The voice was not that of a lady. I should have said without hesitation, had I heard the voice under any other circumstances, that the speaker had been born within the sound of Bow Bells.

'Had I?'

It was a man's voice which put the question. There was something about the tone in which the speaker put it which reminded one of the line in the people's ballad, 'It ain't exactly what 'e sez, it's the nasty way 'e sez it.' The question was put in a very 'nasty way' indeed.

'Yes, my boy, you had.'

'Indeed?'

'Yes, you may say "indeed", but if you don't I tell you what I'll do – I'll spoil you.'

'And what, my dear Gertie, am I to understand by the mystic threat of spoiling me?'

'I'll go straight to your wife, and I'll tell her everything.'

'Oh, you will, will you?'

There was a movement of a chair. The male speaker was getting up.

'Yes, I will.'

There was a slight pause. One could fancy that the speakers were facing each other. One could picture the look of impudent defiance upon the woman's countenance, the suggestion of coming storm upon that of the man. It was the man's voice which broke the silence.

'It is odd, Gertrude, that you should have chosen this evening to threaten me, because I myself had chosen this evening, I won't say to threaten, but to make a communication to you.'

'Give me a match.' The request came from the woman.

'With pleasure. I will give you anything, my dear Gertrude, within reason.' There was another pause. In the silence I seemed to hear my wife holding her breath – as I certainly was holding mine. All at once there came a sound of scratching, a flash of light. It came so unexpectedly, and such was the extreme tension of my nerves, that, with a stifled exclamation, I half rose in bed. My wife pressed her hand against my lips. She held me down. She spoke in so attenuated a whisper that it was only because all my senses were so keenly on the alert that I heard her.

'You goose! He's only striking a match.'

He might have been, but who? She took things for granted. I wanted to know. The light continued flickering to and fro, as a match does flicker. I would have given much to know who held it, or even what was its position in the room. As luck had it, my face was turned the other way. My wife seemed to understand what was passing in my mind.

'There's no one there,' she whispered.

No one, I presumed, but the match. I took it for granted that was there. Though I did not venture to inquire, I felt that I might not have such perfect control over my voice as my wife appeared to have.

While the light continued to flicker there came stealing into my nostrils – I sniffed, the thing was unmistakable! – the odour of tobacco. The woman was lighting a cigarette. I knew it was the woman because presently there came this request from the man, 'After you with the light, my dear.'

I presume that the match was passed. Immediately the smell of tobacco redoubled. The man had lit a cigarette as well. I confess that I resented – silently, but still strongly – the idea of two strangers, whether ghosts or anybody else, smoking, uninvited, in my cabin.

The match went out. The cigarettes were lit. The man continued speaking.

'The communication, my dear Gertrude, which I intended to make to you was this. The time has come for us to part.'

He paused, possibly for an answer. None came.

'I need not enlarge on the reasons which necessitate our parting. They exist.'

Pause again. Then the woman.

'What are you going to give me?'

'One of the reasons which necessitate our parting – a very strong reason, as you, I am sure, will be the first to admit – is that I have nothing left to give you.'

'So you say.'

'Precisely. So I say and so I mean.'

'Do you mean that you are going to give me nothing?'

'I mean, my dear Gertrude, that I have nothing to give you. You have left me nothing.'

'Bah!'

The sound which issued from the lady's lips was expressive of the most complete contempt.

'Look here, my boy, you give me a hundred sovereigns or I'll spoil you.'

Pause again. Probably the gentleman was thinking over the lady's observation.

'What benefit do you think you will do yourself by what you call "spoiling" me?'

'Never mind about that: I'll do it. You think I don't know all about you, but I do. Perhaps I'm not so soft as you think. Your wife's got some money if you haven't. Suppose you go back and ask her for some. You've treated me badly enough. I don't see why you shouldn't go and treat her the same. She wouldn't make things warm for you if she knew a few things I could tell her – not at all! You give me a hundred sovereigns or, I tell you straight, I'll go right to your house and I'll tell her all.'

'Oh, no, you won't.'

'Won't I? I say I will!'

'Oh, no, you won't.'

'I say I will! I've warned you, that's all. I'm not going to stop here, talking stuff to you. I'm going to bed. You can go and hang yourself for all I care.'

There was a sound, an indubitable sound – the sound of a pair of shoes being thrown upon the floor. There were other sounds, equally capable of explanation: sounds which suggested – I wish the printer would put it in small type – that the lady was undressing. Undressing, too, with scant regard to ceremony. Garments were thrown off and tossed higgledy-piggledy here and there. They appeared to be thrown, with sublime indifference, upon table, chairs, and floor. I even felt something alight upon the bed. Some feminine garment, perhaps, which, although it fell by no means heavily, made me conscious, as it fell, of the most curious sensation I had in all my life – till then – experienced. It seemed that the lady, while she unrobed, continued smoking. From her next words it appeared that the gentleman, also smoking, stood and stared at her.

'Don't stand staring at me like a gawk. I'm going to turn in.'

'And I'm going to turn out. Not, as you suggested, to hang myself, but to finish this cigarette upon the roof. Perhaps, when I return, you will be in a more equable frame of mind.'

'Don't you flatter yourself. What I say I mean. A hundred sovereigns, or I tell your wife.'

He laughed very softly, as though he was determined not to be annoyed. Then we heard his footsteps as he crossed the floor. The door opened, then closed. We heard him ascend the steps. Then, with curious distinctness, his measured tramp, tramp, as he moved to and fro upon the roof. In the cabin for a moment there was silence. Then the woman said, with a curious faltering in her voice –

'I'll do it. I don't care what he says.' There was a choking in her throat. 'He don't care for me a bit.'

Suddenly she flung herself upon her knees beside the bed. She pillowed her head and arms upon the coverlet. I lay near the outer edge of the bed, which was a small one, by the way. As I lay I felt the pressure of her limbs. My sensations, as I did, I am unable to describe. After a momentary interval there came the sound of sobbing. I could feel the woman quivering with the strength of her emotion. Violet and I were speechless. I do not think that, for the instant, we could have spoken even had we tried. The woman's presence was so evident, her grief so real. As she wept disjointed words came from her.

'I've given everything for him! If he only cared for me! If he only did.'

All at once, with a rapid movement, she sprang up. The removal of the pressure was altogether unmistakable. I was conscious of her resting her hands upon the coverlet to assist her to her feet. I felt the little jerk; then the withdrawal of the hands. She choked back her sobs when she had gained her feet. Her tone was changed.

'What a fool I am to make a fuss. He don't care for me – not that.' We heard her snap her fingers in the air. 'He never did. Us women are always fools – we're all the same. I'll go to bed.'

Violet clutched my arm. She whispered, in that attenuated fashion she seemed to have caught the trick of –

'She's getting into bed. We must get out.'

It certainly was a fact, someone was getting into bed. The bedclothes were moved; not our bedclothes, but some phantom coverings. We heard them rustle, we were conscious of a current of air across our faces as someone caught them open. And then! – then someone stepped upon the bed.

'Let's get out!' gasped Violet.

Chapter III

She moved away from me. She squeezed herself against the side of the cabin. She withdrew her limbs from between the sheets. As for me, the person who had stepped upon the bed had actually stepped upon me, and that without seeming at all conscious of my presence. Someone sat down plump upon the sheet beside me. That was enough. I took advantage of my lying on the edge of the bed to slip out upon the floor. I might possess an unsuspected capacity for undergoing strange experiences, but I drew the line at sleeping with a ghost.

The moonlight streamed across the room. As I stood, in something very like a state of nature on the floor, I could clearly see Violet cowering on the further side of the bed. I could distinguish all her features. But when I looked upon the bed itself – there was nothing there. The moon's rays fell upon the pillow. They revealed its snowy whiteness. There seemed nothing else it could reveal. It was untenanted. And yet, if one looked closely at it, it seemed to be indented, just as it might have been indented had a human head been lying there. But about one thing there could be no mistake whatever – my ears did not play me false, I heard it too distinctly –

the sound made by a person who settles himself between the sheets, and then the measured respiration of one who composes himself to slumber.

I remained there silent. On her hands and knees Violet crept towards the foot of the bed. When she had gained the floor she stole on tiptoe to my side. 'I did not dare to step across her.' I felt her, as she nestled to me, give me a little shiver. 'I could not do it. Can you see her?'

'What a fool I am!' As Violet asked her question there came this observation from the person in the bed – whom, by the way, I could not see. There was a long-drawn sigh. 'What fools all we women are! What fools!'

There was a sincerity of bitterness about the tone, which, coming as it did from an unseen speaker – one so near and yet so far – had on one a most uncomfortable effect. Violet pressed closer to my side. The woman in the bed turned over. Overhead there still continued the measured tramp, tramping of the man. We were conscious, in some subtle way, that the woman lay listening to the footsteps. They spoke more audibly to her ears even than to ours.

'Ollie! Ollie!' she repeated the name softly to herself, with a degree of tenderness which was in startling contrast to her previous bitterness.

'I wish you would come to bed.'

She was silent. There was only the sound of her gentle breathing. Her bitter mood had been but transient. She was falling asleep with words of tenderness upon her lips. Above, the footsteps ceased. All was still. There was not even the murmur of the waters. The wife and I, side by side, stood looking down upon what seemed an empty bed.

'She is asleep,' said Violet.

It seemed to me she was: although I could not see her, it seemed to me she was. I could hear her breathing as softly as a child. Violet continued whispering –

'How strange! Eric, what can it mean?'

I muttered a reply –

'A problem for the Psychical Research Society.'

'It seems just like a dream.'

'I wish it were a dream.'

'S-sh! There is someone coming down the stairs.'

There was – at least, if we could trust our ears, there was.

Apparently the man above had had enough of solitude. We heard him move across the roof, then pause just by the steps, then descend them one by one. It seemed to us that in his step there was something stealthy, that he was endeavouring not to arouse attention, to make as little noise as possible. Half-way down he paused; at the foot he paused again.

'He's listening outside the door.' It almost seemed that he was. We stood and listened too. 'Let's get away from the bed.'

My wife drew me with her. At the opposite end of the cabin was a sort of little alcove, which was screened by a curtain, and behind which were hung one or two of our garments which we were not actually using. Violet drew me within the shadow of this alcove. I say drew me because, offering no resistance, I allowed myself to be completely passive in her hands. The alcove was not large enough to hold us. Still the curtain acted as a partial screen.

The silence endured for some moments. Then we heard without a hand softly turning the handle of the door. While I was wondering whether, after all, I was not the victim of an attack of indigestion, or whether I was about to witness an attempt at effecting a burglarious entry into a houseboat, a strange thing happened, the strangest thing that had happened yet.

As I have already mentioned, the moon's rays flooded the cabin. This was owing to the fact that a long narrow casement, which ran round the walls near the roof of the cabin, had been left open for the sake of admitting air and ventilation; but, save for the moonbeams, the cabin was unlighted. When, however, we heard the handle being softly turned, a singular change occurred. It was like the transformation scene in a theatre. The whole place, all at once, was brilliantly illuminated. The moonbeams disappeared. Instead, a large swinging lamp was hanging from the centre of the cabin. So strong was the light which it shed around that our eyes were dazzled. It was not our lamp; we used small hand-lamps, which stood upon the table. By its glare we saw that the whole cabin was changed. For an instant we failed to clearly realise in what the change consisted. Then we understood it was a question of decoration. The contents of the cabin, for the most part, were the same, though they looked newer, and the positions of the various articles were altered; but the panels of the cabin of the *Water Lily* were painted blue and white. The panels of this cabin were coloured chocolate and gold.

'Eric, it's the *Sylph!*'

The suggestion conveyed by my wife's whispered words, even as she spoke, occurred to me. I understood where, for Inglis, had lain the difficulty of recognition. The two cabins were the same, and yet were not. It was just as though someone had endeavoured, without spending much cash, to render one as much as possible unlike the other. In this cabin there were many things which were not ours. In fact, so far as I can see, there was nothing which was ours.

Strange articles of costume were scattered about; the table was covered with a curious litter; and on the ingenious article of furniture which did duty as a bed, and which stood where our bed stood, and which, indeed, seemed to be our bed, there was someone sleeping.

As my startled eyes travelled round this amazing transformation scene, at last they reached the door. There they stayed. Mechanically I shrank back nearer to the wall. I felt my wife tighten her grasp upon my hand.

The door was opened some few inches. Through the aperture thus formed there peered a man. He seemed to be listening. It was so still that one could hear the gentle breathing of the woman sleeping in the bed. Apparently satisfied, he opened the door sufficiently wide to admit of his entering the cabin. My impression was that he could not fail to perceive us, yet to all appearances he remained entirely unconscious of our neighbourhood. He was a man certainly under five feet six in height. He was slight in build, very dark, with face clean shaven; his face was long and narrow. In dress and bearing he seemed a gentleman, yet there was that about him which immediately reminded me of what Inglis had said of the man Bush – 'he looked as though he had something to do with horses.'

He stood for some seconds in an attitude of listening, so close to me that I had only to stretch out my hand to take him by the throat. I did not do it. I don't know what restrained me; I think, more than anything, it was the feeling that these things which were passing before me must be passing in a dream. His face was turned away. He looked intently towards the sleeping woman.

After he had had enough of listening he moved towards the bed. His step was soft and cat-like; it was absolutely noiseless. Glancing down, I perceived that he was without boots or shoes.

He was in his stockinged feet. I had distinctly heard the tramp, tramping of a pair of shoes upon the cabin roof. I had heard them descend the steps. Possibly he had paused outside the door to take them off.

When he reached the bed he stood looking down upon the sleeper. He stooped over her, as if the better to catch her breathing. He whispered softly –

'Gerty!'

He paused for a moment, as if for an answer. None came. Standing up, he put his hand, as it seemed to me, into the bosom of his flannel shirt. He took out a leather sheath. From the sheath he drew a knife. It was a long, slender, glittering blade. Quite twelve inches in length, at no part was it broader than my little finger. With the empty sheath in his left hand, the knife behind his back in his right, he again leaned over the sleeper. Again he softly whispered, 'Gerty!'

Again there was no answer. Again he stood upright, turning his back towards the bed, so that he looked towards us. His face was not an ugly one, though the expression was somewhat saturnine. On it, at the instant, there was a peculiar look, such a look as I could fancy upon the face of a jockey who, towards the close of a great race, settles himself in the saddle with the determination to 'finish' well. The naked blade he placed upon the table, the empty sheath beside it. Then he moved towards us. My first thought was that now, at last, we were discovered; but something in the expression of his features told me that this was not so. He approached us with an indifference which was amazing. He passed so close to us that we were conscious of the slight disturbance of the air caused by his passage. There was a Gladstone bag on a chair within two feet of us. Picking it up, he bore it to the table. Opening it out, he commenced to pack it. All manner of things he placed within it, both masculine and feminine belongings, even the garments which the sleeper had taken off, and which lay scattered on the chair and on the floor, even her shoes and stockings! When the bag was filled he took a long brown ulster, which was thrown over the back of a chair. He stuffed the pockets with odds and ends. When he had completed his operations the cabin was stripped of everything except the actual furniture. He satisfied himself that this was so by overhauling every nook and corner, in the process passing and repassing Violet and me with a perfect unconcern which was more and more amazing. Being apparently at last clear in his mind upon that point, he put on the ulster and a dark cloth cap, and began to fasten the Gladstone bag.

While he was doing so, his back being turned to the bed, without the slightest warning, the woman in the bed sat up. The man's movements had been noiseless. He had made no sound which could have roused her. Possibly some sudden intuition had come to her in her sleep. However that might be, she all at once was wide awake. She stared round the apartment with wondering eyes. Her glance fell on the man, dressed as for a journey.

'Where are you going?'

The words fell from her lips as unawares. Then some sudden conception of his purpose seemed to have flown to her brain. She sprang out of bed with a bound.

'You shan't go,' she screamed.

She rushed to him. He put his hand on the table. He turned to her. Something flashed in the lamplight. It was the knife. As she came he plunged it into her side right to the hilt. For an instant he held her spitted on the blade. He put his hand to her throat. He thrust her from him. With the other hand he extricated the blade. He let her fall upon the floor. She had uttered a sort of sigh as the weapon was being driven home. Beyond that she had not made a sound.

All was still. He remained for some seconds looking down at her as she lay. Then he turned away. We saw his face. It was, if possible, paler than before. A smile distorted his lips. He stood for a moment as if listening. Then he glanced round the cabin, as if to make sure that he was unobserved. His black eyes travelled over our startled features, in evident unconsciousness that we were there. Then he glanced at the blade in his hand. As he did so he perceptibly shuddered. The glittering steel was obscured with blood. As he perceived that this was so he gasped. He seemed to realise for the first time what it was that he had done. Taking an envelope from an inner pocket of his ulster he began to wipe the blood from off the blade. While doing so his wandering glance fell upon the woman lying on the floor. Some new aspect of the recumbent figure seemed to strike him with a sudden horror. He staggered backwards. I thought he would have fallen. He caught at the wall to help him stand – caught at the wall with the hand which held the blade. At that part of the cabin the wall was doubly panelled half-way to the roof. Between the outer and the inner panel there was evidently a cavity, because, when in his sudden alarm he clutched at the wall, the blade slipped from his relaxing grasp and fell between the panels. Such was his state of panic that he did not appear to perceive what had happened. And at that moment a cry rang out upon the river – possibly it was someone hailing the keeper of the lock – 'Ahoy!'

The sound seemed to fill him with unreasoning terror. He rushed to the table. He closed the Gladstone with a hurried snap; he caught it up; he turned to flee. As he did so I stepped out of the alcove. I advanced right in front of him. I cannot say whether he saw me, or whether he didn't. But he seemed to see me. He started back. A look of the most awful terror came on his countenance. And at that same instant the whole scene vanished. I was standing in the cabin of the *Water Lily*. The moon was stealing through the little narrow casement. Violet was creeping to my side. She stole into my arms. I held her to me.

'Eric,' she moaned.

For myself, I am not ashamed to own that, temporarily, I had lost the use of my tongue. When, in a measure, the faculty of speech returned to me –

'Was it a dream?' I whispered.

'It was a vision.'

'A vision?' I shuddered. 'Look!'

As I spoke she turned to look. There, in the moonbeams, we saw a woman in her nightdress, lying on the cabin floor. We saw that she had golden hair. It seemed to us that she was dead. We saw her but a moment – she was gone! It must have been imagination; we know that these things are not, but it belonged to that order of imagination which is stranger than reality.

My wife looked up at me.

'Eric, it is a vision which has been sent to us in order that we may expose in the light of day a crime which was hidden in the night.'

I said nothing. I felt for a box of matches on the table. I lit a lamp. I looked round and round the cabin, holding the lamp above my head the better to assist my search. It was with a feeling of the most absurd relief that I perceived that everything was unchanged, that, so far as I could see, there was no one there but my wife and I.

'I think, Violet, if you don't mind, I'll have some whisky.'
She offered no objection. She stood and watched me as I poured
the stuff into a glass. I am bound to admit that the spirit did me good.
'And what,' I asked, 'do you make of the performance we have
just now witnessed?' She was still. I took another drink. There
can be no doubt that, under certain circumstances, whisky is a
fluid which is not to be despised. 'Have we both suddenly become
insane, or do you attribute it to the cucumber we ate at lunch?'
'How strange that Mr Inglis should have told us the story only
this afternoon.'
'I wish Mr Inglis had kept the story to himself entirely.'
'They were the voices which I heard last night. They were
the voices Mason heard. It was all predestined. I understand it
now.'
'I wish that I could say the same.'
'I see it all!'
She pressed her hands against her brow. Her eyes flashed fire.
'I see why it was sent to us, what it is we have to do. Eric, we
have to find the knife.'
I began to fear, from her frenzied manner, that her brain must
in reality be softening.
'What knife?'
'The knife which he dropped between the panels. The boat has
only been repainted. We know that in all essentials the *Sylph* and
the *Water Lily* are one and the same. Mr Inglis said that the weapon
which did the deed was never found. No adequate search was
ever made. It is waiting for us where he dropped it.'
'My dear Violet, don't you think you had better have a little
whisky? It will calm you?'
'Have you a hammer and a chisel?'
'What do you want them for?'
'It was here that he was standing; it was here that he dropped
the knife.' She had taken up her position against the wall at the
foot of the bed. Frankly, I did not like her manner at all. It was
certainly where, in the latter portion of that nightmare, the fellow
had been standing. 'I will wrench this panel away.' She rapped
against a particular panel with her knuckles. 'Behind it we shall find
the knife.'
'My dear Violet, this houseboat isn't mine. We cannot destroy
another man's property in that wanton fashion. He will hardly

accept as an adequate excuse the fact that at the time we were suffering from a severe attack of indigestion.'

'This will do.'

She took a large carving-knife out of the knife-basket which was on the shelf close by her. She thrust the blade between the panel and the woodwork. It could scarcely have been securely fastened. In a surprisingly short space of time she had forced it loose. Then, grasping it with both her hands, she hauled the panel bodily away.

'Eric, it is there!'

Something was there, resting on a little ledge which had checked its fall on to the floor beneath – something which was covered with paint, and dust, and cobwebs, and Violet all at once grew timid.

'You take it; I dare not touch the thing.'

'It is very curious; something is there, and, by George, it is a knife!'

It was a knife – the knife which we had seen in the vision, the dream, the nightmare, call it what you will – the something which had seemed so real. There was no mistaking it, tarnished though it was – the long, slender blade which we had seen the man draw from the leather sheath. Stuck to it by what was afterwards shown to be coagulated blood was an envelope – the envelope which we had seen the fellow take from his pocket to wipe off the crimson stain. It had adhered to the blade. When the knife fell the envelope fell too.

'At least,' I murmured as I stared at this grim relic, 'this is a singular coincidence.'

The blood upon the blade had dried. It required but little to cause the envelope to fall away. As a matter of fact, while I was still holding the weapon in my hand it fell to the floor. I picked it up. It was addressed in a woman's hand, 'Francis Joynes, Esq., Fairleigh, Streatham.'

I at once recognised the name as that of a well-known owner of racehorses and so-called 'gentleman rider'.

Not the least singular part of all that singular story was that the letter inside that envelope, which was afterwards opened and read by the proper authorities, was from Mr Joynes's wife. It was a loving, tender letter, from a wife who was an invalid abroad to a husband whom she supposed was thinking of her at home.

Mr Joynes was never arrested, and that for this sufficient reason: that when the agents of the law arrived at his residence Mr Joynes was dead. He had committed suicide on the very night on which we saw that – call it vision – on board the *Water Lily*. I viewed the corpse against my will. I was not called in evidence. Had I been, I was prepared to swear, as was my wife, that Mr Joynes was the man whom I had seen in a dream that night. It was shown at the inquest that he had suffered of late from horrid dreams – that he had scarcely dared to sleep. I wonder if, in that last and most awful of his dreams, he had seen my face – seen it as I saw his?

It was afterwards shown, from inquiries which were made, that Mr Joynes and 'Mr Bush', tenant of the *Sylph*, were, beyond all doubt, one and the same person. On the singular circumstances which caused that discovery to be made I offer no comment.

DAME INOWSLAD

by

R. Murray Gilchrist

As with so many other Victorian authors, R. Murray Gilchrist (1868–1917) faded into oblivion when he died, despite a collected volume of his works appearing nine years after his death. Yet some of his fiction was the most original of its time and I think he is an unrecognised master of the macabre story. At a time when most authors in this vein were producing simple ghost stories and horror tales, Gilchrist wrote a book of the most remarkable and subtle fiction ever published.

Born in Sheffield, R. Murray Gilchrist began writing at an early age. His greatest inspiration came from his visits to Derbyshire, where he was fascinated by the people of the Peak District. In later years he spent much time in a remote part of the High Peak, studying the local people and writing several books about them and their dialect. One of them was factual: The Peak District (1910) but the rest were fictional, and included Natives of Milton (1902), Goodbye to Market (1908) and A Peakland Faggot (1897). The last title was also used for the collected volume of his High Peak tales published in 1926.

Gilchrist had first started writing fiction for The National Observer where several of the stories from his first book The Stone Dragon (1894) appeared. His later fiction included some fine novels such as Weird Wedlock (1913), The Abbey Mystery (1898) and The Labyrinth (1902). But The Stone Dragon was without doubt his most remarkable work, all the more notable as he never again attempted anything like it.

I have used stories from it in previous anthologies and would recommend anyone interested in reading more of Gilchrist's work to try 'The Basilisk' (in Terror by Gaslight) and 'Witch-in-Grain' (in The Thrill of Horror). This fine little story from The Stone Dragon casually but skilfully works around to a final paragraph of chilling brevity. If only Gilchrist had written more like this, I am certain his name would have survived a lot longer.

Sycamores and beeches surrounded the inn; elders, still green-flowered, leaned over the grass-grown roads. The belt of sward was white with lady-smocks, but in the damp hollows marsh-marigolds radiated essential sunlight. The blackbirds sang, and loudly, yet without the true strain of mirth: sang like blackbirds that must sing, but of rifled nests. Even the grasshoppers had some trouble: never had they chirped so pathetically before.

On the green the gilded figure of a bull hung from two uprights; it swung from side to side in the light breeze. The copper bell on a twisted pole hard by was green with mould: a-swing from it was a rusty chain; it had been used in the old posting days, and many a yeoman had heaved himself into his saddle from the worn mounting-block beside it.

For the inn itself, it was vast and rambling, dwarfed by the towering trees. For miles in every direction lay the old forest of Gardomwood, a relic of primeval woodland, rich in glades and streamlets: hazy in the clearings, where sheer-legs, like the trivets of witches' cauldrons, and tents and blue-smoking heaps told of charcoal-burners and their ever-shifting trade.

The Golden Bull with its beautiful precincts took me back to that fading Arcady whose shepherdesses and swains felt the end of the joy-time coming. It was utterly sad; but I was caught in the meshes of its melancholy, and for the while could not escape. Twilight fell, and I ceased from exploring, and went indoors. In the parlour was a great square piano. Its music, while acidly discordant, was yet plaintive with the curious speech such old things often own. I played a few Robin Hood ballads – of the Outlaw and Little John, of the Bishop of Hereford and Robin's pleasing escape. Then the hostess entered with a great Nottingham jar full of white lilac. She set this down between the firedogs, and stood leaning one hand on a chair-back and listening to the music. When I stopped she sighed heavily: I left the piano, and offered her a chair. She was middle-aged and deformed; her shoulders were humped, her face was shrivelled, but she had large grey eyes and a wistful smile.

'I thank you, sir,' she said. ' 'Twas the music drew me in.

Nobody's played since last summer, when Sir Jake Inowslad stayed here. His taste was sonatas and fugues – things pretty enow, but only pleasing at the time. Give me a melody that I can catch – almost grasp in my hand so to speak.'

'Do you play?' I asked, half hoping to hear some air she had loved in her youth.

'No, I cannot play. I was still room maid at Melbrook Abbey, so I never had opportunity.'

As she spoke, a girl came in with the snuffer-tray and candles. She was pale and tall and of a tempting shape. Beautiful she was not, yet the sad strangeness of her face impressed me more than great beauty would have done. Her eyes were like the other woman's, but clearer and more expressive; her lips were quaintly arched; long yellow hair hung down her back. She seemed, although she walked erect, to be recovering from some violent illness. When she had gone the hostess spoke again. 'My niece is not strong,' she said, laying an unnecessary emphasis on the word *niece*. 'The air does not suit her.'

'Was not she bred in the country?' I inquired.

'Ah, no! She is not without money – her father endowed her well. Until two years back she was at the convent of the Sisters of Saint Vincent de Paul for her education. 'Tis in the hill-country, and I think that coming to the flatness of Gardomwood has done her harm.'

The girl came in again: this time I noted her grace of movement; it had something of the wearied goddess. 'Aunt,' she said quietly, 'I wish to go into the woods – you can spare me? All I had to do is done; the women are sewing in the kitchen.' She went to the further end of the room, where a cloak of rose-coloured silk hung, ermine-lined, from a nail in the panelling. She donned it at her leisure; her long and narrow hands were of a perfect colour. She tied the broad ribands of the collar; she lighted two candles that hung before a tarnished mirror, and gazed at her shadow; then, her lips moving silently, she left the room.

'Ever the same,' the elder woman said. 'Night after night does she leave the house and travel about like an aimless thing. Come back, Dinah,' she called, 'come back.' But the thin voice went wavering through the empty passages unanswered. So the hostess rose and with a half-apologetic 'Goodnight,' left me alone. I sat down in the deep recess of the window behind a heavy curtain.

A copy of Denis Diderot's *Religieuse* lay on the little table. I took it up, and was soon engrossed in it: for of all books this is the most fascinating, the most disappointing, the most grim. A light came glimmering at the end of the vista before me: it grew and grew, and the moon uplifted herself waist-high above the trees. And when I had watched her thus far, I returned to my nun and reached page twenty-two of the second volume, where I read the following sentence: 'After a few flourishes she played some things, foolish, wild, and incoherent as her own ideas, but through all the defects of her execution I saw she had a touch infinitely superior to mine.' Then in the shaded window-seat I fell asleep....

The striking of a tall clock near the hearth awakened me: I had slept till midnight. The candles had been removed from the table to the piano; those in the girandole had guttered out or been extinguished. A young man sat at the piano on the embroidered stool. His back was towards me; I saw nothing but high, narrow shoulders and a dome-shaped head of dishevelled black hair plentifully besprinkled with grey. From the road outside came a noise of horses whinnying and plunging. I looked out, and there was a lumbering coach drawn by four stallions which, black in daylight, shone now like burnished steel.

The would-be musician turned and showed me a long painful face with glistening eyes and a brow ridged upward like a ruined stair. It was a face of intense eagerness; the eagerness of a man experimenting and praying for a result whereon his life depends. Without any prelude he played a dance of ghosts in an old ballroom: ghosts of men and women that moved in lavoltas and sarabands; ghosts that laughed at Susanna in the tapestry; ghosts that loved and hated. When the last chord had sent them crowding to their graves he turned and listened for a footstep. None came. He lifted a leather case from the side of the stool and, unfastening its clasps, took out a necklace which glistened in the candlelight like a fairy shower of rain and snow. 'Twas of table diamonds and margarites, the gems as big as filberts. He spread it across the wires, and after an instant's reflection began to play. The carcanet rattled and jangled as he went: it was as an advancing host of cymbal-women. When he listened again, great tears oozed from his eyes. He took up the jewel and played a melody vapid at first, but so subtle in its repetitions that none might doubt its meaning: thus and not otherwise would sound a lyke-wake sung in a worn voice after a night of singing. And whilst he played, the door opened silently, and I saw Dinah, there in her nightgown, holding the posts with her hands. She took one swift glance, then disappeared again in the darkness, and came back carrying in her arms a bundle swathed in pure linen and strongly redolent of aromatic herbs. Holding this to her breast, she approached the man. Her shadow fell across the keys, and he lifted his head. From both came a long murmur: his of love and joy and protection, hers of agony. He rose and would have clasped her, but she drew back and placed her burden in his outstretched hands.

'It is the child,' she said. 'Three months ago I gave birth to her, none knew save myself.... She was all that remained of you: all that I had, and I dared not part with her.... But now – now that I have seen you again – take her away – leave me – leave me in peace.'

'Dinah,' he said proudly, 'listen to me.'

'Nay,' she whispered, 'not again. If I listen I may forget your wickedness; I might be weak again. Leave me, Jake.'

'Dinah, you must hear me. Why, out of all the love you held and hold for me, can you condemn? When I left you I fell mad; for the year I have been mad, and only yesterday did they set me loose. See, I have brought you all the diamonds; tomorrow you will be Dame Inowslad.' And he laid the dead thing on a table, and caught the mother to his bosom. Her figure was shaken with sobs.

'Oh,' she cried, 'it has been hard; but my trial has brought the true reward of happiness. Only once have I missed seeing the place where you promised to meet me – the place where you said you loved me; and that was on the night of my lonely travailing.'

Outside the horses plunged and snorted: a shrunken postillion swaying at the neck of the off-leader. In the hollows of the road lay sheets of mist, and the moonlight turned them into floods. A long train of startled owls left the hollow sycamores and passed hooting...hooting...down the glade.

'Let us go,' Sir Jake said; 'by morning light we shall be in sight of Cammere, where Heaven grant us a happy time; – a year of joy for each week of pain. Do not wait to dress; rich robes and linen are inside the coach; I have brought many of my mother's gowns.'

Dinah extricated herself from his embrace, and went to find her cloak. During her absence a strange and terrible look came into Inowslad's face and he smote his forehead. He smiled at her reappearing. 'Dinah,' he said, looking downwards, so that she might not see his eyes, 'Dinah, I am so happy that I can scarce see. Lead me from the house.'

He took up the dead little one in his right arm, and carried it as believers carry relics. The outer door closed softly; they descended the mossgrown steps, and entered the coach. The horses leaped forward, half drowning the sound of a chuckle. A glint of the moon pierced the coach windows, and I saw a brown hand, convulsed and violent, gripping a long white throat.

THE MOUNTAIN OF SPIRITS

and

THE GOLDEN BRACELET

Anonymous *

Now for two very odd items indeed. I can't tell you much about them at all, except that they come from an anonymous anthology entitled The Best Terrible Tales from the Spanish, *published by a gentleman called William Reeves around 1891. The book was part of a series which included the best terrible tales from Germany, France and Italy. No author is ascribed to the stories, or a translator, so that is all I can find out about them.*

Anonymous ghost stories were, of course, not uncommon in Victorian days. Such forms of literature were still strictly infra dig with many writers, but I wonder just how many of them turned out the odd ghost story under another name? The magazines of the day were full of them, and there were many books of ghost stories by writers who, rather suspiciously, never seemed to write any other books. We can only surmise, of course, but it is worth recalling that the author of Little Women, *Louisa May Alcott, wrote thrillers and tales of terror under the pseudonym A. M. Bernard – and that was not discovered until a few years ago.*

So here are those two anonymous terrible Spanish tales. I don't think the 'terrible' relates to the quality, incidentally; in fact, they stand up very well even now. But who wrote them? Read them and wonder. . . .

THE MOUNTAIN OF SPIRITS

On the night of the Dead I listened, till I know not what hour, to the tolling of the bells. Their sound, monotonous and everlasting, brought to my mind that legend which I had heard at Soria.

I wished to go to sleep, but it was impossible. Once aroused,

* We know better now. See note on p.162

one's imagination is a steed which takes the bit between its teeth, and it is of no avail to try to restrain it. In order to pass the time I decided to set to work and write, and what I wrote is here.

I heard the story told at the place where the events are said to have taken place, and I have written it down, turning my head many times with fear when I heard the window creak as the cold night wind dashed against it.

I

'Call back the dogs, blow the horns, so that the hunters may gather again, and let us go back to the town. The night comes on. Today is All Saints' Day, and we stand on the Mountain of Spirits!'

'Well! What then!'

'Upon any other day I would not leave without making an end of that band of wolves driven from their dens by the snow of Montcayo, but today it is impossible. In a moment the bell will sound from the chapel of the Templars calling to evening prayer, and the spirits of the dead will commence to toll the bell of the mountain chapel.'

'Of that ruinous chapel? Bah! You want to frighten me!'

'No, my beautiful cousin. You are ignorant of what has taken place on this spot, to which you have come from so far only a year past. Rein in your palfrey, I will make my horse walk at a like pace, and I will tell you this history while we are on the road.'

The pages formed themselves into joyous noisy groups, the counts of Borges and Alcudiel mounted their superb horses, and followed together their children, Beatrice and Alonso, who headed the procession.

As they went on Alonso narrated the promised story in these words—

'This mountain, which is now called the Mountain of Spirits, belonged once upon a time to the Templars, whose convent you can see from here on the bank of that river. The Templars were at that time warriors and monks. Soria had been conquered by the Arabs, and the king gathered troops together from far-off parts in order to defend the town upon the side of the bridge, giving by this great offence to the nobles of Castile, who would themselves have been able to defend it, as afterwards they themselves were able to reconquer the land.

'Between the troops who came from afar belonging to the

powerful order and the nobles of the town a great hatred existed, which was hidden for some years, but which afterwards plainly showed itself. The former reserved to themselves this mountain, desiring to possess for their own wants and pleasures the abundance of game there was to be found there. The latter determined to organise a great hunt within the reserved ground in defiance of the severe prohibitions that the "spurred priests", as they called the strangers, had issued. Nothing was heard but the language of defiance. On the one side the love of the chase was irrestrainable, on the other was an equally uncontrollable desire for combat. The projected expedition took place. It would not be remembered by the beasts of the forest, but its memory is ever present in the minds of the mothers who weep the fate of their sons. It was not a hunt, it was a terrible battle. The mountain was heaped with bodies, and the wolves that should have been exterminated held a sanguinary feast. At length the king interposed his authority. He declared the mountain, which had been the cause of so much bloodshed, interdicted, and the chapel of the monks, situated in the same mountain in which were buried together friends and enemies, began to fall into ruin.

'Since that time it is said that upon All Saints' night the bell of the chapel sounds of itself, and the spirits of the dead, clad in their grave clothes, sweep in weird hunt over the craggy ground and thickets. The deer cry sadly, the wolves howl, snakes utter horrible hissings, and when the day breaks one may see imprinted on the snow the tracks of skeleton feet. That is why in Soria this mountain is called the Mountain of Spirits, and why I wish to leave it before night has fallen.'

Alonso finished his tale just as he and his cousin arrived at the bridge by which access is obtained from that side of the mountain to the town. There they awaited the arrival of the others, and having been joined by them, the whole company disappeared in the narrow winding streets of Soria.

II

The servants had cleared away the banquet; the high Gothic fireplace of the palace of the counts of Alcudiel was filled with a good fire lighting up the groups of dames and lords who were chatting together around the fire, and the wind beat against the panes of the windows of the hall.

Two persons alone had retired from this general conversation. Beatrice followed with her eyes the leaping of the flames, absorbed in deep thought; Alonso looked upon the reflection of the fire in the blue eyes of Beatrice.

The two remained for some time without speaking a word.

The old women told, as befitted the night of the dead, terrible stories in which spectres and apparitions acted the chief part, and one could hear afar off the sound of the bells of the churches of Soria tolling monotonously and sadly.

'Beautiful cousin', said Alonso, at last breaking the long silence, 'soon we shall be separated, perhaps for ever. The sandy plains of our Castile, the rude and warlike customs, the manners, simple and patriarchal, will not please you, I am sure. I have several times heard you sigh; was it for some far off gallant of your neighbourhood?'

Beatrice made a gesture of cold indifference. All the woman's character showed itself in the disdainful contraction of her little lips.

'It was perhaps for the pomp of the French court where you have lived till now,' went on the young man. 'In one manner or another, I presage it will not be long before I lose you. Before, however, we separate I would like to give you something in memory of me. Do you remember when we went to the church to return thanks to God for giving you your health again – which you came to seek in this country – the brilliant which fastened the plume of my cap then attracted your attention? How fine it looked when it served as a fastening for the veil which was thrown over your dark hair! A bride has already worn it. My father made a present of it to her who gave me life, and she wore it as she went to the altar. Would you like it?'

'I do not know the custom of your country,' said the girl, 'but in mine to receive a present entails an obligation. One can only accept on a ceremonial day a present from one's father.'

The cold tone in which Beatrice pronounced these words for a moment troubled the young man, but recovering himself, he said sadly –

'I know that, cousin, but today they celebrate the fête of all the saints, and yours is one of the chief amongst them. We are then arrived today at a time of ceremony and of presents. Will you accept mine?'

Beatrice bit her lip lightly as she held out her hand to receive the jewel, but said not a word.

The two were again silent. One could once more hear the voices of the old folk talking of wizards and hobgoblins, the sighing of the wind as it beat against the windows, and the lugubrious, monotonous tolling of the bells.

After some moments the interrupted conversation was renewed in this fashion –

'Before the end of the fête of all the saints, which comprehends both yours and mine, since you may without compromising your wishes, give me some memorial of you; will you refuse it me?'

As he spoke he looked at his cousin, whose face, illuminated as a terrible idea occurred to her, shone as if lighted by a lightning flash.

'Why should I not,' said she, taking the young man's right hand, and pretending to search amongst the folds of her large velvet mantle embroidered with gold. Then she said, with the air of a disappointed child –

'You remember the azure blue ribbon which I wore today during the hunt? You remarked that its colour was emblematic, the colour you most loved.'

'Yes.'

'Well, then! It is lost; it is lost, and I was thinking of giving it to you as a present!'

'It is lost! Where?' cried the young man, rising from his seat with an expression of fear and of despair.

'I do not know – perhaps upon the mountain.'

'Upon the Mountain of Spirits?' murmured he, growing pale and sitting down again, 'upon the Mountain of Spirits!'

After a pause, he said in a husky low voice –

'You know, for you have heard it a thousand times, in the city, in all Castile, that I am called the king of the hunters. Not having the opportunity to show my skill, like my ancestors, in actual combat, I have found a vent in this pastime, which is the imitation of war, for all my manly strength, all the hereditary ardour of my race. The carpet pressed by your feet is made of the skins of fierce beasts slain by my hand. I know their lurking-places and their habits. I have fought them by day and by night, on foot and on horseback, alone and with others, and no one can say that he has ever seen me shun danger on any occasion. On any other night I would go in search of that ribbon, I would go as if to a feast – but this night, this night why should I seek it? I fear. Listen! The bells are tolling. One can hear the bell of San Juan del Duero sound. The spirits of the mountain commence now to lift their yellow skulls above the weeds which grow upon their graves – spirits, of whom the very sight is able to make the blood of the bravest run cold, to turn his hair white; spirits who are able to drag him helplessly on in the wild sweep of their fantastic hunt, like a leaf which the wind carries one knows not whither.'

While the young man spoke, an almost imperceptible smile played on the lips of Beatrice, who, when he had finished, said in a tone of indifference, looking at the fireplace where the flames gleamed and leaped, sending up sparks of a thousand colours –

'Oh no! certainly! What nonsense! To go to the mountain at such a time for such a trifle! Such a dark night, the night of the dead, and with the roads, too, full of wolves!'

She spoke these last words with so strange an accent that Alonso could not but feel their bitter irony. Moved as by some invisible power, he sprang upon his feet. He passed his hand over his brow as if to wipe away whatever fear still dwelt within his brain, for none was in his heart. Then, in a firm voice, addressing the beautiful girl, bent towards the fire, and still occupied in watching the smoke eddying up, he said –

'Goodbye, Beatrice. Goodbye!'

'Alonso! Alonso!' said she, turning quickly.

But when she wished, or appeared to wish, to detain him, the young man had disappeared.

At the end of a few minutes the noise of a horse's hoofs was heard going at a gallop. The beautiful girl listened to the sound, a radiant expression of satisfied pride colouring her cheeks, till the noise became faint and at length died away.

The old folk, meanwhile, continued their tales of terrible apparitions, the wind sighed around the building, and the bells of the town could be heard afar off.

III

An hour passed – two, three. Midnight was about to sound, and Beatrice retired to her chamber. Alonso had not returned. He had not returned, although he should have come back in less than an hour.

'He has been afraid to go,' said the young girl, closing her book of prayers and going towards the bed, after having endeavoured in vain to offer up some of those prayers set apart by the Church for the day of the dead, for those who are no more.

She put out the light, drew the double curtains of silk, and went to sleep. She slept, but restlessly, lightly, troubled.

Midnight sounded from the lock of the postern, Beatrice heard in her dreams the vibrations of the bell – slow, solemn, sad, and she opened her eyes. She though she heard some one at that moment speak her name, but it seemed far off, very far off, and in a voice hoarse and plaintive. The wind sighed around the window.

'It was the wind!' she said, and placing her hand over her heart, she sought to repress its throbbing. Every moment, however, it beat the more and more. The larch-tree doors to the chambers began to grate on their hinges with a sharp grinding – prolonged, harsh!

At first one, and that the nearest of the doors, and then all the doors which led to the place, shook in their turn, these with a low grave noise, those with something like a groan – prolonged, piercing. Then all was quiet – a quiet filled with strange sounds. The silence of midnight, with the monotonous murmur of distant water, the baying of far-off hounds, confused voices, unintelligible words, echoes of steps coming and going, the rustling of robes brushing the floor, weary sighings, incomprehensible tremblings such as announce the presence of some one whom one cannot see, but of whom one divines the approach in spite of the dark around.

Beatrice, frozen, trembling, put her head from between the curtains to listen for a moment. She heard a thousand different sounds. She passed her hand over her forehead and listened again. There was nothing! All was quiet!

If, with that phosphorescence which attaches to the pupil in moments of extreme nervousness, she saw what looked like a body moving in all directions, when she fixed her dilated eyes on any one point there was nothing – all was darkness, impenetrable shadow.

'Bah!' she cried, turning away and laying her beautiful head upon the blue satin pillow, 'shall I be as big a coward as the poor folk, whose hearts beat with terror, even under armour, while they listen to the story of an apparition?'

She closed her eyes, determined to go to sleep; but the effort was a vain one. She became more pale, more restless, more terrified. It was surely no more a delusion. The hangings, worked with gold and with silk before the door, were parted, and slow steps resounded upon the carpet. The noise of those steps was low, almost imperceptible, but continual, and accompanying them was a sound like the cracking of wood or bone. They came on, they came on, and the *prie-Dieu* at the head of the bed was shaken. Beatrice uttered a sharp cry, and plunging down under the clothes of her bed, hid her head and held her breath.

The wind howled around the windows. The water of the fountain fell, fell with an eternal monotonous sound, the baying of the dogs swelled out upon the gusts, and the bells of the town of Soria, one near at hand, others afar off, tolled dolefully for the souls of the dead.

So passed an hour, two – the night, an age; for that night seemed eternal to Beatrice. At last the morning appeared, and recovering from her fear she opened her eyes to the first rays of the light. After a night sleepless and full of terror how beautiful, was the clear white light of day! She parted the curtains around her bed, and she felt disposed to laugh at her past fearfulness, when all of a sudden a cold perspiration bathed her limbs, her eyes dilated beyond themselves, and the pallor of the dead stole over her cheeks. Upon the *prie-Dieu* she saw, bloody and torn, the piece of blue ribbon which she had lost upon the mountain, the blue ribbon that Alonso had gone to seek!

When the affrighted servants came to announce to her the death of the first-born of Alcudiel, who it seemed had been devoured by wolves in the wild parts of the Mountain of Spirits, they found her motionless, clinging with her two hands to one of the ebony columns of her bed, her eyes fixed, her mouth open, her lips white, her limbs rigid – dead, dead of horror!

THE GOLDEN BRACELET

I

She was beautiful – beautiful with that beauty which makes one mad; beautiful with that beauty which strikes one as supernatural, but yet is such as one never ascribes to the angels in one's dreams. It was a diabolic beauty, such as the Evil One gives to such as are to work his purposes on earth.

He loved her – loved her with a love which knows no curb nor limit. He loved her with the love which seeks delight and finds nought but pain, with that love which assimilates itself to felicity, and yet, notwithstanding, is such as heaven inspires in a man in expiation of a crime.

She was capricious – capricious and extravagant, like most women.

He was superstitious and valiant, as were all the men of his time.

She was called Maria Antunez.

He, Pedro Alfonso de Orellana.

Both were of Toledo, and both of them lived in the town in which they had been born.

The tradition which deals with their remarkable history has descended to us through many years, but it tells us no more respecting who its heroes were.

In my character of a faithful chronicler, I shall not add a word of my own for the purpose of better introducing them.

II

He found her one day in tears and said to her –

'Why do you weep?'

She dried her eyes, and looking at him fixedly, sighed and commenced again to weep.

Pedro, astonished, approached Maria, took her hand, and leaning on the Arabic balustrade whence the beautiful girl had been watching the current of the river, he again asked her –

'Why do you weep?'

At the foot of the building the Tagus rolled, fretting itself against the rocks on which the imperial city is situated. The sun was sinking behind the neighbouring mountains, and the mist of evening floated around like a delicate azure veil. The monotonous murmuring of the water alone broke the deep stillness.

'Do not ask me why I weep, do not ask me. I should not know what to reply, nor if I answered you would you comprehend me. There are desires which lie hidden in women's hearts which are not revealed even in a sigh – foolish dreams which fly through our imagination; which cannot find expression in words; incomprehensible phenomena of our mysterious nature which a man has no power to conceive of. Do not, I beg of you, ask me the cause of my sorrow. If I were to tell it to you I daresay you would but laugh.'

Having spoken these words she bent down her head, and he again repeated his question.

The girl remained obstinately silent for a while, but at length she said to him in a low voice broken by sobs –

'Do you wish it? I am about to tell you of a foolish thing, but that does not matter. I will tell it you since you so wish it.

'Yesterday I went to church. They were celebrating the festival of the Virgin. Her image, placed in the centre of the altar, upon a ledge of gold, shone like burning coal. The notes of the vibrating organ swelled, echoing, echoing through all the church, and in the choir the priests were singing the *Salve Regina*.

'I prayed and prayed, absorbed in religious thought, when mechanically lifting my eyes they fell upon the altar. I do not know how it was that my eyes fixed themselves upon the image – no, not upon the image, but upon an object which till then I had never seen, an object which, by some inexplicable attraction, absorbed all my attention. Do not laugh! This object was the golden bracelet worn by the Mother on the arm on which reposed her divine Son. I tore my eyes away, and bent them down in prayer. Impossible! My eyes involuntarily returned to the same place. The lights from the altar, reflected in the thousand faces of the diamonds, were multiplied in a wonderful fashion. Numberless sparks of lights – red, azure, green yellow – danced around the precious stones like a whirlwind of fiery atoms, like a bewildering dance of spirits of flame, fascinating by their brilliancy and their terrible restlessness.

'I left the church, I came home, but I did so full of thought of what I had seen. I threw myself down to sleep. I could not. The night passed, but the thought never quitted me. In the morning my eyes closed themselves, and, would you believe it? even in my sleep there passed before me a woman – a woman brown and beautiful, wearing a bracelet of gold and of diamonds. A woman! Yes, but it was not the Virgin whom I adore and before whom I bow. It was a woman – a woman like myself, who laughed at me and seemed to mock me. "Do you see it?" she appeared to say, pointing to her bracelet. "How it shines! It looks like a circlet of stars stolen from the sky during a summer's night! Do you see it? Well, it is not for you, and it never shall be, never, never! You may have others, more beautiful, richer, if such is possible, but this which sparkles in a manner so fascinating, so fascinating – never, never!" I awoke, but the vision remains ever fixed in my mind, it is there like a burning nail, diabolic, not to be withdrawn, an inspiration no doubt of Satan himself. Well, then? Why are you silent, and why do you hang your head? Does my foolishness make you dumb?'

Pedro, with a convulsive movement, clutched the hilt of his sword, lifted his down-bent head, and said in a low voice –

'What Virgin was it that wore the bracelet?'

'That of Sagrario,' replied Maria.

'That of Sagrario!' repeated the young man in a voice of terror, 'that of Sagrario in the cathedral!'

The tumult of passion that raged within him showed itself in the motion of his features. He was buried in thought.

'Ah! Why was it not worn by some other?' he went on, loudly, passionately. 'Why did not the archbishop wear it on his mitre, the king on his crown, or the Evil One himself bear it in his hands! For you I would have torn it from them at the price of my life, or at the loss of my soul. But from the Virgin of Sagrario, from our patron saint – I, I who was born in Toledo. It is impossible, impossible!'

'Never!' murmured Maria, in scarcely perceptible tones, 'Never!'

And she commenced to weep again.

Pedro fixed a stupefied look upon the current of the river – upon the current which slowly went on, ceaseless, before his straining eyes, murmuring against the foot of the building – against the rocks on which stands the imperial city.

III

The cathedral of Toledo! Imagine to yourself a forest of gigantic palm-trees which, interlacing their branches, form a colossal magnificent roof, in the shade of which lurk, living with the life that genius has given to them, a multitude of carvings of things, imaginary and real.

Figure to yourself an indescribable mingling of shadow and of light, mixing and blending in the corners of the nave, while the rays of colour stream from the stained windows. There the light of the lamps struggles and loses itself in the shadows of the sanctuary.

Figure to yourself a mountain of stone, immense like the spirit of our religion, sombre as its traditions, enigmatic as its parables, and then you will have but a feeble idea of this eternal monument of the enthusiastic faith of our ancestors, upon which the folk of centuries have poured out, in emulation, the treasures of their belief, of their inspiration, and of their art.

In it dwells the silence, the majesty, the mystic poetry, and the religious awe opposing themselves to worldly thought and the mean passions of the world.

Consumption is checked when one breathes the pure air of the mountains, and irreligion should be cured by breathing the atmosphere of faith.

But however great, however imposing the cathedral may seem to us at whatever hour we enter its mysterious and sacred precincts, never does it produce so profound an impression as on those days when in it are displayed all the splendour of religious pomp, when its altars are covered with gold and precious stones, its paths with carpets, and its pillars with hangings.

Then, when a thousand silver lamps throw around streams of light; when the air is laden with a cloud of incense, the voices of the choir, and the notes of the organ; and the bells in the tower make the building tremble from the lowest depths of its foundation to the highest point of its crown, then may one comprehend, feeling it in one's heart, the tremendous majesty of God who dwells within us, in the spirit by which one breathes, filling one with the reflection of His omnipotence.

A scene such as we have described might have been witnessed on the occasion when the last day of the great octave of the Virgin was being celebrated in the cathedral of Toledo.

The religious feast had brought together a vast congregation of worshippers; but the crowd had now dispersed itself in all directions. The wax tapers were being extinguished in the various chapels and on the high altar, and the great gates of the church clattered on their hinges, closing themselves behind the last Toledan. Then, from out of the shadow emerged a man, white, more ghastly than the figure on the tomb upon which he leaned for an instant in order to master his emotion. He waited a moment, and then glided cautiously to the screen which separated the choir. The light of a lamp shone upon him as he stole by.

It was Pedro.

What had passed between the two lovers before he could summon resolution to put into execution a scheme the very thought of which had made his hair bristle with horror, no one will ever know. There, however, he stood, ready to carry out his audacious scheme. In his restless gaze, in the trembling of his limbs, in the large drops of perspiration which stood upon his forehead, was written the nature of his thoughts.

The cathedral was deserted – quite deserted, and all was profound silence.

Nevertheless at times there could be heard confused sounds. Perhaps the creaking of the timbers or the murmuring of the wind. Who knows? The high-strung senses of the imagination see and hear, in its exaltation, things which do not exist. However that may be, near him, afar off, sometimes behind him, sometimes in front of him, there seemed to be stifled sighs, the rustling of vestments sweeping upon the ground, the sound of steps which came and went without cessation.

Pedro, with an effort, went on his way. He came to the screen and took his first step towards the great altar. Around this portion of the building are the tombs of the kings, of whom the statues of stone, the hand on the hilt of their swords, seem to watch night and day in the shadow of the sanctuary where they lie till eternity.

'Onward!' he whispered in a low voice, and he would have gone on but he could not. It seemed as if his feet were glued to the stone pavement. He cast down his eyes, and his hair bristled with horror. The floor of the chapel was composed of large dull sepulchral stones. For a moment he thought that a hand, icy and fleshless, held him to the spot with an irresistible force. The dying out lamps, which glittered in the background of the nave like stars lost in clouds, swam before his eyes; the statues on the tombs, the images on the altar, seemed to move, and the whole place with its granite arches and its pillars of hewn stone appeared to reel.

'Onward!' said Pedro again, beside himself, and he went on

towards the altar. He climbed up it until he came to the pedestal on which stood the Virgin. Around him was a dream of chimerical and horrible forms. All was dark or dim light more dreadful than darkness itself. The Queen of Heaven alone, over whom streamed the soft light of a golden lamp, appeared to smile, tranquil, loving, serene in the midst of such horror.

Then, however, that smile, mute, immobile, which had calmed him for a moment, in the end inspired him with terror – a stranger terror, a deeper terror, than any he had ever yet felt.

He strove to recover himself, and turning away his eyes so that he should not see the image, he put out his hand with a convulsive motion, and tore away the golden bracelet, the pious offering of a saintly archbishop – the golden bracelet that was worth a fortune!

The thing was in his possession. His nervous fingers clutched it with a supernatural strength. Now he had only to fly – to fly with it. To do that, however, it was necessary he should raise his eyes, and Pedro dared not look. He dared not look upon the image, upon the kings at their tombs, upon the demons on the cornices, upon the grotesque figures of the columns, on the shadow and the rays of light which, like white gigantic phantoms, slowly moved in the background of the naves, peopling them with terror-striking mysterious beings.

At last, opening his eyes, he threw a look around, and a sharp cry broke from his lips.

The cathedral was full of forms – of forms which, clothed in strange garbs, had come down from their niches, and filled the whole place. They looked at him with their empty eye-sockets.

Saints, nuns, angels, demons, warriors, dames, pages, cenobites, and clowns, crowded and mixed together in the nave and up to the altar. At its foot officiated, in the presence of the kings kneeling on their tombs, the marble archbishops whom he had but lately seen lying immovable on their graves, while, crawling over the flag-stones, creeping up the pillars, sitting on the dais, hanging from the vaults, living like the worms of an immense corpse, were a whole world of granite reptiles and animals, fantastic, deformed, horrible.

He could no longer resist. His temples throbbed with a fearful force. A mist of blood floated before his eyes. He uttered a second cry, a cry harsh, half human, and fell fainting on the altar.

When on the following day the sacristans discovered him at the foot of the altar, holding still the bracelet of gold in his hand, seeing them approach he cried out, with a peal of hideous laughter –

'For her! for her!'

The man was mad.

EDITOR'S NOTE

As I asked in the introduction to these two stories: who wrote them? My question was answered in 1992 by a reader in America, Eduardo Zinna (who wrote to me from Cambodia where he was working for the United Nations). He identified the stories as being the work of the Spanish poet Gustavo Adolfo Bécquer (1836-1870), taken from his collection LEYENDAS (1857-1864). The Dover edition of this book is the first chance I've had to correctly ascribe the tales, and I am indebted to Mr. Zinna for his kind letter.

– HL

THE TYBURN GHOST

by

The Countess of Munster

As with Lady Dilke, Wilhelmina FitzClarence, the Countess of Munster (1830–1906) has been completely overlooked by bibliophiles and anthologists since her death. This is regrettable, for there can be fewer truly representative collections of Victorian ghost stories than her Ghostly Tales *(1896).*

The daughter of Lady Augusta FitzClarence and the second son of the 12th Earl of Cassillia, Wilhelmina married her cousin, the second Earl of Munster in 1855. In her childhood she had known William IV, who was a family friend, and she recalled her younger experiences in My Memories and Miscellanies *(1904).*

Her first novel was Dorinda *(1889) and two years later she published her only other novel* A Scotch Earl *(1891).* Ghostly Tales *is possibly her best work, being an interesting set of ghost stories, many with London settings. 'The Tyburn Ghost' is a surprisingly grim little piece, proving that Wilhelmina FitzClarence was yet another forgotten Victorian expert in the art of chilling the spine. There can be fewer lines more frightening than that used to describe her apparition's lips!*

Some years ago a lady and her three daughters, who generally resided in the country, had reason to visit the metropolis. After some trouble in the way of house-hunting, they settled in a lodging located in a small street in close proximity to the Marble Arch, Hyde Park.

It was summertime, about the middle of July, and the heat being intense, the atmosphere (or the want of it!) in a small lodging-house was very oppressive. Mrs Dale, however, was not very sensitive to 'stuffiness'; besides which, had she been so, she was not well enough off to afford a more spacious dwelling. Indeed, had it not been for the landlady's obliging disposition, and readiness to accede to some alterations suggested by Mrs Dale, in the arrangement of the apartment, the latter lady would have been forced to seek a *pied-à-terre* in a still less fashionable locality than even Dash-street.

But to make our story clear, we must describe the relative positions of the rooms in Dash-street, as well as what were the slight alterations suggested by Mrs Dale, and carried out by the obliging Mrs Parsons; who, knowing that the season was more than half over, felt it was better to put herself out a little, than not to let her rooms at all.

No. 5 Dash-street was a tenement of the most conventional furnished-apartment type; and the rooms hired by Mrs Dale consisted of two small sitting-rooms on the drawing-room floor, with folding doors between them, and one tolerably good sized bedroom, on the upper storey, situated exactly above the front sitting-room. There was a large 'four-poster' in this upper bedroom, in which the two elder young ladies agreed to repose – together; and Mrs Dale persuaded the landlady to allow another 'four-poster' to be placed in the back-sitting room for her convenience and that of her youngest daughter – they also electing to sleep therein together.

This was an economical arrangement, necessitating the use of only two beds instead of four (or at least of three), and, as lodging-house keepers charge according to the number of the beds used, the arrangement was a satisfactory one for Mrs Dale.

Upon the appointed day, rather late in the evening, the Dale family arrived in Dash-street. Mrs Dale had had some business to transact in the City; so, after a frugal supper, they began to think of retiring for the night. Mrs Parsons, being a busy, hard-working woman, was nothing loth, and soon brought in the extra bed, toilet table, etc., and after bidding her lodgers a hearty goodnight, left them to themselves.

Mrs Dale had already thrown herself into the expectant arms of an inviting *fauteuil*, intent upon enjoying a free-and-easy yawn, when she suddenly noticed for the first time that there was a balcony outside the window which ran along the whole row of the Dash-street houses. Not being of an imaginative temperament, however, the only nocturnal danger which presented itself to the lady's innocently conventional mind, was – cats! Thereupon the following colloquy took place between her and her daughter Minny, who was to be her bed-fellow:

'Minny, mind you shut that window!'

'By all means, mother!'

'And mind you lock it, too; for I am terrified at cats!'

Minny was a very dutiful daughter; but all the same she could not but think, in her 'inner consciousness', that if the window were shut, it would take a very uncommon cat to open it, even if it were *not* locked! She, however, silently and humbly obeyed orders, and, after much straining and struggling, managed to shut and lock the window, thus imprisoning within the stuffy little room the pleasing odour of the evening meal (which had consisted of pickled salmon and Welsh rare-bit!) and also effectually preventing the entrance of the least breath of fresh air!

'And now that we are comfortable,' said Mrs Dale, whose complexion was shining from a 'combination of heat and eat', 'we may as well go to bed!'

Accordingly, having kissed and dismissed her two daughters, who were to sleep upstairs, she and Minny commenced disrobing themselves in the back sitting-room.

'I think,' said Mrs Dale, after pondering a little, 'that if we lock both the doors which open into the drawing-rooms from the staircase, we might safely sleep with the folding-doors open between the two rooms and so be cooler; and we shall get more air,' – (i.e., the atmosphere of the pickled salmon, etc.) – 'don't you think?'

'We will do so,' said the obedient Minny, flinging open the folding-doors; she then kissed her mother affectionately, and got into bed.

Now the room was small, and the 'four-poster' was large; so it had been found necessary to place the latter almost in the centre of the former. There was just room for one chair between the bed and the wall on Minny's side, and only a little larger space, occupied by an ottoman and a small table, upon Mrs Dale's side.

By this time Minny, who was the most active and efficient sister of the three, and upon whom the principal responsibilities of the family were laid, was very tired, and soon, very soon (after she had felt her mother lie down by her side) she fell fast asleep.

The ladies were lying back to back – Minny's face being turned to the wall, and her mother's towards the ottoman, on the other side of the room.

Suddenly Minny was awakened by a sharp exclamation of seeming terror from her mother, and turning round she beheld the old lady sitting bolt upright in the bed; her teeth were chattering, her night-cap was awry, and she was shaking in every limb.

'What's the matter, mother?'

'I've – I've seen something!' she gasped.

'But, what? *What?*'

'An old hag! – with a villainous face, and hanging lips!'

'Oh! mother, don't you think it's fancy? You know you never sleep well in a strange bed!'

'It *wasn't* fancy!' answered the terrified woman; 'she passed along there,' pointing with a shaking hand along the wall, 'and when she turned and saw me looking at her, she came close to me in a threatening way, and put her horrid putrid-looking face close into mine. Faugh! I smelt Death! She also nodded viciously, and laughed at my fright, shewing black, slimy teeth! Then she pointed jeeringly with her brown skeleton finger close to my face, and curtsied very low;' and the perspiration poured off the poor old lady's face at the recollection.

'Dearest mother,' said Minny tenderly, 'you are over-tired and nervous! Come and sleep this side of the bed – for no one can get at you here, between the bed and the wall!'

And the good daughter helped her mother over into her place, while she lay down in her mother's, feeling convinced that the old lady was suffering from the effects of – pickled salmon!

Minny slept peacefully for some time, when suddenly *she* awoke, feeling curiously uneasy, and for some reason she dreaded to open her eyes! Then, after a second or two, she began to realise that something – someone – was very close to her; that in fact *a face* was almost touching hers; for she smelt a fœtid breath, like to what (she fancied) must be the odour of the grave!

With an effort, she opened her eyes and beheld the figure of an old woman, who, as the terrified girl started into a sitting posture, retreated to the foot of the bed, seemingly prepared, however, to spring upon its occupant; for she clung to both the bed-posts with her brown, claw-like hands, both arms distended, and her head bent slightly forward; her small, lithe body meanwhile swaying to and fro, as though to give it the necessary impetus.

The hag's face was the wickedest Minny had ever seen, and was mottled and brown in colour, as though in a state of decomposition. She wore an old-fashioned mob-cap, trimmed with a wreath of roses (an incongruous head-dress for so ghastly a head!) and a malicious grin parted the charred and blackened lips. She was dressed in a brown silk *sacque*, embroidered all over with pink roses, and Minny fancied she heard the tapping of high-heeled shoes, as the detestable apparition seemingly changing its intention, relinquished the bed-posts and once more began to approach her – curtseying ironically, as though enjoying the girl's terror!

But Minny, being religiously courageous, pulled herself together, and the sacred words seemed to spring solemnly to her lips: 'In the name of the Father, the Son, and the Holy Ghost, I bid thee be gone!'

A mingled expression of fear and malignant hatred appeared in the evil hag's face, as Minny slowly uttered these words; then the figure shrank, crouched against the wall, and finally disappeared.

Minny knew now that she had seen an evil spirit, and was also convinced that her adjuration had had effect, and that she should never be troubled again in the same way! Those sacred words would always (she felt) have power – complete power – over the devil and his angels. So, in peace she lay down and slept till morning.

She deemed it best to say nothing to her mother of what she had seen, and when the old lady, while dressing the next morning, reiterated her assertion that what she had seen was 'not a dream, nor had it been nightmare', – all that Minny answered was, 'She hoped her mother would not relate her experiences to the two sisters who slept upstairs, as it was no use to frighten them.' To this Mrs Dale agreed.

The old lady felt nervous all the same for a night or two after the strange occurrence; but being troubled no more by the unpleasant nocturnal visitor, she became quite bold, and began to think that, after all, it might have been the fault of the pickled salmon, and that the Welsh rare-bit might also have had something to do with it! Having also a great deal of business to transact in the City, and the rooms being convenient, she decided to stay a fortnight longer in Dash-street.

One day, the second sister (Janet) asked for a private word with Minny, and told her that she (Janet) felt 'very ill', and that both she and the other sister (Mary by name) fancied there must be 'something unwholesome' in the bedroom in which they slept, as they had neither of them 'felt well' since their *séjour* in Dash-street.

Minny looked anxiously at her sisters, and could not but acknow-ledge to herself that they both looked ill; and reproached herself for not having noticed it before. The fortnight was, however, nearly over, so she spoke to her mother, and it was settled that they should leave the very next day; but that they must send for the landlady and tell her so, as she was expecting them to stay a day or two longer.

Mrs Parsons was much put out at the news, and asked the reason of so sudden a departure? Was there anything she could do? Or had she left anything undone? As she spoke she looked in a strangely suspicious manner at Mrs Dale, and murmured, 'she hoped if there was any reason of complaint that the ladies would tell her.'

'Oh no, Mrs Parsons,' answered Mrs Dale, 'we have been most comfortable, but my daughers fancy there is a smell in their bed-room upstairs, and that consequently it is not quite wholesome. Can you account for this?'

'I hope the young ladies will tell me exactly from what they suffer? Is there anything else besides the smell?'

Minnie turned to Janet, who looked as though she could barely stand and gasped out: 'Yes, I *will* tell the truth, and – Mary, come here and corroborate what I say! for I can bear it no longer! Mrs Parsons, every night for the last week or more, between the hours of one and three, I and my sister are visited by a villainous old hag,' and at the remembrance of what she had gone through, of distress and terror, Janet so nearly swooned that after a few minutes Mary was compelled to become spokeswoman.

'Yes!' she said, 'what Janet says is true! but we kept silence, knowing it was an object to mother to remain here! The old hag,' Mary continued, shuddering, 'looks like – a Devil! and as though she had mouldered for years in her grave! Her lips look as though they were falling off – horrible! – horrible!'

'Enough!' said Mrs Parsons, holding up her hand, 'I know it all! – and this cursed house has been my ruin. I ought never to have stayed here; but what *can* a poor widow do! I got it cheap, as it had a bad name – and now, see!'

She then related that the house had been sold to her cheap by a relative – who had warned her it was haunted by the old woman whom the Dale family had seen. *She* had never seen the ghost her-

self, and would not believe in it, but upon making anxious researches she had discovered that the house was built on the very
site of Tyburn, and once when, for sanitary purposes, excavations
had been made, a lot of charred bones had been unearthed – thereby
attesting to the truth of what she had been told.

After hearing her story Mrs Dale felt sorry for the woman, and
before leaving made her a small present in money – at the same
time impressing upon her that it was scarcely fair or honourable
for her, under the circumstances, to receive lodgers. She also offered
to help her always in any small way she could – and she felt glad
afterwards to think she hád done so; for not many months later,
she read in the papers that No. 5, Dash-street, had been burnt to
the ground, and that the poor landlady's body had been found
among the ruins, bearing incontestable signs of the unfortunate
woman having (mercifully) been suffocated.

Years later, as some workmen were digging on the same spot for
fresh foundations, an old coffin was unearthed, and upon its being
opened, it was found to contain fragments of a female skeleton –
a brown silk gown, in wonderful preservation, some human teeth,
and a wreath of artificial roses!

REMORSELESS VENGEANCE

by

Guy Boothby

Though he wrote over fifty books, Guy Boothby (1867–1905) is now remembered for just five. These were a series of novels about the sinister Dr Nikola, who chased the secret of immortality all around the world, and they were best-sellers in their day. Boothby was one of the first Australian writers to find success, and he left behind many short stories which are gradually being hunted out again.

Born in Adelaide, Boothby was the descendant of English emigrants, and it was decided that he would be educated in England. He was sent here at the age of seven and stayed until he was seventeen. On his return to Australia, he held several jobs, at one time being private secretary to the mayor of Adelaide but it was writing that attracted him and he published his first book in 1894, the same year moving back to England and settling in Bournemouth. From then on, as well as farming, Boothby wrote a string of successful books, some of them based on his Australian experiences, including Bushigrams *(1897) and* Billy Binks, Hero *(1898). He died suddenly at the age of thirty-seven.*

Boothby's short stories are still neglected, despite their quality and quantity. Among the best of his many collections were The Lady of the Island *(1904),* A Royal Affair *(1906),* For Love of Her *(1905) and* Uncle Joe's Legacy *(1902), from which I have selected 'Remorseless Vengeance'. Set in the South Seas, which Boothby obviously knew well, it is a splendid ghost story, in the Victorian tradition but with some added Australian spice.*

To use that expressive South Sea phrase, I have had the misfortune to be 'on the beach' in a variety of places in my time. There are people who say that it is worse to be stranded in

Trafalgar Square than, shall we say, Honolulu or Rangoon. Be that as it may, the worst time I ever had was that of which I am now going to tell you. I had crossed the Pacific from San Francisco before the mast on an American mail boat, had left her in Hong Kong, and had made my way down to Singapore on a collier. As matters did not look very bright there, I signed aboard a Dutch boat for Batavia, intending to work my way on to Australia. It was in Batavia, however, that the real trouble began. As soon as I arrived I fell ill, and the little money I had managed to scrape together melted like snow before the mid-day sun. What to do I knew not – I was on my beam ends. I had nothing to sell, even if there were anyone to buy, and horrible visions of Dutch gaols began to obtrude themselves upon me.

It was on the night of the 23rd of December, such a night as I'll be bound they were not having in the old country. There was not a cloud in the sky, and the stars shone like the lamps along the Thames Embankment when you look at them from Waterloo Bridge. I was smoking in the brick-paved verandah of the hotel and wondering how I was going to pay my bill, when a man entered the gates of the hotel and walked across the garden and along the verandah towards where I was seated. I noticed that he was very tall, very broad-shouldered, and that he carried himself like a man who liked his own way and generally managed to get it.

'I wonder who he can be?' I said to myself, and half expected that he would pass me and proceed in the direction of the manager's office. My astonishment may be imagined, therefore, when he picked up a chair from beside the wall and seated himself at my side.

'Good evening,' he said, as calmly as you might address a friend on the top of a 'bus.

'Good evening,' I replied in the same tone.

'Frank Riddington is your name, I believe?' he continued, still with the same composure.

'I believe so,' I answered, 'but I don't know how you became aware of it.'

'That's neither here nor there,' he answered; 'putting other matters aside for the moment, let me give you some news.'

He paused for a moment and puffed meditatively at his cigar.

'I don't know whether you're aware that there's an amiable plot on hand in this hotel to kick you into the street in the morning,' he went on. 'The proprietor seems to think it unlikely that you will be able to settle your account.'

'And, by Jove, he is not far wrong,' I replied. 'It's Christmas time, I know, and I am probably in bed and dreaming. You're undoubtedly the fairy godmother sent to help me out of my difficulty.'

He laughed – a short, sharp laugh.

'How do you propose to do it?'

'By putting a piece of business in your way. I want your assistance, and if you will give it me I am prepared to hand you sufficient money not only to settle your bill, but to leave a bit over. What's more, you can leave Batavia, if you like.'

'Provided the business of which you speak is satisfactory,' I replied, 'you can call it settled. What am I to do?'

He took several long puffs at his cigar.

'You have heard of General Van der Vaal?'

'The man who, until lately, has been commanding the Dutch forces up in Achin?'

'The same. He arrived in Batavia three days ago. His house is situated on the King's Plain, three-quarters of a mile or so from here.'

'Well, what about him?'

Leaning a little towards me, and sinking his voice, he continued: 'I want General Van der Vaal – badly – and tonight!'

For a moment I had doubts as to his sanity.

'I'm afraid I haven't quite grasped the situation,' I said. 'Do I understand that you are going to abduct General Van der Vaal?'

'Exactly!' he replied. 'I am going to deport him from the island. You need not ask why, at this stage of the proceedings. I shouldn't have brought you into the matter at all, but that my mate fell ill, and I had to find a substitute.'

'You haven't told me your name yet,' I replied.

'It slipped my memory,' he answered. 'But you are welcome to it now. I am Captain Berringer!'

You may imagine my surprise. Here I was sitting talking face to face with the notorious Captain Berringer, whose doings were known from Rangoon to Vladivostock – from Nagasaki to Sourabaya. He and his brother – of whom, by the way, nothing had been heard for some time past – had been more than suspected of flagrant acts of piracy. They were well known to the Dutch as pearl stealers in prohibited waters. The Russians had threatened to hang them for seal-stealing in Behring Straits, while the French had some charges against them in Tonkin that would ensure them a considerable sojourn there should they appear in that neighbourhood again.

'Well, what do you say to my proposal?' he asked. 'It will be as easy to accomplish as it will be for them to turn you into the street in the morning.'

I knew this well enough, but I saw that if he happened to fail I should, in all probability, be even worse off than before.

'Where's your vessel,' I asked, feeling sure that he had one near at hand.

'Dodging about off the coast,' he said. 'We'll pick her up before daylight.'

'And you'll take me with you?'

'That's as you please,' he answered.

'I'll come right enough. Batavia will be too hot for me after tonight. But first you must hand over the money. I must settle with that little beast of a proprietor tonight.'

'I like your honesty,' he said, with a sneer. 'Under the circumstances it is so easy to run away without paying.'

'Captain Berringer,' said I, 'whatever I may be now, I was once a gentleman.'

A quarter-of-an-hour later the bill was paid, and I had made my arrangements to meet my employer outside the Harmonic Club punctually at midnight. I am not going to say that I was not nervous, for it would not be the truth. Van der Vaal's reputation was a cruel one, and if he got the upper hand of us we should be likely to receive but scant mercy. Punctually to the minute I reached the rendezvous, where I found the captain awaiting me. Then we set off in the direction of the King's Plain, as you may suppose keeping well in the shadow of the trees. We had not walked very far before Berringer placed a revolver into my hand, which I slipped into my pocket.

'Let's hope we shan't have to use them,' he said; 'but there's nothing like being prepared.'

By the time we had climbed the wall and were approaching the house, still keeping in the shadow of the trees, I was beginning to think I had had enough of the adventure, but it was too late to draw back, even had the Captain permitted such a thing.

Suddenly the Captain laid his hand on my arm.

'His room is at the end on this side,' he whispered. 'He sleeps with his window open, and his bed is in the furthest corner. His lamp is still burning, but let us hope that he is asleep. If he gives the alarm we're done for.'

I won't deny that I was too frightened to answer him. My fear, however, did not prevent me from following him into the clump of trees near the steps that led to the verandah. Here we slipped off our boots, made our preparations, and then tiptoed with the utmost care across the path, up the steps, and in the direction of the General's room. That he was a strict disciplinarian we were aware, and that, in consequence, we knew that his watchman was likely to be a watchman in the real sense of the word.

The heavy breathing that came from the further corner of the room told us that the man we wanted was fast asleep. A faint light, from a wick which floated in a bowl of cocoanut oil, illuminated the room, and showed us a large bed of the Dutch pattern, closely veiled with mosquito curtains. Towards this we made our way. On it, stretched out at full length, was the figure of a man. I lifted the netting while the Captain prepared for the struggle. A moment later he leapt upon his victim, seized him by the throat and pinioned him. A gag was quickly thrust into his mouth, whilst I took hold of his wrists. In less time than it takes to tell he was bound hand and foot, unable either to resist or to summon help.

'Bundle up some of his clothes,' whispered Berringer, pointing to some garments on a chair. 'Then pick up his heels, while I'll take his shoulders. But not a sound as you love your life.'

In less than ten minutes we had carried him across the grounds, had lifted him over the wall, where we found a native cart waiting for us, and had stowed him and ourselves away in it.

'Now for Tanjong Prick,' said the Captain. 'We must be out of the islands before daybreak.'

At a prearranged spot some four or five miles from the port we pulled up beneath a small tope of palms.

'Are you still bent upon accompanying me?' asked the Captain, as we lifted the inanimate General from the cart and placed him on the ground.

'More than ever,' I replied. 'Java shall see me no more.'

Berringer consulted his watch, and found the time to be exactly half-past two. A second later a shrill whistle reached us from the beach.

'That's the boat,' said Berringer. 'Now let's carry him down to her.'

We accordingly set off in the direction indicated. It was not, however, until we were alongside a smart-looking brig, and I was clambering aboard, that I felt in any way easy in my mind.

'Pick him up and bring him aft to the cuddy,' said the skipper to two of the hands, indicating the prostrate General. Then turning to the second mate, who was standing by, he added: 'Make sail, and let's get out of this. Follow me, Mr Riddington.'

I accompanied him along the deck, and from it into the cuddy, the two sailors and their heavy burden preceding us. Once there the wretched man's bonds were loosed. They had been tight enough, goodness knows, for when we released him he was so weak that he could not stand, but sank down on one of the seats beside the table, and buried his face in his hands.

'What does this mean?' he asked at last, looking up at us with a pitiable assumption of dignity. 'Why have you brought me here?'

'That's easily told,' said the Captain. 'Last Christmas you were commanding in Achin. Do you remember an Englishman named Bernard Watson who threw in his lot with them?'

'I hanged him on Christmas Day,' said the other, with a touch of his old spirit.

'Exactly,' said Berringer. 'And that's why you're here tonight. He was my brother. We will cry "quits" when I hang you on the yard-arm on Christmas morning.'

'Good heavens, Captain!' I cried, 'you're surely not going to do this?'

'I am,' he answered, with a firmness there was no mistaking. The idea was too horrible to contemplate. I tried to convince myself that, had I known what the end would be, I should have taken no part in it.

A cabin had already been prepared for the General, and to it he was forthwith conducted. The door having been closed and locked upon him, the Captain and I were left alone together. I implored him to reconsider his decision.

'I never reconsider my decisions,' he answered. 'The man shall hang at sunrise the day after tomorow. He hanged my brother in cold blood, and I'll do the same for him. That's enough. Now I must go and look at my mate; he's been ailing this week past. If you want food the steward will bring it to you, and if you want a bunk – well, you can help yourself.'

With that he turned on his heel, and left me.

Here I was in a nice position. To all intents and purposes I had aided and abetted a murder, and if any of Berringer's crew should care to turn Queen's evidence I should find myself in the dock, a convicted murderer. In vain I set my wits to work to try and find some scheme which might save the wretched man and myself. I could discover none, however.

All the next day we sailed on, heading for the Northern Australian Coast, so it seemed to me. I met the Captain at meals, and upon the deck, but he appeared morose and sullen, gave his orders in peremptory jerks, and never once, so far as I heard, alluded to the unhappy man below. I attempted to broach the subject to the mate, in the hope that he might take the same view of it as I did, but I soon found that my advances in that quarter were not likely to be favourably received. The crew, as I soon discovered, were Kanakas, with two exceptions, and devoted to their Captain. I was quite certain that they would do nothing but what he wished. Such a Christmas Eve I sincerely trust I may never spend again.

Late in the afternoon I bearded the Captain in his cabin, and once more endeavoured to induce him to think well before committing such an act. Ten minutes later I was back in the cuddy, a wiser and sadder man. From that moment I resigned myself to the inevitable.

At half-past six that evening the Captain and I dined together in solitary state. Afterwards I went on deck. It was a beautiful moonlight night, with scarcely enough wind to fill the canvas. The sea was as smooth as glass, with a long train of phosphorous light in our wake. I had seen nothing of the skipper since eight bells. At about ten o'clock, however, and just as I was thinking of turning in, he emerged from the companion. A few strides brought him to my side.

'A fine night, Riddington,' he said, in a strange, hard voice, very unlike his usual tone.

'A very fine night,' I answered.

'Riddington,' he began again, with sudden vehemence, 'do you believe in ghosts?'

'I have never thought much about the matter,' I answered. 'Why do you ask?'

'Because I've seen a ghost tonight,' he replied. 'The ghost of my brother Bernard, who was hanged by that man locked in the cabin below, exactly a year ago, at daybreak. Don't make any mistake about what I'm saying. You can feel my pulse, if you like, and you will find it beating as steady as ever it has done in my life. I haven't touched a drop of liquor today, and I honestly believe I'm as sane a man as there is in the world. Yet I tell you that, not a quarter of an hour ago, my brother stood beside me in my cabin.'

Not knowing what answer to make, I held my tongue for the moment. At last I spoke.

'Did he say anything?' I inquired.

'He told me that I should not be permitted to execute my vengeance on Van der Vaal! It was to be left to him to deal with him. But I've passed my word, and I'll not depart from it. Ghost or no ghost, he hangs at sunrise.'

So saying, he turned and walked away from me, and went below.

I am not going to pretend that I slept that night. Of one thing I am quite certain, and that is that the Captain did not leave his cabin all night. Half an hour before daybreak, however, he came to my cabin.

'Come on deck,' he said. 'The time is up.'

I followed him, to find all the ghastly preparations complete. Once more I pleaded for mercy with all the strength at my command, and once more I failed to move him. Even the vision he had declared he had seen seemed now to be forgotten.

'Bring him on deck,' he said at last, turning to the mate and handing him the key of the cabin as he spoke. The other disappeared, and I, unable to control myself, went to the side of the vessel and looked down at the still water below. The brig was scarcely moving. Presently I heard the noise of feet in the companion, and turning, with a white face, no doubt, I saw the mate and two of the hands emerge from the hatchway. They approached the Captain, who seemed not to see them. To the amazement of everyone, he was looking straight before him across the poop, with an expression of indescribable terror on his face. Then, with a crash, he lost his balance and fell forward upon the deck. We ran to his assistance, but were too late. He was dead.

Who shall say what he had seen in that terrible half-minute? The mate and I looked at each other in stupefied bewilderment. I was the first to find my voice.

'The General?'

'Dead,' the other replied. 'He died as we entered the cabin to fetch him out. God help me – you never saw such a sight! It looked as if he were fighting with someone whom we could not see, and was being slowly strangled.'

I waited to hear no more, but turned and walked aft. I am not a superstitious man, but I felt that the Captain's brother had been right after all, when he had said that he would take the matter of revenge into his own hands.

THE GREEN BOTTLE

and

AN EDDY ON THE FLOOR

by

Bernard Capes

And to close our tour of the gas-lit graveyard, two stories from an author I consider the most exciting 'discovery' I have made during my researches into the Victorian era, and one whose complete obscurity over the past sixty years is totally without justification.

Bernard Capes was one of the Victorian period's most prolific contributors to magazines, his work appearing in (among others) The Illustrated London News, Pearson's Weekly, Cornhill Magazine, Macmillan's, Lippincott's and The Sketch. His first novel was the delightfully titled The Adventures of the Comte de la Muette During the Reign of Terror (1898), published in Edinburgh. He wrote over thirty-five books, the last being the post-humous novel The Skeleton Key (1919). Capes died in Winchester on 2 November 1918 after a brief illness.

But of all his works, it seems to me that his ghost stories were his finest – and they have been completely overlooked by antholo-gists, probably since his death and perhaps even before. You will not find the name of Bernard Capes in any history of the English ghost story; I hope my use of his work will alter this.

The best of his stories can be found in the five collections At a Winter's Fire (1899), From Door to Door (1900), Plots (1902), Bag and Baggage (1913), and The Fabulists (1915). 'The Green Bottle' comes from Plots and 'An Eddy on the Floor' from At a Winter's Fire. The first story is a gentle fantasy that turns abruptly to suggested but sharp horror; the second is a long ghost story of supernatural vengeance with some gruesome special effects. As far as I am concerned, Bernard Capes was as fine a writer of macabre stories as the Victorian era ever produced; I think you will agree with me.

THE GREEN BOTTLE

My knowledge of Sewell was principally of a fox-nosed, weedy, scorbutic youth who wrote four-to-the-pound pars for the Daily Record. Further, I bore in mind his flaccid palms, his dropping underjaw, and the way in which in Fleet Street bars he would hang – looking, indeed, rather like a wet towel – on the words of any Captain Bobadil of his craft who would condescend to wipe his boots on him, or, for the matter of that, his foul mouth. He had no principles, I think. He was born lacking the sentiments of pride and decency. If he was kicked into the mud, he would make, before rising, a little conciliatory gift of mud pie for the kicker. On close terms with the petty ailments of his own body, the secret discoveries that delighted him were of similar weaknesses in others. The prescriptively unmentionable was his humour's best inspiration; his belief in the real approval underlying the affected disgust of his hearers quite genuine. He was, in short, a sort of editors' pimp, with all the taste and the instinct to *procure* 'copy', in the detestable sense.

At one time he elected, to my sorrow, to attach himself to me, with this justification (from his point of view) that I then happened to be grinding my literary barrel-organ – always adaptable to the popular need – to the tune of a contemporary interest in the problems of criminology; and the mudlark, being himself of a Newgate complexion of mind, had the assurance in consequence to assume a sympathetic bond between us. Now, the difficulty being to convince Sewell that decency was ever anything but a diplomatic pose, and that one did not pursue vice, as dogs hunt foxes, because of the mere bestial attraction to an abominable scent, but with the sole purpose to reach and end the offence, I was led, more contemptuously than wisely, into allowing the assumption of claim by default, with the result that for some weeks the unsavoury thing stuck to me like a jigger. Then, at the climax of the annoyance, just when I had resolved, as an anthropological economy, upon dissecting my torment or himself as the closest possible illustration of my meaning, of a sudden the creature vanished – disappeared *sans phrase*; and Fleet Street and the Daily Record knew no more.

The fact was that Mr Sewell had been left a competence, and had retired into private life.

I did not see the fellow again for some eighteen months, when, one afternoon, he visited me quite unexpectedly at my lodgings. He accepted, as of old, the finger I committed to his clasp, and which I then – hardly covertly, under my desk – wrenched dry between my knees. He was scarcely altered in appearance. The only accent of difference that I could observe was in his tie, which was a spotted burglarious-looking token, in place of the rusty-black wisp that had been wont to depend, loosely knotted, from his neck. For the rest, he was the slack, unwholesome figure, with the sniggering and inward manner, of my knowledge. And yet, scanned again, there was something unusual about him after all – a suggestion, it might be, of excited nervousness, such as one might imagine in a very fulsome Paul Pry bursting, while fearing, to retail a ticklish piece of scandal.

'Well,' I said, after some indifferent commonplaces, 'so you've got your ticket-of-leave? And aren't your fingers itching, in a vacuous freedom, for oakum and the Fleet Street crank again?'

'Oh, Mr Deering,' says he, tittering and twisting, 'I like that metaphor. I come to report myself to you, Mr Deering.'

'H'mph!' said I. 'Well, when all's said, how *do* you manage to kill time?'

'Why, I kill it,' says he, grinning, 'and I lay it out. It's only necessary to have an object in life, Mr Deering. Mine's killing time, that I may lay it out. You'll never guess what I've become.'

'I'll make one shot. A body-snatcher.'

'Tee-hee! Not so far wrong. A collector, Mr Deering. I wish you'd come and see my museum. Will you have dinner with me tonight?'

'Not to be thought of. See here and here! In fact, I've already given you longer than I can spare. Goodbye, till our next meeting. If I'm on the jury, I'll try to forget the worst I know of you.'

He rose, fidgeted, still lingered.

'I do wish you'd dine with me.'

'I tell you I can't. Besides, I'm particular – it's a fad of mine – about my alimentary atmosphere. An unwholesome one balks my digestion.'

I began to be annoyed that the fellow would not go. Suddenly he turned upon me, with more decision than he had yet shown.

'The fact is something – something very odd has happened; quite impossible, you'd say. I don't know; if you'd only come and look.'

I did look – at him – in surprise.

'Odd – that concerns me? Why not tell me now, then?'

'You'd never believe unless you saw.'

'Saw! Saw what? Why, I'm hanged if, by the jaw of you, you aren't thinking to come the supernatural over me!'

'Yes,' he said, fawningly persistent; 'I want you to see. It's a case of horrors or nothing. You'll be able to judge, as you've made it your line.'

'I've done no such thing. I never raised a banshee yet that would deceive so much as a psychist.'

'Well,' said he, 'that's another inducement. You'd not be predisposed to the infection.'

'Infection!' I shouted. 'What, the devil! You've not been laying-out in earnest!'

He wriggled over a laugh.

'No,' said he. 'I meant the infection of fear.'

'Oh, trust me there!' said I.

This was so far a concession that, under the stimulus of a curiosity the creature had succeeded in arousing in me, I presently accepted, though grudgingly, his invitation. Then he took himself away, and I went on with my work – rather peevishly, for there was a bad taste in my mouth, that I endeavoured unsuccessfully to neutralise with tobacco.

At seven o'clock I packed away and went, depressed, to keep my engagement. It was a July evening of that unsavoury closeness that paints faces with a metallic sweat, and vulgarises out of all picturesqueness the motley concerns of life; an evening when fat women are truculent at omnibus doors; when the brassy twang of piano-organs blends indescribably with the sour stench of the roads; when a dive into a sequestered bar brings no consequence as of virtue refreshed, but rather as of self-indulgence rebuked with an added dyspepsia. And, appropriate to the atmosphere, my goal was in that inferno of dreary unfulfilments, Notting Hill. Thither I made my way, and there in the end house of a stuccoed and lifeless-looking terrace, converted (by an S.A. missionary, one might, from its vulgarity, suppose) into flats, came presently to a stop.

There was a bill 'To Let' in the ground-floor window, from which, by inference, my host was engaged to the upper rooms. He himself greeted me at the front door, to which I had mounted by a dozen of ill-laid steps. A second door within, set in a make-shift partition, opened straight upon the stairway that led up to his quarters.

'I hope you won't object to a cold collation, Mr Deering?' said he.

The stairs were so steep, and he looked so down upon me, twisting about from the height at which he led, that his white face seemed to hang like a clammy stone gargoyle from the gloom.

'I wouldn't suggest it's what you're accustomed to,' he said; 'but when one's only slavey goes out with the daylight, and doesn't return till the milk, it can't be helped, you know.'

'It's all right,' I said brusquely, and rudely enough, to be sure. 'I never supposed you kept a retinue. You're the only soul in the house, I conclude?'

We had come to a landing, where the stairs gave a wheel and went up, carpetless, steeper than ever. Looking aloft, it was some unmeaning comfort to me to observe that a skylight, obscured by dirt, took the slope of the ceiling with a wan sheen as of phosphorescence.

Two doorways, a step or so apart, faced us entering upon the landing. Through the nearest of these I caught glimpse of a white tablecloth and our meal set upon it. The second, and further, door, that was opposite the turn of the stairs, was shut.

'Eh!' said Sewell, with a curious intonation. 'The only soul, eh? Well, upon my word, I won't answer for that.'

'What the devil do you mean?' I exclaimed irritably.

'Why,' he answered, propitiatory at once, 'the rooms below are tenantless, if that's what you refer to.'

'What else should I refer to?'

'To be sure, to be sure,' he answered. 'Oh, yes; I'm the only one in possession! I don't mind. Generally speaking – there may be something now and again that makes a difference, you know – but, generally speaking, I think I've got the collector's love of solitude. We sort of hug ourselves over our finds, don't we? and then it isn't nice to have anybody else by, eh? That's my museum – that second door. I'd like you, if you don't mind, just to go cursorily round it now, before we sit down, and see what sort of an impression it makes on you.'

'Is your rotten mystery connected with it?'

'Well, yes, it is.'

'Lead on, then, and let's get it over.'

He obeyed, opening the door gingerly to its full width before entering, as if he half expected something to be there before him. I uttered an instant grunt. A row of unclean faces, their upper prominences so covered with dust as to give one the impression of their posturing over some infernal kind of footlights, leered down upon us from the top of a high bookcase.

'Yes,' said Sewell, though I had not spoken to him, 'they're a pretty lot, aren't they, Mr Deering? I picked 'em up at the Vandal sale – the lunatic specialist, don't you remember, that went mad and cut his own throat in the end? I don't know half their stories; but when I'm in the mood I sit here and try to piece 'em out of their faces. That fellow with the fat wale on his neck, now –'

'Oh, shut your imagination, you anthropophagist! Here, we'll hurry up with this. I see, I see. Absolutely characteristic; and I might have guessed the bent of your virtuosity.'

I found a precursory inspection more than sufficient. The creature had only found himself out of independence. He was become logically an Old Bailey curioso. His collection, disposed about the shelves of that same bookless bookcase and on little tables and whatnots, ranged from housebreakers' tools (miracles of vicious elegance) to a slip from a C.C. open spaces seat, on the branch of a tree above which a suicide had hanged himself. There were murderous revolvers, together with the bullets extracted from their victims. There were knives, lengths of Newgate rope, last confessions, photographs, and bloodstains. And, in inviting me to the discussion of this garbage, Sewell, I believe, was actuated by no inhumanity of malevolence. An unnatural appetite is normal to itself, I suppose.

But all the time his manner was *distrait* – spasmodic – watchful, and not of me, I could have thought.

All at once I felt myself constrained to rise from an examination, and to walk to the window. It looked across to the sordid backs of other converted houses; it looked down into a well of a garden, choked with rank grass, from the jungle of which stiff ears of dockweed stood up, as if picked to the French casement, that I could not see, in the room below. Now the tall buildings so blocked out the sunset that, although day still ruled, the room in which we stood was already appropriated to a livid twilight. I tugged at the window, striving to open it.

'What are you trying?' cried Sewell. 'What are you up to? What's the matter with you?'

He hurried across the room. He looked curiously into my face, as if for confirmation of some hope or fear of his own.

'You can't do it,' he said. 'It's been nailed up. Look here, Mr Deering, we'll feed, shall we?'

'Yes,' I snarled. I was furious with myself. I walked out of the room as stiff as, and bristling like, a baited cat. For the moment I was exalted above the impulse to put my tail between my legs.

Sewell's cold collation was vile. I swear it, though no sybarite, in some explanation of a subsequent nightmare. Macbeth hadn't supped when he saw the ghost of Banquo. How many ghosts he would have seen after a slice of Sewell's steak pie is conjectural. At the fourth mouthful I put down (I might have, dietetically, with scarce more discomfort to myself) my knife and fork.

'Is that beastly door shut?' I said crossly.

He knew, without my explaining, that I meant the door of the museum.

'Yes,' he answered, impervious to my rudeness, and offered no further remark. But, perhaps from a like sentiment of oppression, he turned up the gas above the table.

I made another effort at the pie, and finally desisted.

'Look here,' I said, falling back in my chair, and streaking down the damp hair on my forehead, 'I'm not a fool. D'you hear? I'm not a fool, I say. I want to know, that's all. What the devil's the matter with that bottle?'

'Ah!' he breathed out, with a curious under-inflexion of relief, or triumph. 'The bottle; yes; I thought you'd come to it.'

'Did you, indeed? So that's your Asian mystery?'

'Yes, that's it,' he said quietly. 'You've found it out, Mr Deering, and I wasn't mistaken, it seems.'

'Mistaken? I don't know. What's the matter with it? What infernal trick have you been planning? Take care!' I said bullyingly.

'Shall we go and look at it again?'

He only answered with the soft question.

I half rose, fought with myself, yielded, and dropped back.

'I'm damned if I do,' I said, 'until you've told me.'

'Very well,' he replied, slinkingly moved to govern and applaud me in a breath. 'I'll tell you at once, Mr Deering.'

He felt in his inner breast-pocket, produced a memorandum-book, withdrew a newspaper cutting from it, rose, and crossing to me, placed the slip in my hand. Accepting it sullenly, and taking my reason by the ears, I forced that to focus itself on the lines. They were headed and ran as follows:

THE LAMBETH TRAGEDY

'Mr. Hobbins, the south-western district coroner, held an inquest yesterday on the body of Ephraim Ellis, glass-blower, who, as has been stated, fell down dead at the very moment that the officers of justice entered the premises of his employers, Messrs. Mackay, to arrest him on suspicion of having caused the death of Francis Riddick, a fellow-workman. Ellis, it will be remembered, was actually engaged in blowing bottles at the moment of his arrest. A verdict of death from syncope, resulting on shock, was returned.'

Sewell stood behind me as I read. His long, ropy claw slid over my shoulder, and a finger of it traced along the words 'it will be remembered'.

'Yes,' I muttered, in response to the unspoken query, 'I recollect reading something about it. What then?'

Sewell's finger went on five – six letters, and stopped.

'He was "blowing bottles,"' he said. 'He *was*, Mr Deering. I was standing by him at the time, and he was blowing that very green bottle you saw on the table in the next room. Do you know how they do it? They dip the end of their pipe into the melting-pot that sits in the furnace, and then, having rolled the little knob they've fished up tube-shaped on an iron plate, and pinched it for a neck, they take and blow it into a brass mould until it fits out the shape of the thing. Then they open the mould, and the bottle comes free, but stuck to the pipe, until a touch with a cold iron snaps the two apart. That's the way; but this bottle, you'll say, has a neck like a retort. I'll tell you why, Mr Deering. Ellis had just blown the thing complete, when the policeman put a hand on his shoulder. The pipe was at his mouth. He gave a last gasp into it and went down, the soft bottle-neck bending and sealing itself as the falling pipe dragged it over. Very well; I'd known the

man and something of his story, and I brought away the green
bottle, just as he'd left it, for a memento. But, Mr Deering, I
brought away that in it that I hadn't bargained for. Can't you
guess what it was?'

'No.'

'Why, Ellis's soul, Mr Deering, that passed into it with that last
gasp of his, and was sealed up for anyone that likes to let it out.'

I got to my feet, driven beyond endurance.

'You ass!' I cried. 'Have you drivelled to an end?'

'Oh, dear no!' he whispered, with a little nervous but defiant
chuckle. 'Now, you know, don't you, Mr Deering, that there's
something uncommon about – about that out there? Perhaps you'll
be able to explain it. It was in the hope that I asked you (who've
made such a study of psychological phenomena) to endure my
company for a night. And, to tell you the truth, there's something
more and worse. Wouldn't you like to hear about it, Mr
Deering?'

'Oh, go on!' I said, with a groan. 'I've accepted my company,
as you say, and –'

'Won't you come further from the door?' he asked, truckling
to and hating me, as I believed. 'I can see you aren't comfortable,
and no wonder.'

I ground my teeth on a curse, and slouching to the mantelpiece,
put my back against it. A blue-bottle, droning heavily in labour,
whirled about the room and settled with a buzzing flop on the pie.
The cessation of its fulsome chaunt seemed to embolden unseen
things to stir and giggle in the dark corners of the room.

'*Aren't* you going on?' I said desperately.

'Yes,' he answered; 'I'm going on. From first to last I'll tell you
everything, and then you can form your own conclusions. Mr
Deering, I'd got to know, as I said, the man Ephraim Ellis. How,
don't particularly matter. I'm fond of prowling about at night. I
make acquaintances, and pick up things that interest me. This man
did. There was something suggestive about him – something
haunted, as I'd like to put it. He kept company at one time with a
slavey of mine that died of fits (I've seen her in 'em), and perhaps
that led to my following him up to his work-place and getting
into talk with him. He was a glass-blower, and on night duty.
A queer customer he was, and dark and secret as sin. Sometimes
I'd look at him, red and shifty in the glow, and I'd think, "Are

you calculating the consequences, my friend, of braining me with a white-hot bottle?" He may have been, more than you'd fancy; for I believe the man took me for an unclean spirit sent to goad him to further desperations. "Further", I say; but, mind you, I only go by report. It would never do, would it, Mr Deering, for you and me to be certain, or they might claim us for accessories?' I broke into a hoarse, angry exclamation.

'No, no,' he interrupted me hurriedly, 'of course they couldn't. It was only my fun. But the truth is, Ellis's fellow-workmen were fully persuaded that Ellis had murdered Riddick, who had been found one morning, after he'd relieved Ellis at solitary night duty, with his head melted and run away against the door of a furnace. I don't know; and I don't know what they went upon, seeing the trunk was all right, and that there was no head to examine for trace of injuries. But they made out their suspicions – on technical grounds, I suppose; and, as to the moral – why, Riddick, by their showing, had been a taunting devil, a regular bad lot, who'd made a game of baiting Ellis till he drove the man almost to madness. Anyhow, Ellis was marked down by them, and given the cold shoulder of fear; and so he worked apart (for he was too valuable a hand to be dismissed) – he worked apart – with only me, I really believe, in the wide world to speak to him, until the police, acting upon rumours, or the shadows of 'em, came to lay hands on him.

'But now, I must tell you, before that happened there was something else occurred that was more intimate to the moral, if not to the circumstantial, point. Ellis took to having fits, or seizures, in which he'd rave that Riddick hadn't been got rid of after all, but that he'd all of a sudden be there again, and burrowing into him, and hanging on inside like a bat under ivy, while he'd whisper into his soul blasphemies not fit to be mentioned. He'd not lose his senses – what he's got of 'em – in these states; but he'd sit down staring, with a face on him as if he'd swallowed a live eel. Sometimes I could have burst with laughter at the sight. And then, once upon a time, Mr Deering, he took me all in a moment into his confidence, as I may say. And it was like a deathbed confession, for that night the police came and finished him.

'I had been standing by, watching him at work, when he broke off for a drink of water. The common tap was in a little yard at the back of the premises, and as he went out to it I fancied he beckoned me to follow him. Anyhow, I did, and faced him there

under the starlight. I'm only speaking of three nights ago, so you
may believe the whole thing sticks pretty vividly in my memory.
'He glanced up as I stood before him.
' "Why do you follow me?" he says in a low voice. "Why do
you come and stand there and look at me? Are you Riddick?
My God, I'll melt your head like wax if you are!" says he.
' "Why, Mr Ellis," says I, taken aback, till I jumped to the
humour of the thing, "if Riddick grips you, as he has done, while
I'm looking on, I can't be Riddick, can I?"
' "No, that's true," he says. "What do you want with me, then?"
And, "Oh, my God!" he says, in such a Hamlet's ghost voice as
would have set you sniggering, "can you stand by and see a soul
raving in the grip of damnation and not offer to help it?"
' "Mr Ellis," I answered, "does Riddick really come to you like
that?"
' "He comes and clutches me," he said, "as he clutched me when
he was alive. He holds me and claims me to his own wickedness,
and I must listen and listen, and can't get away. I want to escape,
and he clings on and whispers. And if I strike him down, and
melt his bloody battered face into glass, there he is in a little while
up and at my soul again, struggling with it in my throat, lest it get
away from him and fly free with some last breath I put into my
work."
'He looked at me in a death's-head kind of manner, and I had a
business, as you may guess, Mr Deering, not to explode in his face.
'Well, after a minute he turns round, with a groan, and goes
back to his work. And I followed, as you may suppose.
'Now, he was at his bottles once more, and me standing by
him, when all of a sudden he put down his pipe, and his face
was like soapy pumice-stone.
' "He's entered into me! He's got me again!" he whispered in a
voice like choking.
' "Go on with your work, as if you didn't know," says I, choking
too, though for a different reason. "Then you'll be able to take him
off his guard and blow him out into a bottle."
'I thought that was too tall, even for his reach. But, Mr Deering –
would you believe it? – the mug actually made a run and scramble
to do as I told him. Only I suppose Riddick was holding on so
tight that, when he blew, the two, himself and the other, came
away together. Anyhow, there's the consequences in the next

room – sealed and untouched, as it was left from the corpse's mouth; for the police took him while he was near bursting himself over that, the very last bottle he was ever to mould.'

He brought himself to a stop with a feculent chuckle. Then: 'What you'll judge it to be, I can't tell,' he went on. 'It's as funny as fits, whatever it may mean. I know, for myself, I'd sooner sit and watch it – on the right side of the glass – than I would a little fish in an aquarium setting himself to catch, and lose, and catch again, and suck down by fractions a huge, wriggling worm.'

I came away from the mantelpiece. The room seemed a swimming vortex. I have a notion that I cursed Sewell for an unnamable carrion. But, if I did, my loathing and horror hit him without effect. I can only remember that we were in the museum again, that dusk had gathered there heavy and opaque; and then suddenly Sewell had lit a candle, and was holding it behind the thing on the table, while he invited me with a gesture to advance and inspect.

It was an ordinary claret bottle, but distorted at the neck. The light struck into and through it. And I looked, and saw that its milky-greenness was in never-ceasing motion.

'There they are!' whispered Sewell gluttonously. 'Look, Mr Deering, mightn't it be the worm and the fish, now!' . . .

A little palpitating, shuddering blot of terror, human and inhuman; now distended, as if gasping in a momentary respite; now crouching and hugging itself into a shapeless ball, and always steadily, untiringly followed and sprung upon by the thing that had the appearance, through the semi-opaque glass, of a shambling, fat-lidded . . .

Something gave in me, and with a sobbing snarl I caught the bottle up in my hand.

'Mr Deering!' cried Sewell, 'Mr Deering! what are you going to do?'

'Stand back!' I shrieked, 'stand back!'

He ran round at me, with a little nervous gobble of laughter. 'Don't!' he cried. 'Let's take it away and bury it.'

He caught at my arm, but I flung him aside madly, and with all my force dashed the horror to the floor.

A moment's silence succeeded the ringing crash.

'Oh,' whispered Sewell, giggling, 'listen! It's going up the stairs after the other – there's something beating on the skylight!'

I tore on to the landing. There was a sound as if some sprawling, bloated body were climbing the bare treads in a series of scrambling flops. Higher, it might have been a great moth that fluttered frenziedly against the glass.

The cord of the light hung down to my hand. I wrenched at it demoniacally, and the glass above swung open with a scream.

A whir, receding into the faint stinging whine of a distant organ, vibrated overhead and was gone. Something on the upper stairs – something unseen and shocking – turned, and began to descend towards me. And at that I wheeled, and rushed staggering for escape and release, leaving Sewell to finish conclusions with what remained.

AN EDDY ON THE FLOOR

I had the pleasure of an invitation to one of those reunions or séances at the house, in a fashionable quarter, of my distant connection, Lady Barbara Grille, whereat it was my hostess's humour to gather together those many birds of alien feather and incongruous habit that will flock from the hedgerows to the least little flattering crumb of attention. And scarce one of them but thinks the simple feast is spread for him alone. And with so cheap a bait may a title lure.

That reference to so charming a personality should be in this place is a digression. She affects my narrative only inasmuch as I happened to meet at her house a gentleman who for a time exerted a considerable influence over my fortunes.

The next morning after the séance, my landlady entered with a card, which she presented to my consideration:

MAJOR JAMES SHRIKE,
H.M. PRISON, D——

All astonishment, I bade my visitor up.

He entered briskly, fur-collared, hat in hand, and bowed as he stood on the threshold. He was a very short man – snub-nosed; rusty-whiskered; indubitably and unimpressively a cockney in appearance. He might have walked out of a Cruikshank etching.

I was beginning, 'May I inquire –' when the other took me up with a vehement frankness that I found engaging at once.

'This is a great intrusion. Will you pardon me? I heard some remarks of yours last night that deeply interested me. I obtained your name and address from our hostess, and took the liberty of –'

'Oh! pray be seated. Say no more. My kinswoman's introduction is all-sufficient. I am happy in having caught your attention in so motley a crowd.'

'She doesn't – forgive the impertinence – take herself seriously enough.'

'Lady Barbara? Then you've found her out?'

'Ah! – you're not offended?'

'Not in the least.'

'Good. It was a motley assemblage, as you say. Yet I'm inclined to think I found my pearl in the oyster. I'm afraid I interrupted – eh?'

'No, no, not at all. Only some idle scribbling. I'd finished.'

'You are a poet?'

'Only a lunatic. I haven't taken my degree.'

'Ah! it's a noble gift – the gift of song; precious through its rarity.'

I caught a note of emotion in my visitor's voice, and glanced at him curiously.

'Surely,' I thought, 'that vulgar, ruddy little face is transfigured.'

'But,' said the stranger, coming to earth, 'I am lingering beside the mark. I must try to justify my solecism in manners by a straight reference to the object of my visit. That is, in the first instance, a matter of business.'

'Business!'

'I am a man with a purpose, seeking the hopefullest means to an end. Plainly: if I could procure you the post of resident doctor at D— gaol, would you be disposed to accept it?'

I looked my utter astonishment.

'I can affect no surprise at yours,' said the visitor. 'It is perfectly natural. Let me forestall some unnecessary expression of it. My offer seems unaccountable to you, seeing that we never met until last night. But I don't move entirely in the dark. I have ventured in the interval to inform myself as to the details of your career. I was entirely one with much of your expression of opinion as to the treatment of criminals, in which you controverted the crude and unpleasant scepticism of the lady you talked with. Combining the two, I come to the immediate conclusion that you are the man for my purpose.'

'You have dumbfounded me. I don't know what to answer. You have views, I know, as to prison treatment. Will you sketch them? Will you talk on, while I try to bring my scattered wits to a focus?'

'Certainly I will. Let me, in the first instance, recall to you a few words of your own. They ran somewhat in this fashion: Is not the man of practical genius the man who is most apt at solving the little problems of resourcefulness in life? Do you remember them?'

'Perhaps I do, in a cruder form.'

'They attracted me at once. It is upon such a postulate I base my practice. Their moral is this: To know the antidote the moment the snake bites. That is to have the intuition of divinity. We shall rise to it some day, no doubt, and climb the hither side of the new Olympus. Who knows? Over the crest the spirit of creation may be ours.'

I nodded, still at sea, and the other went on with a smile:

'I once knew a world-famous engineer with whom I used to breakfast occasionally. He had a patent egg-boiler on the table, with a little double-sided ladle underneath to hold the spirit. He complained that his egg was always undercooked. I said, "Why not reverse the ladle so as to bring the deeper cut uppermost?" He was charmed with my perspicacity. The solution had never occurred to him. You remember, too, no doubt, the story of Coleridge and the horse collar. We aim too much at great developments. If we cultivate resourcefulness, the rest will follow. Shall I state my system *in nuce*? It is to encourage this spirit of resourcefulness.'

'Surely the habitual criminal has it in a marked degree?'

'Yes; but abnormally developed in a single direction. His one object is to out-manœuvre in a game of desperate and immoral chances. The tactical spirit in him has none of the higher ambition. It has felt itself in the degree only that stops at defiance.'

'That is perfectly true.'

'It is half self-conscious of an individuality that instinctively assumes the hopelessness of a recognition by duller intellects. Leaning to resentment through misguided vanity, it falls "all oblique". What is the cure for this? I answer, the teaching of a divine egotism. The subject must be led to a pure devotion to self. What he wishes to respect he must be taught to make beautiful and interesting. The policy of sacrifice to others has so long stunted his moral nature because it is an hypocritical policy. We are responsible to ourselves in the first instance; and to argue an eternal system of blind self-sacrifice is to undervalue the fine gift of individuality. In such he sees but an indefensible policy of force applied to the advantage of the community. He is told to be good – not that he may morally profit, but that others may not suffer inconvenience.'

I was beginning to grasp, through my confusion, a certain clue of meaning in my visitor's rapid utterance. The stranger spoke fluently, but in the dry, positive voice that characterises men of will.

'Pray go on,' I said; 'I am digesting in silence.'

'We must endeavour to lead him to respect of self by showing him what his mind is capable of. I argue on no sectarian, no religious grounds even. Is it possible to make a man's self his most precious possession? Anyhow, I work to that end. A doctor purges before building up with a tonic. I eliminate cant and hypocrisy, and then introduce self-respect. It isn't enough to employ a man's hands only. Initiation in some labour that should prove wholesome and remunerative is a redeeming factor, but it isn't all. His mind must work also, and awaken to its capacities. If it rusts, the body reverts to inhuman instincts.'

'May I ask how you –?'

'By intercourse – in my own person or through my officials. I wish to have only those about me who are willing to contribute to my designs, and with whom I can work in absolute harmony. All my officers are chosen to that end. No doubt a dash of constitutional sentimentalism gives colour to my theories. I get it from a human trait in me that circumstances have obliged me to put a hoarding round.'

'I begin to gather daylight.'

'Quite so. My patients are invited to exchange views with their guardians in a spirit of perfect friendliness; to solve little problems of practical moment; to acquire the pride of self-reliance. We have competitions, such as certain newspapers open to their readers, in a simple form. I draw up the questions myself. The answers give me insight into the mental conditions of the competitors. Upon insight I proceed. I am fortunate in private means, and I am in a position to offer modest prizes to the winners. Whenever such an one is discharged, he finds awaiting him the tools most handy to his vocation. I bid him go forth in no pharisaical spirit, and invite him to communicate with me. I wish the shadow of the gaol to extend no further than the road whereon it lies. Henceforth, we are acquaintances with a common interest at heart. Isn't it monstrous that a state-fixed degree of misconduct should earn a man social ostracism? Parents are generally inclined to rule extra tenderness towards a child whose peccadilloes have brought him a whipping. For myself, I have no faith in police supervision. Give a culprit his term and have done with it. I find the majority who come back to me are ticket-of-leave men.

'Have I said enough? I offer you the reversion of the post. The present holder of it leaves in a month's time. Please to determine here and at once.'

'Very good. I have decided.'

'You will accept?'

'Yes.'

With my unexpected appointment as doctor to D— gaol, I seemed to have put on the seven-league boots of success. No doubt it was an extraordinary degree of good fortune, even to one who had looked forward with a broad view of confidence; yet, I think, perhaps on account of the very casual nature of my promotion, I never took the post entirely seriously.

At the same time I was fully bent on justifying my little cockney patron's choice by a resolute subscription to his theories of prison management.

Major James Shrike inspired me with a curious conceit of impertinent respect. In person the very embodiment of that insignificant vulgarity, without extenuating circumstances, which is the type in caricature of the ultimate cockney, he possessed a force of mind and an earnestness of purpose that absolutely redeemed him on close acquaintanceship. I found him all he had stated himself to be, and something more.

He had a noble object always in view – the employment of sane and humanitarian methods in the treatment of redeemable criminals, and he strove towards it with completely untiring devotion. He was of those who never insist beyond the limits of their own understanding, clear-sighted in discipline, frank in relaxation, an altruist in the larger sense.

His undaunted persistence, as I learned, received ample illustration some few years prior to my acquaintance with him, when – his system being experimental rather than mature – a devastating epidemic of typhoid in the prison had for the time stultified his efforts. He stuck to his post; but so virulent was the outbreak that the prison commissioners judged a complete evacuation of the building and overhauling of the drainage to be necessary. As a consequence, for some eighteen months – during thirteen of which the Governor and his household remained sole inmates of the solitary pile (so sluggishly do we redeem our condemned social bog-lands) – the 'system' stood still for lack of material to mould. At the end of over a year of stagnation, a contract was accepted and workmen put in, and another five months saw the prison re-ordered for practical purposes.

The interval of forced inactivity must have sorely tried the patience of the Governor. Practical theorists condemned to rust too often eat out their own hearts. Major Shrike never referred to this period, and, indeed, laboriously snubbed any allusion to it.

He was, I have a shrewd notion, something of an officially petted reformer. Anyhow, to his abolition of the insensate barbarism of crank and treadmill in favour of civilising methods no opposition was offered. Solitary confinement – a punishment outside all nature to a gregarious race – found no advocate in him. 'A man's own suffering mind,' he argued, 'must be, of all moral food, the most poisonous for him to feed on. Surround a scorpion with fire and he stings himself to death, they say. Throw a diseased soul entirely upon its own resources and moral suicide results.'

To sum up: his nature embodied humanity without sentimentalism, firmness without obstinacy, individuality without selfishness; his activity was boundless, his devotion to his system so real as to admit no utilitarian sophistries into his scheme of personal benevolence. Before I had been with him a week, I respected him as I had never respected man before.

One evening (it was during the second month of my appointment) we were sitting in his private study – a dark, comfortable room

lined with books. It was an occasion on which a new characteristic of the man was offered to my inspection.

A prisoner of a somewhat unusual type had come in that day –
a spiritualistic medium, convicted of imposture. To this person I
casually referred.

'May I ask how you propose dealing with the newcomer?'

'On the familiar lines.'

'But, surely – here we have a man of superior education, of
imagination even?'

'No, no, no! A hawker's opportuneness; that describes it. These
fellows would make death itself a vulgarity.'

'You've no faith in their—'

'Not a tittle. Heaven forfend! A sheet and a turnip are poetry
to their manifestations. It's as crude and sour soil for us to work
on as any I know. We'll cart it wholesale.'

'I take you – excuse my saying so – for a supremely sceptical
man.'

'As to what?'

'The supernatural.'

There was no answer during a considerable interval. Presently
it came, with deliberate insistence:

'It is a principle with me to oppose bullying. We are here for a
definite purpose – his duty plain to any man who *wills* to read it.
There may be disembodied spirits who seek to distress or annoy
where they can no longer control. If there are, mine, which is not
yet divorced from its means to material action, declines to
be influenced by any irresponsible whimsey, emanating from a
place whose denizens appear to be actuated by a mere frivolous
antagonism to all human order and progress.'

'But supposing you, a murderer, to be haunted by the present-
ment of your victim?'

'I will imagine that to be my case. Well, it makes no difference.
My interest is with the great human system, in one of whose veins
I am a circulating drop. It is my business to help to keep the system
sound, to do my duty without fear or favour. If disease – say a
fouled conscience – contaminates me, it is for me to throw off
the incubus, not accept it, and transmit the poison. Whatever my
lapses of nature, I owe it to the entire system to work for purity
in my allotted sphere, and not to allow any microbe bugbear to
ride me roughshod, to the detriment of my fellow drops.'

I laughed.

'It should be for you,' I said, 'to learn to shiver, like the boy in the fairy tale.'

'I cannot,' he answered, with a peculiar quiet smile; 'and yet prisons, above all places, should be haunted.'

Very shortly after his arrival I was called to the cell of the medium, F—. He suffered, by his own statement, from severe pains in the head.

I found the man to be nervous, anaemic; his manner character-ised by a sort of hysterical effrontery.

'Send me to the infirmary,' he begged. 'This isn't punishment, but torture.'

'What are your symptoms?'

'I see things; my case has no comparison with others. To a man of my super-sensitiveness close confinement is mere cruelty.'

I made a short examination. He was restless under my hands.

'You'll stay where you are,' I said.

He broke out into violent abuse, and I left him.

Later in the day I visited him again. He was then white and sullen; but under his mood I could read real excitement of some sort.

'Now, confess to me, my man,' I said, 'what do you see?'

He eyed me narrowly, with his lips a little shaky.

'Will you have me moved if I tell you?'

'I can give no promise till I know.'

He made up his mind after an interval of silence.

'There's something uncanny in my neighbourhood. Who's con-fined in the next cell – there, to the left?'

'To my knowledge it's empty.'

He shook his head incredulously.

'Very well,' I said, 'I don't mean to bandy words with you'; and I turned to go.

At that he came after me with a frightened choke.

'Doctor, your mission's a merciful one. I'm not trying to sauce you. For God's sake have me moved! I can see further than most, I tell you!'

The fellow's manner gave me pause. He was patently and beyond the pride of concealment terrified.

'What do you see?' I repeated stubbornly.

'It isn't that I see, but I know. The cell's *not* empty!'

I stared at him in considerable wonderment.

'I will make inquiries,' I said. 'You may take that for a promise. If the cell proves empty, you stop where you are.'

I noticed that he dropped his hands with a lost gesture as I left him. I was sufficiently moved to accost the warder who awaited me on the spot.

'Johnson,' I said, 'is that cell—'

'Empty, sir,' answered the man sharply and at once.

Before I could respond, F— came suddenly to the door, which I still held open.

'You lying cur!' he shouted. 'You damned lying cur!'

The warder thrust the man back with violence.

'Now you, 49,' he said, 'dry up, and none of your sauce!' and he banged to the door with a sounding slap, and turned to me with a lowering face. The prisoner inside yelped and stormed at the studded panels.

'That cell's empty, sir,' repeated Johnson.

'Will you, as a matter of conscience, let me convince myself? I promised the man.'

'No, I can't.'

'You can't?'

'No, sir.'

'This is a piece of stupid discourtesy. You can have no reason, of course?'

'I can't open it – that's all.'

'Oh, Johnson! Then I must go to the fountainhead.'

'Very well, sir.'

Quite baffled by the man's obstinacy, I said no more, but walked off. If my anger was roused, my curiosity was piqued in proportion.

I had no opportunity of interviewing the Governor all day, but at night I visited him by invitation to play a game of piquet.

He was a man without 'incumbrances' – as a severe conservatism designates the *lares* of the cottage – and, at home, lived at his ease and indulged his amusements without comment.

I found him 'tasting' his books, with which the room was well lined, and drawing with relish at an excellent cigar in the intervals of the courses.

He nodded to me, and held out an open volume in his left hand.

'Listen to this fellow,' he said, tapping the page with his fingers:

' "*The most tolerable sort of Revenge, is for those wrongs which there is no Law to remedy: But then, let a man take heed, the Revenge be such, as there is no law to punish: Else, a man's Enemy, is still before hand, and it is two for one. Some, when they take Revenge, are Desirous the party should know, whence it cometh. This is the more Generous. For the Delight seemeth to be, not so much in doing the Hurt, as in making the Party repent: But Base and Crafty Cowards, are like the Arrow that flyeth in the Dark. Cosmus, Duke of Florence, had a Desperate Saying against Perfidious or Neglecting Friends, as if these wrongs were unpardonable. You shall reade (saith he) that we are commanded to forgive our Enemies: But you never read, that we are commanded to forgive our Friends.*" '

'Is he not a rare fellow?'

'Who?' said I.

'Francis Bacon, who screwed his wit to his philosophy, like a hammer-head to its handle, and knocked a nail in at every blow. How many of our friends round about here would be picking oakum now if they had made a gospel of that quotation?'

'You mean they take no heed that the Law may punish for that for which it gives no remedy?'

'Precisely; and specifically as to revenge. The criminal, from the murderer to the petty pilferer, is actuated solely by the spirit of vengeance – vengeance blind and speechless – towards a system that forces him into a position quite outside his natural instincts.'

'As to that, we have left Nature in the thicket. It is hopeless hunting for her now.'

'We hear her breathing sometimes, my friend. Otherwise Her Majesty's prison locks would rust. But, I grant you, we have grown so unfamiliar with her that we call her simplest manifestations *super*natural nowadays.'

'That reminds me. I visited F— this afternoon. The man was in a queer way – not foxing, in my opinion. Hysteria, probably.'

'Oh! What was the matter with him?'

'The form it took was some absurd prejudice about the next cell – number 47. He swore it was not empty – was quite upset about it – said there was some infernal influence at work in his neighbourhood. Nerves, he finds, I suppose, may revenge themselves on one who has made a habit of playing tricks with them.

To satisfy him, I asked Johnson to open the door of the next
cell—'

'Well?'

'He refused.'

'It is closed by my orders.'

'That settles it, of course. The manner of Johnson's refusal was a
bit uncivil, but – '

He had been looking at me intently all this time – so intently
that I was conscious of a little embarrassment and confusion. His
mouth was set like a dash between brackets, and his eyes glistened.
Now his features relaxed, and he gave a short high neigh of a laugh.

'My dear fellow, you must make allowances for the rough old
lurcher. He was a soldier. He is all cut and measured out to the
regimental pattern. With him Major Shrike, like the king, can do
no wrong. Did I ever tell you he served under me in India? He
did; and, moreover, I saved his life there.'

'In an engagement?'

'Worse – from the bite of a snake. It was a mere question of
will. I told him to wake and walk, and he did. They had thought
him already in *rigor mortis*; and, as for him – well, his devotion
to me since has been single to the last degree.'

'That's as it should be.'

'To be sure. And he's quite in my confidence. You must pass
over the old beggar's churlishness.'

I laughed an assent. And then an odd thing happened. As I spoke,
I had walked over to a bookcase on the opposite side of the room
to that on which my host stood. Near this bookcase hung a mirror
– an oblong affair, set in brass *repoussé* work – on the wall; and,
happening to glance into it as I approached, I caught sight of the
Major's reflection as he turned his face to follow my movement.

I say 'turned his face' – a formal description only. What met my
startled gaze was an image of some nameless horror – of features
grooved, and battered, and shapeless, as if they had been torn by
a wild beast.

I gave a little indrawn gasp and turned about. There stood the
Major, plainly himself, with a pleasant smile on his face.

'What's up?' said he.

He spoke abstractedly, pulling at his cigar; and I answered
rudely, 'That's a damned bad looking-glass of yours!'

'I didn't know there was anything wrong with it,' he said, still abstracted and apart. And, indeed, when by sheer mental effort I forced myself to look again, there stood my companion as he stood in the room.

I gave a tremulous laugh, muttered something or nothing, and fell to examining the books in the case. But my fingers shook a trifle as I aimlessly pulled out one volume after another.

'Am *I* getting fanciful?' I thought – 'I whose business it is to give practical account of every bugbear of the nerves. Bah! My liver must be out of order. A speck of bile in one's eye may look a flying dragon.'

I dismissed the folly from my mind, and set myself resolutely to inspecting the books marshalled before me. Roving amongst them, I pulled out, entirely at random, a thin, worn duodecimo, that was thrust well back at a shelf end, as if it shrank from comparison with its prosperous and portly neighbours. Nothing but chance impelled me to the choice; and I don't know to this day what the ragged volume was about. It opened naturally at a marker that lay in it – a folded slip of paper, yellow with age; and glancing at this, a printed name caught my eye.

With some stir of curiosity, I spread the slip out. It was a title-page to a volume, of poems, presumably; and the author was James Shrike.

I uttered an exclamation, and turned, book in hand.

'An author!' I said. '*You* an author, Major Shrike!'

To my surprise, he snapped round upon me with something like a glare of fury on his face. This the more startled me as I believed I had reason to regard him as a man whose principles of conduct had long disciplined a temper that was naturally hasty enough.

Before I could speak to explain, he had come hurriedly across the room and had rudely snatched the paper out of my hand.

'How did this get – ' he began; then in a moment came to himself, and apologised for his ill manners.

'I thought every scrap of the stuff had been destroyed,' he said, and tore the page into fragments. 'It is an ancient effusion, doctor – perhaps the greatest folly of my life; but it's something of a sore subject with me, and I shall be obliged if you'll not refer to it again.'

He courted my forgiveness so frankly that the matter passed without embarrassment; and we had our game and spent a genial evening together. But memory of the queer little scene stuck in my mind, and I could not forbear pondering it fitfully.

Surely here was a new side-light that played upon my friend and superior a little fantastically.

Conscious of a certain vague wonder in my mind, I was traversing the prison, lost in thought, after my sociable evening with the Governor, when the fact that dim light was issuing from the open door of cell number 49 brought me to myself and to a pause in the corridor outside.

Then I saw that something was wrong with the cell's inmate, and that my services were required.

The medium was struggling on the floor, in what looked like an epileptic fit, and Johnson and another warder were holding him from doing an injury to himself.

The younger man welcomed my appearance with relief.

'Heard him guggling,' he said, 'and thought as something were up. You come timely, sir.'

More assistance was procured, and I ordered the prisoner's removal to the infirmary. For a minute, before following him, I was left alone with Johnson.

'It came to a climax, then?' I said, looking the man steadily in the face.

'He may be subject to 'em, sir,' he replied evasively.

I walked deliberately up to the closed door of the adjoining cell, which was the last on that side of the corridor. Huddled against the massive end wall, and half embedded in it, as it seemed, it lay in a certain shadow, and bore every sign of dust and disuse. Looking closely, I saw that the trap in the door was not only firmly bolted, but *screwed into its socket*.

I turned and said to the warder quietly –

'Is it long since this cell was in use?'

'You're very fond of asking questions,' he answered doggedly.

It was evident he would baffle me by impertinence rather than yield a confidence. A queer insistence had seized me – a strange desire to know more about this mysterious chamber. But, for all my curiosity, I flushed at the man's tone.

'You have your orders,' I said sternly, 'and do well to hold by them. I doubt, nevertheless, if they include impertinence to your superiors.'

'I look straight on my duty, sir,' he said, a little abashed. 'I don't wish to give offence.'

He did not, I feel sure. He followed his instinct to throw me off the scent, that was all.

I strode off in a fume, and after attending F— in the infirmary, went promptly to my own quarters.

I was in an odd frame of mind, and for long tramped my sitting-room to and fro, too restless to go to bed, or, as an alternative, to settle down to a book. There was a welling up in my heart of some emotion that I could neither trace nor define. It seemed neighbour to terror, neighbour to an intense fainting pity, yet was not distinctly either of these. Indeed, where was cause for one, or the subject of the other? F— might have endured mental sufferings which it was only human to help to end, yet F— was a swindling rogue, who, once relieved, merited no further consideration.

It was not on him my sentiments were wasted. Who, then, was responsible for them?

There was a very plain line of demarcation between the legitimate spirit of inquiry and mere apish curiosity. I could recognise it, I have no doubt, as a rule, yet in my then mood, under the influence of a kind of morbid seizure, inquisitiveness took me by the throat. I could not whistle my mind from the chase of a certain graveyard will-o'-the-wisp; and on it went stumbling and floundering through bog and mire, until it fell into a state of collapse, and was useful for nothing else.

I went to bed and to sleep without difficulty, but I was conscious of myself all the time, and of a shadowless horror that seemed to come stealthily out of corners and to bend over and look at me, and to be nothing but a curtain or a hanging coat when I started and stared.

Over and over again this happened, and my temperature rose by leaps, and suddenly I saw that if I failed to assert myself, and promptly, fever would lap me in a consuming fire. Then in a moment I broke into a profuse perspiration, and sank exhausted into delicious unconsciousness.

Morning found me restored to vigour, but still with the maggot of curiosity in my brain. It worked there all day, and for many subsequent days, and at last it seemed as if my every faculty were honeycombed with its ramifications. Then 'this will not do', I thought, but still the tunnelling process went on.

At first I would not acknowledge to myself what all this mental to-do was about. I was ashamed of my new development, in fact, and nervous, too, in a degree of what it might reveal in the matter of moral degeneration; but gradually, as the curious devil mastered me, I grew into such harmony with it that I could shut my eyes no longer to the true purpose of its insistence. It was the *closed cell* about which my thoughts hovered like crows circling round carrion.

'In the dead waste and middle' of a certain night I awoke with a strange, quick recovery of consciousness. There was the passing of a single expiration, and I had been asleep and was awake. I had gone to bed with no sense of premonition or of resolve in a particular direction; I sat up a monomaniac. It was as if, swelling in the silent hours, the tumour of curiosity had come to a head, and in a moment it was necessary to operate upon it.

I make no excuse for my then condition. I am convinced I was the victim of some undistinguishable force, that I was an agent under the control of the supernatural, if you like. Some thought had been in my mind of late that in my position it was my duty to unriddle the mystery of the closed cell. This was a sop timidly held out to and rejected by my better reason. I sought – and I knew it in my heart – solution of the puzzle, because it was a puzzle with an atmosphere that vitiated my moral fibre. Now, suddenly, I knew I must act, or, by forcing self-control, imperil my mind's stability.

All strung to a sort of exaltation, I rose noiselessly and dressed myself with rapid, nervous hands. My every faculty was focused upon a solitary point. Without and around there was nothing but shadow and uncertainty. I seemed conscious only of a shaft of light, as it were, traversing the darkness and globing itself in a steady disc of radiance on a lonely door.

Slipping out into the great echoing vault of the prison in stockinged feet, I sped with no hesitation of purpose in the direction of the corridor that was my goal. Surely some resolute Providence guided and encompassed me, for no meeting with the night patrol occurred at any point to embarrass or deter me. Like a ghost myself, I flitted along the stone flags of the passages, hardly waking a murmur from them in my progress.

Without, I knew, a wild and stormy wind thundered on the

walls of the prison. Within, where the very atmosphere was self-contained, a cold and solemn peace held like an irrevocable judgement.

I found myself as if in a dream before the sealed door that had for days harassed my waking thoughts. Dim light from a distant gas jet made a patch of yellow upon one of its panels; the rest was buttressed with shadow.

A sense of fear and constriction was upon me as I drew softly from my pocket a screwdriver I had brought with me. It never occurred to me, I swear, that the quest was no business of mine, and that even now I could withdraw from it, and no one be the wiser. But I was afraid – I was afraid. And there was not even the negative comfort of knowing that the neighbouring cell was tenanted. It gaped like a ghostly garret next door to a deserted house.

What reason had I to be there at all, or, being there, to fear? I can no more explain than tell how it was that I, an impartial follower of my vocation, had allowed myself to be tricked by that in the nerves I had made it my interest to study and combat in others.

My hand that held the tool was cold and wet. The stiff little shriek of the first screw, as it turned at first uneasily in its socket, sent a jarring thrill through me. But I persevered, and it came out readily by-and-by, as did the four or five others that held the trap secure.

Then I paused a moment; and, I confess, the quick pant of fear seemed to come grey from my lips. There were sounds about me – the deep breathing of imprisoned men; and I envied the sleepers their hard-wrung repose.

At last, in one access of determination, I put out my hand, and sliding back the bolt, hurriedly flung open the trap. An acrid whiff of dust assailed my nostrils as I stepped back a pace and stood expectant of anything – or nothing. What did I wish, or dread, or foresee? The complete absurdity of my behaviour was revealed to me in a moment. I could shake off the incubus here and now, and be a sane man again.

I giggled, with an actual ring of self-contempt in my voice, as I made a forward movement to close the aperture. I advanced my face to it, and inhaled the sluggish air that stole forth, and – God in heaven!

I had staggered back with that cry in my throat, when I felt fingers like iron clamps close on my arm and hold it. The grip, more than the face I turned to look upon in my surging terror, was forcibly human.

It was the warder Johnson who had seized me, and my heart bounded as I met the cold fury of his eyes.

'Prying!' he said, in a hoarse, savage whisper. 'So you will, will you? And now let the devil help you!'

It was not this fellow I feared, though his white face was set like a demon's; and in the thick of my terror I made a feeble attempt to assert my authority.

'Let me go!' I muttered. 'What! you dare?'

In his frenzy he shook my arm as a terrier shakes a rat, and, like a dog, he held on, daring me to release myself.

For the moment an instinct half-murderous leapt in me. It sank and was overwhelmed in a slough of some more secret emotion.

'Oh!' I whispered, collapsing, as it were, to the man's fury, even pitifully deprecating it. 'What is it? What's there? It drew me – something unnameable.'

He gave a snapping laugh like a cough. His rage waxed second by second. There was a maniacal suggestiveness in it; and not much longer, it was evident, could he have it under control. I saw it run and congest in his eyes; and, on the instant of its accumulation, he tore at me with a sudden wild strength, and drove me up against the very door of the secret cell.

The action, the necessity of self-defence, restored me to some measure of dignity and sanity.

'Let me go, you ruffian!' I cried, struggling to free myself from his grasp.

It was useless. He held me madly. There was no beating him off: and, so holding me, he managed to produce a single key from one of his pockets, and to slip it with a rusty clang into the lock of the door.

'You dirty, prying civilian!' he panted at me, as he swayed this way and that with the pull of my body. 'You shall have your wish, by G—! You want to see inside, do you? Look, then!'

He dashed open the door as he spoke, and pulled me violently into the opening. A great waft of the cold, dank air came at us, and with it – what?

The warder had jerked his dark lantern from his belt, and now –

an arm of his still clasped about one of mine – snapped the slide open.

'Where is it?' he muttered, directing the disc of light round and about the floor of the cell. I ceased struggling. Some counter influence was raising an odd curiosity in me.

'Ah!' he cried, in a stifled voice, 'there you are, my friend!'

He was setting the light slowly travelling along the stone flags close by the wall over against us, and now, so guiding it, looked askance at me with a small, greedy smile.

'Follow the light, sir,' he whispered jeeringly.

I looked, and saw twirling on the floor, in the patch of radiance cast by the lamp, *a little eddy of dust*, it seemed. This eddy was never still, but went circling in that stagnant place without apparent cause or influence; and, as it circled, it moved slowly on by wall and corner, so that presently in its progress it must reach us where we stood.

Now, draughts will play queer freaks in quiet places, and of this trifling phenomenon I should have taken little note ordinarily. But, I must say at once, that as I gazed upon the odd moving thing my heart seemed to fall in upon itself like a drained artery.

'Johnson!' I cried, 'I must get out of this. I don't know what's the matter, or – Why do you hold me? D—n it! man, let me go; let me go, I say!'

As I grappled with him he dropped the lantern with a crash and flung his arms violently about me.

'You don't!' he panted, the muscles of his bent and rigid neck seeming actually to cut into my shoulder-blade. 'You don't, by G—! You came of your own accord, and now you shall take your bellyful!'

It was a struggle for life or death, or, worse, for life and reason. But I was young and wiry, and held my own, if I could do little more. Yet there was something to combat beyond the mere brute strength of the man I struggled with, for I fought in an atmosphere of horror unexplainable, and I knew that inch by inch the *thing* on the floor was circling round in our direction.

Suddenly in the breathing darkness I felt it close upon us, gave one mortal yell of fear, and, with a last despairing fury, tore myself from the encircling arms, and sprang into the corridor without. As I plunged and leapt, the warder clutched at me, missed, caught a foot on the edge of the door, and, as the latter whirled to with a

clap, fell heavily at my feet in a fit. Then, as I stood staring down
upon him, steps sounded along the corridor and the voices of scared
men hurrying up.

Ill and shaken, and, for the time, little in love with life, yet fearing
death as I had never dreaded it before, I spent the rest of that
horrible night huddled between my crumpled sheets, fearing to
look forth, fearing to think, wild only to be far away, to be
housed in some green and innocent hamlet, where I might forget
the madness and the terror in learning to walk the unvext paths of
placid souls. That unction I could lay to my heart, at least. I had
done the manly part by the stricken warder, whom I had attended
to his own home, in a row of little tenements that stood south of
the prison walls. I had replied to all inquiries with some dignity
and spirit, attributing my ruffled condition to an assault on the part
of Johnson, when he was already under the shadow of his seizure.
I had directed his removal, and grudged him no professional attention that it was in my power to bestow. But afterwards, locked
into my room, my whole nervous system broke up like a trodden
ant-hill, leaving me conscious of nothing but an aimless scurrying
terror and the black swarm of thoughts, so that I verily fancied
my reason would give under the strain.

Yet I had more to endure and to triumph over.

Near morning I fell into a troubled sleep, throughout which
the drawn twitch of muscle seemed an accent on every word of
ill-omen I had ever spelt out of the alphabet of fear. If my body
rested, my brain was an open chamber for any toad of ugliness
that listed to 'sit at squat' in.

Suddenly I woke to the fact that there was a knocking at my
door – that there had been for some little time.

I cried, 'Come in!' finding a weak restorative in the mere sound
of my own human voice; then, remembering the key was turned,
bade the visitor wait until I could come to him.

Scrambling, feeling dazed and white-livered, out of bed, I
opened the door, and met one of the warders on the threshold. The
man looked scared, and his lips, I noticed, were set in a somewhat boding fashion.

'Can you come at once, sir?' he said. 'There's summat wrong
with the Governor.'

'Wrong? What's the matter with him?'

'Why,' – he looked down, rubbed an imaginary protuberance smooth with his foot, and glanced up at me again with a quick, furtive expression – 'he's got his face set in the grating of 47, and danged if a man Jack of us can get him to move or speak.'

I turned away, feeling sick. I hurriedly pulled on coat and trousers, and hurriedly went off with my summoner. Reason was all absorbed in a wildest phantasy of apprehension.

'Who found him?' I muttered, as we sped on.

'Vokins see him go down the corridor about half after eight, sir, and see him give a start like when he noticed the trap open. It's never been so before in my time. Johnson must ha' done it last night, before he were took.'

'Yes, yes.'

'The man said the Governor went to shut it, it seemed, and to draw his face to'ards the bars in so doin'. Then he see him a-lookin' through, as he thought; but nat'rally it weren't no business of his'n, and he went off about his work. But when he come anigh agen, fifteen minutes later, there were the Governor in the same position; and he got scared over it, and called out to one or two of us.'

'Why didn't one of you ask the Major if anything was wrong?'

'Bless you! we did; and no answer. And we pulled him, compatible with discipline, but –'

'But what?'

'He's stuck.'

'Stuck!'

'See for yourself, sir. That's all I ask.'

I did, a moment later. A little group was collected about the door of cell 47, and the members of it spoke together in whispers, as if they were frightened men. One young fellow, with a face white in patches, as if it had been floured, slid from them as I approached, and accosted me tremulously.

'Don't go anigh, sir. There's something wrong about the place.'

I pulled myself together, forcibly beating down the excitement reawakened by the associations of the spot. In the discomfiture of others' nerves I found my own restoration.

'Don't be an ass!' I said, in a determined voice. 'There's nothing here that can't be explained. Make way for me, please!'

They parted and let me through, and I saw him. He stood, spruce, frock-coated, dapper, as he always was, with his face pressed against and *into* the grill, and either hand raised and clenched tightly round a bar of the trap. His posture was as of one caught and striving frantically to release himself; yet the narrowness of the interval between the rails precluded so extravagant an idea. He stood quite motionless – taut and on the strain, as it were – and nothing of his face was visible but the back ridges of his jaw-bones, showing white through a bush of red whiskers.

'Major Shrike!' I rapped out, and, allowing myself no hesitation, reached forth my hand and grasped his shoulder. The body vibrated under my touch, but he neither answered nor made sign of hearing me. Then I pulled at him forcibly, and ever with increasing strength. His fingers held like steel braces. He seemed glued to the trap, like Theseus to the rock.

Hastily I peered round, to see if I could get a glimpse of his face. I noticed enough to send me back with a little stagger.

'Has none of you got a key to this door?' I asked, reviewing the scared faces about me, than which my own was no less troubled, I feel sure.

'Only the Governor, sir,' said the warder who had fetched me. 'There's not a man but him amongst us that ever seen this opened.'

He was wrong there, I could have told him; but held my tongue, for obvious reasons,

'I want it opened. Will one of you feel in his pockets?'

Not a soul stirred. Even had not sense of discipline precluded, that of a certain inhuman atmosphere made fearful creatures of them all.

'Then,' said I, 'I must do it myself.'

I turned once more to the stiff-strung figure, had actually put hand on it, when an exclamation from Vokins arrested me.

'There's a key – there, sir!' he said – 'stickin' out yonder between his feet.'

Sure enough there was – Johnson's, no doubt, that had been shot from its socket by the clapping to of the door, and afterwards kicked aside by the warder in his convulsive struggles.

I stooped, only too thankful for the respite, and drew it forth. I had seen it but once before, yet I recognised it at a glance.

Now, I confess, my heart felt ill as I slipped the key into the wards, and a sickness of resentment at the tyranny of Fate in

making me its helpless minister surged up in my veins. Once, with
my fingers on the iron loop, I paused, and ventured a fearful
side glance at the figure whose crooked elbow almost touched my
face; then, strung to the high pitch of inevitability, I shot the lock,
pushed at the door, and in the act, made a back leap into the
corridor.

Scarcely, in doing so, did I look for the totter and collapse outwards of the rigid form. I had expected to see it fall away, face
down, into the cell, as its support swung from it. Yet it was, I
swear, as if *something* from within had relaxed its grasp and given
the fearful dead man a swingeing push outwards as the door
opened.

It went on its back, with a dusty slap on the stone flags, and
from all its spectators – me included – came a sudden drawn sound,
like wind in a keyhole.

What can I say, or how describe it? A dead thing it was – but the
face!

Barred with livid scars where the grating rails had crossed it, the
rest seemed to have been worked and kneaded into a mere feature-
less plate of yellow and expressionless flesh.

And it was this I had seen in the glass!

There was an interval following the experience above narrated,
during which a certain personality that had once been mine was
effaced or suspended, and I seemed a passive creature, innocent
of the least desire of independence. It was not that I was actually
ill or actually insane. A merciful Providence set my finer
wits slumbering, that was all, leaving me a sufficiency of the
grosser faculties that were necessary to the right ordering of my
behaviour.

I kept to my room, it is true, and even lay a good deal in
bed; but this was more to satisfy the busy scruples of a *locum tenens*
– a practitioner of the neighbourhood, who came daily to the
prison to officiate in my absence – than to cosset a complaint that
in its inactivity was purely negative. I could review what had
happened with a calmness as profound as if I had read of it in a book.
I could have wished to continue my duties, indeed, had the power
of insistence remained to me. But the saner medicus was acute
where I had gone blunt, and bade me to the restful course. He
was right. I was mentally stunned, and had I not slept off my

lethargy, I should have gone mad in an hour – leapt at a bound, probably, from inertia to flaming lunacy.

I remembered everything, but through a fluffy atmosphere, so to speak. It was as if I looked on bygone pictures through ground glass that softened the ugly outlines.

Sometimes I referred to these to my substitute, who was wise to answer me according to my mood; for the truth left me unruffled, whereas an obvious evasion of it would have distressed me.

'Hammond,' I said one day, 'I have never yet asked you. How did I give my evidence at the inquest?'

'Like a doctor and a sane man.'

'That's good. But it was a difficult course to steer. You conducted the *post-mortem*. Did any peculiarity in the dead man's face strike you?'

'Nothing but this: that the excessive contraction of the bicipital muscles had brought the features into such forcible contact with the bars as to cause bruising and actual abrasion. He must have been dead some little time when you found him.'

'And nothing else? You noticed nothing else in his face – a sort of obliteration of what makes one human, I mean?'

'Oh, dear, no! nothing but the painful constriction that marks any ordinary fatal attack of *angina pectoris*. – There's a rum breach of promise case in the paper today. You should read it; it'll make you laugh.'

I had no more inclination to laugh than to sigh; but I accepted the change of subject with an equanimity now habitual to me.

One morning I sat up in bed, and knew that consciousness was wide awake in me once more. It had slept, and now rose refreshed, but trembling. Looking back, all in a flutter of new responsibility, along the misty path by way of which I had recently loitered, I shook with an awful thankfulness at sight of the pitfalls I had skirted and escaped – of the demons my witlessness had baffled.

The joy of life was in my heart again, but chastened and made pitiful by experience.

Hammond noticed the change in me directly he entered, and congratulated me upon it.

'Go slow at first, old man,' he said. 'You've fairly sloughed the old skin; but give the sun time to toughen the new one. Walk in it at present, and be content.'

I was, in great measure, and I followed his advice. I got leave of absence, and ran down for a month in the country to a certain house we wot of, where kindly ministration to my convalescence was only one of the many blisses to be put to an account of rosy days.

> 'Then did my love awake,
> Most like a lily-flower,
> And as the lovely queene of heaven,
> So shone shee in her bower.'

Ah, me! ah, me! when was it? A year ago, or two-thirds of a lifetime? Alas! 'Age with stealing steps hath clawde me with his crowch.' And will the yews root in *my* heart, I wonder?

I was well, sane, recovered, when one morning, towards the end of my visit, I received a letter from Hammond, enclosing a packet addressed to me, and jealously sealed and fastened. My friend's communication ran as follows:

'There died here yesterday afternoon a warder, Johnson – he who had that apoplectic seizure, you will remember, the night before poor Shrike's exit. I attended him to the end, and, being alone with him an hour before the finish, he took the enclosed from under his pillow, and a solemn oath from me that I would forward it direct to you, sealed as you will find it, and permit no other soul to examine or even touch it. I acquit myself of the charge, but, my dear fellow, with an uneasy sense of the responsibility I incur in thus possibly suggesting to you a retrospect of events which you had much best consign to the limbo of the – not inexplainable, but not worth trying to explain. It was patent from what I have gathered that you were in an overstrung and excitable condition at that time, and that your temporary collapse was purely nervous in its character. It seems there was some nonsense abroad in the prison about a certain cell, and that there were fools who thought fit to associate Johnson's attack and the other's death with the opening of that cell's door. I have given the new Governor a tip, and he has stopped all that. We have examined the cell in company, and found it, as one might suppose, a very ordinary chamber. The two men died perfectly natural deaths, and there is the last to be said on the subject. I mention it only from the fear that enclosed may contain some allusion to the rubbish, a perusal of which might check the wholesome convalescence of your thoughts. If you take my advice, you will throw the packet into the fire unread. At least, if you *do* examine it, postpone the duty till you feel yourself absolutely impervious to any mental trickery, and – bear in mind that you are a worthy member of a particularly matter-of-fact and unemotional profession.'

I smiled at the last clause, for I was now in a condition to feel a rather warm shame over my erst weak-knee'd collapse before a sheet and an illuminated turnip. I took the packet to my bedroom, shut the door, and sat myself down by the open window. The garden lay below me, and the dewy meadows beyond. In the one, bees were busy ruffling the ruddy gillyflowers and April stocks; in the other, the hedge twigs were all frosted with Mary buds, as if Spring had brushed them with the fleece of her wings in passing.

I fetched a sigh of content as I broke the seal of the packet and brought out the enclosure. Somewhere in the garden a little sardonic laugh was clipt to silence. It came from groom or maid, no doubt; yet it thrilled me with an odd feeling of uncanniness, and I shivered slightly.

'Bah!' I said to myself determinedly. 'There is a shrewd nip in the wind, for all the show of sunlight;' and I rose, pulled down the window, and resumed my seat.

Then in the closed room, that had become deathly quiet by contrast, I opened and read the dead man's letter.

'Sir, – I hope you will read what I here put down. I lay it on you as a solemn injunction, for I am a dying man, and I know it. And to who is my death due, and the Governor's death, if not to you, for your pryin' and curiosity, as surely as if you had drove a nife through our harts? Therefore, I say, Read this, and take my burden from me, for it has been a burden; and now it is right that you that interfered should have it on your own mortal shoulders. The Major is dead and I am dying, and in the first of my fit it went on in my head like cimbells that the trap was left open, and that if he passed he would look in and *it* would get him. For he knew not fear, neither would he submit to bullying by God or devil.

'Now I will tell you the truth, and Heaven quit you of your responsibility in our destruction.

'There wasn't another man to me like the Governor in all the countries of the world. Once he brought me to life after doctors had given me up for dead; but he willed it, and I lived; and ever afterwards I loved him as a dog loves its master. That was in the Punjab; and I came home to England with him, and was his servant when he got his appointment to the jail here. I tell you he was a proud and fierce man, but under control and tender to those he favoured; and I will tell you also a strange thing about him. Though he was a soldier and an officer, and strict in discipline as made men fear and admire him, his hart at bottom was all for books, and literature, and such-like gentle crafts. I had his confidence, as a man gives his confidence to his dog, and before me sometimes he unbent as he never would before others. In this way I learnt the bitter sorrow of his life. He had once hoped to be a poet, acknowledged as such before the world. He was by natur' an idelist, as they call it, and God knows what it meant to him to come out of the woods, so to speak, and swet in the dust of cities; but he did it, for his will was of tempered steel. He buried his dreams in the clouds and came down to earth greatly resolved, but with one undying hate, It is not good to hate as he could, and worse to be hated by such as him; and I will tell you the story, and what it led to.

'It was when he was a subaltern that he made up his mind to the plunge. For years he had placed all his hopes and confidents in a book of verses he had wrote, and added to, and improved during that time. A little encouragement, a little word of praise, was all he looked for, and then he was redy to buckle to again, profitin' by advice, and do better. He put all the love and beauty of his hart into that book, and at last, after doubt, and anguish, and much diffidents, he published it, and give it to the world. Sir, it fell what they call still-born from the press. It was like a green leaf flutterin' down in a dead wood. To a proud and hopeful man, bubblin' with music, the pain of neglect, when he come to relize it, was terrible. But nothing was said, and there was nothing to say. In silence he had to endure and suffer.

'But one day, during manoovers, there came to the camp a grey-faced man, a newspaper correspondent, and young Shrike nocked up a friendship with him. Now how it come about I cannot tell, but so it did that this skip-kennel wormed the lad's sorrow out of him, and his confidents, swore he'd been damnabilly used, and that when he got back he'd crack up the book himself in his own paper. He was a fool for his pains, and a serpent in his croolty. The notice come out as promised, and, my God! the author was laughed and mocked at from beginning to end. Even confidentses he had given to the creature was twisted to his ridicule, and his very appearance joked over. And the mess got wind of it, and made a rare story for the dog days.

'He bore it like a soldier and that he became hart and liver from the moment. But he put something to the account of the grey-faced man and locked it up in his breast.

'He come across him again years afterwards in India, and told him very politely that he hadn't forgotten him, and didn't intend to. But he was anigh losin' sight of him there for ever and a day, for the creature took cholera, or what looked like it, and rubbed shoulders with death and the devil before he pulled through. And he come across him again over here, and that was the last of him, as you shall see presently.

'Once, after I knew the Major (he were Captain then), I was a-brushin' his coat, and he stood a long while before the glass. Then he twisted upon me, with a smile on his mouth, and says he –

' "The dog was right, Johnson: this isn't the face of a poet. I was a presumtious ass, and born to cast up figgers with a pen behind my ear."

' "Captain," I says, "if you was skinned, you'd look like any other man without his. The quality of a soul isn't expressed by a coat."

' "Well," he answers, "my soul's pretty clean-swept, I think, save for one Bluebeard chamber in it that's been kep' locked ever so many years. It's nice and dirty by this time, I expect," he says. Then the grin comes on his mouth again. "I'll open it some day," he says, "and look. There's something in it about comparing me to a dancing dervish, with the wind in my petticuts. Perhaps I'll get the chance to set somebody else dancing by-and-by."

'He did, and took it, and the Bluebeard chamber come to be opened in this very jail.

'It was when the system was lying fallow, so to speak, and the prison was deserted. Nobody was there but him and me and the echoes from the empty courts. The contract for restoration hadn't been signed, and for months, and more than a year, we lay idle, nothing bein' done.

'Near the beginnin' of this period, one day comes, for the third

time of the Major's seein' him, the grey-faced man. "Let bygones
be bygones," he says. "I was a good friend to you, though you
didn't know it; and now, I expect, you're in the way to thank
me."

'"I am," says the Major.

'"Of course," he answers. "Where would be your fame and
reputation as one of the leadin' prison reformers of the day if you
had kep' on in that riming nonsense?"

'"Have you come for my thanks?" says the Governor.

'"I've come," says the grey-faced man, "to examine and report
upon your system."

'"For your paper?"

'"Possibly; but to satisfy myself of its efficacy, in the first
instance."

'"You aren't commissioned, then?"

'"No; I come on my own responsibility."

'"Without consultation with any one?"

'"Absolutely without. I haven't even a wife to advise me," he
says, with a yellow grin. What once passed for cholera had set the
bile on his skin like paint, and he had caught a manner of cough-
ing behind his hand like a toast-master.

'"I know," says the Major, looking him steady in the face, "that
what you say about me and my affairs is sure to be actuated by
conscientious motives."

'"Ah," he answers. "You're sore about that review still, I see."

'"Not at all," says the Major; "and, in proof, I invite you to be
my guest for the night, and tomorrow I'll show you over the
prison and explain my system."

'The creature cried, "Done!" and they set to and discussed jail
matters in great earnestness. I couldn't guess the Governor's inten-
tions, but, somehow, his manner troubled me. And yet I can
remember only one point of his talk. He were always dead against
making public show of his birds. "They're there for reformation,
not ignimony," he'd say. Prisons in the old days were often, with
the asylum and the work'us, made the holiday show-places of
towns. I've heard of one Justice of the Peace, up North, who, to
save himself trouble, used to sign a lot of blank orders for leave to
view, so that applicants needn't bother him when they wanted to
go over. They've changed all that, and the Governor were instru-
mental in the change.

' "It's against my rule," he said that night, "to exhibit to a stranger without a Government permit; but, seein' the place is empty, and for old remembrance' sake, I'll make an exception in your favour, and you shall learn all I can show you of the inside of a prison."

'Now this was natural enough; but I was uneasy.

'He treated his guest royly; so much that when we assembled the next mornin' for the inspection, the grey-faced man were shaky as a wet dog. But the Major were all set prim and dry, like the soldier he was.

'We went straight away down corridor B, and at cell 47 we stopped.

' "We will begin our inspection here," said the Governor. "Johnson, open the door."

'I had the keys of the row; fitted in the right one, and pushed open the door.

' "After you, sir," said the Major; and the creature walked in, and he shut the door on him.

'I think he smelt a rat at once, for he began beating on the wood and calling out to us. But the Major only turned round to me with his face like a stone.

' "Take that key from the bunch," he said, "and give it to me."

'I obeyed, all in a tremble, and he took and put it in his pocket.

' "My God, Major!" I whispered, "what are you going to do with him?"

' "Silence, sir!" he said. "How dare you question your superior officer!"

"And the noise inside grew louder.

'The Governor, he listened to it a moment like music; then he unbolted and flung open the trap, and the creature's face came at it like a wild beast's.

' "Sir," said the Major to it, "you can't better understand my system than by experiencing it. What an article for your paper you could write already – almost as pungint a one as that in which you ruined the hopes and prospects of a young cockney poet."

'The man mouthed at the bars. He was half-mad, I think, in that one minute.

' "Let me out!" he screamed. "This is a hidius joke! Let me out!"

' "When you are quite quiet – deathly quiet," said the Major,

"you shall come out. Not before;" and he shut the trap in its face
very softly.

'"Come, Johnson, march!" he said, and took the lead, and we
walked out of the prison.

'I was like to faint, but I dared not disobey, and the man's
screeching followed us all down the empty corridors and halls, until
we shut the first great door on it.

'It may have gone on for hours, alone in that awful emptiness.
The creature was a reptile, but the thought sickened my heart.

'And from that hour till his death, five months later, he rotted
and maddened in his dreadful tomb.'

There was more, but I pushed the ghastly confession from me at
this point in uncontrollable loathing and terror. Was it possible –
possible, that injured vanity could so falsify its victim's every tradition of decency?

'Oh!' I muttered, 'what a disease is ambition! Who takes one
step towards it puts his foot on Alsirat!'

It was minutes before my shocked nerves were equal to a re-
sumption of the task; but at last I took it up again, with a groan.

'I don't think at first I realized the full mischief the Governor
intended to do. At least, I hoped he only meant to give the man a
good fright and then let him go. I might have known better. How
could he ever release him without ruining himself?

'The next morning he summoned me to attend him. There was
a strange new look of triumph in his face, and in his hand he held
a heavy hunting-crop. I pray to God he acted in madness, but my
duty and obedience was to him.

'"There is sport towards, Johnson," he said. "My dervish has
got to dance."

'I followed him quiet. We listened when I opened the jail door,
but the place was silent as the grave. But from the cell, when we
reached it, came a low, whispering sound.

'The Governor slipped the trap and looked through.

'"All right," he said, and put the key in the door and flung it
open.

'He were sittin' crouched on the ground, and he looked up at us
vacant-like. His face were all fallen down, as it were, and his mouth
never ceased to shake and whisper.

'The Major shut the door and posted me in a corner. Then he moved to the creature with his whip.

'"Up!" he cried. "Up, you dervish, and dance to us!" and he brought the thong with a smack across his shoulders.

'The creature leapt under the blow, and then to his feet with a cry, and the Major whipped him till he danced. All round the cell he drove him, lashing and cutting – and again, and many times again, until the poor thing rolled on the floor whimpering and sobbing. I shall have to give an account of this some day. I shall have to whip my master with a red-hot serpent round the blazing furnace of the pit, and I shall do it with agony, because here my love and my obedience was to him.

'When it was finished, he bade me put down food and drink that I had brought with me, and come away with him; and we went, leaving him rolling on the floor of the cell, and shut him alone in the empty prison until we should come again at the same time tomorrow.

'So day by day this went on, and the dancing three or four times a week, until at last the whip could be left behind, for the man would scream and begin to dance at the mere turning of the key in the lock. And he danced for four months, but not the fifth.

'Nobody official came near us all this time. The prison stood lonely as a deserted ruin where dark things have been done.

'Once, with fear and trembling, I asked my master how he would account for the inmate of 47 if he was suddenly called upon by authority to open the cell; and he answered, smiling, –

'"I should say it was my mad brother. By his own account, he showed me a brother's love, you know. It would be thought a liberty; but the authorities, I think, would stretch a point for me. But if I got sufficient notice, I should clear out the cell."

'I asked him how, with my eyes rather than my lips, and he answered me only with a look.

'And all this time he was, outside the prison, living the life of a good man – helping the needy, ministering to the poor. He even entertained occasionally, and had more than one noisy party in his house.

'But the fifth month the creature danced no more. He was a dumb, silent animal then, with matted hair and beard; and when one entered he would only look up at one pitifully, as if he said,

"My long punishment is nearly ended." How it came that no inquiry was ever made about him I know not, but none ever was. Perhaps he was one of the wandering gentry that nobody ever knows where they are next. He was unmarried, and had apparently not told of his intended journey to a soul.

'And at the last he died in the night. We found him lying stiff and stark in the morning, and scratched with a piece of black crust on a stone of the wall these strange words: "An Eddy on the Floor." Just that – nothing else.

'Then the Governor came and looked down, and was silent. Suddenly he caught me by the shoulder.

'"Johnson," he cried, "if it was to do again, I would do it! I repent of nothing. But he has paid the penalty, and we call quits. May he rest in peace!"

'"Amen!" I answered low. Yet I knew our turn must come for this.

'We buried him in quicklime under the wall where the murderers lie, and I made the cell trim and rubbed out the writing, and the Governor locked all up and took away the key. But he locked in more than he bargained for.

'For months the place was left to itself, and neither of us went anigh 47. Then one day the workmen was to be put in, and the Major he took me round with him for a last examination of the place before they come.

'He hesitated a bit outside a particular cell; but at last he drove in the key and kicked open the door.

'"My God!" he says, "he's dancing still!"

'My heart was thumpin', I tell you, as I looked over his shoulder. What did we see? What you well understand, sir; but, for all it was no more than that, we knew as well as if it was shouted in our ears that it was him, dancin'. It went round by the walls and drew towards us, and as it stole near I screamed out, "An Eddy on the Floor!" and seized and dragged the Major out and clapped to the door behind us.

'"Oh!" I said, "in another moment it would have had us."

'He looked at me gloomily.

'"Johnson," he said, "I'm not to be frighted or coerced. He may dance, but he shall dance alone. Get a screwdriver and some screws and fasten up this trap. No one from this time looks into this cell."

'I did as he bid me, swetin'; and I swear all the time I wrought I dreaded a hand would come through the trap and clutch mine.

'On one pretex' or another, from that day till the night you meddled with it, he kep' that cell as close shut as a tomb. And he went his ways, discardin' the past from that time forth. Now and again a over-sensitive prisoner in the next cell would complain of feelin' uncomfortable. If possible, he would be removed to another; if not, he was dam'd for his fancies. And so it might be goin' on to now, if you hadn't pried and interfered. I don't blame you at this moment, sir. Likely you were an instrument in the hands of Providence; only, as the instrument, you must now take the burden of the truth on your own shoulders. I am a dying man, but I cannot die till I have confessed. Per'aps you may find it in your hart some day to give up a prayer for me – but it must be for the Major as well.

'Your obedient servant,
'J. JOHNSON.'

What comment of my own can I append to this wild narrative? Professionally, and apart from personal experiences, I should rule it the composition of an epileptic. That a noted journalist, nameless as he was and is to me, however nomadic in habit, could disappear from human ken, and his fellows rest content to leave him unaccounted for, seems a tax upon credulity so stupendous that I cannot seriously endorse the statement.

Yet, also – there *is* that little matter of my personal experience.

A CATALOG OF SELECTED
DOVER BOOKS
IN ALL FIELDS OF INTEREST

A CATALOG OF SELECTED DOVER
BOOKS IN ALL FIELDS OF INTEREST

CONCERNING THE SPIRITUAL IN ART, Wassily Kandinsky. Pioneering work by father of abstract art. Thoughts on color theory, nature of art. Analysis of earlier masters. 12 illustrations. 80pp. of text. 5⅜ x 8½. 0-486-23411-8

CELTIC ART: The Methods of Construction, George Bain. Simple geometric techniques for making Celtic interlacements, spirals, Kells-type initials, animals, humans, etc. Over 500 illustrations. 160pp. 9 x 12. (Available in U.S. only.) 0-486-22923-8

AN ATLAS OF ANATOMY FOR ARTISTS, Fritz Schider. Most thorough reference work on art anatomy in the world. Hundreds of illustrations, including selections from works by Vesalius, Leonardo, Goya, Ingres, Michelangelo, others. 593 illustrations. 192pp. 7⅞ x 10¼. 0-486-20241-0

CELTIC HAND STROKE-BY-STROKE (Irish Half-Uncial from "The Book of Kells"): An Arthur Baker Calligraphy Manual, Arthur Baker. Complete guide to creating each letter of the alphabet in distinctive Celtic manner. Covers hand position, strokes, pens, inks, paper, more. Illustrated. 48pp. 8¼ x 11. 0-486-24336-2

EASY ORIGAMI, John Montroll. Charming collection of 32 projects (hat, cup, pelican, piano, swan, many more) specially designed for the novice origami hobbyist. Clearly illustrated easy-to-follow instructions insure that even beginning papercrafters will achieve successful results. 48pp. 8¼ x 11. 0-486-27298-2

BLOOMINGDALE'S ILLUSTRATED 1886 CATALOG: Fashions, Dry Goods and Housewares, Bloomingdale Brothers. Famed merchants' extremely rare catalog depicting about 1,700 products: clothing, housewares, firearms, dry goods, jewelry, more. Invaluable for dating, identifying vintage items. Also, copyright-free graphics for artists, designers. Co-published with Henry Ford Museum & Greenfield Village. 160pp. 8¼ x 11. 0-486-25780-0

THE ART OF WORLDLY WISDOM, Baltasar Gracian. "Think with the few and speak with the many," "Friends are a second existence," and "Be able to forget" are among this 1637 volume's 300 pithy maxims. A perfect source of mental and spiritual refreshment, it can be opened at random and appreciated either in brief or at length. 128pp. 5⅜ x 8½. 0-486-44034-6

JOHNSON'S DICTIONARY: A Modern Selection, Samuel Johnson (E. L. McAdam and George Milne, eds.). This modern version reduces the original 1755 edition's 2,300 pages of definitions and literary examples to a more manageable length, retaining the verbal pleasure and historical curiosity of the original. 480pp. 5³⁄₁₆ x 8¼. 0-486-44089-3

ADVENTURES OF HUCKLEBERRY FINN, Mark Twain, Illustrated by E. W. Kemble. A work of eternal richness and complexity, a source of ongoing critical debate, and a literary landmark, Twain's 1885 masterpiece about a barefoot boy's journey of self-discovery has enthralled readers around the world. This handsome clothbound reproduction of the first edition features all 174 of the original black-and-white illustrations. 368pp. 5⅜ x 8½. 0-486-44322-1

STICKLEY CRAFTSMAN FURNITURE CATALOGS, Gustav Stickley and L. & J. G. Stickley. Beautiful, functional furniture in two authentic catalogs from 1910. 594 illustrations, including 277 photos, show settles, rockers, armchairs, reclining chairs, bookcases, desks, tables. 183pp. 6½ x 9¼. 0-486-23838-5

AMERICAN LOCOMOTIVES IN HISTORIC PHOTOGRAPHS: 1858 to 1949, Ron Ziel (ed.). A rare collection of 126 meticulously detailed official photographs, called "builder portraits," of American locomotives that majestically chronicle the rise of steam locomotive power in America. Introduction. Detailed captions. xi+ 129pp. 9 x 12. 0-486-27393-8

AMERICA'S LIGHTHOUSES: An Illustrated History, Francis Ross Holland, Jr. Delightfully written, profusely illustrated fact-filled survey of over 200 American lighthouses since 1716. History, anecdotes, technological advances, more. 240pp. 8 x 10¾. 0-486-25576-X

TOWARDS A NEW ARCHITECTURE, Le Corbusier. Pioneering manifesto by founder of "International School." Technical and aesthetic theories, views of industry, economics, relation of form to function, "mass-production split" and much more. Profusely illustrated. 320pp. 6⅛ x 9¼. (Available in U.S. only.) 0-486-25023-7

HOW THE OTHER HALF LIVES, Jacob Riis. Famous journalistic record, exposing poverty and degradation of New York slums around 1900, by major social reformer. 100 striking and influential photographs. 233pp. 10 x 7⅞. 0-486-22012-5

FRUIT KEY AND TWIG KEY TO TREES AND SHRUBS, William M. Harlow. One of the handiest and most widely used identification aids. Fruit key covers 120 deciduous and evergreen species; twig key 160 deciduous species. Easily used. Over 300 photographs. 126pp. 5⅜ x 8½. 0-486-20511-8

COMMON BIRD SONGS, Dr. Donald J. Borror. Songs of 60 most common U.S. birds: robins, sparrows, cardinals, bluejays, finches, more–arranged in order of increasing complexity. Up to 9 variations of songs of each species.
Cassette and manual 0-486-99911-4

ORCHIDS AS HOUSE PLANTS, Rebecca Tyson Northen. Grow cattleyas and many other kinds of orchids–in a window, in a case, or under artificial light. 63 illustrations. 148pp. 5⅜ x 8½. 0-486-23261-1

MONSTER MAZES, Dave Phillips. Masterful mazes at four levels of difficulty. Avoid deadly perils and evil creatures to find magical treasures. Solutions for all 32 exciting illustrated puzzles. 48pp. 8¼ x 11. 0-486-26005-4

MOZART'S DON GIOVANNI (DOVER OPERA LIBRETTO SERIES), Wolfgang Amadeus Mozart. Introduced and translated by Ellen H. Bleiler. Standard Italian libretto, with complete English translation. Convenient and thoroughly portable–an ideal companion for reading along with a recording or the performance itself. Introduction. List of characters. Plot summary. 121pp. 5¼ x 8½. 0-486-24944-1

FRANK LLOYD WRIGHT'S DANA HOUSE, Donald Hoffmann. Pictorial essay of residential masterpiece with over 160 interior and exterior photos, plans, elevations, sketches and studies. 128pp. 9¼ x 10¾. 0-486-29120-0

THE CLARINET AND CLARINET PLAYING, David Pino. Lively, comprehensive work features suggestions about technique, musicianship, and musical interpretation, as well as guidelines for teaching, making your own reeds, and preparing for public performance. Includes an intriguing look at clarinet history. "A godsend," *The Clarinet,* Journal of the International Clarinet Society. Appendixes. 7 illus. 320pp. 5⅜ x 8½. 0-486-40270-3

HOLLYWOOD GLAMOR PORTRAITS, John Kobal (ed.). 145 photos from 1926-49. Harlow, Gable, Bogart, Bacall; 94 stars in all. Full background on photographers, technical aspects. 160pp. 8⅜ x 11¼. 0-486-23352-9

THE RAVEN AND OTHER FAVORITE POEMS, Edgar Allan Poe. Over 40 of the author's most memorable poems: "The Bells," "Ulalume," "Israfel," "To Helen," "The Conqueror Worm," "Eldorado," "Annabel Lee," many more. Alphabetic lists of titles and first lines. 64pp. 5³⁄₁₆ x 8¼. 0-486-26685-0

PERSONAL MEMOIRS OF U. S. GRANT, Ulysses Simpson Grant. Intelligent, deeply moving firsthand account of Civil War campaigns, considered by many the finest military memoirs ever written. Includes letters, historic photographs, maps and more. 528pp. 6⅛ x 9¼. 0-486-28587-1

ANCIENT EGYPTIAN MATERIALS AND INDUSTRIES, A. Lucas and J. Harris. Fascinating, comprehensive, thoroughly documented text describes this ancient civilization's vast resources and the processes that incorporated them in daily life, including the use of animal products, building materials, cosmetics, perfumes and incense, fibers, glazed ware, glass and its manufacture, materials used in the mummification process, and much more. 544pp. 6¹/₈ x 9¹/₄. (Available in U.S. only.) 0-486-40446-3

RUSSIAN STORIES/RUSSKIE RASSKAZY: A Dual-Language Book, edited by Gleb Struve. Twelve tales by such masters as Chekhov, Tolstoy, Dostoevsky, Pushkin, others. Excellent word-for-word English translations on facing pages, plus teaching and study aids, Russian/English vocabulary, biographical/critical introductions, more. 416pp. 5⅜ x 8½. 0-486-26244-8

PHILADELPHIA THEN AND NOW: 60 Sites Photographed in the Past and Present, Kenneth Finkel and Susan Oyama. Rare photographs of City Hall, Logan Square, Independence Hall, Betsy Ross House, other landmarks juxtaposed with contemporary views. Captures changing face of historic city. Introduction. Captions. 128pp. 8¼ x 11. 0-486-25790-8

NORTH AMERICAN INDIAN LIFE: Customs and Traditions of 23 Tribes, Elsie Clews Parsons (ed.). 27 fictionalized essays by noted anthropologists examine religion, customs, government, additional facets of life among the Winnebago, Crow, Zuni, Eskimo, other tribes. 480pp. 6⅛ x 9¼. 0-486-27377-6

TECHNICAL MANUAL AND DICTIONARY OF CLASSICAL BALLET, Gail Grant. Defines, explains, comments on steps, movements, poses and concepts. 15-page pictorial section. Basic book for student, viewer. 127pp. 5⅜ x 8½. 0-486-21843-0

THE MALE AND FEMALE FIGURE IN MOTION: 60 Classic Photographic Sequences, Eadweard Muybridge. 60 true-action photographs of men and women walking, running, climbing, bending, turning, etc., reproduced from rare 19th-century masterpiece. vi + 121pp. 9 x 12. 0-486-24745-7

CATALOG OF DOVER BOOKS

ANIMALS: 1,419 Copyright-Free Illustrations of Mammals, Birds, Fish, Insects, etc., Jim Harter (ed.). Clear wood engravings present, in extremely lifelike poses, over 1,000 species of animals. One of the most extensive pictorial sourcebooks of its kind. Captions. Index. 284pp. 9 x 12. 0-486-23766-4

1001 QUESTIONS ANSWERED ABOUT THE SEASHORE, N. J. Berrill and Jacquelyn Berrill. Queries answered about dolphins, sea snails, sponges, starfish, fishes, shore birds, many others. Covers appearance, breeding, growth, feeding, much more. 305pp. 5¼ x 8¼. 0-486-23366-9

ATTRACTING BIRDS TO YOUR YARD, William J. Weber. Easy-to-follow guide offers advice on how to attract the greatest diversity of birds: birdhouses, feeders, water and waterers, much more. 96pp. 5³/₁₆ x 8¼. 0-486-28927-3

MEDICINAL AND OTHER USES OF NORTH AMERICAN PLANTS: A Historical Survey with Special Reference to the Eastern Indian Tribes, Charlotte Erichsen-Brown. Chronological historical citations document 500 years of usage of plants, trees, shrubs native to eastern Canada, northeastern U.S. Also complete identifying information. 343 illustrations. 544pp. 6½ x 9¼. 0-486-25951-X

STORYBOOK MAZES, Dave Phillips. 23 stories and mazes on two-page spreads: Wizard of Oz, Treasure Island, Robin Hood, etc. Solutions. 64pp. 8¼ x 11. 0-486-23628-5

AMERICAN NEGRO SONGS: 230 Folk Songs and Spirituals, Religious and Secular, John W. Work. This authoritative study traces the African influences of songs sung and played by black Americans at work, in church, and as entertainment. The author discusses the lyric significance of such songs as "Swing Low, Sweet Chariot," "John Henry," and others and offers the words and music for 230 songs. Bibliography. Index of Song Titles. 272pp. 6½ x 9¼. 0-486-40271-1

MOVIE-STAR PORTRAITS OF THE FORTIES, John Kobal (ed.). 163 glamor, studio photos of 106 stars of the 1940s: Rita Hayworth, Ava Gardner, Marlon Brando, Clark Gable, many more. 176pp. 8⅜ x 11¼. 0-486-23546-7

YEKL and THE IMPORTED BRIDEGROOM AND OTHER STORIES OF YIDDISH NEW YORK, Abraham Cahan. Film Hester Street based on *Yekl* (1896). Novel, other stories among first about Jewish immigrants on N.Y.'s East Side. 240pp. 5⅜ x 8½. 0-486-22427-9

SELECTED POEMS, Walt Whitman. Generous sampling from *Leaves of Grass*. Twenty-four poems include "I Hear America Singing," "Song of the Open Road," "I Sing the Body Electric," "When Lilacs Last in the Dooryard Bloom'd," "O Captain! My Captain!"–all reprinted from an authoritative edition. Lists of titles and first lines. 128pp. 5³/₁₆ x 8¼. 0-486-26878-0

SONGS OF EXPERIENCE: Facsimile Reproduction with 26 Plates in Full Color, William Blake. 26 full-color plates from a rare 1826 edition. Includes "The Tyger," "London," "Holy Thursday," and other poems. Printed text of poems. 48pp. 5¼ x 7. 0-486-24636-1

THE BEST TALES OF HOFFMANN, E. T. A. Hoffmann. 10 of Hoffmann's most important stories: "Nutcracker and the King of Mice," "The Golden Flowerpot," etc. 458pp. 5⅜ x 8½. 0-486-21793-0

THE BOOK OF TEA, Kakuzo Okakura. Minor classic of the Orient: entertaining, charming explanation, interpretation of traditional Japanese culture in terms of tea ceremony. 94pp. 5⅜ x 8½. 0-486-20070-1

FRENCH STORIES/CONTES FRANÇAIS: A Dual-Language Book, Wallace Fowlie. Ten stories by French masters, Voltaire to Camus: "Micromegas" by Voltaire; "The Atheist's Mass" by Balzac; "Minuet" by de Maupassant; "The Guest" by Camus, six more. Excellent English translations on facing pages. Also French-English vocabulary list, exercises, more. 352pp. 5⅜ x 8½. 0-486-26443-2

CHICAGO AT THE TURN OF THE CENTURY IN PHOTOGRAPHS: 122 Historic Views from the Collections of the Chicago Historical Society, Larry A. Viskochil. Rare large-format prints offer detailed views of City Hall, State Street, the Loop, Hull House, Union Station, many other landmarks, circa 1904-1913. Introduction. Captions. Maps. 144pp. 9⅜ x 12¼. 0-486-24656-6

OLD BROOKLYN IN EARLY PHOTOGRAPHS, 1865-1929, William Lee Younger. Luna Park, Gravesend race track, construction of Grand Army Plaza, moving of Hotel Brighton, etc. 157 previously unpublished photographs. 165pp. 8⅞ x 11¾. 0-486-23587-4

THE MYTHS OF THE NORTH AMERICAN INDIANS, Lewis Spence. Rich anthology of the myths and legends of the Algonquins, Iroquois, Pawnees and Sioux, prefaced by an extensive historical and ethnological commentary. 36 illustrations. 480pp. 5⅜ x 8½. 0-486-25967-6

AN ENCYCLOPEDIA OF BATTLES: Accounts of Over 1,560 Battles from 1479 B.C. to the Present, David Eggenberger. Essential details of every major battle in recorded history from the first battle of Megiddo in 1479 B.C. to Grenada in 1984. List of Battle Maps. New Appendix covering the years 1967-1984. Index. 99 illustrations. 544pp. 6½ x 9¼. 0-486-24913-1

SAILING ALONE AROUND THE WORLD, Captain Joshua Slocum. First man to sail around the world, alone, in small boat. One of great feats of seamanship told in delightful manner. 67 illustrations. 294pp. 5⅜ x 8½. 0-486-20326-3

ANARCHISM AND OTHER ESSAYS, Emma Goldman. Powerful, penetrating, prophetic essays on direct action, role of minorities, prison reform, puritan hypocrisy, violence, etc. 271pp. 5⅜ x 8½. 0-486-22484-8

MYTHS OF THE HINDUS AND BUDDHISTS, Ananda K. Coomaraswamy and Sister Nivedita. Great stories of the epics; deeds of Krishna, Shiva, taken from puranas, Vedas, folk tales; etc. 32 illustrations. 400pp. 5⅜ x 8½. 0-486-21759-0

MY BONDAGE AND MY FREEDOM, Frederick Douglass. Born a slave, Douglass became outspoken force in antislavery movement. The best of Douglass' autobiographies. Graphic description of slave life. 464pp. 5⅜ x 8½. 0-486-22457-0

FOLLOWING THE EQUATOR: A Journey Around the World, Mark Twain. Fascinating humorous account of 1897 voyage to Hawaii, Australia, India, New Zealand, etc. Ironic, bemused reports on peoples, customs, climate, flora and fauna, politics, much more. 197 illustrations. 720pp. 5⅜ x 8½. 0-486-26113-1

THE PEOPLE CALLED SHAKERS, Edward D. Andrews. Definitive study of Shakers: origins, beliefs, practices, dances, social organization, furniture and crafts, etc. 33 illustrations. 351pp. 5⅜ x 8½. 0-486-21081-2

THE MYTHS OF GREECE AND ROME, H. A. Guerber. A classic of mythology, generously illustrated, long prized for its simple, graphic, accurate retelling of the principal myths of Greece and Rome, and for its commentary on their origins and significance. With 64 illustrations by Michelangelo, Raphael, Titian, Rubens, Canova, Bernini and others. 480pp. 5⅜ x 8½. 0-486-27584-1

PSYCHOLOGY OF MUSIC, Carl E. Seashore. Classic work discusses music as a medium from psychological viewpoint. Clear treatment of physical acoustics, auditory apparatus, sound perception, development of musical skills, nature of musical feeling, host of other topics. 88 figures. 408pp. 5⅜ x 8½. 0-486-21851-1

LIFE IN ANCIENT EGYPT, Adolf Erman. Fullest, most thorough, detailed older account with much not in more recent books, domestic life, religion, magic, medicine, commerce, much more. Many illustrations reproduce tomb paintings, carvings, hieroglyphs, etc. 597pp. 5⅜ x 8½. 0-486-22632-8

SUNDIALS, Their Theory and Construction, Albert Waugh. Far and away the best, most thorough coverage of ideas, mathematics concerned, types, construction, adjusting anywhere. Simple, nontechnical treatment allows even children to build several of these dials. Over 100 illustrations. 230pp. 5⅜ x 8½. 0-486-22947-5

THEORETICAL HYDRODYNAMICS, L. M. Milne-Thomson. Classic exposition of the mathematical theory of fluid motion, applicable to both hydrodynamics and aerodynamics. Over 600 exercises. 768pp. 6⅛ x 9¼. 0-486-68970-0

OLD-TIME VIGNETTES IN FULL COLOR, Carol Belanger Grafton (ed.). Over 390 charming, often sentimental illustrations, selected from archives of Victorian graphics–pretty women posing, children playing, food, flowers, kittens and puppies, smiling cherubs, birds and butterflies, much more. All copyright-free. 48pp. 9¼ x 12¼. 0-486-27269-9

PERSPECTIVE FOR ARTISTS, Rex Vicat Cole. Depth, perspective of sky and sea, shadows, much more, not usually covered. 391 diagrams, 81 reproductions of drawings and paintings. 279pp. 5⅜ x 8½. 0-486-22487-2

DRAWING THE LIVING FIGURE, Joseph Sheppard. Innovative approach to artistic anatomy focuses on specifics of surface anatomy, rather than muscles and bones. Over 170 drawings of live models in front, back and side views, and in widely varying poses. Accompanying diagrams. 177 illustrations. Introduction. Index. 144pp. 8⅜ x11¼. 0-486-26723-7

GOTHIC AND OLD ENGLISH ALPHABETS: 100 Complete Fonts, Dan X. Solo. Add power, elegance to posters, signs, other graphics with 100 stunning copyright-free alphabets: Blackstone, Dolbey, Germania, 97 more–including many lower-case, numerals, punctuation marks. 104pp. 8⅛ x 11. 0-486-24695-7

THE BOOK OF WOOD CARVING, Charles Marshall Sayers. Finest book for beginners discusses fundamentals and offers 34 designs. "Absolutely first rate . . . well thought out and well executed."–E. J. Tangerman. 118pp. 7¾ x 10⅝. 0-486-23654-4

ILLUSTRATED CATALOG OF CIVIL WAR MILITARY GOODS: Union Army Weapons, Insignia, Uniform Accessories, and Other Equipment, Schuyler, Hartley, and Graham. Rare, profusely illustrated 1846 catalog includes Union Army uniform and dress regulations, arms and ammunition, coats, insignia, flags, swords, rifles, etc. 226 illustrations. 160pp. 9 x 12. 0-486-24939-5

WOMEN'S FASHIONS OF THE EARLY 1900s: An Unabridged Republication of "New York Fashions, 1909," National Cloak & Suit Co. Rare catalog of mail-order fashions documents women's and children's clothing styles shortly after the turn of the century. Captions offer full descriptions, prices. Invaluable resource for fashion, costume historians. Approximately 725 illustrations. 128pp. 8⅜ x 11¼. 0-486-27276-1

HOW TO DO BEADWORK, Mary White. Fundamental book on craft from simple projects to five-bead chains and woven works. 106 illustrations. 142pp. 5⅜ x 8.
0-486-20697-1

THE 1912 AND 1915 GUSTAV STICKLEY FURNITURE CATALOGS, Gustav Stickley. With over 200 detailed illustrations and descriptions, these two catalogs are essential reading and reference materials and identification guides for Stickley furniture. Captions cite materials, dimensions and prices. 112pp. 6½ x 9¼. 0-486-26676-1

EARLY AMERICAN LOCOMOTIVES, John H. White, Jr. Finest locomotive engravings from early 19th century: historical (1804–74), main-line (after 1870), special, foreign, etc. 147 plates. 142pp. 11⅜ x 8¼. 0-486-22772-3

LITTLE BOOK OF EARLY AMERICAN CRAFTS AND TRADES, Peter Stockham (ed.). 1807 children's book explains crafts and trades: baker, hatter, cooper, potter, and many others. 23 copperplate illustrations. 140pp. 4⅝ x 6.
0-486-23336-7

VICTORIAN FASHIONS AND COSTUMES FROM HARPER'S BAZAR, 1867–1898, Stella Blum (ed.). Day costumes, evening wear, sports clothes, shoes, hats, other accessories in over 1,000 detailed engravings. 320pp. 9⅜ x 12¼.
0-486-22990-4

THE LONG ISLAND RAIL ROAD IN EARLY PHOTOGRAPHS, Ron Ziel. Over 220 rare photos, informative text document origin (1844) and development of rail service on Long Island. Vintage views of early trains, locomotives, stations, passengers, crews, much more. Captions. 8⅞ x 11¾. 0-486-26301-0

VOYAGE OF THE LIBERDADE, Joshua Slocum. Great 19th-century mariner's thrilling, first-hand account of the wreck of his ship off South America, the 35-foot boat he built from the wreckage, and its remarkable voyage home. 128pp. 5⅜ x 8½.
0-486-40022-0

TEN BOOKS ON ARCHITECTURE, Vitruvius. The most important book ever written on architecture. Early Roman aesthetics, technology, classical orders, site selection, all other aspects. Morgan translation. 331pp. 5⅜ x 8½. 0-486-20645-9

THE HUMAN FIGURE IN MOTION, Eadweard Muybridge. More than 4,500 stopped-action photos, in action series, showing undraped men, women, children jumping, lying down, throwing, sitting, wrestling, carrying, etc. 390pp. 7⅞ x 10⅝.
0-486-20204-6 Clothbd.

TREES OF THE EASTERN AND CENTRAL UNITED STATES AND CANADA, William M. Harlow. Best one-volume guide to 140 trees. Full descriptions, woodlore, range, etc. Over 600 illustrations. Handy size. 288pp. 4½ x 6⅜. 0-486-20395-6

GROWING AND USING HERBS AND SPICES, Milo Miloradovich. Versatile handbook provides all the information needed for cultivation and use of all the herbs and spices available in North America. 4 illustrations. Index. Glossary. 236pp. 5⅜ x 8½.
0-486-25058-X

BIG BOOK OF MAZES AND LABYRINTHS, Walter Shepherd. 50 mazes and labyrinths in all–classical, solid, ripple, and more–in one great volume. Perfect inexpensive puzzler for clever youngsters. Full solutions. 112pp. 8⅛ x 11. 0-486-22951-3

PIANO TUNING, J. Cree Fischer. Clearest, best book for beginner, amateur. Simple repairs, raising dropped notes, tuning by easy method of flattened fifths. No previous skills needed. 4 illustrations. 201pp. 5⅜ x 8½. 0-486-23267-0

HINTS TO SINGERS, Lillian Nordica. Selecting the right teacher, developing confidence, overcoming stage fright, and many other important skills receive thoughtful discussion in this indispensible guide, written by a world-famous diva of four decades' experience. 96pp. 5⅜ x 8½. 0-486-40094-8

THE COMPLETE NONSENSE OF EDWARD LEAR, Edward Lear. All nonsense limericks, zany alphabets, Owl and Pussycat, songs, nonsense botany, etc., illustrated by Lear. Total of 320pp. 5⅜ x 8½. (Available in U.S. only.) 0-486-20167-8

VICTORIAN PARLOUR POETRY: An Annotated Anthology, Michael R. Turner. 117 gems by Longfellow, Tennyson, Browning, many lesser-known poets. "The Village Blacksmith," "Curfew Must Not Ring Tonight," "Only a Baby Small," dozens more, often difficult to find elsewhere. Index of poets, titles, first lines. xxiii + 325pp. 5⅝ x 8¼. 0-486-27044-0

DUBLINERS, James Joyce. Fifteen stories offer vivid, tightly focused observations of the lives of Dublin's poorer classes. At least one, "The Dead," is considered a masterpiece. Reprinted complete and unabridged from standard edition. 160pp. 5³⁄₁₆ x 8¼. 0-486-26870-5

GREAT WEIRD TALES: 14 Stories by Lovecraft, Blackwood, Machen and Others, S. T. Joshi (ed.). 14 spellbinding tales, including "The Sin Eater," by Fiona McLeod, "The Eye Above the Mantel," by Frank Belknap Long, as well as renowned works by R. H. Barlow, Lord Dunsany, Arthur Machen, W. C. Morrow and eight other masters of the genre. 256pp. 5⅜ x 8½. (Available in U.S. only.) 0-486-40436-6

THE BOOK OF THE SACRED MAGIC OF ABRAMELIN THE MAGE, translated by S. MacGregor Mathers. Medieval manuscript of ceremonial magic. Basic document in Aleister Crowley, Golden Dawn groups. 268pp. 5⅜ x 8½. 0-486-23211-5

THE BATTLES THAT CHANGED HISTORY, Fletcher Pratt. Eminent historian profiles 16 crucial conflicts, ancient to modern, that changed the course of civilization. 352pp. 5⅜ x 8½. 0-486-41129-X

NEW RUSSIAN-ENGLISH AND ENGLISH-RUSSIAN DICTIONARY, M. A. O'Brien. This is a remarkably handy Russian dictionary, containing a surprising amount of information, including over 70,000 entries. 366pp. 4½ x 6⅛. 0-486-20208-9

NEW YORK IN THE FORTIES, Andreas Feininger. 162 brilliant photographs by the well-known photographer, formerly with *Life* magazine. Commuters, shoppers, Times Square at night, much else from city at its peak. Captions by John von Hartz. 181pp. 9¼ x 10¾. 0-486-23585-8

INDIAN SIGN LANGUAGE, William Tomkins. Over 525 signs developed by Sioux and other tribes. Written instructions and diagrams. Also 290 pictographs. 111pp. 6⅛ x 9¼. 0-486-22029-X

ANATOMY: A Complete Guide for Artists, Joseph Sheppard. A master of figure drawing shows artists how to render human anatomy convincingly. Over 460 illustrations. 224pp. 8⅜ x 11¼. 0-486-27279-6

MEDIEVAL CALLIGRAPHY: Its History and Technique, Marc Drogin. Spirited history, comprehensive instruction manual covers 13 styles (ca. 4th century through 15th). Excellent photographs; directions for duplicating medieval techniques with modern tools. 224pp. 8⅜ x 11¼. 0-486-26142-5

DRIED FLOWERS: How to Prepare Them, Sarah Whitlock and Martha Rankin. Complete instructions on how to use silica gel, meal and borax, perlite aggregate, sand and borax, glycerine and water to create attractive permanent flower arrangements. 12 illustrations. 32pp. 5⅜ x 8½. 0-486-21802-3

EASY-TO-MAKE BIRD FEEDERS FOR WOODWORKERS, Scott D. Campbell. Detailed, simple-to-use guide for designing, constructing, caring for and using feeders. Text, illustrations for 12 classic and contemporary designs. 96pp. 5⅜ x 8½. 0-486-25847-5

THE COMPLETE BOOK OF BIRDHOUSE CONSTRUCTION FOR WOOD-WORKERS, Scott D. Campbell. Detailed instructions, illustrations, tables. Also data on bird habitat and instinct patterns. Bibliography. 3 tables. 63 illustrations in 15 figures. 48pp. 5¼ x 8½. 0-486-24407-5

SCOTTISH WONDER TALES FROM MYTH AND LEGEND, Donald A. Mackenzie. 16 lively tales tell of giants rumbling down mountainsides, of a magic wand that turns stone pillars into warriors, of gods and goddesses, evil hags, powerful forces and more. 240pp. 5⅜ x 8½. 0-486-29677-6

THE HISTORY OF UNDERCLOTHES, C. Willett Cunnington and Phyllis Cunnington. Fascinating, well-documented survey covering six centuries of English undergarments, enhanced with over 100 illustrations: 12th-century laced-up bodice, footed long drawers (1795), 19th-century bustles, 19th-century corsets for men, Victorian "bust improvers," much more. 272pp. 5⅜ x 8¼. 0-486-27124-2

ARTS AND CRAFTS FURNITURE: The Complete Brooks Catalog of 1912, Brooks Manufacturing Co. Photos and detailed descriptions of more than 150 now very collectible furniture designs from the Arts and Crafts movement depict davenports, settees, buffets, desks, tables, chairs, bedsteads, dressers and more, all built of solid, quarter-sawed oak. Invaluable for students and enthusiasts of antiques, Americana and the decorative arts. 80pp. 6½ x 9¼. 0-486-27471-3

WILBUR AND ORVILLE: A Biography of the Wright Brothers, Fred Howard. Definitive, crisply written study tells the full story of the brothers' lives and work. A vividly written biography, unparalleled in scope and color, that also captures the spirit of an extraordinary era. 560pp. 6⅛ x 9¼. 0-486-40297-5

THE ARTS OF THE SAILOR: Knotting, Splicing and Ropework, Hervey Garrett Smith. Indispensable shipboard reference covers tools, basic knots and useful hitches; handsewing and canvas work, more. Over 100 illustrations. Delightful reading for sea lovers. 256pp. 5⅜ x 8½. 0-486-26440-8

FRANK LLOYD WRIGHT'S FALLINGWATER: The House and Its History, Second, Revised Edition, Donald Hoffmann. A total revision–both in text and illustrations–of the standard document on Fallingwater, the boldest, most personal architectural statement of Wright's mature years, updated with valuable new material from the recently opened Frank Lloyd Wright Archives. "Fascinating"–*The New York Times.* 116 illustrations. 128pp. 9¼ x 10¾. 0-486-27430-6

PHOTOGRAPHIC SKETCHBOOK OF THE CIVIL WAR, Alexander Gardner. 100 photos taken on field during the Civil War. Famous shots of Manassas Harper's Ferry, Lincoln, Richmond, slave pens, etc. 244pp. 10⅝ x 8¼. 0-486-22731-6

FIVE ACRES AND INDEPENDENCE, Maurice G. Kains. Great back-to-the-land classic explains basics of self-sufficient farming. The one book to get. 95 illustrations. 397pp. 5⅜ x 8½. 0-486-20974-1

A MODERN HERBAL, Margaret Grieve. Much the fullest, most exact, most useful compilation of herbal material. Gigantic alphabetical encyclopedia, from aconite to zedoary, gives botanical information, medical properties, folklore, economic uses, much else. Indispensable to serious reader. 161 illustrations. 888pp. 6½ x 9¼. 2-vol. set. (Available in U.S. only.)　　　Vol. I: 0-486-22798-7　　Vol. II: 0-486-22799-5

HIDDEN TREASURE MAZE BOOK, Dave Phillips. Solve 34 challenging mazes accompanied by heroic tales of adventure. Evil dragons, people-eating plants, blood-thirsty giants, many more dangerous adversaries lurk at every twist and turn. 34 mazes, stories, solutions. 48pp. 8¼ x 11.　　　　　　　　　0-486-24566-7

LETTERS OF W. A. MOZART, Wolfgang A. Mozart. Remarkable letters show bawdy wit, humor, imagination, musical insights, contemporary musical world; includes some letters from Leopold Mozart. 276pp. 5⅜ x 8½.　　　0-486-22859-2

BASIC PRINCIPLES OF CLASSICAL BALLET, Agrippina Vaganova. Great Russian theoretician, teacher explains methods for teaching classical ballet. 118 illustrations. 175pp. 5⅜ x 8½.　　　　　　　　　　　　　　　0-486-22036-2

THE JUMPING FROG, Mark Twain. Revenge edition. The original story of The Celebrated Jumping Frog of Calaveras County, a hapless French translation, and Twain's hilarious "retranslation" from the French. 12 illustrations. 66pp. 5⅜ x 8½.
0-486-22686-7

BEST REMEMBERED POEMS, Martin Gardner (ed.). The 126 poems in this superb collection of 19th- and 20th-century British and American verse range from Shelley's "To a Skylark" to the impassioned "Renascence" of Edna St. Vincent Millay and to Edward Lear's whimsical "The Owl and the Pussycat." 224pp. 5⅜ x 8½.
0-486-27165-X

COMPLETE SONNETS, William Shakespeare. Over 150 exquisite poems deal with love, friendship, the tyranny of time, beauty's evanescence, death and other themes in language of remarkable power, precision and beauty. Glossary of archaic terms. 80pp. 5³⁄₁₆ x 8¼.　　　　　　　　　　　　　　　　0-486-26686-9

HISTORIC HOMES OF THE AMERICAN PRESIDENTS, Second, Revised Edition, Irvin Haas. A traveler's guide to American Presidential homes, most open to the public, depicting and describing homes occupied by every American President from George Washington to George Bush. With visiting hours, admission charges, travel routes. 175 photographs. Index. 160pp. 8¼ x 11.　　　　0-486-26751-2

THE WIT AND HUMOR OF OSCAR WILDE, Alvin Redman (ed.). More than 1,000 ripostes, paradoxes, wisecracks: Work is the curse of the drinking classes; I can resist everything except temptation; etc. 258pp. 5⅜ x 8½.　　　0-486-20602-5

SHAKESPEARE LEXICON AND QUOTATION DICTIONARY, Alexander Schmidt. Full definitions, locations, shades of meaning in every word in plays and poems. More than 50,000 exact quotations. 1,485pp. 6½ x 9¼. 2-vol. set.
Vol. 1: 0-486-22726-X　　　Vol. 2: 0-486-22727-8

SELECTED POEMS, Emily Dickinson. Over 100 best-known, best-loved poems by one of America's foremost poets, reprinted from authoritative early editions. No comparable edition at this price. Index of first lines. 64pp. 5³⁄₁₆ x 8¼. 0-486-26466-1

THE INSIDIOUS DR. FU-MANCHU, Sax Rohmer. The first of the popular mystery series introduces a pair of English detectives to their archnemesis, the diabolical Dr. Fu-Manchu. Flavorful atmosphere, fast-paced action, and colorful characters enliven this classic of the genre. 208pp. 5³⁄₁₆ x 8¼.　　　　0-486-29898-1

THE MALLEUS MALEFICARUM OF KRAMER AND SPRENGER, translated by Montague Summers. Full text of most important witchhunter's "bible," used by both Catholics and Protestants. 278pp. 6⅝ x 10. 0-486-22802-9

SPANISH STORIES/CUENTOS ESPAÑOLES: A Dual-Language Book, Angel Flores (ed.). Unique format offers 13 great stories in Spanish by Cervantes, Borges, others. Faithful English translations on facing pages. 352pp. 5⅜ x 8½. 0-486-25399-6

GARDEN CITY, LONG ISLAND, IN EARLY PHOTOGRAPHS, 1869–1919, Mildred H. Smith. Handsome treasury of 118 vintage pictures, accompanied by carefully researched captions, document the Garden City Hotel fire (1899), the Vanderbilt Cup Race (1908), the first airmail flight departing from the Nassau Boulevard Aerodrome (1911), and much more. 96pp. 8⅞ x 11¾. 0-486-40669-5

OLD QUEENS, N.Y., IN EARLY PHOTOGRAPHS, Vincent F. Seyfried and William Asadorian. Over 160 rare photographs of Maspeth, Jamaica, Jackson Heights, and other areas. Vintage views of DeWitt Clinton mansion, 1939 World's Fair and more. Captions. 192pp. 8⅞ x 11. 0-486-26358-4

CAPTURED BY THE INDIANS: 15 Firsthand Accounts, 1750-1870, Frederick Drimmer. Astounding true historical accounts of grisly torture, bloody conflicts, relentless pursuits, miraculous escapes and more, by people who lived to tell the tale. 384pp. 5⅜ x 8½. 0-486-24901-8

THE WORLD'S GREAT SPEECHES (Fourth Enlarged Edition), Lewis Copeland, Lawrence W. Lamm, and Stephen J. McKenna. Nearly 300 speeches provide public speakers with a wealth of updated quotes and inspiration–from Pericles' funeral oration and William Jennings Bryan's "Cross of Gold Speech" to Malcolm X's powerful words on the Black Revolution and Earl of Spenser's tribute to his sister, Diana, Princess of Wales. 944pp. 5⅜ x 8⅜. 0-486-40903-1

THE BOOK OF THE SWORD, Sir Richard F. Burton. Great Victorian scholar/adventurer's eloquent, erudite history of the "queen of weapons"–from prehistory to early Roman Empire. Evolution and development of early swords, variations (sabre, broadsword, cutlass, scimitar, etc.), much more. 336pp. 6⅛ x 9¼. 0-486-25434-8

AUTOBIOGRAPHY: The Story of My Experiments with Truth, Mohandas K. Gandhi. Boyhood, legal studies, purification, the growth of the Satyagraha (nonviolent protest) movement. Critical, inspiring work of the man responsible for the freedom of India. 480pp. 5⅜ x 8½. (Available in U.S. only.) 0-486-24593-4

CELTIC MYTHS AND LEGENDS, T. W. Rolleston. Masterful retelling of Irish and Welsh stories and tales. Cuchulain, King Arthur, Deirdre, the Grail, many more. First paperback edition. 58 full-page illustrations. 512pp. 5⅜ x 8½. 0-486-26507-2

THE PRINCIPLES OF PSYCHOLOGY, William James. Famous long course complete, unabridged. Stream of thought, time perception, memory, experimental methods; great work decades ahead of its time. 94 figures. 1,391pp. 5⅜ x 8½. 2-vol. set.
Vol. I: 0-486-20381-6 Vol. II: 0-486-20382-4

THE WORLD AS WILL AND REPRESENTATION, Arthur Schopenhauer. Definitive English translation of Schopenhauer's life work, correcting more than 1,000 errors, omissions in earlier translations. Translated by E. F. J. Payne. Total of 1,269pp. 5⅜ x 8½. 2-vol. set. Vol. 1: 0-486-21761-2 Vol. 2: 0-486-21762-0

CATALOG OF DOVER BOOKS

MAGIC AND MYSTERY IN TIBET, Madame Alexandra David-Neel. Experiences among lamas, magicians, sages, sorcerers, Bonpa wizards. A true psychic discovery. 32 illustrations. 321pp. 5⅜ x 8½. (Available in U.S. only.) 0-486-22682-4

THE EGYPTIAN BOOK OF THE DEAD, E. A. Wallis Budge. Complete reproduction of Ani's papyrus, finest ever found. Full hieroglyphic text, interlinear transliteration, word-for-word translation, smooth translation. 533pp. 6½ x 9¼. 0-486-21866-X

HISTORIC COSTUME IN PICTURES, Braun & Schneider. Over 1,450 costumed figures in clearly detailed engravings–from dawn of civilization to end of 19th century. Captions. Many folk costumes. 256pp. 8⅜ x 11¼. 0-486-23150-X

MATHEMATICS FOR THE NONMATHEMATICIAN, Morris Kline. Detailed, college-level treatment of mathematics in cultural and historical context, with numerous exercises. Recommended Reading Lists. Tables. Numerous figures. 641pp. 5⅜ x 8½. 0-486-24823-2

PROBABILISTIC METHODS IN THE THEORY OF STRUCTURES, Isaac Elishakoff. Well-written introduction covers the elements of the theory of probability from two or more random variables, the reliability of such multivariable structures, the theory of random function, Monte Carlo methods of treating problems incapable of exact solution, and more. Examples. 502pp. 5⅜ x 8½. 0-486-40691-1

THE RIME OF THE ANCIENT MARINER, Gustave Doré, S. T. Coleridge. Doré's finest work; 34 plates capture moods, subtleties of poem. Flawless full-size reproductions printed on facing pages with authoritative text of poem. "Beautiful. Simply beautiful."–Publisher's Weekly. 77pp. 9¼ x 12. 0-486-22305-1

SCULPTURE: Principles and Practice, Louis Slobodkin. Step-by-step approach to clay, plaster, metals, stone; classical and modern. 253 drawings, photos. 255pp. 8⅛ x 11. 0-486-22960-2

THE INFLUENCE OF SEA POWER UPON HISTORY, 1660–1783, A. T. Mahan. Influential classic of naval history and tactics still used as text in war colleges. First paperback edition. 4 maps. 24 battle plans. 640pp. 5⅜ x 8½. 0-486-25509-3

THE STORY OF THE TITANIC AS TOLD BY ITS SURVIVORS, Jack Winocour (ed.). What it was really like. Panic, despair, shocking inefficiency, and a little heroism. More thrilling than any fictional account. 26 illustrations. 320pp. 5⅜ x 8½. 0-486-20610-6

ONE TWO THREE . . . INFINITY: Facts and Speculations of Science, George Gamow. Great physicist's fascinating, readable overview of contemporary science: number theory, relativity, fourth dimension, entropy, genes, atomic structure, much more. 128 illustrations. Index. 352pp. 5⅜ x 8½. 0-486-25664-2

DALÍ ON MODERN ART: The Cuckolds of Antiquated Modern Art, Salvador Dalí. Influential painter skewers modern art and its practitioners. Outrageous evaluations of Picasso, Cézanne, Turner, more. 15 renderings of paintings discussed. 44 calligraphic decorations by Dalí. 96pp. 5⅜ x 8½. (Available in U.S. only.) 0-486-29220-7

ANTIQUE PLAYING CARDS: A Pictorial History, Henry René D'Allemagne. Over 900 elaborate, decorative images from rare playing cards (14th–20th centuries): Bacchus, death, dancing dogs, hunting scenes, royal coats of arms, players cheating, much more. 96pp. 9¼ x 12¼. 0-486-29265-7

MAKING FURNITURE MASTERPIECES: 30 Projects with Measured Drawings, Franklin H. Gottshall. Step-by-step instructions, illustrations for constructing handsome, useful pieces, among them a Sheraton desk, Chippendale chair, Spanish desk, Queen Anne table and a William and Mary dressing mirror. 224pp. 8⅛ x 11¼. 0-486-29338-6

NORTH AMERICAN INDIAN DESIGNS FOR ARTISTS AND CRAFTSPEOPLE, Eva Wilson. Over 360 authentic copyright-free designs adapted from Navajo blankets, Hopi pottery, Sioux buffalo hides, more. Geometrics, symbolic figures, plant and animal motifs, etc. 128pp. 8⅜ x 11. (Not for sale in the United Kingdom.) 0-486-25341-4

THE FOSSIL BOOK: A Record of Prehistoric Life, Patricia V. Rich et al. Profusely illustrated definitive guide covers everything from single-celled organisms and dinosaurs to birds and mammals and the interplay between climate and man. Over 1,500 illustrations. 760pp. 7½ x 10⅛. 0-486-29371-8

VICTORIAN ARCHITECTURAL DETAILS: Designs for Over 700 Stairs, Mantels, Doors, Windows, Cornices, Porches, and Other Decorative Elements, A. J. Bicknell & Company. Everything from dormer windows and piazzas to balconies and gable ornaments. Also includes elevations and floor plans for handsome, private residences and commercial structures. 80pp. 9⅜ x 12¼. 0-486-44015-X

WESTERN ISLAMIC ARCHITECTURE: A Concise Introduction, John D. Hoag. Profusely illustrated critical appraisal compares and contrasts Islamic mosques and palaces–from Spain and Egypt to other areas in the Middle East. 139 illustrations. 128pp. 6 x 9. 0-486-43760-4

CHINESE ARCHITECTURE: A Pictorial History, Liang Ssu-ch'eng. More than 240 rare photographs and drawings depict temples, pagodas, tombs, bridges, and imperial palaces comprising much of China's architectural heritage. 152 halftones, 94 diagrams. 232pp. 10¾ x 9⅞. 0-486-43999-2

THE RENAISSANCE: Studies in Art and Poetry, Walter Pater. One of the most talked-about books of the 19th century, *The Renaissance* combines scholarship and philosophy in an innovative work of cultural criticism that examines the achievements of Botticelli, Leonardo, Michelangelo, and other artists. "The holy writ of beauty."–Oscar Wilde. 160pp. 5⅜ x 8½. 0-486-44025-7

A TREATISE ON PAINTING, Leonardo da Vinci. The great Renaissance artist's practical advice on drawing and painting techniques covers anatomy, perspective, composition, light and shadow, and color. A classic of art instruction, it features 48 drawings by Nicholas Poussin and Leon Battista Alberti. 192pp. 5⅜ x 8½. 0-486-44155-5

THE MIND OF LEONARDO DA VINCI, Edward McCurdy. More than just a biography, this classic study by a distinguished historian draws upon Leonardo's extensive writings to offer numerous demonstrations of the Renaissance master's achievements, not only in sculpture and painting, but also in music, engineering, and even experimental aviation. 384pp. 5⅜ x 8½. 0-486-44142-3

WASHINGTON IRVING'S RIP VAN WINKLE, Illustrated by Arthur Rackham. Lovely prints that established artist as a leading illustrator of the time and forever etched into the popular imagination a classic of Catskill lore. 51 full-color plates. 80pp. 8⅜ x 11. 0-486-44242-X

HENSCHE ON PAINTING, John W. Robichaux. Basic painting philosophy and methodology of a great teacher, as expounded in his famous classes and workshops on Cape Cod. 7 illustrations in color on covers. 80pp. 5⅜ x 8½. 0-486-43728-0

CATALOG OF DOVER BOOKS

LIGHT AND SHADE: A Classic Approach to Three-Dimensional Drawing, Mrs. Mary P. Merrifield. Handy reference clearly demonstrates principles of light and shade by revealing effects of common daylight, sunshine, and candle or artificial light on geometrical solids. 13 plates. 64pp. 5⅜ x 8½. 0-486-44143-1

ASTROLOGY AND ASTRONOMY: A Pictorial Archive of Signs and Symbols, Ernst and Johanna Lehner. Treasure trove of stories, lore, and myth, accompanied by more than 300 rare illustrations of planets, the Milky Way, signs of the zodiac, comets, meteors, and other astronomical phenomena. 192pp. 8⅜ x 11. 0-486-43981-X

JEWELRY MAKING: Techniques for Metal, Tim McCreight. Easy-to-follow instructions and carefully executed illustrations describe tools and techniques, use of gems and enamels, wire inlay, casting, and other topics. 72 line illustrations and diagrams. 176pp. 8¼ x 10⅞. 0-486-44043-5

MAKING BIRDHOUSES: Easy and Advanced Projects, Gladstone Califf. Easy-to-follow instructions include diagrams for everything from a one-room house for bluebirds to a forty-two-room structure for purple martins. 56 plates; 4 figures. 80pp. 8¾ x 6⅜. 0-486-44183-0

LITTLE BOOK OF LOG CABINS: How to Build and Furnish Them, William S. Wicks. Handy how-to manual, with instructions and illustrations for building cabins in the Adirondack style, fireplaces, stairways, furniture, beamed ceilings, and more. 102 line drawings. 96pp. 8¾ x 6⅜. 0-486-44259-4

THE SEASONS OF AMERICA PAST, Eric Sloane. From "sugaring time" and strawberry picking to Indian summer and fall harvest, a whole year's activities described in charming prose and enhanced with 79 of the author's own illustrations. 160pp. 8¼ x 11. 0-486-44220-9

THE METROPOLIS OF TOMORROW, Hugh Ferriss. Generous, prophetic vision of the metropolis of the future, as perceived in 1929. Powerful illustrations of towering structures, wide avenues, and rooftop parks–all features in many of today's modern cities. 59 illustrations. 144pp. 8¼ x 11. 0-486-43727-2

THE PATH TO ROME, Hilaire Belloc. This 1902 memoir abounds in lively vignettes from a vanished time, recounting a pilgrimage on foot across the Alps and Apennines in order to "see all Europe which the Christian Faith has saved." 77 of the author's original line drawings complement his sparkling prose. 272pp. 5⅜ x 8½. 0-486-44001-X

THE HISTORY OF RASSELAS: Prince of Abissinia, Samuel Johnson. Distinguished English writer attacks eighteenth-century optimism and man's unrealistic estimates of what life has to offer. 112pp. 5⅜ x 8½. 0-486-44094-X

A VOYAGE TO ARCTURUS, David Lindsay. A brilliant flight of pure fancy, where wild creatures crowd the fantastic landscape and demented torturers dominate victims with their bizarre mental powers. 272pp. 5⅜ x 8½. 0-486-44198-9

Paperbound unless otherwise indicated. Available at your book dealer, online at **www.doverpublications.com**, or by writing to Dept. GI, Dover Publications, Inc., 31 East 2nd Street, Mineola, NY 11501. For current price information or for free catalogs (please indicate field of interest), write to Dover Publications or log on to **www.doverpublications.com** and see every Dover book in print. Dover publishes more than 500 books each year on science, elementary and advanced mathematics, biology, music, art, literary history, social sciences, and other areas.